A Thousand Li:
The Second Expedition

A Cultivation Novel
Book 4 of A Thousand Li Series

By

Tao Wong

Copyright

A Starlit Publishing Book
Published by Starlit Publishing
PO Box 30035
High Park PO
Toronto, ON
M6P 3K0
Canada
www.starlitpublishing.com

Ebook ISBN: 9781989994092
Paperback ISBN: 9781989994108
Hardcover ISBN: 9781989994115 and 9781778550300

Books in A Thousand Li series

The First Step

The First Stop

The First War

The Second Expedition

The Second Sect

The Second Storm

The Third Kingdom

The Third Realm

The Third Cut

Short Stories

The Favored Son

The Storming White Clouds Sect

On Gods and Demons

Clifftop Crisis and Transformation

Imperial March

Villages & Illnesses

Descent from the Mountain

The Divine Peak

Fish Ball Quest

Ten Thousand and One Fates

Table of Contents

What Happened Before

As the war between the States of Wei and Shen continue to heat up, Wu Ying continued his training with the Verdant Green Waters Sect. However, realizing that his family could be in danger of the upcoming warring season, Wu Ying planned and conducted an extraction operation of his family and the village to the Sect itself.

Forced to bargain with Lord Wen, the group journeyed into the state of Wei itself, to conduct a daring raid to retrieve the bloodline scrolls and cultivation methods for the Lord. To do so safely, the group joined the war efforts, doing battle with rival Sect leaders.

Having successfully retrieved the cultivation method, Wu Ying and team brought the village back to the Sect, only to find that the war itself had swept by with little effect. Amused by the vagaries of fate, and enlightened upon the futility of humanity's plans, Wu Ying settled himself into a period of study, intent on progressing his cultivation base and setting aside mortal concerns.

Chapter 1

The compressed earth path up the mountain was wide and well trampled, countless feet having worn away any greenery. Clad in dark-colored cloth shoes, the two martial artists hiked up the winding trail, shaded from the late evening sun by the towering dove trees with their heart-shaped leaves on either side of the bare trail. Wisps of clouds occasionally covered the sun as a light breeze rustled dried leaves and brought the scents of blooming flowers and fresh flowing water to the pair of immortal cultivators.

As they climbed, the occasional whistle of birds chirping to one another filtered through the undergrowth, breaking through the on-going argument between the pair.

"Did you really have to carry all that?" Tou He said, exasperation clear in his voice as he strolled alongside his friend, his wooden staff over one muscular shoulder.

"It's not hard. And I need the contribution points," Wu Ying, the other cultivator, said defensively.

He glanced at his bald friend, clad at last in the pale green and blue robes of the inner sect. Sometime after their return last autumn, Tou He had stopped wearing his signature orange monk robes and had begun wearing the inner sect attire of the Verdant Green Waters Sect. He had continued to keep his head shaved and his prayer beads around his neck though, unwilling to give up all aspects of his past.

"But all of it?" Tou He said, pointing at the burden Wu Ying carried. "Shouldn't you leave something for the others?"

Wu Ying made a face as his feet dug into the ground again, the multiple rice bags strapped together shifting precariously on his back. He shifted his weight sideways, keeping balanced the entire makeshift-backpack that was twice his height and three times his weight. The motion was automatic, his breathing only hitching a little. Doing so was no more difficult than the strength training they regularly practiced in the inner sect. Feats of such strength and endurance were nothing, not for a pair of Energy Storage cultivators.

"This isn't all! There's a ton more to take." Wu Ying protested. "There's still beans, fish, tofu, and more. I even saw a ship coming in on the river from Shazi Po. I bet that has the new sect robes."

Tou He shook his head. "Still, how many points is this? Ten? Twelve?"

"Seven." Wu Ying exhaled before taking the next step, feeling the ground beneath his feet give way and compress under the added weight. Once more, he made a note to himself to practice his qinggong exercises. Of all the aspects he was working on, the "light foot" exercises had been the most difficult to grasp since his ascension to the Energy Storage realm. "They lowered the amount last month."

"Did they?" Tou He frowned then shrugged, letting the matter go.

For the ex-Buddhist monk, the struggle for contribution points had never been a concern. The tea master had always had more than he needed. The materials for tea ceremonies – at his level—didn't require much in terms of contribution points. And as an honorary martial specialist, Tou He had more than sufficient opportunities to earn sect contribution points by dealing with wandering spirits and demonic beasts.

Wu Ying sighed as he exhaled, then he wiped the dirt off his tanned face, pushing aside long hair that had come loose from its ties as he took the next step. He felt a flash of jealousy rising up and squashed it, knowing it had nothing to do with his friend.

His own desperate need for contribution points was no fault of Tou He's. The ex-monk had smartly chosen not to set up an entire displaced village. He also didn't have a secondary occupation as a budding apothecarist, an occupation that was known to eat contribution points and materials like a taotei[1].

Between those two factors, Wu Ying had spent the entirety of his spring and summer running Sect quests, trying to rebuild his bank of contribution points. With what he owed the Sect, and with the village only beginning to get on its feet, the last few months had left him little time for practice. He'd only managed to consolidate his gains, ensuring that his cultivation base and his meridians were thoroughly cleansed.

"Yeah. We took in more outer sect members than usual. It seems the villages are looking to dump as many as they can to us and the other sects," Wu Ying said.

That was no surprise if one considered things. Which, Wu Ying had to admit, was not something he'd thought of until lately.

Cultivation sects were often protected from the vagaries of war, for while they might offer a few members to the war efforts, they rarely saw the wholesale destruction or disruption villages might experience. Few kingdoms, no matter their strength, wanted to start the escalating conflict that sect destruction entailed. A single angry and determined survivor could wreak significant damage. Assassinations, brutal attacks against the bureaucracy of a nation, even delving into darker daos and massacring entire villages were well-worn tactics by the vengeful. Never mind the karmic issues of such destruction, or its effect on diplomatic relations in the future for such a kingdom.

Better to let your own allied sect handle attacks on other sects, and, in turn, receive the brunt of the displeasure such genocide might result in.

"So why?" Tou He said.

---

[1] Taotei – a mythological (or, in our case, real) beast from Chinese folklore that has an unending hunger.

"Seven contribution points is above average," Wu Ying said. "I have needs. I need to pay off Bao Cong. I also want to bank enough points so I don't have to keep worrying about it all."

Wu Ying shook his head. The worry about his finances, about how many contribution points he had, kept him up late into the night most days. It affected his training, affected the way he progressed on his contemplation of the Dao. Perhaps, it was his master's—Elder Cheng's—influence, but he could feel the burdens of his past relationships bind him, slowing down his cultivation speed. Even his weekly visits to his parents had begun to feel constrictive.

Cultivation, in itself, was a selfish endeavor. It went against the needs of the family, of friends and society. After all, cultivation focused on the progress of an individual, outside the bounds of society. The use of cultivation materials, the endless hours of practice, of meditation, of drawing in chi from the world. It took away from time spent with family, aiding your village or company, or progressing one's kingdom.

Cultivation, at its heart, was selfish. The desire to become immortal was against the very rules of heaven. It defied the natural order, while still being part of the Dao.

For the Dao encompassed all things, all possibilities. As such, the possibility of becoming immortal was part of the Dao. It had to be. It was just a small, almost unimportant, portion of it when one compared it to the entirety of the Dao[2].

Yet, balanced against the needs of the family, of society at large, the pursuit of immortality could wreck a family, a nation, a society. Numerous

---

[2] Dao when capitalized is talking of the true Dao, the *Way* that encompassed the heavens and earth and everything in between. It is the Way that is natural and that cannot be explained. For in explaining, one misses the point.

kingdoms had fallen due to the selfish pursuit of its ruler, families left broken. Some cultivators, like his Master, cut ties with all. Trying, as best as he could, to be free of such obligations. Others, like Wu Ying himself, tried to walk that razor edge between familial and societal duty and personal desire. Both, in their own ways, tried to grasp the Dao.

"How much more do you need?" asked Tou He, interrupting Wu Ying's musings.

"With my latest gathering? And this mission completion? This should be enough." Wu Ying shifted his weight forward a little, letting the pack that dwarfed him in both size and weight shift as well. He had to admit, perhaps this was a little much.

But he had chosen to grab the rice bags as much for nostalgia as the contribution points. After all, seven points was but a single handful of Spirit Grass.

"Good." Tou He rubbed his bald head. "Running all these quests with you has been rather tiring."

Wu Ying flashed his friend a grin, gratitude welling up within his chest. Since his breakup with Li Yao, Wu Ying had few that he could rely on to run the more dangerous combat and gathering missions. While he could and did join the other groups that formed within the Sect, it was always good to have someone you could rely on. After all, none of the Sect missions offered to them by the nobility and the villagers were safe.

If they were, they wouldn't have been offered.

"Thank you, once again."

"No need. That's what friends are for," Tou He said. "Now, come on. I'm getting hungry."

So saying, the cultivator sped up, leaving his friend behind. Wu Ying glared at the departing back before he hunkered down, circulating his chi within his dantian, and pushed forward. He was getting hungry too.

***

Under the paifang that marked the official start of the Sect grounds, Wu Ying spotted the gate guardian, Elder Lu. The old man sat under the brownish-red column of the paifang, long pipe held in hand, tobacco smoke drifting upward and polluting the fresh mountain air. Wu Ying could just catch the edges of the pipe smoke scent, the sweet, cloying taste of tobacco and burnt herbs tickling his nose and staining his taste buds.

"Elder Lu." Wu Ying put his hands together, palm over fist, as he bowed to the Elder. He had to shorten the bow significantly or risk tipping over. Even with the chi that flowed through him from his opened and cleansed meridians, from the single open energy storage meridian in his body, Wu Ying still had to contend with the physics of the universe. When Elder Lu nodded back in acknowledgement of his greeting, Wu Ying continued. "Is that a new blend?"

"It is. But you don't have time for these pleasantries." Elder Lu took his pipe out of his mouth, leaning forward as the ends of his long beard fluttered in the wind. "Your martial sister is looking for you."

"She's back?" Wu Ying said. His Master and his martial sister, Fairy Yang, had left at the start of the year on a personal quest. They hadn't informed Wu Ying of their intentions, leaving him to manage his own business. Wu Ying understood. He was still too junior to help.

"Yes. Your Master is injured," Elder Lu murmured, a trace of concern in his dark brown eyes.

Wu Ying's eyes widened, and he struggled with the straps on his back. Frustrated, he yanked on them hard, tearing the ropes free and dumping the entire package. It tilted dangerously for a second before Tou He moved, grabbing hold of it and balancing the entire burden of rice sacks. When Wu Ying looked at his friend, he received a single, simple nod.

Assured of the rice's delivery, he took off running at full speed headed for his Master's residence. A small worm of worry burrowed into his chest as he ran. What kind of injury could it be that had sent two Core cultivators back to the Sect in ignominious retreat? What kind of enemy had they met that could injure them so badly?

He had no answers. He would not, until he found his Master.

***

Wu Ying ascended the mountain swiftly, feet pounding into the ground. As he rushed up the path, he passed outer sect members in their dark green and light striped robes, taking care of the chores that kept the Sect functioning. Those chores ranged from mundane tasks like sweeping the cobblestone paths, trimming hedges and trees, cooking, and running errands to more exotic, immortal sect-only tasks like caring for the occasional Spirit beast pet, tending to the spiritual herb gardens, or rebuilding damaged martial training halls.

Amidst all that, he spotted classes of outer sect members learning new martial forms, studying classical cultivation and philosophical texts, and of course, cultivating. So many of them were either seated cross-legged or standing in horse stance, breathing in quiet rhythm to the world or their own heartbeats. Drawing the chi of the heaven and earth into their bodies to filter through their meridians and collect in their dantians. All to gain even an ounce more progress on their journey.

Through all these, Wu Ying ran, taking himself farther and farther up the mountain. Past the outer sect halls and training grounds to where the inner sect members, like himself, resided. Their halls and training grounds were similar in nature, though larger and more ornate. Their classes, their lectures were led by Elders more often than not, their cultivation practices held in secluded courtyards as each cultivator progressed their individual techniques.

Inner sect members weren't put through a mass training program, instead receiving individual training in their cultivation methods. As inner sect members, they were expected to be able to progress their cultivation individually. Those who failed, and failed too long and too often, might find themselves demoted. Or, in the worst cases, removed from the Sect's main headquarters.

It was to other, smaller branches, scattered throughout the land, that these forsaken, discarded members would be sent. Their cultivation journey cut short, their prospects removed. They'd have to struggle, aid the local villages, and perhaps, in that way, progress their cultivation. They would no longer have easy access to well-paying assignments, no longer be able to purchase cultivation pills or access the library with ease.

Still, it wasn't entirely impossible even for these "banished" cultivators to continue. Sometimes the change of pace was all that was required for a cultivator to grow. Occasionally, a few cultivators found inspiration in such external work. And so, the Elders said, this practice was good for individuals, while helping the Sect grow its influence.

On Wu Ying ran, passing the inner sect library and the armory that hosted the collected spiritual weapons and equipment of the outer and inner sect members. Upward, offering quick nods to Elders, as he passed the busy assignment hall, where he was to report the completion of his mission. And as he sprinted, breathing in deep, he caught whiffs of smoke and ash, felt the touch of fire chi as the distant ring of hammer on metal signaled the presence of the blacksmithing halls.

No smell from the apothecary halls, of course. They dealt with much more dangerous materials, and without proper ventilation, without proper wards in place, they might accidentally poison the entire Sect. More than one failed apothecarist's mixture had poisoned its creator.

No, no scent from the apothecarist halls, even as he passed them and climbed higher and higher, leaving behind the inner sect buildings until he reached the stupendous heights of the residences of the Elders. Each house was a small compound containing training rooms, apothecarist buildings, resting places, and kitchens for the Elders. Each of whom had their own servants, drawn from the outer sect or, sometimes, the mundane servants who served the Sect itself.

Up, until he reached two-thirds of the way to the peak of the Elders' residences. Until he finally reached, panting, his Master's residence. Outside the building, Wu Ying paused before the barred wooden doors, staring at the elaborate golden lion knockers. He drew deep breaths to calm his breathing, to settle his heart, and have his chi stop churning. He readied himself for what came next. For he had a sudden premonition that what came next would change his life forever.

Again.

Chapter 2

The residence that his Master lived in was one of the larger complexes in the Sect. It was also set farther back in the grounds, the pathway to it almost hidden, the building blending into its surroundings. As was typical, the layout of the residence was in the formal siheyuan style of architecture. This consisted of a northern main residence with its entrances facing the south with buildings on the side along the east and west axis. The side buildings were connected to the main house via pathways, all of which faced in toward a main courtyard.

Due to space constraints, rather than sprawling across a large amount of land, most residences on the mountain grew vertically. As an important Elder, Elder Cheng's house consisted of a second floor for the main building and a second courtyard offering him extra space for guests. The building itself was made of wood, with pounded earth lower walls and wooden supports.

For a moment, Wu Ying stood before the main gate, staring at the large wooden barricade and its couple of door knockers. A sense of dreadful anticipation filled him before he pushed on the door knockers. The dull, metallic thud roused the servants within, one of whom opened and greeted Wu Ying in quick order, ushering him into the main residence.

To Wu Ying's surprise, he found his Master lying on the divan in his living room beside his open plan bedroom, pale but lucid, a bound paper book beside him. Wu Ying bowed low, offering formal greetings which were swiftly returned.

"Ah. I see that you have heard," Elder Cheng said, shaking his head slightly. "You do not need to concern yourself. It is a minor injury. It will heal itself in time."

Wu Ying frowned, staring at his Master. The usual masculine set of his jaw and the long, swordsman's arms were still there. But his face was paler, gone from a perfect, unblemished white to a sallow, sickly yellow. Small trembling movements on those long fingers as they held the book across his body were easy to discern, and the casual lounging robes his Master wore stank of old sweat.

"What happened?" Wu Ying hesitated and added, "If you can tell me."

"I cannot. Not in detail. But your sister is fine. We managed to escape with minimal injury." Elder Cheng let his hand drop, placing the book by his side as he focused on Wu Ying. "The rest you are not ready for yet."

"If they came for you..." Wu Ying hoped the allusion to his own vulnerability could extract further information from his Master.

"They would not dare to attack the Sect." In a softer, quieter voice that Wu Ying did not expect his Master to think he heard, Elder Cheng added, "At least, not yet."

"And is there not anything I can get for you?" Wu Ying said. "Herbs, some special pills?"

Elder Cheng shook his head. "I am well provisioned. The poison will dissipate. Enough about me. Show me what you have learned."

With a small exertion of strength, Elder Cheng stood and walked toward the doors and the entrance to the courtyard. His movements were small, careful as he guided himself to a nearby bench, where he sat again, facing the inner courtyard.

Wu Ying, trailing behind his Master, took position in the courtyard, in the center of the training ring. At a nod from his Master, Wu Ying drew his ever-present jian, saluting him then the shrine to Guan Yu. The long, straight sword was Wu Ying's favorite weapon, perfect for carrying on a daily basis, and one that he had studied since childhood with his father. At his Master's urging, he began the sword form of his family.

The Long family sword style had once been famed across the kingdom, a powerful style that had been wielded by one of his ancestors in the Nascent

Soul stage. That, over time, his family had not been able to showcase another cultivator of that strength had lost them much prestige, eventually resulting in them ending up as peasants, as their ancestor had once been. Still, the style itself was powerful, well developed in its form. It just required a practitioner who could bring its full strength to the fore.

The story of a great ancestor and the family's subsequent fall from grace was a familiar one for many other families, as Wu Ying was growing more and more cognizant of. In a nation as large as this, everyone had a family member who was rumored or known to have been strong at some point. Bloodlines, hidden knowledge, it was less uncommon than you would think. Only those families who had broken away from the main branches or those who had lost their heritage entirely could not quote a fabled ancestor.

From form to form, Wu Ying flowed. Dragon unsheathes its Claws, transformed to Dragon swiping at the Clouds, to Return in the Snow, to Dragon sweeping its Tail. With each motion, chi informed his use. And as Wu Ying practiced the forms more, he realized that each form was as varied as his own imagination.

What could be a block in one situation could be the start of a trap in another or a feint the next time it was used. A simple lunge, the Sword's Truth, could begin or end a form, or in some cases, even be a feint to be followed by a controlled retreat.

Ever since he had gained his first Energy Storage meridian, his projection of sword intent, the sword chi that he gained and passed through his weapon, had grown stronger. He could wield the sword intent with as much strength, as much grace as he could his own body. With a sliver more understanding of the weapon, of the jian, Wu Ying knew he was only a step away from achieving the Heart of the jian.

From form to form, he flowed, his breathing matching his motion. Explosive when needed, deep and steady when required. He was so caught in his art, he forgot where he was until the form was done and he sheathed his weapon.

A slow clap rose from his Master. "Better. Much better. You have grown comfortable in the basic form. You have integrated your sword intent into the form itself. It seems that allowing you to run to your parents has borne fruit."

Wu Ying bowed in gratitude. "Yes, Master. The experience, fighting the Wei, the spirit beasts, has opened my eyes to the basic form."

"Good. Very good." Master Cheng's face then grew serious as he leaned forward and fixed Wu Ying with a disapproving glare. "Then what of your third form? How has that progressed?"

Wu Ying winced. The Long family sword style did not consist of a single form, but multiple forms. Unfortunately, while Wu Ying had studied each form in detail, he had focused practice on only the first one. Of the five that he had access to, one was a generic sword style, meant for use with both the dao and the jian, and the other four focused entirely on the jian itself.

He had a passing knowledge of the first and second forms, had practiced the third on occasion, and had only studied the motions of the fourth and fifth. He had not even gone as far as memorizing them—mostly because the fourth and fifth forms were not meant for those at his cultivation level. But the third form, like the second, could be utilized by those who had yet to reach Core cultivation stage. As his Master well knew.

"I have practiced it somewhat," Wu Ying offered.

"But not enough to show me?"

"It's... it's not up to standard, Master." Wu Ying admitted ruefully.

"Show me."

It was not a request, but a command. And so, Wu Ying went through the motions. With his Sense of the Sword, he did not embarrass himself completely, but compared to the fluid, rehearsed motions of the second form, he moved like a child given a stick for the first time. His previous form had been filled with intent and consideration in each action, the forms flowing fluidly from motion to motion, perfectly positioned and balanced at all times. With the third form, each of his actions lacked intent, lacked strength. To a layman, it might look acceptable, but to a master of the weapon, like Elder Cheng, it was a travesty.

Three quarters of the way through, Master Cheng finally had enough. "Unacceptable. Continue practicing this form in the evening and morning. The third form takes full advantage of your energy meridians and should be practiced now that you have gained access to them in full. They can only help your cultivation. Which, I note"—Elder Cheng's voice grew even more angry—"you have stalled on. Again."

Wu Ying winced. His obligations had slowed down his progress. Wu Ying knew his Master saw little to be gained in all the time he spent running back and forth on missions, spending time with his family. Even though his Master had allowed Wu Ying to indulge his sense of honor and duty, it was a point of contention between them. Sometimes, Wu Ying wondered about the fate that had led him to this master. In so many ways, the pair of them had conflicting ideologies.

As Wu Ying stayed bowed in acknowledgement of his Master's scolding, Elder Cheng spoke. "Ah Yuan, now that we are back, I want you to keep an eye on him. He should not be allowed to slack off on his cultivation. You know why."

In surprise, Wu Ying straightened. He spotted Fa Yuan, his martial sister, who had arrived without a single noise in the entrance of the residence at some point. And, as he turned, he spotted the knowing glance that passed between the pair.

"Yes, Master. But you should be resting." There was a tone of chiding in Fairy Yang's voice. "I shall see to him."

"Yes, yes," Master Cheng said, waving.

He pushed himself up, taking the young lady's offered hand and muttering about impudent students. Still, he allowed her to take him into his residence while Wu Ying put his weapon away and cleared the courtyard. His movement to join them within had been waved back by his martial sister, so he waited.

When Fa Yuan exited, she raked her eyes over Wu Ying before she nodded. "Come. We shall leave our Master to his rest. We have much to speak of."

***

The pair adjourned to the top floor of the teahouse, taking one of the private rooms within. The doors were left ajar for propriety's sake, though the privacy formations were activated. It blurred the faces of anyone within, ensuring that others could not see subtle reactions or read lips, while also blocking all noise from within the formation. It was a suitable compromise for privacy's sake to ensure Wu Ying did not gain any additional aggravation. After all, Fairy Yang had gained her nickname because of her great beauty.

As a single child, Wu Ying thought that this was perhaps what those with elder sisters experienced. Both being marveled at for their luck in having a beautiful female in residence and pitied, for they would be forever out of touch. Of course, as martial brothers and sisters, they were not blood siblings and could potentially form a close relationship. But the cultural mores around such fraternization were nearly as strong as those around true blood relations.

As Wu Ying served the requisite tea to his martial sister, he let his gaze roll over her heart-shaped face, the exquisite, unblemished pearl-white skin, the slight, delicate nose, the perfectly sculpted eyebrows, and the long, lustrous black hair. Even her martial robes, green and grey as befitted an Elder, did little to hide her slim and well-proportioned, athletic body.

Yes, he knew, he was definitely pitied. But Wu Ying was also grateful, for he had, occasionally, traded on her infamy for his own use in gaining some small advantage in the assignment hall.

"Our master is gravely injured," Fairy Yang said, broaching the topic after she had thanked him for the tea.

Wu Ying nodded, not at all surprised. After all, as much as Elder Cheng had tried to hide it, Wu Ying had noted the damage. At Elder Cheng's cultivation level, the injuries must be significant to last this long. Otherwise, he would've expected Elder Cheng to be cultivating, speeding up the healing process, rather than lying on his divan in his residence.

"What can we do?" Wu Ying said.

"Do you know why he refused to acknowledge the injury?" Fairy Yang said.

"He did not want me to be beholden to him further. Or vice versa."

"A little of that. But he also worries about you." Fa Yuan paused, swirling the teacup and its contents. "Our mission, it was dangerous. Involving you at your cultivation level would be reckless."

"Good thing I'm young and reckless." Wu Ying flashed her a grin, trying for rakish insouciance. "Cultivation is not a safe path. Choosing the safest way is only a choice to a dead-end."

Fa Yuan shook her head, but a slight smile pulled at her lips. "Are you certain?" When Wu Ying nodded firmly, she sighed. "Very well. Both your Master and I have noticed a rise in tensions between the States of Wei and Shen. We believe the rise is not a natural increase but due to the machinations of a dark sect."

Wu Ying frowned. Dark sects were one of the four types of sects: orthodox, heretical, demonic, and dark. Of those, the first two were relatively benign. The Verdant Green Waters Sect was an orthodox sect, though not as much as the famed Wudang Sect.

Heretical sects might be unusual in their teachings and sometimes destructive, but not necessarily wrong – just uncommon for the norms of society. Even demon sects were part of the Dao, though their presence in the natural world often resulted in its warping. It was the dark sects—those that followed the darker, evil forms of acquiring power—that were regularly suppressed by all.

Dark sects were rarely spoken of—mostly because their very existence was hotly debated. Obviously, certain historical tragedies could be laid at their door. The fall of the Huang Empire. The Red Petal Rebellion. The two-decade drought of the northern kingdom of Yi. But those were old tragedies and their instigators located, prosecuted, and destroyed.

Dark sects in the modern day were nonexistent. Adults did not take the idea of such sects seriously. They were like children's nighttime stories, bandied about as nightmare fuel. Those who would progress their dao via violence, bloodshed, sacrifice, and necromancy had been driven out. Or so it was believed.

As such, when his martial sister spoke of the existence of such a sect, Wu Ying could not help but doubt her words. "Are you certain?"

He was quite proud his voice did not even shake when he asked the question.

"No. Of course not. But the poison our Master has had inflicted upon him has increased our certainty. It is the Three Seasons poison."

Even though Fa Yuan had said the name of the poison as though it held great meaning, Wu Ying could not place it.

When he pointed that out, Fairy Yang sighed. "It is a fabled poison, one whose manufacture was supposedly lost long ago. It was used by the dark sects in the past as a way of dealing with those who stood in their way. The Three Seasons poison guarantees the death of the poisoned in three seasons.

"The first season, the poisoned individual is wracked with colds, fevers, and trembling of the hands. They grow tired easily and lack appetite. Their chi flows slow down, and they struggle to continue cultivating. The second season, they grow even more ill, often bedridden, as their chi grows stagnant. The poisoned individual might even regress in their cultivation during this period. In the third and final season, the poisoned individual grows stronger, the earlier symptoms seeming to have faded away. They are able to use their chi again without fear of failure. But they aren't able to replenish it—not at a sustainable rate. Those who reach the third season die in short order, as even existing starves them of the energy of the world."

Wu Ying's eyes dropped in consternation. "What can we do? You didn't tell me this just to warn me, did you?"

"There is a solution to his poisoning. But finding the necessary herbs and spirit stone will be difficult." Fairy Yang leaned forward, fixing Wu Ying with a flat gaze. "Impossible, for someone at your level to do alone. But together, we might have a chance. For I will need your help, your skills as a Gatherer. If you are willing."

As much as Wu Ying and his Master might have different views on relationships, he was still his Master. He had set Wu Ying's feet on the path to immortality. The debt Wu Ying owed could not be repaid in this lifetime. And so, he spoke simply.

"When do we start?"

Chapter 3

The pair discussed their options through the day and late into the night. The servants kept the tea flowing, along with a wide array of snacks and, later on, full meals. Mostly, Wu Ying kept silent, listening to Elder Yang as she detailed their plans over the next few months. In the muted environment of the room, she almost glowed with her passion for the conversation, black eyes gleaming as she spoke.

"These ingredients…" Wu Ying frowned, staring at the notes before him. "The Sun Lotus blossom, the Heart of a Chan Chu,[3] and the Spirit Stone of a Ben[4]. They are all rare ingredients, aren't they?"

He had at least heard of the first, though he could not place where or when. It was probably some random note in one of the many, many manuals on wild herbs and ingredients that he had read in the past couple of years. Unfortunately, many authors had the bright idea to relate the description of one plant with another, as if the reader would know both plants like the original author. Thankfully, most also added a small drawing, though the artistic skills of the scholar varied. And, Wu Ying had to admit, when the relation of descriptions worked, it worked very well.

"They are," Fa Yuan confirmed. "The Ben is a flying monster, a three-legged crane. It migrates from the north to the south during the winter months, so we can only wait for them to return. If we are lucky enough, we might learn of an auction hosting a spirit stone. The only advantage is that when they are available, they are often in large numbers as they travel in flocks.

"The Chan Chu is a spirit frog whose heart we will need to take and store. It's a three-footed frog whose skin is impervious to normal weapons. Only

---

[3] In Chinese legends, a beautiful maiden that was turned into a frog with three legs and sent to the moon

[4] A white magpie with three eyes, six legs, and a glittering red tail

Energy Storage cultivators or higher can injure it. It lives in wetter, unpolluted environs in general, so we'll have to travel far to find it."

Wu Ying rubbed his chin as he considered. "And you need me to help gather the Blossom and keep it alive." At Fa Yuan's nod, he grimaced. "I don't entirely understand why it's so dangerous."

"Because where the Chan Chu resides, there is only wilderness. The monsters we will face while traveling will be stronger than even the taotei you met. You will need more than a single meridian open to survive. On top of that, we will have to travel fast as our schedule will be tight when the Ben arrive. In your current state, you would not be able to keep up."

Wu Ying grimaced again. He felt a flash of regret at having "wasted" his time.

Soon the pair were hammering out details, working out how long they could afford to wait for Wu Ying to prepare, to strengthen himself. They had to balance between training to ensure that they could complete the mission, and the progression of the poison in their Master's veins. Luckily, this was a slow-acting poison, giving them at least nine or ten months.

They talked long into the night, until their initial plans were finally being settled. There was much still to be learned, and while Fa Yuan had already begun the research, there was much she did not know.

In the end, the waitress arrived and politely indicated the closing of the teahouse. They rose, each with their own objectives, knowledge of the necessities, and their plans weighing on their minds. The next few months would be packed with training, with research, and, for Wu Ying, even more assignments.

***

The next morning, after waking up and finishing his morning ablutions, Wu Ying made his way to his gathering teacher's residence. When he realized last night that the conversation with his martial sister would take a while, he'd made sure to have the various herbs and plants he had gathered on his latest expedition sent along to her, but he still wanted to ascertain that they had arrived. More importantly, he also needed to ask Elder Li about the Sun Lotus blossom.

He found Elder Li, his gathering master and the Elder in charge of the growth of the spiritual herbs that supplied the main sect, walking her expensive farm, using her cane to gently raise leaves, push apart tall bushes, and test the soil for correct moisture content by pressing upon it. The old woman did this with every step she took, rattling off recommendations to the long-suffering disciple who trailed behind her.

Senior Goh Ru Ping bobbed his head at every sentence, memorizing the orders and the knowledge she imparted with every step. Like Wu Ying, Ru Ping was an ex-farmer, one whose paunchy, tanned jowls wobbled with each nod. It still amused Wu Ying that for all the labor and cultivation they had faced, Ru Ping had somehow managed to keep that layer of prosperity[5].

The gardens and fields of spiritual herbs stretched out behind the smaller residences of Elder Li, sparkling in the light of the gathered chi of the mountain. They started from the back of her main residence and sprawled all the way to the edge of the mountain slope before rising.

Terraced, manicured fields allowed the Elder to separate the various herbs and plants she grew, while greenhouses, packed with earth on one side and smoky, frosted glass on the other, allowed plants to survive the mild

---

[5] It's a minor joke, that when someone gets fat (and old) Chinese people will say they've grown :prosperous." After all, you could only grow fat if you were well fed and thus prosperous.

winters that the Sect faced in the State of Shen. Even in the early morning light, gardeners and gatherers tended to the plants, watering, pruning, and weeding as necessary.

As Wu Ying walked through the farm, he received nods of appreciation and recognition from many of those within. Unlike most of those who studied under Elder Li, Wu Ying was a wandering Gatherer. He trained to pick wild herbs and plants in areas of high environmental chi. It was an important job, as some plants didn't prosper well under the guidance of human hands or just grew so slowly that wild plants were constantly required to keep up with demand. It was a dangerous job that required both skill in recognition of the plants and martial prowess to survive the wild animals and demonic beasts that littered the wilds.

It was also, to Wu Ying's gratification, a well-paying job. The skill set required was narrow and lacked prestige. Few were willing to take on this occupation, preferring the more popular, more famous occupations like blacksmithing, apothecary, or just general martial arts.

"How is your Master?" Elder Li asked Wu Ying the moment he neared her.

Wu Ying, after he finished bowing and greeting both the Elder and Ru Ping, answered, "He is as well as can be expected. I'm sorry that I did not deliver the materials myself."

"It is understandable. Do not make this a regular occurrence, but they were packed adequately," Elder Li replied. She waved, dismissing Senior Goh who moved away, already calling to the other students the orders he'd received. He did not stray far though, knowing they had to finish the morning inspection. "Did you and Elder Yang have a good conversation?"

"We did." Wu Ying hesitated, only to see Elder Li frown and gesture for him to continue. "We have decided to acquire the necessary ingredients for the cure."

"And you need information on the Sun Lotus." At Wu Ying's acknowledgement, the Elder twisted her hand slightly. A slight fluctuation in the ambient chi, and a small scroll appeared in her hand, which she offered to Wu Ying. "Everything that I can recall, including three locations that should be accessible to you both. They might still contain the Sun Lotus."

"Might?" Wu Ying said.

"It is explained within, but the Sun Lotus is a very delicate plant. Even minor changes in the ambient environment can force it to go into dormancy, not blooming further."

"Thank you, Master." Wu Ying made the document disappear into his own storage ring, mentally grimacing at the lack of space within. His had been acquired two years ago, a gift from a grateful group of merchants. But it was only the size of a closet—a small closet at that. Yet he had not had time to acquire a larger spirit ring.

In truth, he was holding out for a spiritual storage ring much like Elder Li's, one which allowed the storage of plants and other cuttings in an optimal environment. Most plants could not be stored in the quasi-real environment of the average spiritual storage ring.

"Go. Read. Ru Ping will have your tasks soon."

Cognizant of his dismissal, Wu Ying bowed again and scurried off, offering Senior Goh a quick nod as he passed. Wu Ying found an empty table and carefully brushed the dirt and plant clippings off the wooden surface before he extracted the document from Elder Li. It was not a long scroll, so it didn't take Wu Ying long to read and memorize its contents.

First was an intricately detailed sketch of the plant itself. Beside the sketch was a quicker one of the surrounding environment, including common plant types that grew nearby. Next was a written description, with specific characteristics, of the plant and potential plants that could be mistaken for the Sun Lotus and a description of the most unique and outstanding surrounding plants. After that, additional details on the plant itself were listed.

These details included things like the growing season, the various stages of growth, the various parts of the plant, and most importantly for Wu Ying, the gathering method. Even with all the other details Elder Li had crammed into the scroll, her calligraphy beautiful and exact, the gathering method itself took a large portion of the remaining scroll. Elder Li had gone deeply into detail not only about when, and how, one must approach the plant, but the tools and the requisite chi flows to ensure the optimal gathering.

Next up was a description of the uses for the Sun Lotus. As a fire chi aspected flower, it was often used with other metal or earth ingredients in a variety of purifying pills and potions, as well as poisons. Its ability to melt and warm the ingredients—and the body that ingested it—was highly prized. It was even used in some of the more extravagant healing pills and medicinal baths as a warming ingredient, replacing the need for a spirit flame.

When Wu Ying reached the end of the document, he winced. The storage requirements for the Sun Lotus were detailed and intricate. They also required specific items, including a Spirit-level white jade enchanted storage container. As for the final lines on the three locations, they were just as painful, for even Wu Ying had garnered the knowledge of where at least two of those locations were. Far away and in highly dangerous, spirit beast-dominated areas.

On another slip of paper, one that had been left loose in the scroll, Wu Ying found a list of books. He knew this was her way of providing Wu Ying even more homework, since neither party trusted Elder Li's memory entirely. It was a habit she had taught him—review the original documentation always. A single mistake in identification could result in significant problems, for too many plants had no, or even opposite, effects when mixed in an apothecarist's cauldron.

Before he could read the document for a third time, a familiar voice called to Wu Ying. A moment later, a dirt-encrusted hand clapped down on his shoulder. "Enough reading. There's work to be done."

Wu Ying looked up at Senior Goh, who offered him a wide smile as he retracted his hand. Scrambling to his feet and storing the scroll, Wu Ying looked down on the shorter cultivator. "Of course, Senior. Just tell me what I need to do."

Even in these times, Wu Ying had his own obligations to fulfill to Elder Li. As his Gatherer teacher, she too was a master, a teacher that he owed obligations and fealty towards After all, her help, her education, did not come without a price.

"Good. Now, there is a batch of Cold Eel Spirit Grass that needs transplanting and harvesting," Senior Goh said, pointing at the highest level of the terraced farms.

Wu Ying could not help but wince. It was going to be a long, cold day, it seemed.

***

It was late that evening when Tou He found Wu Ying in his own residence. Unlike the grand buildings the Elders lived in, the inner sect members had smaller, single courtyard houses. Still, the amount of land given to them, especially for their expansive training courtyards, was larger than Wu Ying's former family home. As a peasant, he had lived in a single-story mud-walled house with a pair of wings on either side of the entrance. There was no courtyard to hide away within. For them, they had the entirety of their rice farm to enjoy the outdoors.

The ex-monk stood quietly in the courtyard, waiting for his friend to exit his meditation. While Wu Ying could, and did, cultivate as he moved, it was still not as effective as the seated, still meditation that most practiced. As Wu Ying grew more and more mindful of his moving cultivation method, he knew that his ability to cultivate during it would increase, but it was still a relatively new form of cultivation. In that sense, with his need to improve his cultivation rank in a short period, Wu Ying had once again turned back to the tried-and-true method of still cultivation.

With each breath he took, Wu Ying drew in the ambient chi of the world. As it flowed through the air toward him, it rebounded off his aura, which only allowed some of the chi to enter his body. This recent addition to his cultivation practice ensured that only the correctly aspected chi would enter. As there were five elemental chi types—fire, wood, water, earth, and metal—Wu Ying had to push aside all five types and only tap into the sixth unaspected chi element.

After all, using the Yellow Emperor cultivation method, Wu Ying had yet to attune his body to a specific chi type. That meant that he could absorb all types of chi, convert it into unaspected chi, and make it part of his own to control. But such a conversion took time. It also meant that he lacked some of the other advantages the aspected cultivators gained.

For example, Tou He was fire aspected. When he fought, he could imbue his staff, even his aura, with flames. He also handled both heat and cold much better than Wu Ying, the chi within his body keeping Tou He well insulated. In hot weather, Tou He managed to cultivate faster, and would likely blossom in deserts and volcanic mountains.

On the other hand, someone like Senior Goh, who was of the wood aspect, had a steadiness to both his emotions and his presence that fire or air chi individuals lacked. He was able to impart some of his own chi into plants directly, sensing their conditions, allowing him to manipulate their growth. It made him a good gardener, since his attunement could spread across the entirety of the farm.

As for Wu Ying, he had yet to choose. Of course, attuning to achieve an aspect was not just about choice, but also one's dao. Some individuals were naturally more in tune with one type of chi. Finding the right type with certainty could be tricky.

In either case, using the Never Empty Wine Pot cultivation exercise, Wu Ying could increase the amount of chi coming into his body, allowing him to speed up his cultivation. Over the past few months since he had learned the exercise, he had achieved the Major Level of achievement. That meant that he regularly cultivated at a faster rate than before, refilling his empty dantian and meridians after each exercise. The continual process of refilling and emptying was part of cultivation, as he attempted to achieve a higher level of control and standard cultivation amounts.

It was a pity there were no numbers, no graphic imagery that could tell Wu Ying exactly how much more control, how close he was to achieving his next breakthrough. All he had were feelings, the intuitive understanding one gained of his own body and mind, that allowed him to understand that he had improved.

Eventually, Wu Ying found a quiet spot in his cultivation, a time when the ambient chi had stopped flowing toward him and the flow of energy was level. The gap allowed him to end his cultivation with a simple calming of his energy. A long, slow exhalation and Wu Ying opened his eyes, spotting his friend.

"I made sure to visit the assignment hall, so you should have gotten your points," Wu Ying assured his friend. After all, the pair of them had taken the assignment together. Both cultivators were required to register the completion of an assignment when taken together for either to receive the rewards. It helped to ensure that jobs were done correctly.

"I know. I wasn't concerned." Tou He took a seat opposite Wu Ying, crossing his legs on the bare ground and smoothing out his silk robes. "I heard about your Master. My Master and I send our condolences."

"Condolences? He's not dead yet," Wu Ying snapped.

"We didn't mean, I didn't mean to imply…" Tou He said, flustered. He drew a breath, muttered *Amithabha* under his breath to calm himself, and continued. "I'm here to offer whatever help I can."

Wu Ying shook his head. "No need. I'm sorry. I should not have snapped. It's just never seems to end, does it?"

Tou He cocked his head to the side before he shrugged. "The heavens will what they will. I do not think they care or ask what we think."

Wu Ying could not help but laugh, knowing how true that was. Heaven willed and mortals filled. "Thank you. You're a good friend. But don't you have your own troubles?" Wu Ying looked down at Tou He's abdomen.

Tou He shrugged. "We are looking into exercises for my dantian."

"And?" Wu Ying pressed.

"Accessing another sect's library is… complicated." Tou He made a face. "We've already looked through a couple of the smaller sects, those who owe allegiance to the Verdant Green Waters, or who Master Yun has ties to, but…" The ex-monk shrugged. "It's difficult."

"What do you mean difficult?"

"My situation is a little unique." Tou He chuckled. "Not that all these exercises are not unique in themselves. After all, it's unusual to need the exercises, so they are all made for a specific case. And so when we try to find an exercise…"

"You're trying to fit something that's unique into your own unique situation," Wu Ying finished. The pair fell silent, contemplating the issue. Eventually, Wu Ying asked the obvious question. "Then why not make an exercise that is unique for you?"

"Oh, I should just do it like that?" Tou He said, snapping his fingers. The sound bounced around the small courtyard, filling in the silence "The kind of individuals who can make such exercises are uncommon. A badly created exercise could do as much damage as it fixes. In fact, many of the exercises I've read thus far all have their… drawbacks."

"Drawbacks?"

"Mmm… some damage the dantian—often on purpose. Others make the resulting Core fragile. Some can cause chi deviations, changing personalities. Meridians, especially the blocked Energy Storage meridians, can be clogged further as new corruption is introduced during the process." Tou He dropped his voice, leaning closer to his friend. "Many are just expensive. They require ingestion of some terribly expensive—and horrendous tasting—herbal supplements."

Wu Ying frowned. "How would you know how it tastes?"

"We've tested a few," Tou He said, scratching his bald head. "Sometimes the only way to see if they'd work was to test."

Wu Ying sighed. "I'm sorry. I wish I could help."

"Oh, you will." Tou He's eyes glittered with amusement. "I did say most of these required esoteric and expensive herbal supplements, didn't I?"

Wu Ying paused, then barked a laugh. "Yes, yes, I'll be your little dove. I'll carry the stones and sticks to fill your unending sea[6]." He sobered after a moment. "It's the least I can do, after all you've done."

"Between friends, there are no favors," Tou He said peacefully. "Now, tell me about your plans."

Wu Ying shook his head. "We have two months to learn everything we can about our targets. To find the details about the ingredients we need, their locations, and to plan our journey." He looked away from his friend, taking in his small training hall, eyes resting on the wooden jian in the corner that he practiced with every day. "Two months for me to get stronger."

"Your cultivation level?"

"Yes. I need to open more meridians."

"And...?"

"I'm probably at least a month away from the next one," Wu Ying said.

It was hard to tell, but to break the next meridian, he needed to draw in sufficient chi to fill his dantian to nearly over-bursting. Then he could push aside the clogs inside his next Energy Storage meridian. Without sufficient chi in his dantian, he would have no way to create enough pressure to cleanse it. And thus, a month was his best guess.

"A month," Tou He repeated. "And then, the next. Another six months? A year?"

"Maybe less, if I can find a way to improve my cultivation speed," Wu Ying said. Pills would help, increasing the flow in his dantian, clearing out polluted sections of his body. Cultivation exercises like his Never Empty Wine Pot. And of course, the constant practice of his cultivation method,

---

[6] This is a reference to Nüwa, drowned in Chinese mythology in the Eastern Sea. Enraged by her cruel death, she transformed into a bird (the jingwei) and carries twigs and stones in her mouth, dropping them into the ocean to fill it up. She continues that act to this day.

allowing him to refine his abilities and to increase the density and volume of chi within. "Which is why I want to focus on my cultivation exercise."

Tou He nodded. "Well, if you're going on another expedition, then we'll all need to get ready." Tou He pointed at his friend's stomach. "Get cultivating."

"Yes, sir!"

Chapter 4

With his regular duties to Elder Li completed at the moment, Wu Ying made his way to the sect library the next day. He expected to find information on the two creatures they would need to locate. To Wu Ying's marginal surprise, Fa Yuan was also within the large, elaborate, high-ceilinged wood-and-marble-pillars building.

Among the numerous stacks filled with bound paper books, rolled up scrolls, and handwritten journals lay tables for the cultivators to study on. The inner sect library was larger, more elaborate than the one dedicated to the outer sect, where less important, less useful works were kept. In fact, the inner sect library also held works on the outer world, over and above the basic classics that all sect members were expected to memorize.

In the library, among the numerous books, Wu Ying found Elder Yang poring over a laid-out map of the kingdom. He blinked in surprise, curious why the Elder was there and not in the library above. And then, realization struck him. The Elder library likely held little documentation for the kinds of assignments that inner sect members ran, nor the maps of the outer world. The Elder library probably only consisted of the most important information—cultivation manuals and exercises at the Core and above stage.

Fairy Yang looked up, meeting Wu Ying's gaze with placid eyes before waving him over. Wu Ying ambled closer then looked at the map. For the first time, Wu Ying surveyed a detailed, topographic map of the kingdom and the surrounding lands. It even had markings on the wildlands where spirit beasts roamed, the numerous areas local rulers had yet to exploit.

In truth, those lands took up a vast portion of any claimed kingdom. Road stretched through unclaimed forests, around looming hills and valleys. So much of the lands were untouched by human hand, their virgin expanses guarded by powerful Core and sometimes Nascent level spirit beasts. Lakes might be fished, rivers crossed, but sea dragons, water-aspected turtles, and flame carp ruled the deep waters.

In the wilds, humanity was still outnumbered, the invader into a vast and primeval environment.

Standing beside the beautiful young lady, Wu Ying stared at the warm, slightly browned parchment map. Bamboo slats on each edge of the paper held the document flat, while a large stack of books tottered on the edge of the table beside Fa Yuan.

Small flags had been inserted into clay bases and set on multiple locations. Each of the flags was colored differently: some red, some blue, and a single green. Most of these indicators were spread across the entirety of the map, in what at first sight seemed a haphazard manner. Certainly, Wu Ying saw no order to their allocation.

"Elder sister," Wu Ying said, bowing to Fa Yuan. During the course of the last evening together, she had insisted he switch to their more informal, less distant mode of address. No longer was he to call her Elder Yang, especially if they were to work together on this expedition.

"Perfect timing." Fa Yuan pointed at the end of the map. "Did you learn about the Sun Lotus from Elder Li? I'm marking locations for the other creatures."

"Yes. But the colors…?"

"Indicating age and reliability. Some, I have more than one source showing the presence of our targets. Others are but old news or rumors. Come. Show me where we are going," Fa Yuan said, gesturing for Wu Ying to speak.

In short order, Wu Ying had passed on the three locations his Master had provided. Of course, he made sure she knew that he had yet to confirm any of it. Fa Yuan waved away his words of caution even as she marked with green flags all the locations mentioned.

Assuming the green flags meant trusted sources, Wu Ying began to understand the map. He studied it for a time, rubbing his chin as he considered travel times, the dangers, and the geography ahead of them.

Farthest to the west, taking up the majority of the kingdom, was the mountain range the Sect was located in. To the south, the mountain range petered out into rolling hills, in which the majority of the grains that fed the kingdom grew. It was down south that Wu Ying's village had been located. Crisscrossing the land below was the river that led from the mountain range, headed south and east, and met up with the river Li.

Running across the north of the kingdom and starting from the same mountain range was the third major river that crisscrossed the kingdom. Here, it was fed by the mountainous, silver-laden hills which the nobility guarded. Farther north, between the valley and the river, was a no-man's-land in which lay another mountain range, much taller than the one to the east. On the other side of the mountain range was where the State of Khoo began.

East was, of course, the State of Wei with which they constantly battled. To the north and east of the state of Wei lay the State of Cai. To the west, past the mountain range that the Verdant Green Waters Sect was part of, was the State of Wu. Luckily for the State of Shen, they had significant, and peaceful, mercantile ties. Due to the significant presence of demon beasts in their state, the State of Wu had difficulty producing enough food for their people. Because of this, the men of Wu often left their country to act as mercenaries or to trade-in demon beast stones they had acquired.

As for the south, there lay the State of Ying. It was a small state, focused mostly on their maritime activities with just enough land to allow production of rice for their own kingdom. The kings of Shen had, on occasion, chosen to conquer the State of Ying. That conquest never lasted more than a generation or two before the independent fishermen rose up in rebellion and overthrew their conquerors.

Added to that were the ongoing difficulties of ruling a land that was regularly struck by typhoons, and for the last few generations, the State of Ying had been left to their own devices. In truth, even the current king of the State of Ying was king in name only. His words had little standing among the independent fishing villages and the few cities outside his capital.

Wu Ying considered the many locations before he turned his gaze back to the markers. Hills, bamboo forests, mountainous regions, and small and large lakes all contained a flag. Furthermore, to Wu Ying's chagrin, he could not see any pattern, especially when he tried to tie-in the green flags and their locations between the various materials they needed to gather.

"Can we even do this?" Wu Ying said, concern carrying through his voice as he stared at the map. He drew a deep breath, catching the scent of old ink, dry parchment paper, and the hint of a floral perfume coming from Fa Yuan.

"At present? Probably not." In contrast to her words, she looked nonplussed. "The heart will be the most difficult. That must be fresh. Even a few days would reduce its effectiveness significantly. We'll have to collect that last."

"Then—"

"We continue to gather information. This? This is just the start." Fa Yuan flashed Wu Ying a quick smile. A hand waved at the table beside him. "Now, you should see if I missed anything."

Wu Ying sighed, then turned to the books she'd gestured at. Fa Yuan turned away, beckoning one of the librarians to come over. Unlike Wu Ying, she did not have to wait. After all, she was an Elder. They, the inner sect librarians, were there to serve her. And as she rattled off her list of requirements, they jumped to it.

***

The Chan Chu was a demonic frog with three legs, the third leg positioned at the back of its body in slightly different angles. Each kind of frog was aspected to a different element, so it was simple enough—if you memorized the leg positions and coloration—to tell which genus a particular demonic beast was from.

Numerous drawings and detailed information from the scrolls and books, laid out before Wu Ying, showcased this information. A smaller stack of paper beside the cultivator allowed him to complete his own sketches and notes. Along with the information on the uses of various body parts from the Chan Chu, with references to particular alchemical potions and pills, were detailed notes on habitat, eating preferences, prey and predator types for the demonic beasts, and the signs of its whereabouts. All of this, Wu Ying noted and memorized.

Just as important were notes by former hunters on how best to fight the Chan Chu. Traps—generally metal-imbued talisman traps—were a common method. That allowed the hunters to hunt multiple members of the demonic frogs. However, that obviously only worked for certain types of the frogs.

Metal aspected Chan Chu could sense the talismans. Earth aspected beasts were often tough enough to deflect the simple attacks with their bodies. Only the fire, wood, and water Chan Chu were vulnerable. It also meant that the hearts and other body parts of those genus were more readily available on the markets.

In truth, battling the creatures was less troublesome than luring them out from their watery abodes. The Chan Chu were extremely aggressive and would fight one another constantly, often leading to their deaths. Since the creatures all began with cores in the late Body Cleansing stage and grew quickly to late Energy Storage stages, they dominated whichever locale they lived within. Some, a rare few, even reached the Core cultivation level.

In fact, the advancement of a creature, along the various stages of cultivation, had as much to do with its bloodlines and environment as its own progress in the Dao. That was why it was often difficult to rear such creatures for their spirit or demon cores—the very change in their environment saw to their lack of progress.

Truth be told, Wu Ying did not understand the Dao as experienced by creatures, especially demonic creatures. But then again, he didn't really understand the Dao at all.

In either case, finding, locating, and finally ending a Chan Chu would be difficult. Especially since they couldn't use the heart of just any animal. For greatest effectiveness, they had to find one in the late Energy Storage Stage, potentially even Core.

Drawing a deep breath, Wu Ying exhaled and set the document aside to dry. He rose from his seat, searching for the library attendants. Next up was information on the Ben.

***

"Let me understand this," Wu Ying said, leaning forward as he spoke to the old library attendant seated before him. "You only have a single book with a picture of the Ben?"

"Yes," the attendant said. His long whiskers twitched as Wu Ying glared at him, and the attendant met the young man's irritation with the calm of one who knew his position was secure.

"And that's because another Elder—Elder Hua—took most of the documents twelve years ago on an expedition. And never came back," Wu Ying said.

"Yes."

"And you didn't see the need to have more copies acquired in that time," Wu Ying said.

"Yes."

"Why?" Wu Ying said, exasperatedly throwing his hands in the air.

"Because the Ben is a migratory animal whose core can often be found on the open market. In addition, while rare, the actual uses of the Ben's core are limited. As such, demand for the core itself is extremely low. Many recipes have found more efficient ingredients," the attendant replied.

"So?"

"There's no need to spend limited funds learning of a bird that has no use."

"Well, that worked out well, didn't it?" Wu Ying snapped sarcastically. "What of the other documents my martial sister—Elder Yang—was reading?"

"Expedition notes. Old ones," the attendant replied. "A few notes from current wandering cultivators and the like."

"And they don't have sketches or details?" Wu Ying said.

"Not that I know. Though I have not read them all. Obviously."

Wu Ying's eyes thinned before he sighed. "Fine. Just show me where to find them. I'll gather them again to read."

"That will not be necessary. Elder Yang has requested we set those notes aside for you." He gestured to Wu Ying to follow, leading him to the pile of documents.

Grumbling under his breath, Wu Ying took hold of the documents and made his way back to his table. Hopefully the document was more enlightening than the library attendant. Otherwise... well. Otherwise, things would be interesting.

Bending his head, Wu Ying focused. As the day's sun grew low and spirit lamps were lit in the library, Wu Ying made notes. There was nothing to it but to learn, study, and hopefully succeed on the expedition. They could only do what they could do, for now.

Chapter 5

Wu Ying drew in a deep breath, inhaling the clean mountain air as he lightly ran up the mountain. As he breathed, he filtered the chi coming into his lungs through his body, sending it into his meridians and to his dantian, working to cleanse the aspected chi and trying to make the unaspected energy his own. The Never Empty Wine Pot cultivation exercise continued to allow him to filter much of the aspected chi that tried to enter his body, allowing him to continually progress as he ran.

Over the last weeks, Wu Ying's life had grown into a routine. He trained in the morning, cultivating for an hour then doing combat training with the few martial specialists left in the inner sect. He practiced forms in the martial halls, sparred with those available, occasionally taking on two or more Body Cleansing cultivators when Energy Storage cultivators were not available, and worked on the projection of his sword chi. After spending the early portions of the day training his physical body, he scarfed down a quick meal and began the second portion of his day—studying. That began in Elder Li's gardens.

Together with Elder Li, he practiced picking wild herbs, new growing formations for the herbs, the use of enchanted, specialized gardening implements—ones filled with chi, ones made of special material—and the recognition of various plants in the surroundings. With his Master, he journeyed outside the Sect into the back reaches of the mountain range, traversing the untamed wilderness at a run, spotting and picking herbs left untouched by the ignorant.

His Master often spoke of additional expeditions in the future, to map out and exploit the lands below for the Sect. Older maps were available and were updated on their treks, but many were decades, if not centuries, old. The lower the level of the herbs, the more out of date the maps were. Still, Elder Li left the matter to Wu Ying's discretion. After all, many of the plants near the Sect were of little use to her at her stage of cultivation and level of wealth.

By the time Wu Ying was done training with Master Li, it would be late afternoon at the earliest. Other times, he'd finish late into the evening, running with the last glimmers of sunlight at his back as he raced down the stone pathways. He'd consume a late dinner at the nearest dining hall before making his way to the inner sect library. He would join Fa Yuan if she was at the table, or if not, continue his own research.

After a few hundred years of collection, the Sect had accumulated a significant number of documents detailing past exploits, mercantile purchases, and expeditions carried out by various members and ancillary groups. All that information had to be filtered for the details that Wu Ying and Fa Yuan required. Even though various outer sect members had been tasked with the assignment of reading the documents, the final pieces of information, the correlation of the data had to be done by them.

The information they searched for was wide and varied. Locations of the needed materials, the monsters and their habitats, their weaknesses and strengths. Sects known to be able to produce the final compound when the material was acquired. Even hints of the antidote that might still be kept in a sect vault. It was this work that saw Wu Ying working late into the evenings. Meals would often be served at the library table, allowing them to work uninterrupted.

In between the dry scholarly work, Wu Ying often took breaks to cultivate, exercise, and work on the new cultivation technique Fa Yuan had insisted he learn.

It was this technique that Wu Ying practiced as he ran. The Twelve Eastern Gales Movement technique was a qinggong exercise of some repute. Almost all the Sect members learned this particular technique for it was a well-balanced movement technique. It improved swiftness of the feet and lightness of the body by altering the environmental chi via the projection of internal chi.

It was even usable in combat to some small degree. Like most movement techniques, continued use of the Twelve Gales should become part of a cultivator's existence, much like breathing. Each level of the Twelve Gales denoted both strength in a cultivator's understanding and grasp of the qinggong method's use and the level of integration into a cultivator's existence.

All that meant, in the end, was that Wu Ying spent every waking moment he could trying to integrate the new exercise into his daily routine. Thankfully, his earlier cultivation exercises—the Iron Bones and the Aura Restraint techniques—had achieved the level of Greater Achievement. As such, using them by reinforcing his body and restraining his aura was now as simple as letting one's heart beat.

Wu Ying ran up the mountain, his cloth-bound feet pushing against the smooth paving stones of the pathway. Around him, trees loomed, their leaves dripping with the last of the midday rainstorm that had just passed by. Wu Ying's clothes were slightly damp, since he had been caught by the tail end of the shower as he exited the dining hall.

In a change of routine, Wu Ying was making his way to the Elders' residences to take one of his infrequent lessons on apothecary. His study of apothecary had been set aside ever since Fa Yuan had returned with his Master. As much as he desired to progress in the occupation, Wu Ying did not have the time to devote himself to the matter.

Still, to ensure his skills did not deteriorate, he chose to take private lessons with his favorite senior—Liu Tsong. Rather than take public classes, the private lessons allowed Wu Ying to continue learning at his own pace and his own schedule.

Furthermore, Liu Tsong was able to adjust her lessons such that she provided him theoretical instruction that aided him in his development as a Gatherer. In turn, as payment, Wu Ying searched for the ingredients Senior Li required for her studies. It was, to Wu Ying's amusement, the start of what his Master had called the beneficial relationships of a Spirit Gatherer.

As Elder Wei's senior disciple, Liu Tsong had taken over her residence during Elder Wei's secluded cultivation. She cleaned, cared for, and used her Master's cauldrons and apothecarist lab, tasks that the servants and outer sect members could not be trusted with.

Ever since the expedition, Elder Wei had not been seen, spending her time readying herself for ascension to the Nascent Soul stage. Her period of secluded cultivation could last a year or ten or a century. The time period needed truly depended on how much chi she managed to accumulate and if she was certain she had achieved a suitable understanding of the Dao she would build her Nascent Soul around.

It was the last that stymied so many cultivators.

Doubt about one's understanding, uncertainty, and fear—all could kill just as easily as a sword's blade. Calming one's mind, firming one's resolve, it was not a matter that one could put a timeline upon. And all too often, cultivators failed. For the Heavens were jealous of their prestige and desired not to share it.

Footsteps pounding against bare rock sent Wu Ying flying up the hill, passing by cultivators with each breath. With each exhale, he expelled aspected and untouched chi. With each inhale, he brought in new chi to be churned through his body. Each moment, he drove chi through his feet into the paving stones.

Each motion created a puff of wind, a quick gust that picked up leaves and set passing cultivators' clothing fluttering. Combining his own aspected chi and the environmental chi allowed him to influence the world around him. It was what made the Twelve Gales such a powerful movement technique. Expelling chi through one's feet, through one's body to lighten it all the time would have been exhausting for those not in the Core cultivation stage if it relied solely on one's own chi. But by borrowing the environmental chi, weaving one's own energy through it, even Energy Storage cultivators could lighten their footsteps.

Of course, the process of weaving one's chi into unaspected chi was akin to weaving silk while moving, each breath, each footstep a new skein and a new chance to make a mistake. It was why Wu Ying's feet occasionally impacted the ground with greater force, making his footsteps play out the uncoordinated drumbeat of a distracted musician.

And if the failure stung, it also did not matter. For each breath of air, each passing Elder that Wu Ying bowed to as he ran past, was just another step, just another moment, as he progressed his understanding of the cultivation exercise.

Finally, he came to the end of his run, slowing before the barred gates of Elder Wei's residence. Wu Ying stopped in front of the building, brushing himself down and grimacing as he swept aside droplets of rain. Once more, he considered purchasing new robes that would shed the rain, keeping him dry in such light weather. Then he dismissed it. Again.

He had an extra set of robes in his storage ring. Cheaper, faster, and simpler to change into new, dry clothing than to waste tens of contribution points on nicer clothing. He had better things to do with his points, and so long as he had access to free laundry, there was no reason to waste funds.

Even if, occasionally, he got wet.

Pushing aside those thoughts, Wu Ying rapped on the door and smiled at the servant who let him in. In short order, Wu Ying was guided to a changing room where he discarded his wet clothing, leaving it for the servants to dry, and put on his spare robes. As he belted the middle sash, securing it tightly around his body, Wu Ying took a moment to admire himself in the provided mirror.

His long hair tied up in a high knot and wrapped around his head had not come loose in the rain. Black, just like his eyes, set a contrast to his skin, deeply tanned from hours spent working the fields, tramping through woods in search of herbs, and training in the martial arenas. Even as he progressed his cultivation, it seemed he would never gain that pale, ideal beauty of a noble and a gentleman. He ran a finger and thumb along the side of his slender jaw, touching the stubble on his chin, and made note to shave again tomorrow. He kept forgetting, never needing to do it often.

Wu Ying shifted slightly to study his profile. Long hours of exercise, often with added weights, had not added much bulk to his body. The advantages of cultivation and an already muscular form. He'd always had wideset shoulders in comparison to most noblemen and gentleman scholars. After all, they'd only practiced the martial weapons. Wu Ying had had to carry wood, lift stone, shift grain bags, and build dykes all his life.

After a moment's more consideration, Wu Ying could only shrug. In the end, he cared more about his actual strength than how he looked. If he was no ideal beauty, he was still acceptable. After all, at least one young lady had thought him good-looking.

At that, Wu Ying's placid and admiring demeanor fell. A flash of pain and regret rose, twisting his face into a grimace. Wu Ying missed her, his ex-girlfriend. Li Yao. They had not done much as a couple. Fought together, went on an expedition or two. But then, they had broken up. By his choice—and hers in a way.

Since then, he had not seen much of her. Li Yao had spent much of her time running assignments for the Sect or in secluded training. Only occasionally would Wu Ying catch a glimpse of her, and she would often hurry away.

Sometimes, Wu Ying would wander by her residence, late at night after his studies. He'd stop, stare, and then, finally, move on. Some paths, some fates, were not meant to be.

***

Class was held in the privacy of Elder Wei's residence, in a separate building with reinforced, enchanted walls and specially designed airflow. The design and the formations inset into the building created a minor, but noticeable, breeze that spiraled the smoke and other pollutants into the air, keeping the room itself mostly clear. It was a safeguard against poisonous and other potentially toxic by-products of experimentation and production.

In this particular case, Wu Ying and Liu Tsong were mostly working with non-toxic specimens. In fact, there were few reasons for them to be in this room, other than the practical access to the various cauldrons and storage materials within. The methods to verify age, freshness, and potency of herbs and other spiritual materials used required burning, dissolving, crushing, and mixing the materials. That often meant a large number of containers, mortars and pestles, and chopping boards were used. A well-stocked apothecarist workstation had all such equipment on hand.

As class was over, Wu Ying was cleansing the cauldrons and jade mortars, washing them with soap mixed with cleansing Sage Grass and drying them.

The water had to be repeatedly replaced from the correct water barrel, each barrel containing water from different springs. Even in the process of cleansing the equipment, the appropriate water and cleaning materials were required.

Bending back, Wu Ying let his gaze traipse over the room. In the center, dominating the room, was the main apothecarist cauldron, this one with multiple vents and nearly eight feet wide. Made of imperial gold, inset with jade and emerald gems, the cauldron was a Saint level artifact. The first that Wu Ying had ever laid eyes on. Carvings of dragons and phoenixes played across the cauldron cover and sides, while enchanted cores were embedded in the eyes and mouths of the figurines. Inside the cauldron, Wu Ying knew, lay another layer of enchanted Spirit cores, all powering runic script that helped the apothecarist work with volatile, poisonous, and chi infused materials.

Next to the primary cauldron was a smaller, three-foot-diameter cauldron. This cauldron was made of beaten steel, beautiful in its simplicity. There were two vents in this cauldron, its top perfectly fitted to seal in all vapor until it was ready for release. This was the cauldron they used when Wu Ying actually undertook practical lessons. This cauldron was Liu Tsong's prize possession, and unlike her smaller, hardier travel equipment, it never left the Sect.

At each of the room's four cardinal points, the four entrance doors stood closed. Jade inlays on the insides of the doors helped seal the room while handcrafted metal locks ensured their privacy. All four doors, each carved from a single piece of wood, had metal reinforced barriers and was inscribed with jade and gold. Each was barred from the inside, with small wooden flaps at the bottom raised or lowered to control airflow as necessary.

Where the doors were not, along the walls of the building were closed-faced cupboards, all of which contained specimens in glass, stone, or jade jars. Most were carefully tended and checked over on a regular basis by Liu Tsong, ensuring potency and freshness. When they degraded, they would be replaced, the material transferred to Liu Tsong for her use. In this way, the Senior apothecarist would produce pills or concoctions from the materials, improving her own practice and providing for the Sect at the same time.

It was because of this largess that Liu Tsong's ability as an apothecarist was growing by leaps and bounds in the absence of her Master. If her own senior brothers and sisters had been present in the Sect, they would have taken on this advantageous task. However, of the three Senior apothecarist who studied under Elder Wei, one was in closeted meditation. One had left the Sect entirely for the last two decades, setting up his own shop to cater to the nobles and rich merchants after his failure to progress in his immortal cultivation. And the last was on an expedition, wandering the lands and seeking inspiration for his own dao.

"Pink dangshen is highly prized while purple should be stored in black stone. Black dangshen should be discarded," Wu Ying muttered to himself as he worked. "Be careful, verify potency against nearby plants for the Yellow Creeping Ivy of Liang can alter the potency of the dangshen. Regular price, generally by the catty, is seven taels."

"Good," Liu Tsong said, overhearing Wu Ying's mutterings as she put away the last of the ingredients in one of the cupboards. She then took the time to secure it, pulling the split metal padlock key from the padlock and checking that the doors were secure. A slight fluctuation in the ambient chi told Wu Ying that she had stored the key with the rest of her belongings in her spirit ring. "Pay attention to the number of petals on the dangshen as well. The preference is for three and five. Sorting beforehand will likely garner you a higher price per catty, since otherwise—"

"Some poor outer sect member will have to do it," Wu Ying said in unison with Liu Tsong. They broke into wide grins, sharing the inside joke.

"Yes. You're learning fast, though your actual concocting technique is still miserable to watch," Liu Tsong said as she walked back through the room, dodging the myriad wooden and stone tables set in the room. The tables were positioned throughout the room, surrounding the main cauldron, not only for efficiency's sake but also to aid the flow of chi. It thus made travel through the room somewhat more haphazard than a straight line.

"Nothing to be done about it." Wu Ying sighed. "There's so much to learn, and little time to do it in."

Liu Tsong shook her head. "You rush, rush, rush from one cultivation level to another. One technique to the next. It is less than ideal. Cultivation is a multi-decade endeavor, not this headlong rush."

Wu Ying could only offer his Senior a shrug. It was not as if he wanted to be rushing, feeling harried all the time. It was just the Heavens choosing to harry him with events.

"Have you considered my Senior's request further?" Wu Ying asked, changing the subject.

"To join the expedition?" Liu Tsong flashed Wu Ying a smile before she shrugged. "I have. I also know that my Master would feel obligated to help. But I have my duties here. If I left, it would leave my Master vulnerable and her workshop unattended. Doing so would also be leaving the Sect with one fewer high-level apothecarist on hand."

Wu Ying grimaced. She was correct, especially in the lack of apothecarists. While Elder Wei was not the only apothecarist elder, she was the highest level one. And as such, the standards of her students were generally better. With the ongoing war drawing down the Sect's stores of healing and replenishment pills, they desperately needed all the high-level apothecarists they could get. No number of low-level apothecarists could replace a single high-level one and the pills they could make.

"But if we could get you, the pill... it'll be more effective if made immediately."

Liu Tsong shook her head. "I'm not my Master, Wu Ying. I cannot just eye the environment, the flow of chi within a terrain, and make adjustments as I concoct a high-level pill. I need to take careful measurements, ensure the flow of chi around me is taken into account, even set up talismans and enchantments to ensure it stabilizes, to even consider such an attempt. And even then, I would likely fail at the production." She gestured around the room. "This room is perfectly managed. The flow of chi here is a stable constant at all times and completely known to me. Even then, I've failed making Saint class pills, like the one you requested, nine out of ten times. And on the tenth? It was barely considered a pass."

Wu Ying offered his friend a guilty smile as he'd forced her to admit her weakness. "Still..."

"I doubt your Senior would be willing to risk my failure," Liu Tsong said. "I'm sure she is making other arrangements. At the worst, she can always work with Elder Tan when she returns."

Wu Ying winced. If Elder Wei was irascible and prone to outbursts, at least she was reliable. Elder Tan, on the other hand, was as prone to blow off prior obligations as she was to cook up a batch of high-level pills in a fortnight. She was well-known to work when inspiration struck her and only then.

"It'll be fine," Liu Tsong assured Wu Ying. "Elder Tan isn't as unreliable as you think."

Wu Ying raised an eyebrow, having finished cleaning all the implements. He dried his hands on a nearby towel, setting the washcloth aside while he waited for Liu Tsong's answer to his silent query. When she just gave him a strange grin, he decided not to push further. Even in the privacy of this room, certain opinions should not be said out loud, especially by those in the same profession.

Wu Ying could only sigh and hope that his Senior had a better option.

***

Later that evening, he related his conversation with Liu Tsong to Fa Yuan, and she offered him a single nod of acknowledgment.

"Unfortunately, it is all too common these days for apothecarists to refuse to go on expeditions." Fa Yuan sighed. She glanced around the library, then raised a hand to send her chi into the air and block the sound of her next words from those around. "Ever since the great purges, the Guild has slowly discouraged its members from taking part. While there are anomalies, the small number of apothecarists has seen them elevate their overall importance in our society."

Wu Ying rubbed his chin, tracing fingers over the growing stubble. He knew little of the history she spoke of. About a hundred thirty years ago, a series of purges across the various kingdoms had been enacted, almost all in unison. The formation of the Apothecarist Guild in the wake of the purges had seen the rise in importance of the secondary occupation while streamlining their studies and the guild itself.

"Why did the purges happen?" Wu Ying asked.

"Before the purges, apothecarists were not legislated. Anyone could work as one. There were numerous charlatans, conmen, and fools, all of whom regularly took advantage of others. This was just the way it was, and buying pills back then was much more dangerous." Liu Tsong pursed her lips as she recalled the matter. "That all changed when the dark sects took advantage of the chaos. They plied the kingdoms with a large number of false apothecarists, at first providing pills and potions that gave a boost to cultivation speeds and level. Unlike many of the pills and concoctions others sold, these worked."

Wu Ying frowned. Her words seemed harmless enough, but anything to do with the dark sects never was.

"It took nearly two decades before the whispers grew to a cacophony that could not be ignored," Fa Yuan said.

"Whispers?"

"Yes. Of cultivations that had stalled, of meridians damaged. Cores, corrupted. Some even lost their way on their dao paths, growing angry and twisted." She paused, eyeing Wu Ying before she continued in a rush. "Much of this period is in our historical records. Though few read about it these days. Most apothecarists do not like discussing this period. They think it is a bad mark against their occupation and not a warning against dark sects."

Wu Ying shivered, looking about the bright, open room of the library. Once again, the mention of the dark sects, like stories of ghosts and demons told to frighten children. Amoral cultivators, walking a dao path of anger, corruption, and evil. Who sought not even just vengeance but petty revenge, the deaths of others in pain and torture to advance themselves.

The Dao was myriad, it was plentiful, and it encompassed all things. From the growing of plants on a hot summer day to the bitterest winter nights when rats ate their children to survive the long cold. This too was the Dao.

And because the Dao encompassed all, but humanity was limited, there were darker paths, things that the demons and the human mind sought.

Paths of pain and envy, jealousy and anger. Things that were done in wars and behind closed doors, that saw minds warped and lives destroyed.

Some said that this too was part of the Dao, just the way the universe worked. Even the brightest light casts the darkest, deepest shadow. And where there was shadow, there were humans who would seek it out, searching for strength and their way to immortality.

"What happened?" Wu Ying said, then he realized the answer. "The purges."

"Yes. It began with the Sects, with their own apothecarists at their beck and call. They sought out the corrupt within their own ranks, then spread the culling to the lands they controlled. Kings and nobles took part too when they realized the damage done to them and their families." Fa Yuan's face grew grim. "Many innocent apothecarists were falsely accused and killed. Even more were hounded out of the occupation when the Guild was created." Wu Ying blinked at her words, and she offered him a thin-lipped smile. "Those who do not seek to bow to the bureaucracy of the masses will always be crushed under its yoke, if they do not hide their opposition."

"The ox that will not pull in a straight line will be whipped until he does," Wu Ying muttered.

"Yes. Or something less... peasant-like," Fa Yuan replied, though the smile on her lips and the crinkles along her eyes showed that she was joking. "In any case, after the purges, the Guild rose in prominence. But since then, becoming an apothecarist has taken more time and skill, as well as resources. It's why wandering apothecarists, ones not affiliated with Sects, have become a thing of the past. For the most part."

Wu Ying nodded. Even he knew that those without the appropriate Guild seal could not sell their pills or potions or ply their trade in most kingdoms. No serious cultivator would use their wares and no merchant would buy them. Those found to be selling medicines from non-Guild sources were often censured, left without a regular supply, or in some cases, pressured in more direct manners.

"So do our apothecarist students have to take the exams too?" Wu Ying said with a frown.

"Of course. But they are only held once a year, with the location rotating between a set of kingdoms. That way the Guild can ensure there is no favoritism," Fa Yuan replied. "We send our students out when it is viable, and they have reached a sufficient level. The cost of examinations is high, so we do not register them unless they pay the contribution points or reach a high enough level that their pills would bring a return on the open market."

Wu Ying recalled how the vast majority of the pills made by the apothecarists in the Sect were for internal use. No need to be concerned about registration or Guild acknowledgement when everyone was using it internally. It was not as if Elder Wei or Tan would let them slack off in quality. And this way, even the lowest quality pill found residence.

"Do we have another option then?" Wu Ying asked. "If not Liu Tsong?"

"I'm exploring options and requesting help. The problem is that those apothecarists with the requisite skill are often booked many months ahead. And we"—she gestured to the map displayed on the table, numerous new flags placed on it. As they continued their research, they had continued to add potential locations where they could acquire the necessary materials—"do not yet know our final destination. Until then, we can only make inquiries."

Wu Ying grimaced. "If that's the case, and if the potency drops…"

"We should acquire the…" Fa Yuan searched through the notes on the table.

Wu Ying spoke from memory. "A Thrice-Enchanted Ice Jade storage box for the heart. Otherwise, a Fire Bark Encrusted storage box filled with Yang Water from the Nine Abyss Hot Springs."

"Yes." Fa Yuan made a face. "I don't really know where we'd find either though…"

Wu Ying shrugged his shoulder, then seeing the expectant look on her face, sighed. "I'll speak with the armorers tomorrow."

Fa Yuan flashed Wu Ying a wide smile, and he rolled his eyes. Still, all this experience at setting up an expedition was quite an eye-opener. Even if he was not taking part in the recruiting of members.

Chapter 6

Late that night, Wu Ying walked the lamp-lit pathways, one hand holding a spirit lantern aloft. The moon was well past full, leaving the waning moon on the twenty-fourth day to provide its weak illumination. On the cobbled pathway, he spotted the occasional returning inner sect member, having finished their midnight assignations or, in a few unfortunate cases, assignments.

The leaves rustled in the late-night breeze that carried the smell of new greenery. Slivers of moonlight and the reflected light from his spirit lamp amplified the shadows along the mountain path. Even so, for all the stark beauty on offer, Wu Ying paid it no mind.

Instead, he turned over and over his musings on the Dao and that of the presence of the dark sects. It was clear that such sects were real. That their beliefs, while contemptible by common morality, had some truth to them. After all, there was a darker pantheon of immortals, those who were not demons, who were not guards, who lounged among the celestial hierarchy. They had their own residences, their own places of power. And though those immortals among the celestial bureaucracy and the demons were at war, it was impossible to deny that their beliefs must be part of the Dao.

Stories of the world above, the immortal battles that eventually filtered down to the earth below were all glimpses of what could be. That stories that these battles were waged, the fights between the demons below and the immortals above, were less common now did not mean they were any less true. And in all these stories, the darker hierarchy was as often the allies of the celestial empire as enemies.

As much as Wu Ying wanted to deny the truth, to deny the darker impulses within him, the dark sects were part of the Dao. Nature was cruel. Any who ever had watched a cat play with its prey, releasing the rat to run and catch it, dragging it back and batting it around before repeating the action could say as much. How many animals lay dying slowly from the venom of a snake, felt their bodies dissolve as spiders readied their meals? Even plants could be cruel, for the climbing ivy could kill a tree as easily as a woodcutter's axe.

Nature was cruel, and so, the Dao was too. Yet in nature, animals were just creatures who dwelt not on reason nor morality in their actions. If they were cruel, that cruelty often had a place, a reason. The spider sucked upon dissolved flesh for food. The cat played with its prey to learn its nature. The ivy climbed for its own survival.

Humanity though, humanity could choose. In their choices, they could stray from the Dao. They could transact with demons for power, apply great cruelty and great kindness in equal order, without care for consequences. But where was the line? If the Dao encompassed everything, even the evil in man and nature, how could one then be not part of it?

If the Dao was the way, the true way, of what nature and the world should be, then how did one know when one strayed? Not right or wrong—because duality, the nature of creating boxes, of thinking and knowledge, strayed from the simple and encompassing nature of the Dao. If you judged an action to be evil or wrong or good, then such thinking was no longer of the Dao.

But if one did not judge, then how did one understand?

If the world was, in all its glory, in all its nightmares, a part of the Dao, then were not all men, were not all actions, part of it?

Wu Ying did not know. He did not grasp, could not grasp, the differences. The Dao was everything, but it was also only the right way. If one strayed from it, one walked the wrong path. But knowing the right path, knowing the Dao, was a journey.

And he was only eighteen.

This question, this answer, escaped even the most erudite of scholars and the wisest of sages. Mortal man cannot grasp the Dao in its entirety. Those who did were no longer mortal men, but a Sage in truth, an immortal. Mortal man could not grasp both the darkness and the light, hold them in his hand and yet offer no judgment of either.

And so, cultivators like Wu Ying only strove to understand a sliver of the Dao. Understand, grasp, and eventually immortalize it within their own selves. By doing so, they achieved immortality, becoming part of the Dao, becoming part of the celestial bureaucracy. And if they were less than a Daoist Sage in their understanding of the world, they were more than mortals.

Wu Ying laughed, tilting his head up to the cold night sky, breathing in the fresh air. He laughed, for he knew that none of this mattered to him. Not yet. Not truly.

Perhaps there was a path to immortality, one that led through darker paths, that was part of the Dao. Perhaps these dark sects were part of the Dao, part of all that was, is, and could be. But it was a path that Wu Ying rejected. It was not for him to be cruel and callous, to set himself far above others and seek immortality not just selfishly but over the blood and bones of others. He could not stand aside and watch others be hurt. He could not help but judge the dark sects as evil and wrong for what they did.

Perhaps that meant that he would never be a Sage, never truly understand the Dao, never truly understand the heavens above, the hells below, and everything in between. But that was okay. After all, Wu Ying was just a peasant who had grown up digging dirt, planting rice, and squabbling with his parents.

He was no monster, no sage, no demon. He was just a man making his way through the paths of cultivation, seeking his own little slice of the Dao to embody.

Wu Ying exhaled. He turned his head down, taking in the worn cobblestones, the doors to his own residence. Briefly, he wondered how long he had been standing before his wooden doors, lost in thought. Then he chuckled again.

As he did so, he cast aside any doubts, any concerns as he closed one door to immortality. His steps, taking him into his own courtyard on his way to his rooms, paused. A foot hung in mid air, refusing to move as Wu Ying sensed the change.

For long moments, Wu Ying stood with one foot raised. His mind turned, his body thrumming with breathless anticipation. Then he moved. He dropped into a cross-legged position, hands positioned on either leg, thumb and forefinger touching as they rested on his knees. He breathed in and allowed the rush of chi to enter his body.

Enlightenment, as fickle as the wind, arrived. Enlightenment, seeking only an entrance, found him as he shut a door. Enlightenment arrived.

And with it, the approval of the heavens.

***

Wu Ying woke the next day, having collapsed asleep after breaking through another meridian. His dantian, normally drained of chi when he opened a new meridian, was nearly full still. The process of breaking through while showered by the benediction of the heavens was a different experience entirely.

As he stood, Wu Ying grimaced at the soiled clothing that stuck to his body, peeling from his skin with each movement. The filth from within his body had pushed outward as the blockages from his Energy Storage meridian cleared, coating him with their filth. It would need to be dealt with, but for now, Wu Ying had other matters to attend to.

First, he considered his energy levels and where he stood. He felt the pulse of energy in his newly cleared meridian, felt the way energy recharged him. Wu Ying could also tell that not only was he close to breaking through to another meridian, the one he had cleared last night was almost fully cleansed. He could not help but smile even as he walked toward the bathroom.

"My apologies, young Lord. The water in the bath has grown cold. I had expected that you would be awake earlier," said Auntie Yee, the white-haired, mortal servant who took care of his daily tasks. Her presence as his servant, Wu Ying knew, was meant to be a subtle insult. She was, after all, the oldest living mortal servant among the inner sect. As such, she was considered unfit for the more prestigious nobles within the Sect.

Wu Ying was, in fact, grateful for this subtle insult. Auntie Yee was a good cook, one who had many years of practice, and her many years of serving the Sect meant that she understood more of the history and the subtle interactions of the nobles and the cultivators, the Elders and the inner sect members than newer servants. Her presence, and her quiet coaching, had helped Wu Ying grasp many areas of his new life that he might have missed otherwise.

"No need to apologize," Wu Ying said. "I can bathe cold." He had before, more often than not. In the winter, cold baths were the only kind of baths available in his village.

After shooing her out of the way, Wu Ying stripped his clothing, leaving them in a hamper for Auntie Yee to clean later. In the meantime, he stepped into the raised circular wooden bathtub, grasping the soap beads set aside in their wooden container, and washed. Even if he was late for practice, he could not turn up filthy.

A short while later, Wu Ying climbed out of the bath, drying his hair with the laid-out towels. A flicker of annoyance and jealousy ran through him as he wished he had the ability to control the water. Those with the water aspect could easily dry themselves with the right chi exercise. He had to do it the hard way.

In fact, for all his studies, he had yet to learn many useful chi skills. He knew part of that was that he was hurrying along, desperate to catch up with his Seniors. His focus had entirely been on combat, Gathering skills, and apothecary. Even his cultivation exercises were focused on making him able to cultivate faster or more martial.

But chi skills were not just about cultivation. Qinggong skills allowed one to move faster, to run across water, bamboo, and even leaves blowing in the wind. They made journeying through the world easier. At the highest levels, one could even ride spirit swords, flying through the air with ease.

Certain types of Body Cultivation skills did more than just reinforce the body. They also increased the sensitivity of the body to the natural world. Gourmands were particularly focused on such skills, allowing them to truly savor the meals they searched for. Other skills allowed one to shield their body from falling rain, cleanse the blood, or even aid in the healing of others.

Chi was the living force of nature that which made all things one. In that sense, it was clear why cultivation exercises would be wider and more expansive than just combat exercises. Even if that was his own focus, even in Gathering, there were multiple minor skills that could be learned.

Flowing internal wood chi combined with a little bit of water chi could help promote growth in plants. Proper use of wood and fire chi might allow you to pluck certain plants and herbs that would not be viable otherwise. Metal chi on its own could shield one against the thorns of numerous plants. Even his own unaspected chi could be made to work with all those skills, even if it was at a much lower efficiency.

And while Wu Ying had picked up such techniques, he had yet to learn any true skills. Even from Elder Li. After all, his focus was on the understanding and grasp of the plants and their parts. In time, he knew, he would have to learn such skills. Learn to transmit his chi into the earth, especially for plants in the Saint and Immortal level.

But that was for later. For now, Wu Ying had a new meridian to test. Grinning, he slipped on a new pair of robes, then he hurried out, headed for the martial training grounds. Even if he hadn't learned any useful utility skills, he still had martial ones. And perhaps he could win a few duels with his new improvements.

***

The training grounds of the martial specialists had changed. Not in the physical sense. It was still a large courtyard with multiple raised dueling platforms, some platforms with enchanted chi shields to protect bystanders from the fighters within and others just plain for Body Cleansing cultivators and less vigorous training. Looming buildings around the courtyard hosted additional indoor training grounds, along with changing rooms, a simple first aid room, storage sheds for the weapons, and an archery center. It was the largest and most expansive of the inner sect training grounds and one that was, mostly, staffed by the martial specialists.

No, the grounds hadn't changed physically. It was the specialists themselves, the ones who filled the grounds from sunrise to sunset and sometimes afterward. There was now an edge, an intensity that had not been present before, to their training. There were also new faces—much younger new faces—among familiar ones. Those new faces were those who had risen from the outer sect to fill empty spots created by their losses in the war.

The war, always on and off, had grown in intensity in the last two years. During the last recruiting session, nearly three dozen of the outer sect members had been introduced to the inner sect. Another dozen and a half, many of them wandering cultivators, had been added directly as well. More than two-thirds of the new inner sect members had gone on to join the martial specialists, all of them receiving intense, focused training by their Seniors and Elders.

In one of the sandy pits, Wu Ying watched with slight interest as a trio of cultivators were thrown around, grappled and locked down by a familiar Elder. The darker-skinned, shorter Elder Hsu was one of the many new volunteers training the new martial specialists. Of course, his unarmed Snail grappling style was well-hated by all who'd had their faces squashed by his impressive—and hairy—bare chest.

Turning aside before Elder Hsu spotted his regard, Wu Ying made his way to the sparring rings. Elevated off the ground, the circular dueling rings were filled with energetic martial cultivators. Many of the new inductees from the outer sect trained in the unprotected dueling rings, practicing martial forms that didn't see much energy projection. On the other hand, the wandering cultivators and older martial specialists trained in the protected sparring rings.

Wu Ying slowed as he neared the hidden demarcation splitting the sparring rings by type, eyeing the attendees. Of course, his normal victim—

friend—Tou He was not around as he was out on another mission as per his Master's behest. The same could be said for Li Yao. Yin Xue was with the vast majority of the martial specialists—serving in the armies. Ever since his return, Yin Xue's cultivation had progressed at an astounding speed, making full use of his family's cultivation method during the quiet winter months. These days, he was considered one of the strongest non-martial specialists in the inner sect. His progress had seen him forced to take part in the war directly, as he sought to stabilize his cultivation through real world experience and increase his sect contribution.

Other than a few familiar faces, most of those present were strangers to Wu Ying. Some utilized martial skills that Wu Ying had never seen before, styles uncommon to the Sect. He could not help but stare, playing their forms, their preferences, through his mind and setting them against his own style.

"Are you just watching today?" a voice called to Wu Ying. It was a little on the higher pitched side, the words shot out like the spray from a waterfall, unending and indiscriminate. The speaker had a large, flowing beard and, surprisingly, had his hair shorn tight to his scalp except for a single line down the center.

It was uncommon for individuals to cut their hair. Most held to the old ways, keeping their hair uncut as a sign of respect to their ancestors, their parents, who had given them their body. But time and practicality had worn at the edges of this tradition for some. Of course, there were also the mountain clans and other small groups of individuals who kept to their own traditions, putting needles in their faces, marking their skin, and cutting their hair. Wu Ying could not help but wonder which group the speaker was from.

"Well, no. I was hoping to spar," Wu Ying replied.

Wu Ying looked down, noting the man's pair of hook swords. The shuang guo were uncommon weapons, requiring great skill to use. The hook swords had a single straight blade rising from the substantial crescent guards that the wielder could hold, their hands protected by the crescent blades. A hook was formed at the end of the straight blade, allowing the weapon to catch, twist, and strip weapons. Certain styles even used the hooks to extend the range of the weapon, hooking each pair of blades together by their ends. At the bottom of the sword guard, a spike jutted out, allowing the wielder to strike his opponent in close proximity. The entire weapon had multiple forms of attack, but all of them required great skill to weave together.

"Are you available?" Wu Ying said.

"Obviously. We'll take ring three," the man said, striding away without waiting for Wu Ying to follow. Confident that Wu Ying would do so.

Wu Ying shrugged, seeing no reason to delay. He had to admit, he was quite interested in playing with the man. While his father had described the weapons to him, he had yet to experience them himself. Shuang guo were an eclectic weapon, more suited for a civilian than a soldier. And, Wu Ying added to himself, a cultivator. After all, few cultivators were required to fight in an army rank.

The pair ascended the empty platform, hopping up the edge and landing on the stone floor. They both placed their hands on the starting enchantment, channeling their chi into the barrier. In this way, the enchantments could form the necessary protection, utilizing both the fighters' and the environmental chi as a source of fuel.

"Wang Yu Kun, inner sect cultivator. Using the Seven-Star Mantis[7] form," Yu Kun said, announcing his style as he raised and saluted his training weapons.

---

[7] Yes, that's a real style. It's actually the most common praying mantis style.

74

"Long Wu Ying, inner sect cultivator. Using the Long family sword style," Wu Ying replied as per tradition. He too raised the training weapon he'd drawn from his spirit ring. While they could use real weapons, it was generally frowned upon. In recent days, the Elders had put a stop to such practices almost entirely. They could ill afford to allow their new martial cultivators to be injured during this time of need.

They started out slow, circling one another. Watching each other for their movements. Wu Ying rejoiced as he circled, feet never crossing one another, feeling the thrum of new energy from the meridian he had opened. He was now a quarter of the way to the next step—the formation of his Core—and he would soon open the third out of eight Energy Storage meridians.

But that was for later.

For the moment, Wu Ying tested his opponent. He tested his speed, his reactions, his style. Wu Ying offered his blade as he closed, watched as Yu Kun beat at his sword in quick sweeps, attempting to catch the blade at the forward half. Each twist of the hooked weapons attempted to trap his jian, forcing Wu Ying to withdraw his own sword, to make small disengages to keep his sword free.

In turn, Yu Kun rotated the swords around each wrist as he kept the cuts coming at Wu Ying. He stepped closer to Wu Ying with each movement, attempting to cut Wu Ying off. Wu Ying focused on keeping his sword pointed at his opponent's chest, at cutting off the line of attack by leaving his sword a threat.

But all this was the opening act of their duel. A twist of the wrist brought one hook sword close, beating Wu Ying's jian. A second hook sword caught Wu Ying's already disengaging jian as it circled in the same direction. It pulled the sword high, off-line from Yu Kun's body as the cultivator stepped close. The first hook sword kept moving, cutting toward Wu Ying's neck.

When faced with two swords, one must act quickly and decisively, stepping into the gap your sword created or retreat. But with retreat cut off by the edge of the platform, Wu Ying had only one choice. He dropped low, sliding his body along with his foreleg, shifting forward while maintaining the lower level as he struggled to bring his sword back in line. At the same time, Wu Ying brought his free hand upward.

Dragon strokes the Painting was the technique he executed. It was a dangerous—almost insanely so—defense against a weapon. It required you to catch the sword as it cut, deflecting the blade by pushing against the flat of the blade. In some scenarios, the worst-case scenarios, you pushed at the blade itself. So long as you managed to touch the blade at the same spot throughout its motion, the lack of motion would ensure the blade itself did not cut you. It was the same reason one could tap the edge of a kitchen knife, checking for sharpness, and yet not cut oneself.

Unless said knife was extremely sharp, or the force was extremely high, or you made a mistake and let the blade slide the distance of the edge of a grain of rice. Which, when one considered that all this had to be done at speed, was likely to happen. If not for the light coating of chi that Wu Ying wrapped his hand with, if not for his training in the Iron Body Technique, if not for the fact that this was a practice blade, if he had any other choice, he would not have chosen to take the risk.

But he had none. And so, he Stroked the Painting, sending the hook sword skimming alongside his body. He neared Yu Kun, slamming his freed shoulder into the midriff of his opponent. It forced Yu Kun back, giving Wu Ying a momentary opening as he brought his sword in-line. A second more, and he'd…

A sharp pain along the back of his shoulder as the hook of the second sword dug into his back. Wu Ying hissed, then rolled his shoulder, freeing the weapon and letting it slide past. The blunt instrument skidded along his body, following Yu Kun's retreat.

"Your win," Wu Ying said.

"A beautiful deflection," Yu Kun praised.

Wu Ying raised his hand, flexing it slightly and spotting the slight redness from the action. He'd felt it, the way Yu Kun had infused a little metal chi into his weapon, making it sharper, easier to handle. Against a real weapon… "Not that beautiful. I'd have been cut."

"But still, you'd have deflected it."

Wu Ying considered the question and nodded. If he'd had a second weapon, if he'd shifted to a pommel strike… well. Many possibilities. "Again?"

Yu Kun grinned, raising his sword and saluting Wu Ying. A quick reply and the pair began again, this time with the initial feeling out period much shorter. Blades flashed as Wu Ying worked to stay on the outside of Yu Kun's body, forcing him to turn again and again. This time around, Wu Ying took the fight to the other.

And if he was grinning just a little… well, sparring was fun. And his body, his senses were so much stronger than before.

***

As the pair of combatants hopped out of the fighting ring, passing through the fading barrier, they fought to control their breathing. Wu Ying sighed internally, making a note to spar with Yu Kun further. As he had suspected would happen, Wu Ying had lost more than he had won. The cultivator's eclectic, flashy style with the hook swords and their ability to grab, twist, and deflect Wu Ying's jian had been a new experience. Add to that Yu Kun's higher cultivation and his own Sense of the Sword, and Wu Ying was more than matched. There was nothing to be done about it. Only experience would bridge the gap between them.

"Did you recently breakthrough?" Yu Kun asked after he had stored his weapons. Already, both their breathing was normalizing as chi and air entered their lungs.

"I did. Why did you ask?" Wu Ying said, cocking his head.

"Your movements were sometimes off. As if you expected to be a little closer or a little farther with each movement." Yu Kun gestured with his hands, trying to describe Wu Ying's motions. "They improved as we fought. The differences became smaller."

"Ah…" Wu Ying grimaced and nodded. That too was true. Being stronger was good, but when one fought for each chi[8], the most minor of deviations could cause problems. A cut that would seriously injure might only offer the barest of grazes, a dodge that was to position yourself for a better strike might instead put you in a more vulnerable location for a second attack if you misjudged your position by inches. "Yes. It's taking time to relearn."

"It always does." Yu Kun nodded. "It is one of the greatest struggles at this stage."

"Speaking as if you know what it is like in the other stages," Wu Ying said, teasing the man as they finally arrived at a nearby table. Wu Ying poured a glass of water out, then offered it to Yu Kun as the victor.

"No, no, Senior should not—"

---

[8] Traditional Chinese measurement. I won't use it again probably, since without the tone variation, it looks the same. The actual size varied depending on the age, but in the modern period, it's been standardized to 32mm so, about an inch and a quarter

"Har! Senior only by chance. I can tell you're stronger," Wu Ying replied. He had no need to check his aura again, for their fight had made it clear that Yu Kun had cleared more of his Energy Storage meridians.

"Still, it would not be right." Yu Kun pushed the cup back to Wu Ying.

Seeing that Yu Kun's protestations were not just out of courtesy[9] but out of actual conviction, Wu Ying relented and drank the water. His thirst was probably driving him as much as his desire to get over the courtesies. At least among those in the village, such courtesies were generally shortened. After all, everyone knew everyone, so the gesture was more important than the actual outcome, which, in most cases, was already foreordained.

"Are you a martial specialist, Senior Long?"

"No need to be so formal. We are both inner sect members," Wu Ying said, punctuating his words with a gesture. It was weird, especially since Yu Kun was at least five years older. "And no, I just have an interest in the martial arts."

"Ah. Myself too," Yu Kun said, touching his chest. "It is hard to survive on the road without such skill."

"You were one of the wandering cultivators?" Wu Ying asked. He had guessed, but it was better to verify.

Yu Kun nodded.

"Might I ask why you joined us?" When he saw Yu Kun freeze, looking uncomfortable, Wu Ying shook his head. "My apologies. That was rude. Your reasons are your own."

---

[9] Courtesy refusals do happen. In fact, there are long tracts in classic books like *Water Margin* about how various people decline the courtesy of eating, of insisting of paying. Depending on their families, even modern day Chinese do this. Though the process (at least in my experience) is significantly shortened. We don't take hours on figuring out who is paying the bill.

"The Sect has much to offer, and storm clouds gather," Yu Kun said. "While we might flitter from province to province, some storms are too large to run from."

Wu Ying opened his mouth to inquire further but was interrupted as a pair of cultivators appeared beside them.

"Are you open to trading partners? We just finished a duel," one of the cultivators said, gesturing between himself and his partner.

Yu Kun nodded, gesturing for a partner to come with him back to stage three. That left Wu Ying with the other, expectant cultivator. Pushing aside his concerns about what storms Yu Kun sensed, Wu Ying nodded. After all, he still had to practice and make his new cultivation level his own.

Chapter 7

The inner sect armory, holder of mortal, spirit, and saint equipment and weapons was a mysterious building to Wu Ying. No matter how many times he visited, he had never made it past the viewing rooms. Those simple stone-and-marble rooms, with their peaceful paintings on the walls and large, wooden tables to set potential equipment upon, were all that he had ever seen. The building was expansive and likely went miles under the ground.

The attendants who waited upon the visitors saw more of the armory. They took orders, made suggestions, perused through the files of what the armory contained, and took care of those items within. And even then, many only saw small portions of the armory, relegated to care for specific rooms, given specific levels of knowledge.

In this way, the Sect was able to ensure the secrecy of what magical and immortal equipment they held. This level of secrecy, of care, was needed in some cases. After all, a single Saint level sword could engender a bloodbath among noble houses as they strove to provide for their younger generation. A Saint level weapon could raise the level and ability of its user from Core to Nascent Soul. How powerful then would a Nascent Soul level cultivator be with such a weapon?

Sects that flaunted their wealth only made others want to eat vinegar[10] and would only guarantee their eventual downfall. Better to hide their wealth so that both friends and enemies had little to complain of. Of course, such a convoluted establishment of knowledge meant that one was better off speaking with the Elder in charge or one of the Senior disciples when one needed information.

---

[10] From the Chinese term '吃醋' that directly translated means "eat vinegar" or more correctly, jealousy or envy. It comes from a story that Emperor Taizong from the Tang dynasty decided to choose a concubine for his premier Fang Xuanling. Xuanling's wife was so jealous that, given the choice between accepting the concubine or drinking a poison, she drank the poison. She only learned later that the Emperor had switched the poison with vinegar to test her resolve and loyalty.

That was, unless you knew exactly what you were looking for.

"Are you sure you don't have those storage boxes?" Wu Ying asked.

"There are none. And none of similar quality," the attendant said. He waved the document in front of Wu Ying's face, scribbled marks on it written in an internal code that Wu Ying could not decipher. "Elder Shin herself replied to this."

"Can you buy one? For our use?" Wu Ying pleaded.

"A request has been made. These things take time," the attendant replied, raising his chin and looking down at Wu Ying from his nose. "It's not as simple as beating on a piece of metal. Such items are rare and require craftsmen to make."

Wu Ying frowned at that rather random accusation. And then he realized his tanned skin and his muscular arms likely had given the attendant the wrong impression—that he was a blacksmith. Certainly, he looked more like one than an effete apothecarist whose majority ranks were filled with nobles.

"And the rest of our request?"

"Simple enough. They are all gathered, awaiting payment." The attendant glared at Wu Ying. "You do have payment, don't you?"

Wu Ying snorted, extracting the companion token that Elder Yang had given him. He handed it to the attendant, who verified its authenticity against the spirit tablet before deducting the required number of contribution points.

Wu Ying was grateful that his Elder Sister was the one paying for the expedition. The sheer amount of goods that were required—from the mundane items like the rental of the horses, backpacks, and foodstuff, to esoteric talismans, spiritual maps and beacons, and guardian markers— would have bankrupted him twenty times over. And this did not, of course, include the specialized equipment they needed in order to extract and care for the materials they were searching for.

"Is that it?" the attendant said when Wu Ying had taken back the jade token. He glanced impatiently at the door, obviously looking to move on to his next customer.

"Thank you for your time." Wu Ying bowed, acknowledging the rude attendant. He might be on an errand for an Elder, but so were at least half the inner sect members arriving. Better to be polite than to raise a fuss when not needed.

***

"Do you think he knows?" Wu Ying asked Fa Yuan as the pair of them walked up the mountain. They'd been requested to visit their Master from the library by a harried-looking servant who'd promptly left afterward, leaving the pair of conspirators to wonder about the abrupt summons.

"It's possible. While Master Cheng has been resting, he also has been meeting with the other Elders," Fa Yuan said, looking as pretty and serene as normal.

Wu Ying's eyes narrowed at Fa Yuan's blithe answer. But asking further for reassurance would sound like whining and would not change matters. As much as he wanted it to.

"I guess we'll find out…" Wu Ying muttered to himself, mentally playing out the potential consequences of defying his Master's wishes. Being disowned was the worst option by far, though the least likely.

Making their way into their Master's abode was a simple matter. To his surprise though, the sight of their Master reclining on his bed was shocking. Master Cheng was no longer the long-limbed, muscular, and graceful individual Wu Ying remembered, but a thin, drawn individual. One whose scent, whose very aura, made Wu Ying's nose twist in distaste.

"Master," the pair greeted him together, offering low bows as they stepped into the room and waited for his acknowledgement. At the weak wave of his arm, the pair walked toward his bed, staring at the pale, sweating figure.

"Good. Come closer." Even Master Cheng's voice was weak as he gestured them close. They took position next to his bed and, at his gesture, leaned closer. He spoke, his voice dropping with each word. "Closer. I have something to say…

"You idiots!" The formerly weak hand moved with blinding speed, rapping the pair of bowed heads with the end of a closed fist, using the edge of his knuckles. "What do you think you're doing? Did I ask you to look for a cure?"

"Tsifu!" The pair groaned, moving their heads back and chorusing in unison.

"I—" Fa Yuan started.

"We—" Wu Ying said, then stopped, realizing they were speaking over one another. He fell silent, as was his place, but Fa Yuan was interrupted before she could speak.

"You both defied me. Kowtow[11] and pay respects if you truly think yourself my students!" Elder Cheng roared.

Wu Ying could tell the burst of energy Elder Cheng's rage had achieved was weak and fading. Still, Wu Ying and Fa Yuan complied, getting on their hands and knees and pressing their foreheads to the floor. They raised

---

[11] The kowtow is a very subservient form of a bow, where the individual gets on their hands and knees and places their head on the ground. Generally used for the Emperor or when paying respects to those in high authority, or during prayers. Which, I guess, is the same thing. Almost never done now in the modern day outside of temples at most and unless you're trying to humiliate someone.

themselves up partially then bowed again, repeating the actions a total of three times before they stayed bent.

"Master, we meant no disrespect. It is because you are so dear to us that we defied you," Fa Yuan replied.

"And my wishes!"

"Are in error," Fa Yuan said softer, her voice muffled by being spoken to the floor. Even so, Wu Ying could hear them loud and clear. As could Master Cheng.

"How dare you…" Master Cheng stopped, coughing as he tried to regain his breath. His coughing went on and on, such that Wu Ying eventually looked up from the floor to see his Master holding a silk handkerchief to his mouth.

"You have always desired to ensure that the majority may ascend with their karma untethered," Fa Yuan said, her head raised like Wu Ying. "But what we were doing, what they are doing…" Fa Yuan glanced at Wu Ying and shook her head. "Our mission is more important than your personal ties. If small holes are not fixed, bigger holes will bring despair."

Master Cheng frowned, then sighed. "I do not care for your decisions. But… you are correct. It is your dao to decide. And while we rest…" He looked away at the writing brush and paper on his bedside table. His gaze grew contemplative, then flicked to Wu Ying. He shook his head slightly before gesturing with his hand. "Get up, get up. And tell me, where are you on this?"

"We have located multiple possible locations for the ingredients for the cure, but…" Fa Yuan hesitated as the pair clambered to their feet and stood at attention beside his bed.

"Many of those will not be available right now, not until late autumn when the Ben return," Master Cheng replied. "I know. And your preparations?"

"Coming along." Fa Yuan listed the work they had both done, going into detail about the mundane preparations they had set up.

Wu Ying stayed silent, for Fa Yuan did a good job of listing their accomplishments. In addition, it was the first time he was getting a clear picture of their entire expedition, from the resources and contribution points spent, to the letters and correspondence Fa Yuan had conducted to smooth their journey. Everything from speaking with local magistrates, alerting them of their potential visit and requesting help to keep an eye out for the materials they required, to contacting local sect Elders, asking much the same.

Sister Yang was even perusing the messages that flowed back and forth from the Verdant Green Waters Sect to the numerous smaller sects that littered the kingdom, searching for information about the kinds of goods they had for sale. The last was mostly done via official channels, as the Elders in charge of such correspondence sent regular lists between each sect, offering trades and hiding specific needs within a slew of others. It was all very conspiratorial, Fa Yuan explained to Wu Ying's inquiry, as no sect wanted to expose weaknesses or desperate needs. And yet, at the same time, the trading of such rarities and treasures between sects made them all stronger.

"It's why Elder Li pushes you so hard," Master Cheng said. "A Gatherer at the Core cultivation stage would be a real coup for the Sect. As it is, we do a brisk business with the herbs and pills we create from her garden."

"Surely other sects have Gatherers and Spiritual Farmers?" Wu Ying said.

"Of course, but at her level of expertise?" Master Cheng shook his head. "Even if they did, consider our gardens. How we balance the needs of the Sect."

Wu Ying paused as he recalled idle conversations with Senior Goh. His eventual garden that he'd create on a nearby—but not too close—mountain was one of his Senior's favorite topics. What he'd do to alter the chi flows, what plants he'd grow, which mountain he'd pick. Even now, the gardens that Elder Li controlled took up a significant portion of the chi flowing through the Sect, chi that was gathered by the sect arrays from their surroundings. The need to balance security, growth of their personnel, and the growth of the spiritual herbs was one that continued at the highest level. Eking the most out of their allotted amount of environmental chi to push the growth of the plants without affecting the rest of the Sect was a constant battle.

In the end, there was a limit. And thus, wandering Spirit Gatherers, like Wu Ying, who went into the wild places and picked wild spiritual herbs would always be needed to supplement a sect's needs.

Or at least, that was the theory. Wu Ying had many years left to go before he reached the point where his actions were a true supplement.

"As for our expedition members," Fa Yuan said, once she was certain the pair had finished their side conversation, "it is myself and Wu Ying at the moment. I am speaking with the Sect Leader, but he has refused my request for additional Elders." She frowned.

"Good. This is already too much of a burden on the Sect," Master Cheng said. At Fa Yuan's unhappy glare, he continued blithely. "They are needed on the front lines. Or cultivating. For next year."

Fa Yuan made a face but nodded. The war ground on, and while they had lost much ground in the north this year, with the potential of a new city taken and controlled over the border river, the fight next year would be even more intense.

"But two is insufficient. Can you not find others?" Master Cheng turned toward Wu Ying. "Do you not have friends in the inner sect?" He then turned to Fa Yuan. "Have you not put up a mission?"

"I do!" Wu Ying protested. "Tou He has already offered."

"The monk." Master Cheng nodded. "Good." He raised an eyebrow at Sister Yang.

Fa Yuan made a face. "I have been holding off. It is not time yet, and... well, I am a little low on contribution points."

Master Cheng sniffed. "I told you those Elixirs of White Marble Complexion are too expensive."

"I didn't see you complaining when we got into Wei Zhou because of that merchant." Fairy Yang glared at Master Cheng. "And my ointments and elixirs have nothing to do with my current predicament. If I was conducting my usual routines—"

Master Cheng winced and raised a hand in supplication. "My apologies. Your Master was wrong. I should not have said anything."

Fa Yuan nodded, crossing her arms. A little smile danced on her lips though, and Wu Ying noted it was on Master Cheng's too. Somehow, he got the idea that this discussion and fight was something they'd done before.

"I'll make arrangements for the assignment to appear in the Hall, and the payment of the goods. I believe we need a proper storage method for the heart..." At Wu Ying's nod, Master Cheng muttered to himself before he nodded. "I might know someone. I'll send some letters..."

His next words were too low to hear properly, but Wu Ying caught something along the line of "grumpy old man." Wu Ying smiled at his Master's burst of energy. Still, he also noted how much quieter his Master had grown as they talked, how his gestures had become less vigorous. When Wu Ying shot a concerned glance at Fa Yuan, she nodded and tapped the bed with her hand, drawing Master Cheng's attention to her.

"We should go. It is late," Fairy Yang said.

"Late?" Master Cheng peered outward, then seemed to realize how dark the night had grown. With a wave, he dismissed the pair, muttering about how he'd send the letters tomorrow.

By the time the pair had reached the door to his bedroom, he'd fallen asleep. Head lolling to the side, the once-energetic swordsman slept, flickers of pain making his face twitch now that he was unconscious.

"Will he be fine?" Wu Ying asked softly as they left the residence. To see his Master so tired, so damaged, to smell the reek of his damaged chi... it worried him.

"He will be," Fa Yuan said fiercely. Then, quieter, she added, "He has to be."

Wu Ying could only nod in agreement. Even if it was more hope than belief, they would try to make it true.

Chapter 8

With Master Cheng throwing his support behind them, preparations sped up. A few days after his talk with his Master, Wu Ying found himself breaking through and opening his third Energy Storage meridian. This time around, no portentous enlightenment had provided him aid. Instead, good old hard work had seen his progress. But that meant Wu Ying was low on refined chi in his dantian again. A third breakthrough without enlightenment was unlikely to occur before they left. But at least he was no longer lagging his friends.

Just as futile as hoping to breakthrough was Wu Ying's search for aid among his friends. Outside of the ever-reliable Tou He, his allies were of no help. Li Yao avoided Wu Ying at every chance, spending her time running long-term assignments. Liu Tsong had declined outright when he pressed further, while the other martial cultivators he spoke to were either caught up in their own training or serving on the front lines like Yin Xue.

Bao Cong had gone so far as to laugh in Wu Ying's face. He then made Wu Ying spend the rest of the afternoon helping him pump the bellows while he regaled Wu Ying with the many, many reasons he would not be journeying outside of the Sect again, including on-going aches in his previously injured bones every cold morning.

Bereft of options, the pair could only hope that the additional contribution points offered in the assignment by their master would draw some of the more adventurous inner sect cultivators. Meanwhile, the pair discussed what they could do to push ahead and strengthen what could be a small expedition, while reviewing the information on material gathering spots and planning the trip.

To Wu Ying's surprise, one of the potential routes would bring them to a city he knew well. Remembering his first ever assignment, Wu Ying took the time to write a letter to an old friend, sending it off with the next ship that left for Hinma.

As research on potential locations returned fewer and fewer reliable locations, Wu Ying – at the urging of Sister Yang—returned to cultivating more fully. Only by strengthening himself would he be able to reduce the burden he was on the Elder during the expedition.

After acknowledging the potential dangers awaiting them, Elder Cheng had turned Wu Ying toward a new series of training exercises. His Master had even opened the doors of his own cultivation library, passing on to Wu Ying a series of simple, yet fundamental, cultivation exercises. They were all focused upon using the chi in Wu Ying's Energy Storage meridians. It was those cultivation exercises that Wu Ying focused upon—when he was not refining additional chi.

Late in the evening, at a time when he would have been working in the library with Fa Yuan, Wu Ying sat in his abode, legs crossed, hands resting on his knees, three fingers extended, thumb and forefinger touching one another. High above, thunderclouds rolled as dragons cavorted and raindrops fell. Wu Ying cultivated, drawing in the chi of the world and circulating it within himself before expelling the refuse.

Once he had set up the basic flow of his cultivation, Wu Ying gently took his mind off the act itself, just as he did when he was moving, and focused on his new exercises. First one, then the other.

Even as rain struck the roof, bouncing off paving stones and splashing against fine sand, it refused to touch his skin. For the most part. Wu Ying controlled his aura, doing his best to tighten it around himself and ward off the falling raindrops. Unfortunately, each time Wu Ying failed to keep his aura tightened around himself, failed to release the energy within him and firm up his aura, raindrops entered, soaking him.

This cultivation exercise had many names, even an official name, but no one called it anything other than the aura umbrella. The cultivation exercise was simple in theory, difficult in practice. But in mastering it, a cultivator could ward off basic environmental factors. Heat, cold, and, of course, rain.

It also laid the groundwork for more powerful defenses at both the Energy Storage and Core Formation stages. Complex, detailed, and involved cultivation exercises of the same form at the Core Formation stage allowed cultivators to reinforce their auras to such an extent that it was as though they had the strongest suit of armor around them at all times. It was such strength that made Core Formation cultivators dangerous to mobs of mortals and Body Cleansing cultivators.

Of course, even Energy Storage cultivators could practice such exercises, but few had the chi to keep such defenses running or the control over their manipulation of their chi to make it work. Furthermore, much like his Iron Body technique, these defensive techniques could be split between passive and active kinds. The aura umbrella was an active defense requiring constant exertion of chi. His Iron Body technique, as a refinement technique, was passive and much more manageable.

Unfortunately, even though Wu Ying had significant experience in aura manipulation and had grasped the initial stages of this exercise quickly, he still lacked the fine control of drawing chi directly from his meridians at a steady rate. On top of that, he lost a significant portion of the energy he sent to his aura membrane as it leaked out to the world. As such, it was not long before he had to stop and allow the rain to strike him unhindered while he replenished his chi reserves.

Still, that time was not wasted. Then Wu Ying practiced the second of the cultivation exercises his Master had passed to him. Much like the utility aura exercise, the chi-sensing exercise given to him was meant to improve a cultivator's ability to utilize the energy in his meridians.

In this case, chi-sensing exercises helped one sense the flow of chi within the external environment and the internal body. There were numerous types of such exercises—one for each kind of sense with multiple schools of training for each. Of course, certain senses were more useful. Sight had thousands of schools of training exercises, while taste had only a score that were well-known.

Unlike the common sight or hearing exercises, or even the personal-touch-based one, Wu Ying's Master had passed on a cultivation exercise focused on the sense of smell. The exercise required making it part of Wu Ying's existence, like breathing, seeing, or hearing. It required Wu Ying to "smell" in a different direction, as if he had to listen in a different direction and locate a noise without seeing it. But, of course, it was a new scent he was trying to note. Yet at the same time, it was not new. For he had "smelled" it all his life.

Fire was ash and flame, heat that scorched and reminded him of campfires. Water was fresh and bright, the scent in the morning or the feeling in the nose as you stood by a waterfall as it pounded away at the rocks below. Metal was the tang of blood and rusted metal, of the slide of oil on his sword. Earth was the most familiar—overturned soil and the musky smell of good compost. On the other hand, air was the most difficult, the most elusive. It was the barest hint of the cold wind from the north, the taste of the sea from the east, a mixture of spring and winter.

And all of it was mixed together and had grades, different scents depending on where he was, who he was with. The chi that erupted from the earth, that blew through the sky, that congregated around the wood and metal of his sword. It lived everywhere and shifted with the tide of the dragon lines beneath his feet. It was everywhere, and yet, it was a flitting presence except when it encountered an individual.

And perhaps that was why Elder Cheng had given him this particular exercise. For once he mastered it, the scents of others would make it much harder to surprise Wu Ying. Very few cultivators thought to hide their scent of their chi. Hiding a physical scent was easily forgotten, so a metaphysical scent like chi? How much easier to ignore.

While hiding a chi scent was similar to the way one suppressed their aura, it was also different. For with exhalation, each movement or gust of wind, the world was stained with the loss of one's chi to the external environment, the extraction of chi through simple existence and cultivation.

Wu Ying knew he could have spent hours puzzling through chi scents, the way personal chi and environmental chi interacted. In fact, learning to control his own and the way his aura was suppressed would aid his own cultivation. At the same time, it was also time-consuming, and improvements could only happen on the margins. Slowly.

In truth, that could be said for all his cultivation exercises. They built upon his fundamentals, allowing him to make use of the Energy Storage meridians more efficiently. In turn, in time, he would be able to move faster, last longer, and project attacks much more powerfully. But all of that was in time.

A journey of a thousand li started with the first step. And so, Wu Ying pushed the thoughts aside and focused deeper, doing his best to make every moment of practice count.

***

Where new skills and exercise might slowly evolve his use of chi, continued practice and repetition with care allowed Wu Ying to build upon the foundation of his martial skills. Integrating disparate forms into a whole style that was his own—an interpretation of the Long family style that diverged from the founders. He spent hours working his way through the forms, exploring chi projection as he switched sword forms, of fighting with the remaining martial specialists.

Among the new recruits to the inner sect, Wu Ying found the most use in training against. Their unique weapons and styles added a flush of clean water to the stagnant fields of martial cultivation in the Sect. In this new water, Wu Ying's martial expertise grew as though spring had arrived once again.

Days turned to weeks as Wu Ying trained. Time slipped by as face after face before his blade changed. He'd forgotten the name of his current opponent already as the pair sparred this hot summer day.

Like himself, his opponent was a jian wielder. Unlike Wu Ying, his opponent was six and three quarters of a foot tall and had an appropriately sized jian, giving him an incredible reach advantage. Added to that, Wu Ying's opponent made use of a second weapon—a gauntlet of metal he kept equipped for when Wu Ying closed the distance.

"You can't win if you keep running," the martial specialist taunted good-naturedly. His jian kept stabbing, each strike light by his standards, but heavy on Wu Ying's arms as he deflected the fast-moving tip.

Like Wu Ying, he'd refined his body, but he'd refined it for strength, not durability. Most annoying of all, even more than his taunts, was that his opponent did not even have a specialized style. Self-taught, self-trained in actual combat, his fighting style was a sloppy affair that should not work but did.

A duck and a light push of Wu Ying's sword captured his opponent's jian. The man's control of his tip and his positioning was not optimal. It allowed Wu Ying to step into the man's outside line, forcing the weapon away from his body while allowing him to seek his opponent's heart with his tip as he closed the distance.

But just as Wu Ying neared, his opponent released the strength in his blade entirely, letting the entire thing collapse backward. Wu Ying controlled his own tip, which wanted to follow the line of his opponent's sword, ensuring his attack did not go off-line, but the opponent was already twisting, curling his body around the collapsing blade as he brought his gauntleted fist around. His fist closed and Wu Ying's blade ground to a halt as his opponent bent the blade.

Then, rather than following up with sword or fist, his opponent stepped forward and head-butted Wu Ying. Or at least, attempted to.

Wu Ying dropped low, letting his body bend backward and yank the sword from the opponent's light grip. Wu Ying followed the rest of his motion, legs rising and seeking his opponent's chin and missing. Finishing the backflip, Wu Ying sighed at missing his attack. But at least he was safe. If out of measure once more.

While these non-specialist ex-wandering cultivators had exploitable gaps in their fighting techniques, they also often utilized new attacks from angles that Wu Ying would never have considered. Other times, they chained attack forms that were unorthodox but effective. At least, after so many months fighting them, Wu Ying was beginning to be less surprised when they did something different.

A dozen passes later, Wu Ying collapsed, tired. Most sparring matches ended when one or the other's stamina or concentration was exhausted. Other times, they ended because an opponent became bored. That was a reason only the most arrogant or new cultivator chose though.

For Wu Ying, even with the most untaught of opponents, his father had drilled into him that there was a lesson to be learned. Whether by constricting one's own movements or attacks, or by otherwise practicing timing or footwork, you could always learn. If you were willing.

Soon after they finished, Wu Ying's opponent left, making his thanks before searching for a drink. After multiple passes, Wu Ying had picked out the most common techniques his opponent relied upon. After that, exploiting them had been easy. Wu Ying had even introduced a couple of new variations of his own, though many of them had failed. But that was the advantage of sparring. Failure did not result in bloody injury or death.

And unlike true battles, Wu Ying had long minutes to study and learn. In a real battle, a single surprise attack could end a fight. A bad duelist might make a great fighter. It was a lesson Wu Ying reminded himself of constantly as he fought these new Sect members.

As cool water slid down his parched throat, as chi refilled his dantian, a new scent behind Wu Ying made him turn. Tilting his head, Wu Ying smiled. "Yu Kun."

Over the last few weeks, they'd met often on the training ground and had struck up a friendship of blades. Yu Kun was the perfect kind of opponent for Wu Ying at this time—slightly stronger, using a different weapon and a unique but orthodox style. With his varied and wider fighting experience, Wu Ying had to push himself to win.

"You here for another match?" Wu Ying asked.

"Mmmm… eventually. But I wanted to ask about an assignment I noticed."

"Our expedition?" Wu Ying said with some hope in his voice.

"Yes. It seems dangerous."

"I guess. The monsters we intend to fight should be manageable, with planning."

"But the locations you are going to…"

"Might be more difficult. Thus, the high contribution points. And we won't leave until later, so there's time to train further," Wu Ying reassured Yu Kun.

"When?"

Wu Ying hesitated. "In a week or two. We need to do a little more research, but we should go soon. Otherwise, we won't have time to collect the material."

Yu Kun cocked an eyebrow at the words but eventually nodded. "Very well."

"Will you join us?"

"I believe so. I'll apply later today." Yu Kun's lips quirked into a grin. "Though it'll depend if Elder Yang chooses me."

"Chooses you?" Wu Ying frowned. "I thought we'd find it difficult to get many." Wu Ying glanced around pointedly at the quiet training grounds. "The points and the danger—"

"Are high. But you forget, you have one attraction many other assignments are missing." As Wu Ying raised an eyebrow, Yu Kun grinned. "You have a Fairy."

Wu Ying sighed. Of course. He had a sudden premonition of what they'd see when they finally started the selection process.

"So I expect you to put in a good word for me, yes?" Yu Kun grinned.

"Well… only if you can beat me. Wouldn't want to burden the Fairy…"

"Now you're asking for it," Yu Kun said, pointing at the nearby fighting stage. "Let me show you who beats who!"

Laughing, the pair ambled over. As humorous as their words were, Wu Ying gave his best in the fight. He could not forget that this entire expedition was to save his Master's life. And they really did need the best they could find.

***

Days later, Wu Ying and Fa Yuan were seated in a small room off the Assignment Hall's main room. The private room they had been assigned would allow them to interview the prospective expedition members in peace. Beside them, a teapot steamed as the leaves within brewed, bringing a light, floral scent to the surroundings.

Wu Ying was seated perpendicular to Fa Yuan, as she was to lead the interviews. While his comments and opinions were valued, he was only a new inner sect member. Compared to his martial sister, Wu Ying had little experience in managing and picking out suitable applicants.

Wu Ying held the paper sheaf, reviewing the names within. Fa Yuan had dictated them to him over the last few minutes as she had finished browsing through the applicants' information. On a bamboo scroll supplied by the Assignment Hall was each applicant's past history of assignments. Details of the assignments, the applicants' levels, and any skills learned or known by the Sect were included, allowing Fa Yuan to quickly highlight those who were not suitable. It was this list of undesirables that Wu Ying held.

"About Yu Kun," Wu Ying said hesitantly. "I know he hasn't completed as many assignments as others, but he is a good fighter."

Fa Yuan raised an eyebrow. "We have a lot of good fighters."

"But he's a wandering cultivator. Or was. He has more experience outside the Sect," Wu Ying tried again.

"So do I."

He cajoled his brain, trying to find another reason for Fa Yuan to choose the man. To Wu Ying's continued surprise, the number of applicants had beaten even his revised expectations. He had, once again, underestimated the appeal of Fairy Yang. That the applicants included as many women as men only mildly surprised Wu Ying. While female courters for Fairy Yang were common at the higher levels, women at the lower levels of cultivation seemed to be more reserved. Perhaps they had better judgment of their chances.

"Is he that important to you?"

"Yes," Wu Ying replied automatically. Then he paused, letting his brain go over the question again before he nodded firmly. "Not like Tou He. But I believe he will be an asset. I trust him."

Fa Yuan gestured at his document. "Then take him off."

"Really!?!"

"You are as much a part of this as I."

Wu Ying struck the name from the document and stood immediately. "I'll announce the names then."

He strode out of the room and regarded the throng of potential applicants. They packed the corridor, some standing alone, others in small groups. All regarded the others with caution, though a few of the more extroverted were trying their luck with the female candidates.

"Those names read out, we will not need you. Thank you for applying though," Wu Ying called, quieting the crowd.

Rather than allowing them to build disgruntlement, he read the names immediately after his declaration. By the time Wu Ying had finished reading the names on his list, only a dozen applicants were left. Of those, nearly half were women.

Wu Ying could not help but wonder, was it on purpose? Did Fa Yuan assume that the woman applying were less likely to desire her company or were less likely to be jealous of her status? If so, were they then expected to be more competent? Or was it just chance? Wu Ying almost considered perusing the documents, but in this case, the full information provided was limited to the Elder. There were some things an inner sect cultivator was not allowed to know.

He could only shrug in defeat before beckoning the closest surviving applicant to follow as he stepped within. As Wu Ying turned, he could not help but notice that Yu Kun was grinning. And could not help but return the smile.

It would be good to have friends for this expedition.

Chapter 9

A week and a half later, Wu Ying and the rest of the team gathered underneath the red paifang that denoted the start of the Sect and its inner grounds. Unlike the last expedition he had been on, there was no large gathering of Elders, no waiting around for a blessing. This was a smaller, informal expedition, one that was not backed by the Sect in great weight.

After all, the loss of Master Cheng would be a tragedy, but they already faced a significant drain on their resources. Throwing resources into a potential cure, one that might not be sufficient or possible—and losing another Elder to the cause—was already troublesome. Adding additional aid to this would be a bad return on their investment. It did not help their cause that their Master's remoteness from the Sect's majority decisions—in his quest to keep his own karmic ties constrained—meant he had few strong allies in the Sect.

Without a formal sendoff, Wu Ying and the team stood awaiting Fa Yuan as sunlight slowly crept across the horizon. As he waited, Wu Ying scoped out his teammates in more detail. Tou He had his staff and a small bag of foodstuff over one shoulder, the ex-monk quietly chatting with Yu Kun. The pair knew one another somewhat, having dueled and made acquaintances over the last few months. It was not a true bond, but closer than what they had with the other two members of the expedition.

The first was a young lady who stood, arms hidden in the long sleeves of her robe, staring at the early morning mist that wrapped around the edges of the mountain. Her lustrous light brown hair fell behind her in a genteel wave, strands floating in the wind. Sadly, her chin was more pointed and her cheekbones less pronounced than ideal, making her miss the mark of gorgeous and ending in the mediocre pits of beautiful.

Obviously, it was more than sufficient for her current suitor, the other expedition member who had been added during the interviews. He stood nearby, staring at the young lady with wide eyes, blinking long, graceful lashes at her as he regaled the disinterested beauty on the merits of a specific apothecarist potion over another. Even Wu Ying, with his background in the subject, had been lost about five interminable minutes ago, never mind the young lady. But oblivious to her lack of interest, the man continued to speak, waving long, thin, soot-stained fingers.

"Enough, Lei Hui," Fa Yuan scolded as she strode up. "Leave Wang Min alone."

Lei Hui stepped away from Wang Min and bowed to Fa Yuan. Yet Lei Hui's gaze kept darting toward the young lady, and he even went so far as to lick his lips. Wu Ying frowned and made note to keep an eye on the man. His amorous intentions were a little blatant, even to the inexperienced teenager. If not for the fact that he was the most skilled apothecarist who had applied, Fa Yuan likely would have kicked him off the team.

"Good." She nodded at the man, then glanced around. "We will leave now. Make sure to pay your respects to Elder Lu and the Sect before you go. We will be gone for many months."

The group nodded at once, making sure to stop by Elder Lu and show him their Sect tokens and permission passes before they bowed inward to the Sect. Wu Ying hesitated as he came up out of his bow, casting a glance at the gatekeeper. But for once, the elderly gatekeeper had no words of wisdom for Wu Ying, just gesturing with his long pipe for them to go. And if Wu Ying wondered when Elder Lu actually slept or left his post, he kept it to himself.

In short order, the group began the long trek down to the city. Hurrying forward to where his martial sister strode at the front, her steps so light that she was almost floating down the mountain, Wu Ying spoke as he caught up.

"There is no hurry. The ship we booked will not leave until midday."

"Best to be early in case they are too." Fa Yuan flashed Wu Ying a smile and added, "Forgive my impatience, if you will. I am eager to be off after all this time waiting."

Wu Ying smiled, acknowledging her point. He too felt some of that impatience, the need to move. And if they burnt a little energy now, it certainly was not as if they would not be bored once they made it onto the ship. In fact, they would be spending a significant amount of time on the river vessels for the first part of the trip.

"So we'll be going with the initial plan?" Wu Ying said, just to reassure himself.

"Yes. No additional sightings. Our best bet is to visit the auction in Hinma, pick the blossom along the way or immediately afterward, then hope to find a Chan Chu—and a Ben, if we cannot get the heart at auction—nearby," Fa Yuan confirmed.

Wu Ying mentally traced their journey in his mind as they skipped down the winding mountain pathway. They'd be taking the river for the first journey east, then again north, if the crossings were fine. Ever since his adventure in Li county years ago, the number of bandits had decreased, making trade easier. It helped that the Sect had spent some time running out the remaining bandits. It was not the most glamorous of jobs, and it certainly was bloody. But it helped to keep the peace and that was important.

They could head overland through Li county to save time and locate the Sun Lotus. Or they could take the slower but steadier progress of the rivers and canals, making their way across the branching levees to get to their destination. That would be safer, and their chances of chancing upon the Sun Lotus as they traveled would be low anyway.

But the decision to go overland or via ship would depend on the news they gathered as they traveled. If they could catch the right rides, they would continue on the river. If not, an overland journey would be their best choice.

In the end, Wu Ying could only trot aside his martial sister, turning his attention inward as he focused on cultivating. If there was nothing that could be done about the future or what destiny might befall them, then he could only turn to his own self.

When all else failed, when the future was uncertain, the betterment of oneself was a guiding light that had yet to fail Wu Ying.

***

"You are very familiar with the sailors," Lei Hui said as he found Wu Ying leaning against the railing at the back of the boat, watching the city fade in the distance as they followed the river's flow.

Beside Wu Ying, seated on the smoothed wooden floor of the ship, Tou He meditated.

"I've been on this vessel before," Wu Ying said. He smiled slightly, letting his gaze go over the busy sailors. One could say that fate had tied a thread between them, if one didn't know the trouble Wu Ying had taken to ensure their booking of the ship. There was a comfort in familiarity after all.

"Yet I do not lower myself to speak with the uninitiated," Lei Hui said, his gaze flicking over the sailors like Wu Ying's before he dismissed them and turned back to Wu Ying. "Why do you?"

Wu Ying shook his head. "Why not? We once were like them too."

"But we have transformed, journeyed further than them on the mountain of immortality. They will wither and die, while we will continue to climb."

Lei Hui hawked a gobbet of saliva over the side. "They cared not to try, and so they do not deserve our company."

"You're a bit of an ass, aren't you?" Wu Ying looked around, searching for someone to take him—or Lei Hui—from the conversation, but the women were below deck, as was Yu Kun.

"Do you deny that they will die long before us? That we have made more of ourselves than them?" Lei Hui said. "I know your background is like mine. We came from their stock. But unlike them, we were not content to slave away for another."

"We all work for the Sect," Wu Ying rebutted.

"An immortal sect," Lei Hui retorted. "And I am a third-tier apothecarist and you are…" Lei Hui's eyes narrowed. "Well. You're a Spiritual Herb Gatherer. You could do better."

Wu Ying glared at Lei Hui, drawing a breath to scold him. Only to be interrupted by a well-timed utterance from the seated Tou He.

"Amitabha."

Wu Ying shot an aggrieved look at his friend before he let out a sigh. "You don't mince words, do you?"

"Should I?" Lei Hui said. "Would you prefer the truth or well-meaning lies? I speak what I see, and what I see is the truth. You cannot be inexact when working the cauldron. As you know."

"That's not what Senior Li says," Wu Ying remarked. "Apothecary is as much an art, a matter of understanding the flows of the universe and the strengths of your ingredients to create the best product."

"Bah! They are wrong. There is an exact method to our work. That is why our recipes are so exact," Lei Hui said. "We do not say a handful or two of Spirit Grass but three stalks of six chi. We do not ask for the whole flower of the purple hibiscus, but the stamen of one that is at least six months old.

The best recipes are exact, with details about the age and strength of its ingredients.

"It is only because we have yet to ascertain the exact strength of the properties within each ingredient that we are unable to be more exact. For perfection, for the correct formation of Saint and Immortal pills, we must strive for exactness in our recipes. And so, must we do so in our lives!"

"That's how you explain being an ass," Wu Ying said flatly.

"Exactly."

"And lacking all subtlety in your pursuit of our expedition member."

"Exact—wait, what?" Lei Hui exclaimed.

"Your blatant interest in Wang Min wasn't on purpose?" Tou He chimed in, his voice a little incredulous.

"You noticed too?" Wu Ying said.

"Am I blind?" Tou He said. "Even the Abbot would have noticed. And he's been in seclusion all the years I was at the temple."

Lei Hui paled, then muttered, "I-I was not trying to. She was just…"

"Oh, friend…" Wu Ying threw an arm around the man's shoulder, pulling him close. Even if Lei Hui was in his early twenties, it seemed he might have even less experience than Wu Ying. "Let's talk about your approach. And perhaps about the fact we're all on the same expedition…"

"I hadn't—well, I know it was inappropriate, but I meant, after the—"

"Yes, yes," Wu Ying said, grinning slightly. "Just be glad it wasn't Elder Yang you tried that on."

Horrified, eyes wide and his face drained of blood, Lei Hui proclaimed, "I would never! The Elder is far above a poor apothecarist like me!"

Tou He and Wu Ying shared a conspiratorial grin. Perhaps this expedition wouldn't be as difficult as it seemed at first.

***

Later that evening, Fa Yuan found Wu Ying leaning on the railing at the bow of the ship. They sailed down the darkened waterway, pushed by the current with their sails furled and a series of lanterns set around the ship to provide illumination. That provided the first mate and the few lookouts time to watch for potential obstructions, though Wu Ying knew now that most lookouts also trained certain Body Cultivation exercises to aid their vision.

Not that it helped more than marginally, especially compared to general progression in cultivation. But when one was "stuck" at the lower levels of cultivation—due to lack of opportunity, time, or enlightenment—the difference could be significant. At least, compared to other non-sect cultivators or mortals. As for himself, while it was not as bright as daylight, the dark night was not more troublesome than twilight. And so, Fa Yuan found Wu Ying as he watched the play of light on the water, listened to the lap of waves against the hull and the creak of timbers, and cleaned his teeth with his tongue of the soy-sauce chicken and mushroom dinner they'd eaten.

"It was a useful conversation with Lei Hui?" Fa Yuan said, disdaining greetings as she spoke.

"I believe so."

"Good. Will he be a problem?"

"I don't think so. He understands the boundaries. He was just..." Wu Ying frowned, searching for the word.

"Eager?"

He shook his head.

"Arrogant?"

Another shake.

"Foolish?"

"Inexperienced."

She laughed. "If only all pursuers were the same."

"Why did you pick him, if you thought he might be…"

"A risk?"

Wu Ying nodded.

"My personal comfort is a small thing to trade for the success of our assignment. I just did not expect…" She gestured backward.

"For someone not to fall for the Fairy?"

Fa Yuan made a fan appear in her hand, which she used to lightly tap Wu Ying's head. "I am not that arrogant."

"Really?" Wu Ying said. "Then do finish the sentence."

Fa Yuan opened then shut her mouth, searching for the appropriate words. Eventually, she let out a rueful little laugh. "Perhaps you were correct. I might have expected him to seek me out, instead of Wang Min. She is beautiful but…"

"But not you."

An inclination of her head answered Wu Ying's words. He laughed and was shortly joined by his martial sister.

After a time, he could not help but ask, "Is it that troublesome?"

"Being pursued?" Fa Yuan sighed. "It is. My actions are often constrained, my ability to move unnoticed impossible." She gestured at Wu Ying as he stood beside her, swaying with the gentle lap of waves. "I could never take a group of friends and rescue my family." A slight quirk of her lips. "Though my parents have gained much favor by my continued lack of spouse or consort."

He could understand that, especially for the nobles. It was a strange balance, being an immortal cultivator and a female noble. In the normal course of affairs, she would have been a trading piece, one that could garner

109

her family a large bride price. Of course, the family would have to return some of it via the dowry gifted to her, but that would certainly not match the bride price someone as beautiful as Fairy Yang would garner. And none of that would account for the connections that her marriage and the wooing would garner the family.

But as an immortal, her life, to some extent, was her own. Like his ex-girlfriend, Li Yao, her family would support her pursuit of immortality so long as she continued to advance at a decent rate. As an Elder of the Sect, she should have been untouchable, the prestige and influence she garnered more than satisfactory to satisfy any parent, any familial requirement.

Except, of course, she was Fairy Yang.

"Does the inner sect continue their betting?" she asked.

"Yes," Wu Ying replied, seeing no reason to hide the matter. After all, no suitor who came would do so in secret. Each of them arrived with grand pronouncements and gifts. From the stories he'd heard, Fa Yuan's initial suitors were magistrates, nobles and the occasional courtesan. "Every time a new external sect Elder or a core cultivator arrives to exchange pointers with you, it starts up again."

"Exchange pointers." Fa Yuan sighed, her breath misting a little in the cold, humid air. "What a lousy excuse. At least those who are upfront have more courage."

Wu Ying grinned, tracing his fingers along the wood of the bannister. "Well, at least they help provide you with your cultivation resources." His grin widened. "And me."

She could not help but roll her eyes at that. "Yes. Some of them are still providing me Meridian Opening Pills."

Wu Ying chuckled, having benefited from their ill-fitting largesse. Of course, those pills were less than useful for him at this stage, since the Energy

Storage Meridians received a much smaller effect from the pills. They helped soften the blockages, but his problem now was the lack of chi in his dantian, rather than having to cleanse the meridians. Still, they were better than nothing for sure.

"And have none ever caught your eyes?" Wu Ying asked.

Fa Yuan paused, her breath stilling. She turned away from Wu Ying, staring at the passing riverbank in the distance, the way leaves swayed in the light breeze that pushed aside buzzing mosquitos and insects. She was silent for so long, Wu Ying thought he'd overstepped his bounds. While they were martial brother and sister, she was still an Elder.

But eventually, she spoke.

"None. None worth the sacrifice," Fa Yuan said so softly that Wu Ying barely caught her words.

He looked at her profile, and for a second, he sensed the welling up of sadness in her. Of loss and sacrifice, in the past. For relationships could as easily harm one's path as boost it. More easily, in most cases.

"You did well. Keep an eye on Lei Hui. Such aborted feelings can arise at the worst times." And so saying, Fa Yuan turned around and left the deck.

Wu Ying mentally kicked himself. He really should not have asked, for it was not his place. Nor did they have that kind of relationship. But he'd been curious, like so many others. And, perhaps, other than him and his Master, was there anyone she could speak with? Certainly not the other Elders. Nor had he ever seen Fa Yuan with other women in the Sect. Whether it was jealousy, interest, or the barrier of hierarchy, her path was lonelier than his.

Exhaling, Wu Ying shook his head and clutched the bannister. In the end, he could do nothing for her. Her dao—whatever that was or would be—was hers to walk. He could only work on his own strength, and hopefully lighten her load then. Resolved, he breathed, drawing in the chi from around him, and worked through his cultivation manual once more.

Strength. He still needed it.

Chapter 10

Morning three days later saw Wu Ying seated near the bow, cultivating. Beside him, Wang Min and Lei Hui joined him in his morning cultivation. It was early enough that the night watch had just changed, the weary sailors trooping down below to take their breakfast before they crashed for the day. In turn, their replacements inspected the work left behind, ensuring that all was done and grumbling when ropes were left untied or deck pins left untended. Under the shouted commands of the captain, the sails were slowly let down to catch the rising breeze.

None of the activity bothered the trio, not even when a duel began between Tou He and Yu Kun. The ability to cultivate, even in public, was a necessary skill they'd all learned. Some, like Wu Ying, who'd worked to master even moving meditation, were better able to focus. On the other hand, Lei Hui, who'd spent the majority of his time cultivating and working in the Sect, was finding the constant motion of the boat and the noise around him more of a challenge.

All this, Wu Ying could sense as he cultivated and focused on the flow of chi in the surroundings. Both he and Wang Min drew in the chi of the world in a steady fashion. Unlike himself with his filtered aura, Wang Min drew in atmospheric chi in the normal manner, taking all forms of chi and converting it within her body. That resulted in a more regular churn of chi around her.

Lei Hui, on the other hand, had a more interrupted experience where the flow of his chi stuttered to a stop, or a sudden exhalation would occur and a rush of chi would explode from his body. It was not a huge change, subtle enough that Wu Ying only noticed the change because he was paying attention.

Wu Ying's cultivation was steadier but had the occasional bump as his control over his aura and the natural variance in chi types in the environment forced him to adjust his cultivation speed. It was also why there was a greater flow of environmental chi centered around his body.

As the morning sun rose, the cultivators worked on strengthening themselves. Even making good time, they were another four days from their first major stop. Until then, there was little to be done but train.

The first sign of an attack arrived via the trio's extended senses. A shift in the ambient chi, a twist in its flow and the introduction of something slimier with an abundance of water chi. To Wu Ying's nose, the new chi brought with it the smell of something acrid, rotten stagnant water that made his breath hitch a little. His eyes flicked open even as he began the process of calming the flow of chi within his body.

The door below slammed open, Elder Yang striding out, sword drawn. "To arms! Danger approaches from below!"

Wu Ying rose to his feet, his cultivation slowing, the processing becoming a background matter. His two companions were slower, forced to still their cultivation entirely or face a chi backlash. As Wu Ying drew his sword, he searched deck and water for the problem, extending his sense by drawing in deep breaths of the stench.

Sailors scurried about to arm themselves, finding belaying pins, daggers, billhooks, and the occasional spear. They grouped up in small knots, eyes darting about the deck in search of trouble. Yet for all the suddenness of the declaration, none panicked. This was not a world that allowed the panicky to fare well.

The captain, on the foredeck, had his hand on his dao, glaring about him. "Where, Honored Elder?"

"Below us…" Fa Yuan replied, her voice distant as she tilted her head from side to side.

As if called forth, the water around the ship erupted. The creatures that emerged were a well-known threat, their green-scaled bodies and humanoid appearance belying their monstrous nature. A turtle-carapace on their back offered them protection from behind even as the hook-like growths on their knees and the dark-green-striped skin gave the water tigers their name.

"Suiko[12]!" The call rose from all around.

Some of the monsters exploded from the water with such force that they landed on the deck, while others only managed to latch to the hull, clambering upward with their clawed fingers. The first to land beside Wu Ying received a blade in its guts, a simple kick sending the monster flying off the deck and freeing the cultivator's sword.

"Common trash," Lei Hui snapped as he stepped forward and struck one of the suiko with a fist. The monster's chest caved in and it staggered back, its chest heaving as it attempted to breathe. "Ascend to Energy Storage before you dare challenge us!"

Wang Min, on the other hand, was still seated, even as the monsters landed all around. She gestured to the side, and as she did so, a guzheng landed on her crossed legs. Balanced on her knees, the rectangular, twenty-one-stringed instrument was gently caressed by the woman, sending a light trill of notes down its metallic strings.

"Guard me. I must tune this," Wang Min called to the pair of cultivators fighting around her.

"This is not the time to be playing music!" Lei Hui said as he twisted to the side and struck out again with his fist. A tiger head briefly appeared around his hand, formed with brown earth that released on impact, the chi-

---

[12] Translates as water tiger and, yes, it's a real monster. Sometimes called a kappa, though some assert they are two different creatures. For our purpose, only the suiko are real.

and earth-encrusted attack blasting a nearby pair of suiko off the ship just as they rose.

Wu Ying shifted his positioning, putting himself between Wang Min and the majority of the monsters boarding their vessel. He struck again and again, each action a quick attack that sought tendons and vulnerable locations. He sought to injure and disable, knowing that if the monsters were forced off, they would be unable to follow the moving ship.

"Listen to her!" Wu Ying snapped. He could understand Lei Hui's hesitation. He too would be hesitant if he had not been part of the interview and knew what Wang Min intended.

"Insane!" But for all his grumbling, Lei Hui took position beside Wu Ying.

Together, they guarded Wang Min as she tuned her instrument, battling the increasing number of monsters.

In the meantime, Tou He and Yu Kun took the fight to the creatures all along one side of the main body of the ship. They struck, cut, and kicked the suiko attempting to board the ship, aiding the sailors who fought in smaller clusters. In particular, they took care to stop the monsters that managed to separate a sailor from the group and began dragging their victim toward the water.

On the other side of the pair, Elder Yang fought with minimal movements. Her swords hovered, cutting through one neck or the other, flying through the air under the guidance of her fingers before returning to her, where she tapped the sword again. Each touch imparted additional chi, allowing her to control the flying weapon. Under her attacks, Fa Yuan held one side of the ship. Her other blade, she kept with her, held behind her back as she waited.

116

So did the captain, who peered from port to starboard, lower lip caught in his teeth.

"What are they waiting for?" Wu Ying said as he continued to protect Wang Min.

A particularly large suiko rose, ignoring Wu Ying's cuts against its arm as it charged him. Rather than face it directly, Wu Ying let his body drop low, reversed his sword, and pommel-struck it in the center of its stomach. The built-up momentum of the creature and his own attack made it bow over briefly.

A moment later, the suiko recovered and rose to its full height, arms rising above its head to crush the cultivator. Wu Ying rose as well, gripped its arm, and stepped past the large suiko, enacting a throw that used the creature's momentum to send it over backward. A blast of chi as Wu Ying finished his cut sent the monster spinning down the deck, bowling other suiko off their feet.

"Thank you!" Wu Ying called out to the monster snarkily.

"I have no idea why... but they keep coming," Lei Hui was panting now. Rather than conserve his chi throughout the fight, he had been using it liberally, launching impressive and powerful attacks that covered much ground. However, he was flagging now.

In truth, he was not the only one. The sailors, even those who had recently joined the fight from below, were all exhausted. A few minutes of combat was draining in a way a day's worth of sailing could never be. More and more of the sailors were peeled away from their groups, forcing the cultivators protecting them to expend even more energy.

Even Wu Ying had to use his Brilliant Woo Petal Bracer's attack, sending sword energy cutting at groups. As the deck grew coated by green blood, Wu Ying heard a new cry. He stepped forward, striking at his latest opponent

117

and pushing it over the railing before looking about. In the distance, a trio of large suiko had arisen, muscular and larger than the normal monsters. Two took on Elder Yang, their bodies glowing with a pale blue light that helped protect them from her attacks. The other fought Yu Kun, while Tou He aided when he could and dealt with the other monsters attempting to interfere with the fight. No sense of honor, these suiko.

But Wu Ying's attention was mostly focused on his own problems. For another, much larger creature had clambered up the prow, this one standing six feet tall and muscular. Its scales were a darker, deeper green, and on top of its clawed knees, it also had bone protrusions from its elbows and horns on its head. Like the other three monsters, it glowed with power as it infused its own aura with chi. As it opened its mouth, Wu Ying stared at the numerous sharp, pointed teeth and flinched.

Not waiting for the cultivator to recover from his momentary fright, the suiko's muscular legs bunched up and launched it at Wu Ying, claws seeking his throat. Wu Ying fell back, sword weaving in the intricate form Dragon paints the Sunset that blocked each attack, sending dripping claws awry from their targets. But the sudden attack had him retreating, footsteps sliding across the blood-stained, sticky deck.

A sudden trill of strings from behind Wu Ying reminded him of his positioning. He froze, planting his feet. If he continued his retreat, he would run into Wang Min and all the work she'd done tuning her instrument would be wasted.

His choice meant that he was forced to weave and twist his body, shedding claw attacks with body and blade. Sparks flashed as hardened bone met weapon, chi infusions on both sides guarding their weapons. It made the attacks more dangerous, and each blow felt like a hammer strike on his wrist and arms. Forcing more chi into his sword, Wu Ying fought on even as blows slipped past, cutting his arms and torso.

"Done!" Wang Min punctuated her words with a stroke on the guzheng, a trill of metallic strings rising. This was just the prelude to the song she began. It was a fast-moving, high-tempo tune, one that slipped beneath the consciousness of those fighting.

Wu Ying grinned, already feeling the chi she wrapped in each note affecting him. Focusing deep within himself even as he took another clawed attack that cut his robes, he took hold of the chi flowing in his meridians and his aura, tightening his hold on it all.

As if the monstrous suiko before him understood the danger, its attack gained a new tempo, a greater frenzy. Claws and elbows lashed at Wu Ying, attempting to trap his sword darting between them, sometimes blocking, other times threatening the creature's face and chest. At first, they stalemated once more, Wu Ying bleeding as he accumulated additional light wounds. Then the suiko made a new move.

After throwing its right claw at Wu Ying and being deflected, it kept its body rotation even as it hunched its head backward. Offering Wu Ying its back, it then launched itself at the cultivator, trusting in its hardened shell to defeat the cultivator's sword. Caught off guard, Wu Ying was struck by the creature.

Reacting by instinct, Wu Ying gripped the monster's shell with both hands as he allowed his weapon to drop. Even as he was pushed back, he launched himself upward, sending chi to his feet as he triggered the Twelve Eastern Gales Movement qinggong skill to lighten himself and empower his jump.

Together, the joined pair arced over the bowed Wang Min, who continued to play, her fingers flicking with practiced discipline. At the last second, Wu Ying forced one last surge of strength through his arms to throw the monster over his head. He made full use of the creature's body to cushion their fall, even as they crashed into the deck and slid across the blood-clotted deck, bumping into corpses along the way.

Reacting by instinct, using the techniques drilled into him by Elder Hsu, Wu Ying scrambled to roll the suiko over. On top, he then proceeded to attempt to hold the creature down and strike at it. Unlike Elder Hsu, he had not studied the snail style in depth. Nor did he prefer that kind of grappling. Instead, Wu Ying chose to gain a position where he could attack back.

For a few moments, Wu Ying had the advantage. But one issue with fighting monsters was that, in general, they were stronger than cultivators. Pound for pound—and the suiko was heavier than Wu Ying—they were stronger. In their cultivation, they diverted chi into organs, muscles, and tendons rather than meridians. In that sense, a creature just as powerful as Wu Ying—in the Energy Storage level of cultivation—would be physically stronger.

A heave and twist and Wu Ying flew off the monster, tumbling head over heels and bowling over another suiko. Wu Ying struggled to his feet; head slightly woozy as he got himself ready. A moment later, the creature Wu Ying bowled over had struggled up to its feet. Rather than deal with it, Wu Ying spun and kicked the monster in the head, sending it tumbling away again.

Setting himself, Wu Ying conjured another sword from his spirit ring. But before he could deal with the monstrous suiko he had been fighting, Elder Yang had taken action. She flitted over, her other sword wreathed in ghostly flame as she sank it into the creature's chest. It punched through the monster and out its shell with ease, making the creature struggle for a moment before it slumped over.

Even as Elder Yang finished the creature, the other monsters were struggling to stay focused, their eyes heavy, their movements slow. Wang Min's constant strumming, her aural assault, had taken over the chi within their bodies. And as Wang Min slowed the tempo of her playing, lowering both volume and repetition, the creatures found themselves lethargic too.

The sudden change gave the beleaguered defenders a boost in energy, allowing the cultivators to finish the monsters with minimal fuss. As for the sailors… outside of the captain and his first mate, the sailors struggled to shake off her playing. It was only when Wang Min purposely plucked a wrong string that her hold over the men shattered. At that point, most of the surviving monsters woke too, but faced the cultivators' weapons alone.

"Get the sails down! Second shift, to the oars," the captain barked. "We need to make farther distance. And get the signal flags and buoys out."

Elder Yang, having cleaned off her swords, turned to the captain. "These were their leaders. I doubt they'll follow."

"No offense meant, Elder Yang, but I'll sleep better if we have more distance from that nest," the captain replied.

"None taken." Fa Yuan glanced at the bodies some of the sailors were already moving to toss overboard. "Don't." When the sailors acknowledged her words, she turned to Wu Ying. "Can you search for beast stones?"

Wu Ying blinked, making a face as he stared at the monster's bodies. He understood the words. He even understood the need. But digging around through corpses was less than pleasant. Still, as he finished retrieving his original sword, he made his way to the largest body.

"If the Elder doesn't mind, I'd like to do it," Yu Kun called. "I have some experience with these creatures and know where it is best found." A pause, then he grinned. "And for most of these, I can even retrieve the shells for more funds."

His last words slowed the movements of the sailors as they piled the bodies out of the way. Many looked puzzled.

Yu Kun continued. "I know of a few instrument-makers who make good use of these shells. And a few of the stronger ones can be sent to the Hmong,[13] who prize such shields."

More than a few looked puzzled at such an utterance, not having heard of this particular tribe. Not that that was particularly surprising. After all, the lands under heaven were large and expansive, almost impossible to tell the full extent.

Seeing that he had an audience, Yu Kun regaled them with his experiences as he worked. He spoke of the Hmong tribes he'd encountered in his wanderings, tribes that lived dangerous existences in the wild, fighting spirit beasts and shifting their villages as soil gave way or a particularly dangerous spirit beast rose in prominence.

When his stories were exhausted as he showed the sailors and the cultivators how to peel the shells off the suiko backs and clean them, he sang. His voice was surprisingly strong, and in short order, Wang Min joined him on her guzheng.

None of them recognized the words nor the dialect Yu Kun sang in. But his voice and the accompaniment had the group entranced as they worked, for there was a longing in his voice, a sadness that made them listen with care. For a time, the creak of the oars, the snap of the sails, and the song were all that could be heard.

Eventually, Yu Kun ended the song, then flushed a little in embarrassment as the group clapped.

---

[13] The Hmong are an actual ethnic group that lived in China before being pushed out of their original lands. They have a rich cultural history, from their famous embroidery and love songs and a unique traditional dress sense. As always, I'm only using a small portion of their history here.

"What was the song about?" Tou He asked.

"It's a song of parting. Of… loss," Yu Kun replied.

When the group asked further questions, he shook his head and stood. He walked over to Wang Min to thank her for her accompaniment, leaving the other inner sect cultivators and sailors alone.

"Huh…" Wu Ying said. "He has some stories to tell, it seems."

"Indeed," Lei Hui replied as he stared at the talking pair of cultivators, his eyes narrowed.

Wu Ying noted the look but dismissed it for the moment as he eyed the working sailors and cultivators, arms deep in guts and shells. A quick count ensured that he had all the demon stones, including the largest three. Free of the viscera and muscles that held them to the body, the stones were irregular shaped pieces in light and dark blue. Only the larger stones were more regularly shaped, almost as though a bored jewel-maker had begun work on the stones themselves. After cleaning the stones, Wu Ying wrapped them in a handful of silk and headed down the stairs.

Outside Fa Yuan's door, Wu Ying hesitated, feeling the boat move to the slow rhythm of the river. He chuckled, knocking on the slim cabin door as he stood in the narrow hallway. At her request, Wu Ying walked into Fa Yuan's room.

"Sister, the demon stones." He offered them to her.

Taking the cloth, she let it spill open while she spoke. "Did you appraise them?"

"Yes. Two minor Energy Storage stones, dim and mostly used up. The larger stone is an Energy Storage stone too, but brighter. That was taken from the suiko I fought," Wu Ying said. "The rest are Body Cleansing stones."

"And the shells?"

"Yu Kun says he can arrange for their disposal and payment to be sent to the Sect," Wu Ying said.

Fa Yuan nodded, tapping her lips. "Do you trust him to do so?"

"Of course," Wu Ying said. Then, he hesitated. "Should I not?"

"Trust is good, but we know little of him. Or what price these shells might garner," Fa Yuan pointed out. "It is best to trust but verify."

"Verify…?" Wu Ying frowned.

"Speak with some merchants, learn the price we could get for them normally. At the least, we will know the minimum." Fa Yuan leaned forward, fixing Wu Ying with her gaze. "And if the route he opens offers a greater return, his contribution to the Sect will so increase."

"Oh, that's good for him. I should tell…" Wu Ying finally caught on. "I should tell him about the future opportunities available, shouldn't I." The last was stated more firmly. By doing so, he could curtail any potential issues. It might hinder their ability to truly verify if Yu Kun was telling the truth, but the Sect would care more for long term gains than short term benefits.

Fa Yuan smiled and waved Wu Ying out. He exited the cabin with one last bow, closing the door. Through their entire conversation, the door had been left a little ajar, just in case. And so, as he ascended the steps, Wu Ying mulled over the little lesson.

There was much he could learn from his martial sister, it seemed. Including how to skip out on the gross cleanup.

Chapter 11

Days later, the group of cultivators met in a tea house overlooking the harbor, taking one of the few rooms that allowed the group to watch the industrious waterfront. When Wu Ying managed to make his way inside, Fa Yuan was already seated, Wang Min beside her and Tou He perched uncomfortably on a chair nearby. Yu Kun was seated at another table, chatting with a trio of wandering cultivators, while Lei Hui was still missing.

"Are you finished?" Fa Yuan asked Wu Ying as he took a seat next to her.

He smiled as he watched Tou He relax at his presence, the ex-monk putting away the prayer beads he'd been counting. As Tou He sat, he swept his robes aside, his darker and plainer hemp robes a stark contrast to the pale green and blue Sect robes the group wore.

"Yes," Wu Ying said, nodding. "We should be fine to go overland. There are no major bandit groups or beasts along our proposed route. The Sect doesn't have enough horses for all of us though."

Fa Yuan frowned. "Why? I already informed them of our arrival."

"It seems that three of their mares fell ill just yesterday. Some bad feed. The outer sect member involved was whipped," Wu Ying said, shaking his head. Careless idiot hadn't paid attention to what he had been feeding them and hadn't noticed the demon weevils that had spawned.

"Unfortunate," Wang Min, normally quiet, said. "How many do they have?"

"Four that they can lend us," Wu Ying said.

Fa Yuan's lips quirked. "I guess you might be running then."

"Who's running?" Yu Kun said as he returned. "And why? Are we not taking the boats?"

"That still remains to be seen." Fa Yuan's eyes lit upon Lei Hui as the fussy apothecarist arrived. "Clear the table."

The group quickly moved the sample dishes and teacups aside, allowing Fa Yuan to spread out the map she'd brought. By the time Lei Hui took his seat with the others and offered his greetings and apologies, she'd had everything settled.

"The issue of river travel is not our next ship, but the one after," Fa Yuan said, tracing her finger along the river then a canal. "This canal is blocked. It should be cleared by the time we arrive. Or we could help clear it, if we charter a boat. It should not take long…"

Lei Hui made a face, looking almost affronted at the idea of manual labor.

Wu Ying frowned, but for entirely different reasons. "I don't think it's that simple…"

"Oh?" Fa Yuan raised an eyebrow.

"If it's been blocked this long, it might have been a major failure," Wu Ying clarified. "Otherwise, the local villagers would have dealt with it." He pointed farther down the map, where a small village was marked. "Without the canal, they'd face great difficulty with planting. Which makes me think it requires more work than you're assuming."

"It's not a complete blockage," Fa Yuan objected.

"Even so…" Wu Ying trailed off. She too might be right. After all, if there was enough water that the captains were willing to travel upward, it should be fine. Maybe.

"I agree with Wu Ying. Even if we do clear the canal"—Yu Kun traced his finger upward—"won't we need to change again and move upriver here?"

Fa Yuan eyed the location then shook her head. "I'd planned on going overland then. There is a location here"—she tapped on the map farther north—"that has a chance for one of our goals."

"Ah." Yu Kun retrieved his hand and dropped his objection.

"Then we are going by water?" Lei Hui said, sounding less than enthused.

126

"There is one other issue." Wu Ying tapped the map just a little farther north from where they were located. It was off the main road by a significant distance, requiring the group to travel overland to reach it. "There are rumors of a monster living in a marsh here. Most indicate it is a snake of some form, but at least one rumor has it as a poison frog."

Fa Yuan's eyes narrowed. While they had been asking for such information all over the sect and among the merchants, the local rumors were always more important. After all, unless the creature was attacking the local populace, few chose to hunt such monsters. And this particular location was quite a distance away.

"You said most are of a snake?" Tou He said.

"Yes. Three stories, two from traveling merchants and the last from a local woodsman," Wu Ying explained. "It was the woodsman who claimed to see the frog."

Fa Yuan's eyes narrowed a little more. Obviously, the words of a woodsman were more trusted than a merchant. One could more reliably be expected to tell the difference. Though the difference between a monstrous snake and a monstrous toad was significant. Even a lowly merchant should be able to tell the difference.

"Your thoughts?" Elder Yang asked. Mostly though, she focused on Wu Ying.

Wu Ying knew part of the reason she was even letting him speak was so that she could see how he thought, to train him. Otherwise, she would, as Elders were wont to do, make the decision herself.

Wu Ying held his fingers over the map, doing a quick estimate of the distances. This map had been picked specifically for this region, providing more details on the rivers and canals that linked up in the region and even indicating the positions of local villages. Of course, much of the map was marked for the use of traders and merchants. It lacked many of the defining features of the landscape, indications of mountainous or marshy lands. Those, Wu Ying had to mentally fill in from his own experience and his recent conversations. At least the map was roughly accurate in terms of distances, with the local legend giving distances in li.

"Figure about… two weeks to arrive at the destination. It'd add another week or so," Wu Ying said. "And I'm not certain we'd find anything. The Chan Chu is quite different from other demonic frogs."

There were a round of nods. A three-legged frog was rather different than most of its four-legged companions.

"But the Ben have yet to migrate. No word of their arrival has come as yet. And the Sun Lotus blossoms might be locatable farther north." Wu Ying traced his finger away from where the monster was rumored to live to an empty spot on the map. "This area has the required chi density and environment. As for the canals, it is a sure thing we can make it through eventually. But we only save time at the start and lose it later if we have to wait for the Ben to arrive."

Fa Yuan stared at the map, at where Wu Ying's fingers had been. She stayed silent even as the others chimed in with their differing opinions. Lei Hui, realizing they would be forced to trek through wilderness, was suddenly more enthused about the canals. Yu Kun pushed for the overland journey while Wang Min hesitantly voted for the canals, though she offered no reasoning for her choice. As for Tou He, he just sat, smiling and sipping on his tea.

"Is the underbrush too thick for horses?" Fa Yuan asked.

"Unlikely, as one of the merchants made his way through on horses. But it could be tough in the marshes," Wu Ying said.

"Why did they go through there?" Tou He said, suddenly speaking up. "Is there a road or passage we missed?"

Wu Ying shook his head. "One was attempting to cut through to save time on foot. The other—the one with the horses—never explained his reasoning to those I spoke with."

"Is he still around?" Fa Yuan asked.

Wu Ying could only shrug. He hadn't considered asking about that, since he hadn't planned on finding these individuals directly. He'd already spent a few hours moving from tavern to tavern to stable, gathering information.

"Is it important?" Lei Hui said. "Who cares what these mortals do? Their actions are often senseless."

"It might matter, depending on their reasons," Yu Kun retorted.

Fa Yuan nodded, which silenced Lei Hui's objection.

"We'll go over land. Get us the horses we can, and we'll take turns moving on foot," Fa Yuan decided. "We'll stay the night in town and leave tomorrow morning."

"Again, why don't we have enough horses?" Yu Kun said. Wu Ying briefly filled him in on the issue, making the ex-wandering cultivator frown. "Two horses then?" He rubbed his chin. "I'll see what I can do." At Fa Yuan's raised eyebrow, the cultivator shot her a cocky grin. "Don't worry. I have my ways."

As Wu Ying watched the man walk back to his new friends, he could not help but wonder what kind of ways Yu Kun had. Certainly, he seemed to be a store of interesting information. And watching him leave, Wu Ying could not help but consider that his life as a wandering cultivator seemed so free. And relaxed.

And dangerous.

***

The next morning, the group met at the Sect stables where the promised horses were already saddled for them. The stables were set just off the main roads, in an expansive courtyard settlement that also housed the outer sect members who had been relegated to taking care of this location. The entire thing was built from a mixture of wood, packed earth, and foundational pieces of stone, where the pervasive smell of hay and the stink of the animals permeated the structure.

Additional feed was added to the saddlebags placed across the backs of the horses, while each member of the party took additional food into their spirit rings. It was always better to have more supplies than only what their animals could carry. That was something all the expedition members could agree on—except Yu Kun.

That was because the cultivator had not shown up on time. As Fa Yuan stood around, tapping her foot impatiently, the man appeared, leading a pair of saddled horses. At their surprised looks, he pasted on another cocky grin, running a hand over his central strip of hair.

"I told you I had my ways," Yu Kun said.

Wu Ying could not help but grin, striding over to the free animal and taking its reins from Yu Kun's hands. Fa Yuan only glanced at Yu Kun, offering him a single nod of thanks before she gestured for the group to move out. Rather than ride the horses through town, they led them by their reins, the press of bodies on the cobbled streets too great to allow them passage easily.

Like most towns, the city was built along the north-south, east-west axis, with main gates located at each of these compass points. Excluding, of course, the harbor. A simple and slightly taller than head height set of walls contained the bustling civilization within, providing safety from brigands and demonic monsters in equal portion. As a small town, they had no need to raise the twenty-foot-tall walls large cities required.

Even though it was early morning, the residents of the town were awake and bustling from location to location. Housewives carrying baskets of fresh vegetables and meat. Street-side hawkers with their stalls offering fresh-made meals for those laborers in too much of a hurry or lacking wives or kitchens to cook their meals. Farmers arriving from nearby with their vegetables for sale, and fishermen with the rest of their dawn catch, desperate to sell their remnant fish before heading out to acquire more. And of course, alongside the streets were the merchants' stalls with their front doors thrown open, seeking their first sale of the day.

Wu Ying was tempted, knowing that often, one could get an extremely good deal if one was early enough. No merchant wanted to lose their first potential customer of the day. Many believed that doing so would set their luck for the rest of the day. It was a superstition and religion; one occasionally backed by the showering of godly luck and had thus become entrenched among the populace and the merchants themselves.

Tempted as Wu Ying might be, Fa Yuan was not stopping, pulling her horse along and striding through the gaps in the crowd that were created for her. None dared crowd or hinder the passage of the Sect Elder, her robe announcing her presence. Amusingly, Wu Ying, in his dark brown and black hemp robes at the back of the line was crowded out more often, as the public regarded him as but a servant and treated him accordingly. Seeing Wu Ying's difficulty, Yu Kun dropped back, striding alongside Wu Ying. Immediately, the crowd parted, giving the pair more space.

"Why not wear your sect robes?" Yu Kun asked.

"These are sturdier and less likely to be damaged, especially where we are going."

"Did you not purchase the higher-quality robes?" Yu Kun frowned. "Even I have a couple of sets."

Wu Ying could only shrug, not wanting to explain his current predicament and not knowing how to do so without going into too much detail. While not exactly shameful, it wasn't exactly the kind of story he wanted to relate. Even after all this time, not having many contribution points seemed a little embarrassing.

Seeing that Wu Ying was not interested in discussing the matter, Yu Kun dropped the topic. Instead, they turned to discussing the passing goods—so much so that Wu Ying eventually made a brief stop to purchase wrapped steamed buns filled with chives, bean sprouts, and fresh onions, all accompanied by a small portion of roasted pork. He distributed the breakfasts among the group, receiving words of thanks, and in Tou He's case, a joking complaint of the lack of significant meat products.

In short order, the expedition left town, only delayed briefly when the magistrate hurried out to greet and provide regrets at the declined invitation to dine with him. On the open road, they clambered onto their horses and rode. It would be at least a few days before it was time for the group to split off from the well-traveled passage between cities, so they made good time on the well-maintained paved road.

Time, on the horses, passed quickly amidst companionable conversations and moving cultivation. Tou He and Yu Kun both spoke with Fa Yuan and Wu Ying in great detail as they attempted to achieve the same level of comfort in cultivating on the move as Wu Ying and the Elder.

In the meantime, Lei Hui spent his time reading, going through the numerous books and recipes he had brought with him in his spirit ring.

When asked to join the joint moving cultivation lessons, he indicated his lack of interest. He insisted quite sternly that his studies as an apothecarist were more suited to this kind of journey.

Wan Ming also declined, instead spending her time with her pipa, practicing while riding. It was, even to untrained ears, clear that Wan Ming was less conversant with this instrument than she was with the guzheng. The pipa was a four-stringed, pear-shaped wooden instrument with a graceful neck[14] from which Wan Ming would cajole classic and new symphonies to wile away their travel. Only the occasional missed beat or misplucked string marred the beauty of her efforts.

Of course, her playing had the tendency to attract Demon Beasts. Even scared away by Elder Yang's aura, Wan Ming's playing and the subtle tendrils of chi she imparted to each tune drew them close and overrode their fear. In this way, the team found themselves able to provide additional demon beast stones and meat for the pot.

As for Wu Ying, he split his attention between his cultivation exercises and the act of cultivation itself. He constantly churned the chi within his dantian, drawing in environmental, unaspected chi while rejecting other forms of chi and extending his own senses. The various animals that lived in the wild provided him with a new, extensive repertoire of smells, allowing him to progress that particular cultivation exercise at speed. In time, he even picked out the demon beasts as they crept close, lured by Wan Ming's tunes.

All in all, the initial overland journey—stopping at rest houses, occasionally hunting and eating the food they brought or hunted—was idyllic. Until it was time to turn off the road, crossing near a stream that his

---

[14] I had to play with this sentence multiple times while trying not to say "it's a fat guitar with less strings." The pipa is actually quite a beautiful instrument to listen to.

informants had indicated to Wu Ying as the best location to begin their off-trail journey.

From here onward, as Wu Ying's horse set foot on the land across the stream, the expedition would enter the wilds, braving the darkness within the untamed forest. No more would civilization be but a short ride away. In the wild, demon beasts and spirit beasts roamed.

Chapter 12

The initial portion of their off-trail journey into the wild was quiet. The forest around them was busy with undergrowth, the older trees killing off any secondary growth, leaving only bushes and low-level vegetation to clog up the ground. It forced their horses to trample through until they found an animal track. Oak, laurel, and schima trees rose from the forest ground, the evergreen vegetation shrouding them in shadows and floral scents.

Yu Kun had taken the lead, staying about twenty to thirty feet ahead of the group, allowing his horse to pick through the undergrowth and around the dead falls littering the ground. The rest of the group spread out behind him in a roughly straight line, with only Elder Yang choosing to ride away from the main group. In the forest, most of the others had stopped their moving cultivation attempts as they watched for potential threats.

Wu Ying, on the other hand, was able to continue churning his chi, the act of cultivating on the move an almost unconscious action by now. He only stopped when he was actively cultivating, contemplating the Dao, or in the most desperate of fights. On top of all this though, Wu Ying made sure to practice the scent cultivation method passed on to him by Elder Cheng. If nothing else, he needed to gain familiarity with the overflowing scent of wood, earth, and metal chi that pervaded the forest.

As they traveled, no longer did Wang Min play her pipa, nor did the others indulge in casual conversation. While it was unlikely that any demonic beasts would attack a group so large and powerful, one never knew. Unfortunately, while demonic beasts were generally quite dumb and straightforward in their aggression, the spirit beasts that preyed on man often had the intelligence to lay traps. And worse, in the wilds were greater dangers than beasts – for occasionally, demons, true demons, lived.

Knowing that, the expedition members stayed silent and rode on. Under the cover of the looming trees, they listened to the sounds of the forest, the creak of old wood, the chirp of insects, and waited for their next challengers.

Days passed as the group traveled deeper and deeper into the forest. At first, the forest still held minor signs of civilization. The occasional mark of chopped wood, dropped coins, or discarded string and oiled paper. Even the unmistakable stench of human refuse. But soon enough, they left behind all such indicators of humanity as they journeyed deeper into the wilds.

In turn, more signs of wild animals appeared. Few of these signs indicated spirit beasts, most from mundane, unevolved creatures who started at the unexpected presence of humanity. The creatures were all wary, a certain sign that even this deep, the occasional hunter would make his way in.

It was nearly midday on the fourth day since they'd left the road when they met their first spirit beast. There had been indications beforehand that such creatures were within, but most had left long before the group had spotted them. This time, they spotted the creature from a distance through the dense foliage.

"It's gorgeous," Wang Min said as she gazed upon the spirit deer.

There was no doubt in any of the cultivators' eyes that the lone creature was a spirit animal. Even to unaided senses, it blanketed them with a subtle pressure of its chi aura. It was a mixture of wood and earth chi, clearer and cleaner than anything they'd sensed in days.

In addition to its aura, the spirit deer itself was a beautiful specimen, standing five feet tall at its shoulders, with a brilliant white coat that glistened in the sunlight. Its eyes, when it turned to regard them, sparkled with uncommon intelligence, ears flicking as it chewed on a plant.

"I bet it's good eating," Yu Kun said.

"Yes…" Tou He replied, swallowing around saliva that had erupted from his mouth.

"We will not be hunting in here," Fa Yuan said firmly. When the pair of cultivators shot her aggrieved looks, she explained. "The scent of newly spilled blood could attract more danger. Can you not sense the increased flow of ambient chi? We are not in civilized lands anymore."

Her words made the greedy pair pause before reluctantly nodding. The demonic beasts they had met before they'd quickly dealt with, the unrelenting aggression engendered by the corrupted spirit cores leaving no space for peaceful coexistence. However, any demonic beast attracted to their kill this deep into the forest would be much stronger. And while they probably could handle such an attack, there was no reason to risk it.

"Anyway, it would be a shame to kill such a gorgeous creature," Fa Yuan said.

Wu Ying could only nod in agreement, even if Tou He shot him an aggrieved look. After all, Wu Ying was not ruled by his stomach like his friend.

"Let's get moving," Wu Ying said. Putting action to words, he kicked his horse forward, continuing to lead the way through the dense undergrowth.

His action made the deer bound off, leaving in a flash of light that made Wu Ying doubt his friend could even kill it if the Elder had allowed him. All the creature left behind was a serene memory and a small tuft of hair that Wang Min plucked from a branch.

***

For all their concern about attack, the group managed to make their way to the marshlands without great difficulty. A few battles were had with roaming demonic beasts, the most notable being a group of mutated yellow hornets the size of a hand. The two score of creatures struck with little warning, coming late in the day as the evening fog rolled in as they neared the marsh. The expedition quickly dealt with the attack, Wang Min sending a burst of air chi through the sky that disrupted the initial attack before Tou He's staff, burning with flames, crisped the wings of the monsters and left them easy prey for the rest of the team.

As the group came to the beginnings of the marsh, where water lapped against soggy ground, the expedition team finally slowed down. In the front, Wu Ying attempted to goad his mare into entering the marshland but found his ride balking.

"Do not bother, Ah Ying[15]," Fa Yuan called as she guided her horse to a drier section of ground. "They will not enter. Especially in such a place." She leaned down, stroking the neck of her animal as she calmed the nervous stallion. "Though their nervousness likely indicates we might be in luck."

"But the beasts…" Wu Ying waved his hand toward the marsh.

"We will have to wade in ourselves," Fa Yuan said, eyes gleaming. "But we should pick a good spot to do so."

"And the horses?" Tou He said with some concern.

"Someone will have to stay behind," Fa Yuan said.

Lei Hui, who'd looked less than thrilled at the idea of having to wade through the knee-high muddy water, perked up at Fa Yuan's words.

Wu Ying noticed that and, smiling slightly as he turned the horse about, said, "We should probably leave Lei Hui behind with the horses."

Fa Yuan raised an elegant eyebrow at his words.

"We'll not need his services immediately. And the rest of us have martial skills…" Wu Ying said, then winced. "Not that Lei Hui isn't a fighter. He did well against the suiko."

---

[15] Reminder, the "Ah" portion is an honorific only used when one is familiar with said person (or trying to force familiarity). By dropping his generation name and using Ah, it indicates a closer relationship between the two.

138

Lei Hui's face grew darker the more Wu Ying tried to cover for his mistake. "I'll go. I'm a good fighter. You should stay."

"I didn't mean it that way," Wu Ying said.

"I'm sure," Lei Hui growled.

"No, really, I think you did really well..."

While Wu Ying blathered on, Fa Yuan stared at the marsh. The burgeoning argument ground to a halt as they sensed the change in the ambient chi. A light floral scent drew Wu Ying's attention to Fa Yuan, the scent growing stronger as her chi permeated the surroundings. Elder Yang pushed against the environment as she stretched her senses to the maximum. The floral, humid scent of fallen rain and fresh springs rose from his martial sister, almost smothering that of the marsh.

"How far is her spiritual sense range?" Tou He asked Wu Ying as he edged his horse over.

Wu Ying could only shrug. There were too many variables to know for certain, not unless she told him. And since she hadn't, he could only use the estimates given by their teachers. At the Core stage, most practitioners could extend their spiritual sense to a few li, giving them an unparalleled ability compared to the almost blind Energy Storage cultivator's tens of feet.

Then again, that number could change depending not only on the type of sensing exercises one studied, but also the environment. As Fa Yuan was a water practitioner, in the marshlands, she could borrow the ambient water chi to extend her senses even farther than usual.

In silence, the group watched the Core practitioner, trying to learn from her example, from the shifts in energy that surrounded her. Long minutes passed before she finally turned to the group.

"We need to move farther east, but our prey is here," she said.

"A Chan Chu?" Yu Kun said.

"Uncertain, but a large amphibious creature in the late Energy Storage stage. Perhaps even Core," Fa Yuan replied, her brows creasing. "It hides within the mud and earth and shrouds its aura."

Done with the conversation, she waved the group to follow the edge of the shore farther west, taking them along the marshland. The journey became slower, the horses forced to pick through the brambles and sodden ground, careful in the placement of their feet as Fa Yuan led the way. Occasionally, she sent a pulse of chi out to the surroundings, using her spiritual sense to keep track of where they were.

"Won't you alert them doing that?" Wu Ying certainly sensed the shift in environmental chi every time she extended her senses, so the animals who had more powerful senses must do so too.

"It already knows we're here," Fa Yuan said. "But it will not act so long as we stay outside the marsh. Once we enter, we will have to be more careful."

Wu Ying nodded, then watched as she glanced at the water again, her brow creasing. "Is there something wrong?"

"Maybe," Fa Yuan replied truthfully, though she dropped her voice a little. "There's... something else. Maybe."

"Maybe?"

She shrugged. Wu Ying frowned, glancing back at his companions, who rode behind, and could not help but sigh. If she did not know—or would not say—there was nothing he could do but keep an eye on the surroundings.

Eventually, they reached a point in the marshlands that satisfied Fa Yuan. She gestured to the group to dismount, taking hold of her animal's reins and handing them to Lei Hui. The apothecary had calmed down by this point and took the reins without complaint.

"Set up camp a little farther inland." Fa Yuan pointed. "We'll find you after we're done. Keep the animals safe and make sure to prepare for us."

"How long will you be gone?" Lei Hui asked. He took the talisman marks she handed to him, along with the formation flags, all of which he'd use to set up the camp and keep other predators away.

"No more than a day or two," Fa Yuan said. "It will either run or meet us in combat eventually."

The group members were quick to prepare themselves. With spirit rings to hold the majority of their goods, it was only a matter of verifying their weaponry and that they had sufficient food to eat quickly. Wang Min took the longest time, having to change her robes for something a little tighter and less voluminous while also tuning her pipa and guzheng. After she'd verified both were as tuned as they would get for the time being, the group left, leaving Lei Hui with the horses while they journeyed into the marshlands.

***

It was a good thing, Wu Ying had to admit, that there were still solid areas of land they could walk upon. Using their qinggong skills, the Energy Storage cultivators could move across the sodden ground without sinking into the mud. Earth that was too mushy for the mundane was a small impediment for true cultivators like them, though it came with the necessity of continuously circulating their chi.

On the other hand, Fa Yuan, as a Core Formation cultivator and a much more experienced qinggong practitioner, moved across the long grasses and branches of the stubby trees with equal ease. She even ran across the water on occasion as she scouted ahead of the team.

If not for her presence, the team would have bogged down and been forced to reroute—or wade through the water—more than once. With her ahead, the group managed to make good time as they delved deeper into the marshlands, even as wisps of marsh mists rose as the day heated up.

A couple of hours in, the group paused by the edge of the water, debating the best way to cross. Elder Yang had scouted ahead, trying to find the best path for the group. While some of the group could run across water, it cost more chi than they cared to expend at the moment.

"Just let us use your staff," Wu Ying said, pointing at the ground. "If we push it in and jump, we should be able to leap across then toss it back."

"We don't even know how deep the water is!" Tou He protested. He didn't exactly clutch his weapon to his chest, but it was a close call.

"Aren't you a monk? Supposed to be all about discarding desire and material needs?" Yu Kun said, sniffing. "Just give it to us."

"Why don't we cut down a branch?" Wang Min offered.

"No!" Tou He protested. "There's no need to harm the tree." The ex-monk shook his head, but he reluctantly extended his staff.

A flash of motion made Wu Ying turn, his hand dropping to his sword hilt. The sudden explosion of smells, slimy and a little hot, made him draw, executing the Dragon unsheathes his Claws without thinking. His blade caught the first of the leaping white fish. To his surprise, his jian was deflected by what he could only describe as a sword-like snout.

As the fish fell back into the water, Wu Ying glanced at his friends, all of whom were under attack by the jumping fish. Yu Kun, using the hooked portions of his sword, had managed to snatch one of the fish out of the air and slap it down onto the ground. Meanwhile, Tou He had achieved the task of removing fish from water by using the meaty portion of his buttocks.

Only Wang Min, who had been standing farther back, had managed to escape without contact by dodging her attacker.

As Wu Ying fell back toward Wang Min and the center of the small piece of dry ground, Tou He ripped the offending monster from his body. A moment later, the flopping fish landed on the ground and managed to return to the water. As the team regrouped, Wu Ying caught his first proper sight of their attackers.

The fish had a long sword-like rostrum, the snout extending far ahead of its body. Its "sword" gleamed with a metal-like substance, much like its scales, and the fish had one large top fin and three smaller bottom fins. The one that had left Tou He was small but four feet long. Others, like Yu Kun's, were gigantic, nearly nine feet long from the tip of its sword-like rostrum to its tail.

"What are those things?" Wu Ying said, eyes darting around at the water.

Tou He, slapping a hand to his wound, channeled some of his chi to staunch the bleeding. The smell of burning meat permeated the air as he did so, his fire chi interacting with the wounds in a grievous but effective manner. As the ex-monk hobbled back, he held his staff before him. "Baixun[16]!"

"I don't know what that is!" Yu Kun replied as he finished tearing open the side of the baixun's neck that he had managed to ground.

"Good eating! But the juveniles are very aggressive. Once they grow bigger, they're not as tasty, but easier to hunt since they don't lurk in schools anymore." As Tou He spoke, he spun his staff in place, small flames dancing along the staff as it moved.

---

[16] By the way, this is a real fish. Excluding the metallic chi, that is. And the overly aggressive nature. Also, extinct, but they grew up to twenty-three feet in length.

Rippling water in the corner of his vision drew Wu Ying's attention. As if unsatisfied that it had missed the first time, Wang Min's assailant launched itself once more. This time, it came out only partially, shoving its head toward her. Long as it was, it couldn't reach the retreating cultivator. Wu Ying still charged it, intent on skewering the monster before it retreated.

To his surprise, bright light gleamed across its exposed body before a line of lightning exploded toward Wang Min. It struck at her, catching the arm she'd raised to protect herself, and flowing down her body. She let out a long scream as the fish-conjured lightning played across her body.

Unable to stop, Wu Ying finished his lunge, sending both sword intent and his blade into the monster. Sparks of electricity danced across the monster's body, remainder air chi zipping up to numb Wu Ying's arm. But his attack skewered the monster and tore open its side even as it wriggled itself off the blade's edge and landed back in the water.

Wu Ying recovered forward and sent a wave of sword energy into the water, only to see it disperse without hurting anything. Water stained with pale red blood belatedly rose, marking the baixun's retreat. Falling back, worried that he'd be attacked, Wu Ying glanced at his friends.

Working together, Tou He and Yu Kun had managed to catch another monster, hauling it onshore and shattering its back. A few hasty strikes ended the creature's struggles. With two fish corpses before them, the group stared at the water, awaiting the next attack.

Long minutes passed, with Wang Min managing to recover before they'd conceded that the monstrous fish had fled. By the time Fa Yuan returned, having felt the disturbance their fight had caused, Yu Kun had placed a compress on Tou He's injury, wrapping it tightly with cloth.

"Baixun?" Fa Yuan said, eyeing the monsters. "Demonic?"

"No. Spirit," Wu Ying said, having fished out a small spirit stone. It was tiny, having barely started growing in the monster. Finding even one among the two they had managed to kill was surprising.

After pocketing the stone, Fa Yuan said, "I see. Rest, heal yourself quickly, all of you. We cannot turn back for we are close."

In unison, the group sucked in a breath in surprise. Fa Yuan had already turned around, offering her back to them as she watched for additional dangers. As Tou He checked the bandaging and gingerly attempted to move, wincing with each step, Wu Ying cleaned his blade and cursed himself out. If he had been a little faster, warned them instead of attacking...

"Oh, one last thing," Fa Yuan called, never taking her eyes off the water. As the group perked up, she continued. "Finish cleaning the fish. Baixun are good eating."

Chapter 13

"Are you fine?" Wu Ying said softly to Tou He as they ran along the edge of the brackish water, following Elder Yang. Use of qinggong kept them from sinking into the marshy ground, though their movements often kicked fallen leaves and sticks into the flowing water beside them.

"I'll live. It's just a pain in the butt," Tou He said, eyes glinting with amusement. His voice was tight and controlled, a testament to the pain he was obviously in.

Still, Wu Ying sighed theatrically for his friend, choosing to play into the poor joke.

"We will need you to be silent soon," Fa Yuan said as she slowed her stride. She stopped at the edge of the current piece of raised land, turning to the group as her robes flared out behind her. Even the tighter set of martial robes she wore still had a degree of play to preserve modesty. "We will change our plans slightly. Wu Ying, you will join me in fighting the frog. Tou He, you will be in charge of guarding Wang Min while she readies her attack. Yu Kun, watch for additional spirit beasts."

Yu Kun shot an envious glance at Wu Ying but forbore saying anything. Giving Wu Ying the opportunity to fight a powerful Energy Storage creature with the aid of a Core Development cultivator was blatant favoritism for sure. It would mean the danger to him was significantly lowered, while offering him the opportunity to learn. There was only so much one could grasp while watching on the sidelines, and one could never know when inspiration might hit in the midst of combat.

Still, no one complained. In truth, Fa Yuan battling the creature by herself would have been sufficient. Even if it was a Core strength spirit beast, she would, at most, be forced to run away. And if it was a Core strength spirit beast, the inner sect cultivators would be of minimal aid. They had not trained together, nor had they studied any fighting formations that would benefit their attacks.

No, their presence in this expedition was for ancillary reasons. Large fights could draw the attention of other monsters. And while they weren't venturing into the deep wilderness where Core spirit beasts were as common as grains of rice in a paddy field, the scavenger creatures could and would lurk on the edges, watching for their chance to snatch the frog's spirit stone or a few tasty organs. For the inner sect cultivators, offering a show of force would help keep opportunistic beasts away.

"Of course, Elder Yang," Tou He said. His style—the Mountain Resides—was a defensive form with the staff and meant that he was best-suited for guarding or blocking attacks. His position also meant he would need to move less, which would be important with his injury.

In short order, the group set off again, having adjusted their formation. Wu Ying stayed in the front, close to Fa Yuan, while Yu Kun stayed at the back. They journeyed through the marshlands, stepping across murky water, feet lightly touching down on upraised branches or occasionally wading through dirty water when necessary. In short order, all this came to an end. To their surprise, Fa Yuan stopped them at a nearby hillock, focused entirely on the next marshy hill.

Wu Ying stared at the small mound before them. It was brown and grey, like much of the land around them. Sparse tufts of grass grew from the edges, marshy reeds dotting the surroundings before rising toward longer swaying grass at the top. When he opened his mouth to speak, Fa Yuan raised her hand, silencing him. The group held still as she continued to stare. Without anything better to do, Wu Ying focused as well.

It was long seconds, at least a half dozen slow breaths, before he noticed what Fa Yuan had already—small ripples that didn't come from the waves lapping at the edges reflecting back. Dark mud moved at the edges of the hill.

Wu Ying realized that near the water's edge, half submerged before the hill, was their prey. The frog lay deep within the marshy land and held so still that mud itself had washed up on its dotted and slimy body. Along with its mottled grey and yellow skin, the creature had camouflaged itself to such an extent that Wu Ying would have walked right by it.

Fa Yuan turned and raised an eyebrow at Wu Ying. He offered a single, firm nod, acknowledging that he had seen it. When she looked at the others, there were mixed gestures. Rather than speak, she walked back to where a tree dominated the top of the land they stood upon. Once they arrived, Fa Yuan gave them curt orders, describing the scene for those who had missed the signs.

Wang Min was the first to set up. She sat beneath the tree, drawing out her guzheng. She made sure not to strike any of the strings as yet even as she laid it on her portable playing table. Tou He took position next to her, just ahead and in front, while Yu Kun moved to the edge of the land, perpendicular to where the monster lay.

Yu Kun kept the swords on his back sheathed, instead retrieving a bow and a quiver of arrows. Quick motions had him sink those arrows into the mushy soil before setting another to his bowstring. As for Wu Ying, his preparations were much simpler, involving drawing his sword and doing light stretches.

All the while, Elder Yang paid attention to the unmoving frog. Wu Ying wondered whether it was even aware of their presence, or if it trusted its ability to hide such that it's choice to stay motionless was a reasoned decision. In either case, it took no aggressive action as the group readied themselves.

The initial plan was simple. It would also be their first test of Wang Min's ability to manage a creature in the late Energy Storage stage. The frog, whose type they still could not tell, would be attacked by Fa Yuan and Wu Ying.

While they distracted the creature, Wang Min would have time to play a calming, enchanted tune.

Done right, musicians could hypnotize, confuse, and charm others. In this case, the goal was to make the frog's attacks slower, more obvious. Beast trainers were well-known to employ spirit musicians while attempting to capture and train a new spirit beast.

In their case, the expedition was just looking to kill their prey. More involved preparations were wasteful.

A small gesture and a nod was all that was needed between the pair of attackers before Fa Yuan launched herself across the water. Her feet lightly struck the slow-flowing marsh water, small rings of waves expanding from where her feet impacted and pushed off the liquid flooring. She flew straight at the frog, her jian drawn and pointed at the center of the creature's eyes. Beside her body, she held a second sword in readiness.

Wu Ying took a more circuitous route. He ran off at an angle, jumping off floating debris, raised roots, and the occasional solid earth as he made his way to the frog. There were two reasons for his circuitous path. Firstly, he was not as adept as Fa Yuan at qinggong, unable to run across water as yet. Just as importantly, it was safer for him to launch an attack from a blind spot, potentially killing the frog via a surprise attack than face it head-on like his martial sister.

At first, the frog chose not to react. Only at the last few seconds, as the Elder's blade began to threaten its very existence, did it give up the pretense. A ribbit broached the hubbub of the marsh, followed by an explosion of mud and water. A sudden wall of earth and water blocked Fa Yuan's approach, stymieing her attack.

A simple wave of her lead sword cut apart the wall of water and mud. Her momentum arrested, Fa Yuan landed before the parted and falling defense. However, behind the wall, only an empty and slowly filling hole where the frog had once been met her cold gaze.

Even at a distance, Wu Ying felt the splash of falling water, mud splattering his robes and coating him in lukewarm grit. From his angle, Wu Ying spotted the ripples of the creature's passing as it swam under the marsh to attempt to surprise Fa Yuan.

Rather than call a warning, Wu Ying threw a single cut, infusing it with the full strength of his sword intent and chi and adding the Woo Petal Bracer's energy. The Dragon's Breath stroke flew at a slight angle, crossing water and leaving a small ripple of flowing force behind before it impacted. Like a child striking the water, an explosive wave arose as the strike landed and dug into the sneaking frog's body.

"Behind!" Wu Ying finally spoke after he finished his attack.

Fa Yuan was already pivoting on one foot, the other raised by her side. The second blade was still held down by her side, her first blade's guard raised to her face in a salute and in preparation. As blood and pus rose from the water, staining it red and yellow, the frog exploded forth. For the first time, Wu Ying and the other cultivators could see their prey in its full glory.

Slimy skin of mottled yellow and grey covered a creature the size of two water oxen, its bulbous head expanded to its maximum size as it let out an angry call. A single open wound that barely penetrated the creature's pustule-ridden hide spilled blood and pus from its lower back. On the front of the creature's body were two smaller front legs tipped with sharp claws and dripping not just water but an oily, pus-ridden substance. And on its back, to their chagrin, two large and powerful legs were seen.

"Hun dan!" Wu Ying swore, as he watched Fa Yuan and the creature move away from him.

Fa Yuan dodged the leaping frog with a sideways drop step, her sword dragging along its hide. The graceful, deceptively light motion tore open a wound larger than Wu Ying's all-out attack, a testament to both the better quality of her blade and her greater cultivation level. Rather than follow-up, Fa Yuan dodged away while making a face at the rain of pus and blood that had exploded from its body after her attack.

"Yellow-bile demonic frog," Fa Yuan called. "Horrible creatures. But their livers and kidneys are highly prized among alchemists."

"What for?" Wu Ying said as he continued his trek toward dry ground.

"Because it manages to keep even that creature alive from its own infections!"

That was all the time they had for talk, for the monster had turned around again. This time, rather than attempting to jump at Fa Yuan, it spat an attack at her. The water cultivator twisted her hand, cutting at the ground with the blade she held. The transmitted sword chi—attuned with Fa Yuan's own water chi—reacted to the lapping water, repeating the frog's defense. Except unlike the monster's filthy and muddy defense, Fa Yuan's wall of water was indescribably pure.

In retaliation for the attack, Fa Yuan used her other sword to send a slash of sword chi at the monster. However, the frog had moved again, dodging the attack with a quick hop. It was highly agile for something so big. Wu Ying, finally on level ground, found himself facing the leaping creature.

Eyes narrowed, Wu Ying backed off, searching for the trick. For the creature had not jumped far enough to land on him. His caution was rewarded moments later as the yellow-bile frog shot its tongue out at blinding speed. A hasty block sent Wu Ying stumbling back, his hand trembling from the force the late stage Energy Storage monster had packed in its attack.

"Should I shoot it?" Yu Kun called, reminding the pair that they were not the only ones involved. Not that Wang Min's careful tuning, muted by a silencing talisman, was easy to miss even in the midst of battle.

"No. Do your duty!" Fa Yuan ran toward the monster, which hopped backward into the water.

Before the cultivator could reach it, the frog disappeared under the water and swam away, its dark body a shadow in the murky water. Rather than waste chi, Fa Yuan retreated to the hill, swords held before her as she waited.

"Will it run?" Wu Ying asked, somewhat worriedly. Underwater, the frog could easily outpace them.

"Not yet," Fa Yuan said. "We have not injured it enough. We will wait until Wang Min is ready before we go all out."

Wu Ying blinked, glancing at his martial sister. Fa Yuan had been holding back? Then, remembering the fights he had seen on his first expedition, he revised his opinion. Of course she'd been holding back. Though why she felt the need to do so, he was not certain.

"Better to kill it cleanly," Fa Yuan replied, as if reading his mind. "Otherwise you destroy its pustules and bile sacs. Those can kill normal animals for half a li."

Once more, Wu Ying realized the distance between himself and his martial sister. To even consider such matters in the middle of battle... he shook his head and discarded those errant thoughts. Best to stay focused, for it was returning. And unlike Fa Yuan, he had much lower margin of safety in this fight.

***

"Ready!" The shout rose from the small hillock where Wang Min and the other cultivators stayed, waking Wu Ying from his battle stupor. For the last few minutes, he and Fa Yuan had been battling the frog, attempting to keep its attention while not driving it away or injuring it too badly.

"About time," Wu Ying grumbled as he slid backward, letting Elder Yang take over. He drew deep breaths, circulating his chi as he attempted to regain his energy.

As Fa Yuan baited the demonic frog onto land by allowing it to wrap its tongue around her blade, then pulling it to her, she began to lay into the monster fully. Taking her cue, Wang Min played, the tune rising without interruption and filling the marsh with its melody.

Wu Ying grunted, feeling the tug of the slow notes filled with chi entering his body. He closed his aura down, forcing the effects aside with an exertion of will. Unlike the cultivators, the monster had no such defense and immediately flagged in its aggression.

Tethering the monster via its tongue and a blade in its foreleg, Fa Yuan shouted to Wu Ying, "Now! Strike between its forearms."

Wu Ying charged, his sword raised. Remembering her warnings of potential splash back from the pustules, Wu Ying resolved himself to using his sword chi once again, backing it up with the Woo Petal Bracer attack. Just as he neared, Fa Yuan cried out and released the monster, forcing him to abort his attack.

Surprised, Wu Ying turned to regard the Elder fully. His martial sister was no longer in her former position, the coils of a giant snake beside her. The creature had bands of yellow and black along its body, and it had scooped the Elder up in its mouth. A single arrow lodged just beneath its eye, and as Wu Ying watched, a second arrow managed to strike the creature's body and deflect off its scales.

"Cao Nee! It came out of nowhere," Yu Kun cried.

Wu Ying had no more time to pay attention to the new attacker. The yellow-bile frog, released and its tongue injured, now turned its attention to the weaker cultivator, anger flashing in its eyes. Injured and tired or not, it decided to repay the offense by striking with its foreleg. Wu Ying blocked the claws only to be pushed back as the larger and stronger creature continued its attacks.

"Wu Ying!" Tou He called worriedly.

But Wu Ying could only shake his head, long hair flowing behind him as he steadied himself on the marshy ground. Chi pumped out of the soles of his feet, touching the air as he utilized the Twelve Gales technique to lighten his load. His martial sister would handle the other creature. She would be fine. He had to believe that.

It was up to them to deal with this monster.

Chapter 14

Wu Ying hissed, dodging the spray of yellow bile unleashed by its namesake demon frog. He snarled, wondering exactly how much chi it had to produce so much of the noxious substance. It smelled like the worst kind of compost—the one where no one paid attention to what was added, never turning it over and so the meat, vegetables, and feces rotted with impunity. It made the worst fertilizer and would take months of careful tending to set right.

Much like the marshy ground the pair of opponents danced across. Ground bubbled, grass twisted and died as bile impacted it. Occasional arrows would wing their way across, striking the frog but failing to do much more than puncture the numerous pustules on its yellow and brown hide. In the midst of the demonic creature's croaking protests, Wang Min's musical assault continued to dull its senses and calm its chi, forcing the monster to churn ever faster.

For the last few minutes, Wu Ying had fought the creature to a standstill. And the effects of Wang Min's influence were finally showing. Each passing moment, the frog grew slower, the chi embedded in its strikes, in its attacks, less robust. Blows that had forced Wu Ying back initially had grown more manageable.

But in turn, he too was tiring. To match the monster, Wu Ying had burned his own chi without care. Even as he churned his dantian and tried to draw in chi from the external world, tried to cultivate and replenish his body, Wu Ying felt his energy levels dropping. For now, he could match it and more, but soon enough, he would be tapped out.

"I'm coming!" Yu Kun's voice rose from the background noise.

Wu Ying scored another cut on the frog's forearm. This one tore a tendon, making its middle finger flop uselessly. A success, even if the creature had two other fingers to attack him with.

"Okay," Wu Yun breathed out in reply. He wasn't sure if the man heard. The reply was more for him than the other cultivator.

Another block, Dragon shades itself from the Sun, before Wu Ying twisted and launched a kick at the body. One, two, three strikes in rapid succession, all backed up by his chi, made the monster vomit a little bile. Splatters of it hit Wu Ying's pants leg and burned through before the cultivator could jump away.

The attack had a purpose though, winding the monster long enough for Wu Ying to finish retreating. As the frog recovered, Wu Ying executed the Dragon's Breath, cutting from his back leg to the sky. The diagonal cut, backed with chi from the Woo Petal Bracer, sent the monster reeling back as blood and pus blossomed across its chest and lips.

As Wu Ying finished his successful retreat and Yu Kun jumped onto the ground, a resounding boom echoed farther to the north. Even as they recoiled from the pressure of the noise, the wind that pushed at them, huge waves surged, swamping low-waterline hills and knocking over scrawny trees.

"Elder sister!" Wu Ying muttered, his gaze drawn to where the noise had originated.

Even now, Fa Yuan battled the snake that had surprised them. And from the glimpse of its body and the chi that radiated from it, this was no late Energy Storage monster but a spirit beast that had formed its Core. The creature's strength and danger had increased by multiple li, making it a challenge for his martial sister to battle.

While Wu Ying hesitated, Yu Kun had launched himself at the frog. He'd attached his swords to one another, using the hooks on them to extend his reach and create an impromptu whip. In this way, Yu Kun managed to attack and injure the creature while staying outside of its greater reach.

Seeing that his sect mate had things in hand, Wu Ying popped a spirit pill to help speed up his recovery. As he stood there, churning his dantian and drawing in unaspected chi from the environment, Wu Ying regarded their situation

Yu Kun and the frog were evenly matched, though the occasional spit attack managed to disrupt Yu Kun's form. On the other hand, Tou He was now ensnared in his own fight as Fire Lizards and Green Snakes had arrived in search of easy pickings. Rather than get involved in the main battle, they took to attacking the still form of Wang Min, forcing Tou He to protect her.

Thankfully, Wang Min's song continued to suppress the yellow-bile frog and the other monsters in the surroundings. Over the course of the fight, as the monster showed off its cultivation, she had adjusted both the tune and the pitch to better attack the beast.

A cry from ahead drew Wu Ying's attention back to the main fight. Yu Kun was hopping backward, cradling his arm where blood dripped from it. Wu Ying frowned as he joined the man, blade and blade energy flashing as the pair fought. The yellow-bile frog had stopped attacking for a moment, having exploited the full extent of its chi.

"We cannot keep doing this," Wu Ying said. Not only because they were accumulating injuries and losing energy, but they needed to help Elder Yang. Or at least, be ready to do so. "Keep it distracted. I will try to finish this."

Yu Kun offered a quick nod, taking his swords in both hands again. He stepped forward, shifting his stance to put his injured arm behind. Wu Ying felt the solid pulse of chi, the increased strength in Yu Kun's aura as Yu Kun devoted his energy to the attack. With a wordless cry, he threw himself forward while Wu Ying circled toward the frog's back.

The clash between Yu Kun and the bile frog happened quickly, Yu Kun passing between its arms, spinning his swords in an attack and disrupting the monster's rhythm. Each attack was light, barely doing more than score the monster's arms. More importantly, it forced the creature's arms open, changed its stance, and kept it off balance.

Stalking behind the pair, Wu Ying watched for his opportunity. He no longer had any charges in his bracer, which meant this final attack would have to be done using his own energy. Rather than waste it on a Dragon's Breath attack whose energy would disburse, he would have to commit to a physical strike.

A sudden block, a deflection in a swiping attack left the yellow-bile frog's left arm raised. Yu Kun stepped to the same side, pushing against the arm and creating an opening for Wu Ying. Grasping at the opportunity, Wu Ying threw himself forward in the Sword's Truth. A shrill, twisting note struck at the same time, making the creature flinch as it tried to defend itself

A single attack, a perfect lunge. All his energy, all his intent and focus sculpted to a fine point. His body became a single line, the energy that he pushed forward wrapping around himself and his sword. For a brief second, a rainbow of colors formed around Wu Ying as his sword plunged through a gap created by his teammate into the yellow-bile frog's chest.

Between its arms, just below the center line, Wu Ying's sword entered the spirit beast body. It sank through rubbery, slimy flesh, through tough muscle and the lung, before it pierced the heart. A beat, then another that stopped pushed against Wu Ying's arms as his energy petered out. With a twist of his hips and arm, Wu Ying withdrew the weapon, crouching low as he turned to dodge the reflexive swipe by the frog's free arm.

Behind Wu Ying, Yu Kun rolled and recovered, sent tumbling as the dying bile frog freed itself of his harasser. Wu Ying moved backward, barely managing to dodge the creature's explosive vomiting as it died.

158

Breathing hard, the pair of cultivators glanced to the side where their friends still stood. Tou He batted aside another small snake, glaring about him. Around his feet lay the crushed and twitching bodies of his attackers. Others crouched low on the ground or in the water, hissing and trembling as they considered their options.

Wang Min, now freed to attack, turned her attention to a cluster of snakes that slid along the ground and strummed her guzheng. A flurry of sound chi struck the smaller beasts, tearing at skin and tossing the monsters back. Realizing their easy prey was no more and their distraction dead, the opportunistic beasts scattered.

"Is that it?" Wu Ying said, looking around.

The surroundings were a mess with blood and pus scattered across the ground and flowing into the marsh water. Near where the blood and pus had entered the water, dead fish floated, poisoned by the monstrous creature, while hardy weeds and marsh grasses lay withered. Smaller corpses—those Tou He had slain—bobbed and flowed with the slow current, joined by the torn leaves and broken branches their battle had created.

As for the smell… it was best not to think about that.

"It seems so," Yu Kun said. He had his sleeve torn off, a small medicinal flask with powder poured on his wound. After finishing the simple first aid, he used the remnants of his torn sleeve to wrap his arm.

Wu Ying hurried over and aided him.

"When you're done, I could use some help here," Tou He called as he favored his previously injured backside, only to be interrupted by another resounding crash.

Once again, water jumped and a large wave flowed through the marshlands. The group stared into the distance while Wu Ying gripped the sword he'd embedded in the ground while helping Yu Kun.

"Go," Yu Kun said, flexing his arm. "I'll aid Tou He."

Wang Min had placed her musical instrument away, instead retrieving a handheld repeating crossbow. Together, the pair rushed off, dancing across water, corpses, and raised branches as they searched for Elder Yang, led by the noise of continuing battle. Behind, their injured friends treated their injuries and safeguarded their prize.

***

To the pair's surprise, by the time they arrived, the fight between Elder Yang and the snake was over. The corpse of the creature lay across multiple islands, stretching nearly fifty feet from its head to its barely glimpsed tail. The yellow and black bands of the monster were now marred by numerous injuries, some of which seemed like the injury had exploded from within the monster itself.

"Oh, good. You can begin harvesting the material," Fa Yuan said when they arrived. She smiled at the pair, swaying gracefully toward a tree then sitting down, placing her swords over her knees. She began the slow and careful process of cleaning the weapons, cursing when she noticed a chip on one blade.

Wu Ying and Wang Min glanced at one another, perplexed. But given orders by the elder, they had no choice but to take action.

"Skinning or spirit core?" Wu Ying asked.

"Core." Wang Min strode over to the head of the monster, making a face as she noticed the numerous holes jutting from its mouth and skull. She frowned as she pried its mouth open wider and poked her head in, seeing how many of the injuries had erupted from inside the mouth itself.

Wang Min stared at the corpse, seeming to contemplate the best way to acquire the core. Eventually, she put away her repeating crossbow and extracted a cleaver, wielding it over the monster's skull with tendrils of chi. The meaty smacks of the cleaver against skin and bone penetrated the clearing even as Wu Ying skinned the monster itself.

Wu Ying couldn't help but notice that as unperturbed as the Elder had seemed upon their arrival, on closer inspection, many minor tremors ran across her fingers as she cared for her weapon. Surreptitiously, Wu Ying took a deep breath, sensing the chi in the surroundings. His eyes widened as he realized how weak Elder Yang's presence was at the moment.

The only reason for this, the only reason she'd be trembling, would be a lack of chi. It made sense, for the surroundings spoke of a hard-fought battle. Numerous trees had been broken, some shattered by the thrashing of the snake, others pierced by sword light and water spikes. Most of the branches of the remaining foliage were stripped of greenery, leaving naught but bare bark behind. Even birds' nests, firmly entrenched in water or branch, had been cast aside, leaving the young to die.

When dragons fought, peasants bemoaned their fields.

***

Tou He and Yu Kun caught up to the group soon enough. Yu Kun hurried to Wu Ying, extracting his own skinning knife as he did so. Tou He, on the other hand, chose to butcher the monster, laying out slabs of snake meat to be seasoned. Wang Min started a fire nearby while watching over the skinning cultivator and the cultivating Elder. It was at this fire that Tou He began cooking dinner.

In short order, the savory smells of cooking meat filled the clearing. Snake meat was both more tender than beef and had a lighter taste, though this snake had a slight fishy smell from its residence in the water. However, the chi-laced flesh gave the meat its delectable taste. As a Core spirit beast, every inch of its body had been infused with chi, the meat becoming both more energizing and better for their cultivation than any normal meat.

Gourmands often spoke of the enlightenment that eating Core and Nascent Soul Spirit beasts generated. It was no wonder then that many risked life and limb for such treats.

As he worked, Wu Ying could not help but glance at the slowly cooking meat, his mouth salivating from its smell. The snake, unlike the yellow-bile frog, was not poisonous to them, and portions of its flesh would be stored away or carried back. As for the frog, Yu Kun had taken the most important portions before they left. Those would be given to Lei Hui when they returned to allow the apothecary to preserve the alchemical ingredients.

By the time the pair had finished skinning the snake, Tou He had laid out leaf plates of meat. Each portion of the thinly sliced steak was lightly seasoned, using herbs and a dash of soy sauce.

On the second round of consumption, Elder Yang pulled out a wine jar. Wang Min took control of the jar, pouring a cup for each of the cultivators. Wu Ying raised the glass to his nose, catching hints of fragrant jasmine and rice. But he did not drink, waiting for the rest of the group to have their cups filled.

Only when they were ready did Elder Yang speak. "We might have failed to acquire the beast core we were searching for, but we did acquire something just as important."

She waited a beat, seeing if any of the cultivators would speak in the silence. None did as they paid respects to the Elder. A smile crossed her face before it was banished, leaving the same serene and stern appearance that Fa Yuan normally sported.

"We have learned to fight together under the most taxing of circumstances. You have done well, guarding each other's backs and mine. If we continue in this spirit, I am certain we will be successful." Fa Yuan raised her glass, then called the usual cheer. "Ganbei[17]!"

The group downed their drinks after the Elder. As cups were lowered, Wu Ying spotted small smiles on faces all around. As Fa Yuan had said, they might have failed to gather the Chan Chu's heart, but this was only the beginning of the expedition.

---

[17] Cheers. Often shouted out loudly before everyone downs even more alcohol in a show of mutual support. It always puzzles me how a large group of people who can't process alcohol well still have a very strong drinking culture.

Chapter 15

In the morning, the group made their way out of the marsh to meet Lei Hui. Finding his location was a simple enough matter of extending their senses to locate the ripple and subtle interaction of chi against their minds. The talismans in use were meant to nudge spirit beasts and other aggressive animals away from the camp, but for a trained cultivator, they served as a beacon.

Once they entered the clearing, they found the camp set up to the usual standards. Multiple tents, a full campfire and grill, even a section where Lei Hui was practicing his apothecary. The horses were stabled a short distance away, feed bags and a small water trough available for them. Lei Hui had even managed to place a table for them to rest at, shaded by a giant cloth canopy. It was a luxurious camp, worthy of a noble.

"We have some items for you," Yu Kun called to Lei Hui the moment they arrived. He extracted the various valuable portions of the snake and frog, all sealed in enchanted wooden and stone boxes.

"Did you succeed?" Lei Hui asked. He received his answer in the downcast looks among the group and sighed. However, he brightened in short order as he perused the various innards and other portions of the beasts.

After storing his own small pickings, Wu Ying made his way to the pair with more languid steps. Tou He, on the other hand, sat down almost immediately, his breathing having grown ragged as the day had advanced.

Elder Yang, glancing over the group, eyeing their injuries both minor and major, spoke up. "We will rest here for three days before we continue. Lei Hui, finish whatever work you might have within that timeframe." Fa Yuan turned to Tou He. "You will need to be able to ride."

The ex-monk gave her a nod before beginning the process of cultivating and healing himself. He only paused to slip a pill underneath his tongue to feed his body the nutrition and energy he would require.

As three days passed, Tou He and Yu Kun healed, Wang Min practiced, and Wu Ying worked with Lei Hui in prepping the ingredients. Under Lei Hui's careful and exacting precision, the pair prepared and brewed pills, feeding them to the group when necessary and storing others when possible. Occasionally, Wu Ying scoured the nearby region for additional spiritual herbs and ingredients under the watchful eye of his martial sister.

In this high ambient chi environment, he found numerous fields of vegetation and rare plants untouched by Spiritual Gatherers to add to his collection. Some of those he picked, he dried and stored in his spirit ring, but many, he stored outside the dead, spiritless void to ensure their preservation of natural energy.

Once the period of rest was over, the group packed up and left. Thanks to the increased healing properties of an Energy Storage cultivator, Tou He was mostly healed at this point. At this stage of their cultivation, they healed many times faster than a normal mortal, allowing them to recover from what would be crippling injuries in a matter of weeks, if not days. In fact, outside of dismemberment and loss of limbs, their increased cultivation levels allowed most cultivators to fix what would be lingering problems among Body Cleansers.

It was because of these increased healing properties and the general increase in strength and health of the populace that the Yellow Emperor had initiated cultivation training in all the lands. Ever since his initial push, the resulting kingdoms that had arisen after his empire crumbled had continued the tradition.

Even at the risk of rebellion, the might a company of Energy Storage cultivators brought to an army was well worth the trade-off. Of course, in such instances, such companies would be tightly tied to the ruling kingdom through wealth, cultivation incentives, and subtle threats to the cultivators' families.

Now that Tou He had healed enough that he was able to ride alongside the group, they set a vigorous pace. Their days transitioned between early-morning combat training, long rides throughout the day where they ate only the food that had been prepared the night before, and evenings when they would cultivate and take on their own personal developmental tasks.

Progress came fast for some. Yu Kun broke through one morning, forcing the group to wait for him. As if his very act of breaking through clarified something in Wang Min, she froze then pulled forth her pipa. In a flurry of fingers, she played, fingers moving over frets and striking strings. As she did so, enlightenment pressed upon her, the grace of the heavens marking her play.

During one of those endless, repetitive days, Fa Yuan raised the issue of Wu Ying's sword intent. "You study the Long family sword style, do you not?"

"Of course," Wu Ying asserted. "You know that."

"I do. Your lack of a formal swordsmanship master shows, especially now that you are practicing the second form," Fa Yuan said.

"How did you know that?" Wu Ying said, puzzled that she'd managed to dig out information on his family sword style and his teacher. They should still consider his father his teacher.

"Did you think we did not do any research?" Fa Yuan said, shaking her head in disappointment at Wu Ying. She effortlessly moved with the sway of the horse as they made their way through the dense undergrowth of the temperate forest. "Your family style has some history. It took a bit of work, but we learned some details. Including its decline."

Wu Ying shrugged, controlling his horse with a little less grace. After a few years of occasional rides, he had learned how to maneuver the beasts with more skill. It helped that martial skill—and general physical prowess—provided him a decent sense of balance and rhythm. "Are you suggesting I should find a new style?"

Fa Yuan snorted. "Of course not. You have a full set of instruction manuals in a family style. Why would you give that up?" She cocked her head. "You do have a full set of manuals, do you not?" At Wu Ying's reluctant nod, she continued. "Even if you found a master willing to take you in, you would have to work your way up their ranks—and most likely, discard the style you know." Wu Ying made a face at those words and Fa Yuan smirked. "Obviously, you are not willing."

"Obviously." Wu Ying's eyes narrowed as he glanced at the Elder. He considered the reasons why she would bring up the topic. "But I am lacking a teacher for certain aspects. Chi projection through my sword, in particular."

"Yes," Fa Yuan confirmed. "Your father has not the cultivation to teach you, and while the instruction offered in your manuals might provide some help, such instruction can be lacking compared to a real master."

"Would you be willing to help?"

Fa Yuan shook her head, making Wu Ying frown. She held up a hand, then closed her fingers except for the fore and middle finger. Holding them upright and together, she focused, sharpening her aura and bringing forth her chi. She concentrated her aura to a level that the entire area covering her pair of fingers was visible to the naked eye.

"Energy projection comes in many forms, and it differs depending on the cultivation method and the chi aspect one has. My own aspect will conflict with yours," she said. "But in time, you will learn to project chi yourself.

Your cultivation manual and your own exploration will lead you there. No. Your problem does not lie in chi projection."

"Then…?" Wu Ying said, frowning. It was these kinds of talks he needed an Elder for. It was too easy to find oneself pursuing the wrong kind of development. And while it might not take too long to realize the mistake, time lost during the early stages could have significant impact down the road. It was why he was both blessed and cursed by being Master Cheng's disciple.

Blessed, because Master Cheng allowed him a greater leeway in finding his own path. Which, compared to some of the other inner sect members who slaved away at daos and occupations that did not suit them, was certainly preferable. Cursed, because he lacked the ongoing advice that someone like Tou He, whose Master paid more attention to him, gained as a matter of course.

In answer to Wu Ying's question, Fa Yuan swung her fingers. She put so much focus into the action that Wu Ying saw the sword intent as it struck a nearby twig. The thin, leafy branch swayed for a second in the light breeze before gravity took hold and pulled it to the earth. As if she had been waiting, Elder Yang plucked the twig from the air as she rode toward it, then handed the twig to Wu Ying.

The cultivator turned the twig from hand to hand, staring at the shorn edge. It was a perfect cut, the edge so sharp that when he pressed his finger to it, it drew a trace of blood. He pulled his finger away, sucking on it while Fa Yuan spoke.

"Sword intent and energy projection are two sides of the same coin. By understanding the dao of the sword, you understand sharpness, you understand its place within the universe. Chi projection through a weapon allows you to extend your understanding of the sword, of the cuts you throw, the blows it generates into the world."

Wu Ying nodded. What she spoke of was common knowledge, the basics of projecting sword intent. It was why those who had a greater understanding of the sword—people like him with the Sense of the Sword, and others who had the Heart of the Sword—were more dangerous than those who did not.

"But have you considered what sharpness is?" Fa Yuan spoke. "You understand the weight of a weapon. You understand its length, its breadth, you understand even how to take care of it. You may pick up a sword and know instinctively what metals were used to forge it, what strengths and weaknesses it might have, its balance and the care taken by its previous owners. That is the Sense of the Sword, the heart of Sword Dao. But have you considered what it means for a sword to be sharp?"

"It is a weapon that has been honed well." Wu Ying's brows tightened. The answer was immediate and, he knew, wrong. Yet, it was the only answer he had, at least the only answer he knew instinctively.

Behind the pair, a horse neighed, drawing Wu Ying's attention to his friends behind. To his surprise, Yu Kun had moved his horse closer, covering the usual six-foot distance they kept between each other. At Wu Ying's frown, the ex-wandering cultivator offered a guiltless smile.

"Leave him be," Fa Yuan said. She had obviously noticed him earlier and said nothing. In turn, Wu Ying also kept his protestations silent. It was her knowledge to impart. "Tend to your own development. Your answer describes how a blade is made sharp. It does not explain why."

Wu Ying frowned, but looked down at the weapon sheathed at his side. A blade was sharp because one sharpened it. But what was sharpness? Why did the blade cut? Force, strength obviously played a part. But the sharper a blade, the less force one needed. So force was not why a blade could part silk or flesh.

What was sharpness? Wu Ying drew his weapon halfway out its sheath to stare at the edge of his blade. Unconsciously, he guided his horse with his knees and reins as he pondered the question. He barely even noticed when Fa Yuan moved away, leaving him alone.

To ponder the concept of sharpness and cutting. And what a sword did when it parted flesh and branch.

***

Two mornings later, Wu Ying stood before a tree branch. He swung his sword, one filled with chi and sword intent, lightly against the branch. It was a simple wrist cut, the tip meant to barely miss the branch itself. If not for the extension of his chi that coated the weapon, he would miss the branch entirely.

The swinging jian brushed past the wooden branch, leaves trembling as Wu Ying's chi-infused aura struck it. Leaves danced as the entire branch moved. Even as the shorn portion began to fall, Wu Ying threw another cut in the opposite direction. Another wooden chip was sliced off and the branch trembled again, its edges twisting and pulling as gravity took effect.

He stared at the branch, feeling the way his chi had moved, interacted with the wood. The way it split the bark as it passed. Sharpness could be mimicked by controlling one's energy, by sharpening the edge of one's control. But the act of cutting was the splitting of one thing into two. A change in the natural order of the world.

Initially, Wu Ying had felt that change when he layered his blade with sword intent and chi. When metal and branch, when metal and sausage or vegetable met. He had felt the change, the parting of ways. Bread, flesh, or wood. That change had felt all the same to his senses. But it had been muted by the metal in his blade.

And so he had chosen to only use his chi, to feel the change when the sharpened edge of his aura met wood. To understand by feel, by forcing the interaction, the change in the dao of the branch. As he cut, he applied the strength of his cut to a smaller and smaller area, parting the wood.

But why did it part? What was the point of the separation? A force was applied when wood that was whole and true became two parts. And that parting was natural. As if by sharpening his intent, his chi, his aura, he made his intentions clearer to the branch itself. And, understanding his desires, the wood separated.

If he missed, if he still did not grasp the dao of sharpness or the sword, he understood at least a little of what happened. And mayhap, with a little practice, he could understand more. He could apply his intention to the weapon, to the aura and make such a cut a natural portion of the world with even a blunted weapon.

But he was not there yet.

So he cut.

Cut again.

And with each cut, his control, his intent, grew sharper.

Chapter 16

The city walls of Hinma rose before Wu Ying, four times his height. Crenellations and wooden roofs shaded the guards walking the walls, staring down at the throng of visitors that arrived at the south gate. The cultivators, led by Fa Yuan, rode past the growing line while Wu Ying peered around the familiar green countryside at the flowing river to their left and the town.

"You've been here, have you not?" Tou He murmured.

"Yes. This is where I got the wine," Wu Ying confirmed. It was somewhat nostalgic, being back here, though his arrival this time was different from the bedraggled peasant who had arrived in the past.

"Your friend…" Tou He trailed off, forgetting the name.

"Zhong Shei," Wu Ying supplied.

"He lives here then. Will you visit him?"

"If we have time." Wu Ying rose a little in the stirrups, peering to the east to see if he could spot the second river. It was angled such that he could barely see the edges of it, though the presence of a boat making its way downriver gave away its position.

Given birth at the confluence of two rivers, Hinma was a prosperous town, one whose periphery was filled with farmers making use of the plentiful water and whose mills and factories borrowed the strength of the river for the town's abundant industry. The constant flow of liquid also ensured a small breeze ran through the town throughout the day, changing direction as the day and season changed. One advantage of the constant wind flow was that the town smelled better than most places of civilization.

A more traveled cultivator now, Wu Ying was clearer of the city's geographic benefits. He was no longer the uncultured peasant he had been years before. Now, he rode past the waiting farmers and merchants, confident in his place in the world. Or at least, able to fake it sufficiently.

"Elder. Honored cultivators," the lieutenant of the gate guard greeted the group as they arrived before the looming gates. Made of wood and banded with metal, the gates required multiple guards to open and close, even with the use of the pulley system. Of course, there were few reasons to close the gates during the day. Even at night, only the main gates were closed, the postern gates left open for late arrivals. "Welcome to Hinma. Will you be calling upon the magistrate immediately?"

"We would not want to bother His Excellence." Fa Yuan gestured into the town. "A message for when he would be available to see us will be sufficient. We will be staying at the Golden Age Pearl."

"Of course, Honored Elder." The lieutenant bowed to the group, the feathered crest of his helmet bobbing low. As he bent, his gaze swept over the group and he made a quick count of their numbers. His gaze stopped briefly upon Wu Ying, still clad in peasant robes, before skipping away.

As the lieutenant straightened, he beckoned one of his guards close and gave quick orders to the man even as the group rode into the city without concern. Wu Ying absently noted how the guard trotted off, overtaking the slow-moving cultivators as he headed north.

Like most cities, the main roads leading from the compass-set gates were large and well-paved, the center of the town hosting the magistrate's residence and the bureaucratic heart of the city. The well-paved, wide roads ensured that traffic was easily managed, with hawkers and roadside stalls carefully managed by the guards. As a main city, Hinma was governed by the local magistrate rather than a nobleman, and it was this personage that Elder Yang would visit later. After all, it would be impolite for someone of her standing to reside in the city without paying proper respects.

"Wu Ying," Fa Yuan called.

"Yes?" Wu Ying rode up and joined his martial sister at the head of their convoy. He left Tou He eyeing the various street meats on display, already fumbling at his belt. If he'd had time, Wu Ying would have stopped him.

"You will be accompanying me to the magistrate."

Wu Ying nodded.

"Change your clothing."

"I know!" Wu Ying complained. "I'm no child. I know how to dress appropriately."

Fa Yuan smiled tightly, deciding obviously to not publicly disagree. "Hopefully we will be able to hear some good news from him. I had previously written to him, informing him of our arrival for the auction."

"Hopefully," Wu Ying said.

The objective of their visit to Hinma was the cultivator auction. The Magistrate was hosting the event in the hope of generating additional funds for the city and had sent out invitations to all the nearby sects, as well as publicizing the event in nearby counties.

While such auctions were uncommon, they were a good way of acquiring sought-after items for and from wandering cultivators. It was their regular form of trading, and since wandering cultivators were the largest proportion of the cultivator population, the sects gleefully took part as well. After all, it was also a good way for them to discard items that had not received sufficient interest among other sect groups.

"Remember, all of you, do not antagonize any others. You are representing the Sect," Fa Yuan said, raising her voice slightly. She only needed to do so a little, the enhanced senses of the cultivators cutting through the hubbub of the busy street.

As the group murmured their assent to her warning, Wu Ying could not help but crane his neck from side to side as he continued to take in the familiar city. The trundle of oxen, the creak of wagons, and the smells of rotting meat, animal feces, and cooking food mixed in the air. But he also noted small indicators of prosperity, here and there.

Talismans for protection and cleansing, to reduce daytime heat, or to reinforce doorways hung over merchant entrances. The populace was well-fed, their skins healthy and glowing, with only the usual layer of grime among peasants. In the distance, he heard the creak of oars and the snap of sails, all mingling with the closer sounds of the thud of hammers and the crunch of wood being sawed as new buildings, new furniture were constructed.

Hinma had obviously gone through a small growth spurt. It was most likely from the addition of refugees from the east, where the war continued. Small markers of the ongoing war—like the imbalance in the genders, the preponderance of older, less healthy men, and the occasional injured beggar, bereft of limb or sense—could be spotted all around.

Just as interesting were the numerous cultivators. In such a big city, late stage Body Cleansing cultivators and early stage Energy Storage cultivators were expected sights, but the number that Wu Ying spotted was uncommon. If not for the upcoming auction, Wu Ying would have been concerned about the meaning of such density. As he breathed, Wu Ying caught the sharp and dense scent of Core Refinement cultivators deeper in the city.

In short order, the group arrived at their destination. The large inn was walled off on its own plot of land, high walls hiding the inner workings of the inn from prying eyes. Only a single signboard on the outside of the grey walls gave indication to what lay within, though Fa Yuan rode in without hesitation. Waiting servants scrambled to take hold of reins, offering greetings as they did so. All but a single servant, who scrambled inside to inform the proprietor of their esteemed guests' arrival.

Wu Ying and company left the horses to the servants and entered the second inner gate. The entrance hall had a series of jade bowls filled with scented floral water. The cultivators quickly washed their hands and faces with the waiting amenities, drying themselves with the proffered silk face cloths and exhilarating in the cool, clean feeling their faces now exuded.

As Wu Ying half listened to Fa Yuan speak to the proprietor, finalizing the details of their stay, he eyed the receiving room. Multiple servants had scurried in, retrieving the washing bowls and taking them away to be replaced for the next guests. Small, carefully tended plants lay within the receiving room, while watercolor paintings, depicting nearby mist-covered hills, were arranged on the walls. Sparse furnishings allowed those who desired to sit a place to rest, all carefully arranged to ensure the harmonious flow of chi within.

Practiced now, Wu Ying noted the names on the paintings, the gilt edging on the vases and pots, and the hardwood furnishings laid about. And came to a conclusion. Never in his previous life would he have been able to afford even a single night's stay in this inn.

Wu Ying's musings came to an end when a servant scurried over, carrying his bags and the key to his residence. As he was led to his room, Wu Ying inquired about a bath. After all, he would have to clean himself for the upcoming meeting.

***

It was late afternoon when the pair were finally introduced to the magistrate. They were received in his primary waiting room, offered snacks and tea as they entered before the usual preamble of small talk began. For his part, Wu Ying was dressed in his sect robes but was overall silent in the discussion. Much like the magistrate's daughter who accompanied him, they were but a pair of pretty faces in this room.

Wu Ying sipped on the tea, letting the slightly bitter, complex drink settle on the back of his tongue before swallowing. Having spent time with Tou He and been forced to consume ungodly amounts of the brews as Tou He practiced his secondary profession, Wu Ying had gained some subtle appreciation of the types of teas available.

This one, he guessed to be a local brew, picked from the hillside plantations a short ride away. It was slightly harsher than his personal preference, allowed to age longer in the sun than he would have preferred. Still, he was certain it was a high-quality picking, taken from the youngest leaves and carefully sun-dried. But Tou He would really understand the subtleties, while Wu Ying just enjoyed the warmth.

His surface level appreciation extended to the room itself, with its paintings, the mother-of-pearl furnishings, and the few stone carvings. He spotted stonework that represented the eight horses and a depiction of a giant, surfacing turtle carved from jade in the corner. Traditional work, though well done.

"I am grateful that the Verdant Green Waters Sect was so willing to grace my small auction with their presence. Especially sending the graceful Fairy Yang," Magistrate Song said, punctuating his words with a seated bow. It was not a deep one, as befitted a magistrate speaking to an Elder. "If the Elder is willing, I shall be honored if she came to the dinner I am hosting for her and the other cultivators on the night of the auction."

"Of course." Fa Yuan smiled as she spoke.

Wu Ying saw the stern older man melt and return the Fairy's smile. Wu Ying was almost certain he heard the increase in the man's heartbeat as his martial sister graced him with her attention.

"Though, I was hoping," Fa Yuan said, "I could perhaps see the initial list of items?"

The magistrate hesitated before he leaned over and lowered his voice. "You know, I'm not supposed to show all of them..." Wu Ying watched as Fa Yuan let her face collapse in disappointment. And then brighten as the magistrate continued. "But for such a good friend..." He reached into his robe's voluminous sleeves and produced a scroll. "Some rules can be bent."

Even as Fa Yuan thanked him, murmuring words of agreement, Wu Ying noted how the magistrate's daughter's eyes rolled at her father's unabashed flirtation. Catching Wu Ying paying attention to her, she stared back challengingly. Wu Ying could only offer her a crooked smile before he lowered his gaze, not wanting to create any additional problems. After all, he still wasn't entirely certain why the daughter was in this meeting.

"Wu Ying," Fa Yuan said, drawing his attention as she handed him the scroll.

Wu Ying unrolled and perused the list. He took his time, reading each line with care. Partly because he did not want the magistrate to ascertain their specific interest and partly because he might find something of interest to himself.

"And does the Elder of the Verdant Green Waters Sect have anything to add to my small event?" the magistrate asked tentatively.

"Only a small item." Fa Yuan gestured over the table, and after her hand had passed, a single reflective mirror, edged with silver and gold, appeared. "The Mirror of Water and Earth Sight is a Saint-level item that we will entrust to your auction from the Sect. Payment can be sent directly to the Sect."

"Oh!" Magistrate Song's eyes widened as he took hold of the mirror with his hands, turning it over and over again. With the agreement of Fa Yuan, he pushed his chi into the mirror, willing it to show him his own city. A view of the city appeared as if from a bird high above, showing the moving throng below, the swaying lights of torches and spirit lamps and clay roofs. "This mirror is amazing. What is the range?"

"It varies, depending on the amount of chi entrusted to the mirror," Fa Yuan said. "But farther than two hundred li and the image becomes much degraded."

"Two hundred li…." The magistrate breathed out in awe. "This is a stupendous item. Thank you, Elder Yang. Thank your Patriarch as well."

"A small matter. My companions also have some minor demon and spirit cores, spirit beast meat and organs, and some spiritual herbs to add to the auction," Fa Yuan said.

Wu Ying hurriedly pulled the prepared scroll from his spirit ring and offered it with both hands to the magistrate.

Instead of receiving the document directly, the magistrate waved to his daughter. She perused the document quickly before speaking hesitantly. "Much of this… it does not fit our current standards."

"Standards?" Wu Ying said.

"Yes," the daughter said. "For the main auction. We'll buy some of these directly. And have others displayed in a merchant hall during the day for sale directly." She looked at her father.

"If you think that is correct, Ling Ling[18]," Magistrate Song said. He shot a glance at Fa Yuan, who waved, dismissing the scroll as if it was of no matter to her. Relaxing, the magistrate continued. "I'm sure she'll manage the matter and ensure you get the best rate available. I was hoping, perhaps, that Elder Yang might be willing to spend a little time with my little Ling? She is a water-aspected cultivator, much like you."

---

[18] Naming conventions – it's common for parents to use either the personal name twice for children or a nickname rather than the actual name. Again, there's a vastly more complex naming culture in traditional Chinese culture pre-Western colonization that we're not even going to touch.

Fa Yuan frowned, turning to stare at the magistrate's daughter. After a moment, she nodded as she finished sensing the woman. "She is strong enough. I could give her a few pointers."

The magistrate grinned, murmuring words of thanks while his daughter rolled her eyes again and turned to Wu Ying. She pointed at the first of the lines in the document.

Sighing, Wu Ying was grateful he did not have to teach the girl. It was obvious she cared little about progressing her cultivation. But he would pay attention to what she said about their goods. After all, a good portion of the list were the spiritual herbs he had gathered. And every coin they earned would likely be needed for the upcoming auction.

For he'd spotted a Ben Beast Core among the list.

***

"What a pity," Fa Yuan said when the pair left the magistrate's residence, walking back to the inn much later in the day.

"Pity?" Wu Ying said.

"That the child has no interest in cultivation," Fa Yuan said. "Her father has long wanted her to join a sect. She has both talent and ability, but no inclination."

"You know of her?" Wu Ying said.

"I've heard. And noticed her reaction," Fa Yuan said, half-smiling. "She was quite interested in you though."

"Rubbish," Wu Ying retorted. "We were just speaking of the list."

"Mmmhmmm." Fa Yuan looked him over. "You should dress more in the robes. It suits you."

Wu Ying shrugged before he gestured at the split in the road. "If the Elder has nothing more for me, I was thinking of visiting a friend."

Fa Yuan nodded her assent, and Wu Ying moved off with quick steps, disappearing among the crowds with ease. He sighed as he ran his finger along the luxuriant silk of his robes, forced to admit privately that the robes were nice. And certainly were more comfortable than his hemp workmen clothing.

Even if it was more convenient.

Hurrying down the streets, Wu Ying found his way to the Tong family residence. He only had to ask two strangers the direction and only got lost once on the way. Overall, Wu Ying was rather proud of his ability to navigate the unfamiliar city.

It did not take long before Wu Ying found himself seated in the waiting room, awaiting the return of the "Young Master." As he sipped on the tea that had been offered to him, Wu Ying wondered what kind of changes he might find. Three years was not a long time, and yet, at this stage of their cultivation, it was. Would Zhong Shei have progressed far? Was he, like Wu Ying, an Energy Storage cultivator?

If not, would he be jealous?

As his tea cooled and a new pot was brought over, Wu Ying thought over his experiences in this city. Of his quest to find the wine, then the long journey back. The cultivators he had met and what he had learned in the ensuing years. And in that time, the understanding that he had perhaps made more mistakes than he had realized.

It was strange, what life brought. How time changed one's view of the past, where the certainty of youthful righteousness gave way to the realization of weary experience.

His musings were interrupted by a loud voice, full of energy, that called his name as its owner entered. Zhong Shei, clad in the armor of the local city guard, strode in, looking older and grinning wider. Wu Ying stood—only to find the man enveloping him in a hug within seconds. Pushing away, Wu Ying grinned back.

"You look good." Wu Ying narrowed his eyes, feeling the man's aura, drawing a discreet breath as he tested the other. "And you have an aspect!"

"Metal," Zhong Shei said, grinning and slapping his chest. "And I've reached the second stage of Energy Storage Cultivation."

"Congratulations!" Wu Ying said, happy for the man. That single achievement would explain the armor, the signature of a lieutenant's rank. "On your cultivation and your promotion."

"Yes! I don't even have to turn up for regular duty anymore. Now, I only need to cultivate!" At Wu Ying's raised eyebrow, the man shrugged. "They called me back from the frontlines when I broke through. Said I should stay behind and cultivate to gain strength."

Wu Ying nodded, remembering that his friend had been initially part of the war. "Good. The frontlines are dangerous."

"Very true," Zhong Shei said, his face growing unusually serious. He shook his head after a moment, dispersing the darkness and memories. "But my family will ensure I do not return. After all, we still need guards here too."

"For auctions," Wu Ying teased.

"To deal with noisy cultivators," Zhong Shei replied, pushing Wu Ying's shoulder.

Laughing, Wu Ying let himself be pushed back until he took a seat in his original chair. He poured his friend a cup of tea, offering it to the man who sat beside him, a small side table between each other. "Come, let's drink. To reunions."

Zhong Shei stared at the teacup dubiously, then shrugged and drank the warm tea. "This is a good start. But reunions should be drunk with wine, not tea. Tea is for the old men!" Jumping back to his feet, Zhong Shei hauled Wu Ying up. "I know just the place!"

"Not your grandfather's collection!" Wu Ying said quickly.

"Obviously!" Zhong Shei touched his bum, muttering, "I have no desire to be punished again."

Chapter 17

The restaurant Zhong Shei brought Wu Ying to was luxurious to the extreme. The building overlooked the confluence of the two rivers that hemmed in the city. From the third-floor private room they were offered, they could watch the busy waterway below where even in the deepening evening, ships docked under lamplight and cargo was off-loaded.

Waitresses clad in diaphanous gowns waited upon them, bringing in luxurious dishes, plying them with strong wine and pleasant company. It was the kind of indulgent, almost sinful practice that Wu Ying had long considered a mainstay of nobles, and he found the experience both novel and intriguing. Though a small part of him could not help but keep track of how much all this must cost.

As they supped on the delectable dishes, Wu Ying and Zhong Shei spoke of their experiences in the preceding years. Zhong Shei exclaimed, cried out in disbelief, and teased Wu Ying as he detailed both his progress and cultivation, his many adventures since they'd last met, and his regrettable love life.

In turn, Zhong Shei spoke of his own experiences ever since he had left Wu Ying in the Sect years ago. Emboldened and inspired by the cultivators, he had thrown himself into practice. While he did not have the advantages the Sect had, both in knowledge as well as the resources that were readily available, he had done well until he neared the end of the Body Cleansing Levels. There, he finally met his own blockage, unable to clear his last meridian.

It was the onset of the war and the continued encroaching of territory by the State of Wei that had given him the necessary push. Joining the army with his greater than normal cultivation level and his personal connections allowed Zhong Shei to start out as an officer. Then he managed to make a name for himself in a series of tense battles, even succeeding in killing a number of enemy cultivators. Because of these acts, he had managed to acquire additional resources from the army, leading to his eventual breakthrough.

After that, of course, he'd been returned to the backlines to act as a town guard. In this way, he'd have a chance to grow his new cultivation stage, potentially becoming a powerful local guard captain or aid for the bureaucracy that ran the kingdom. The king valued those cultivators who chose to grow within the ranks of his service, or so it was rumored.

"And is that what you want?" Wu Ying asked as his friend finally came to the end of his story.

"It works." The guardsman shrugged. "I have no expectation of becoming like your Master. The life here suits me." He reached over to the young lady seated beside him, pulling her close and giving her a quick squeeze. She burst into a giggle, playing the part set for her. But it seemed to Wu Ying that there was some degree of actual enjoyment and familiarity too. "I have good company. More money than I can spend. And I can keep an eye on my family."

Wu Ying nodded at his friend's words. In truth, he could see that. As an Energy Storage cultivator, Zhong Shei was one of the strongest non-Sect cultivators. That would ensure he had numerous opportunities, both in the government and army if he so chose. If nothing else, if he managed to continue to progress his cultivation over the next few years, he could become the captain of the guard. And at worst, he would be a well-paid lieutenant with few responsibilities.

"To a good life then," Wu Ying said, raising his glass and grinning.

"To a good life," Zhong Shei cried out in return. They toasted and the hostesses quickly refilled their glasses once they'd finished quaffing the wine.

Wu Ying had to admit, he enjoyed the feminine attention. Yet he had more than once gently disengaged from the lady draping herself over him like her companion had on Zhong Shei. While he enjoyed the attention, it was only to a certain extent. A part of him could not help but compare the paid-for companionship with what he'd had with Li Yao. Compare and found it wanting.

If pleasant.

"What about you?" Zhong Shei asked. He barely slurred. Even if they were getting good liquor, and they'd consumed a sizeable portion, they were both strong cultivators. They might be tipsy, but they were not drunk. Yet. "Will you continue pursuing immortality?"

The question made the two women look at Wu Ying with further interest. He could see the envy in their looks, as well as the stark desire. The opportunity given to him was one few would have. And in that sense… "Yes. However far on the road I can walk, I will."

"A tough journey," Zhong Shei said. "And a studious one."

Wu Ying let out a chuckle, remembering how little Zhong Shei had enjoyed practice or studying. Cultivation, while not necessarily aided by scholarly studies, was by itself a boring practice. And in the manuals and documentation of the Sect libraries, one might find hints of a better method or a reason for one's current blockages. Never mind the fact that the simple act of studying could engender enlightenment.

Since cultivation was the slow process of achieving immortality by achieving and embodying a portion of reality—of the Dao—then enlightenment was the fastest way to achieving immortality. Any act that gave one greater understanding of the world might spark true inspiration. Though, Wu Ying had to admit, he'd found more of his enlightenment outside of the library than within the pages of books. But that, perhaps, was a hint of his own path.

"All journeys are tough if you are the one walking them," Wu Ying said. "What we perceive to be hard can only be shaped by the paths we walked before."

Zhong Shei tilted his head, contemplating Wu Ying's drunken wisdom. He then laughed as he spoke. "No. I'm pretty sure I have the easier path."

Zhong Shei leaned over to kiss the young lady, who deflected him with her fan and a tilted head. He laughed again as he readily accepted the tapped rebuke of the fan before he reached for his glass.

A loud meaty sound rose from below, a scream that was cut off, and muffled sobbing. The walls and floors in the restaurant were well-built, but it was impossible to hide the hubbub of other drinkers from the sensitive ears of the cultivators. They'd learned to tune it all out, to get on with life. So the raised voices, the boisterous shouts from nearby diners had been ignored.

But certain sounds drew attention immediately.

Zhong Shei let his hostess go, straightening. He frowned as he stood, a hand reaching for his sword that he'd laid aside. Wu Ying scrambled to his feet a moment later, following his friend. As he slipped his sword into his belt, Wu Ying smelled the ground copper scent of circulating chi as Zhong Shei churned his internal energy to cleanse himself of the drink. Wu Ying followed his example, driving away even the most minute trace of alcohol.

They were halfway down the stairs when they were met by one of the hosts. "Lieutenant Tong, we hate to bother you, but—"

"Which room?" Zhong Shei said.

"The Northern Crane." The host bobbed his head low, pushing his thin body against the wall and out of the way. His pale blue and white robes were covered in a light sheen of sweat, but his eyes glowed with confidence as

Zhong Shei tromped down the remainder of the stairs and turned down the wooden hallway.

Wu Ying followed his friend, a few steps behind. While the entire incident was not his problem, he followed along as much out of curiosity as desire to back up Zhong Shei. Not that Wu Ying expected any issues. After all, as a guard lieutenant, Zhong Shei should be used to dealing with noisy diners.

In short order, they came to the sliding doors that closed off the private room. A single majestic crane was skillfully painted on the door, in the midst of plucking a fish from the pond it rested in. Even in the brief glimpse Wu Ying managed to catch before Zhong Shei pushed the door aside, he noted the level of craftsmanship. But all musings of craft and culture were thrown aside when Wu Ying saw the scene within the private room.

Crouched near the door, her gown slightly torn in the shoulder region, her hand clutching a bruised and bloody face, lay a hostess. Standing above the woman, dressed in silken robes of grey and dark blue stood a towering man, cradling a wine cup in one hand. A cup that he used as a prop as he scolded the woman.

"Dare to say no! Know your place. You are but a lowly entertainer! Do you know who I…" the man trailed off as Zhong Shei strode into the room. The whiskers on his long, well-oiled mustache quivered as he stared at the guard, even as Wu Ying noted the food stain on the sleeve of his left robe. "Who are you? How dare you come in here?"

"City guard Lieutenant Tong," Zhong Shei said, announcing himself. "I heard the commotion and came to ascertain the problem. And you are?"

Behind the standing cultivator, Wu Ying noted three other cultivators, each of them clad in the same grey and dark blue robes and accompanied by a hostess as well. They sat around the round wooden table, regarding Wu Ying and Zhong Shei while plates of food and pots of wine sat on the table, half-consumed. Beside each of them, sheathed swords and a single spear rested, all within easy reach.

Memory tugged at Wu Ying as he tried to recall which sect these robes belonged to. He'd received a number of lectures on the matter, but with dozens of sects in just their kingdom, remembering them all was a challenge. Especially since Wu Ying had had little interaction with them as yet. In either case, Wu Ying could tell from the sense of their auras and the smell of their chi that they were not simple Body Cleansing cultivators but Energy Storage cultivators.

"None of your business. Leave. This is nothing to concern a simple village guard," the cultivator said. He glared at the woman, reaching for her hand to haul her to her feet as she tried to back away.

Even now, the hostess's pupils were too large and unfocused, the side of her face purpling. The strike from the cultivator had done serious damage. A low whimper erupted from the injured hostess as the bearded cultivator reached for her.

Before the man completed the motion, Zhong Shei was there, gripping his arm. He held it still as he said, "I will decide what is my business in my city. And striking women is definitely my business."

"Idiot." The bearded cultivator tried to yank his arm and throw Zhong Shei at the same time. He failed, as he'd underestimated Zhong Shei's strength. Instead, he found himself futilely struggling for a few seconds. "I am Ji Cheng, inner sect disciple of the Northern Lake Pearl!"

Ji Cheng next tried to pull his arm away, and Zhong Shei shoved him backward a little. Stumbling back, Ji Cheng tripped against a chair. A hand reached out to steady himself against the table, inadvertently ending up in a plate of food and staining his robes further.

"Look what you did! You will pay for my robes, you peasant," Ji Cheng snarled, his face twisting.

Zhong Shei shifted his stance, setting himself, while the other cultivators stood, pushing their companions aside—mostly gently. The Northern Lake Pearl sect members all reached for their weapons. Behind, Wu Ying smelled the approach of the host, the acrid stink of his fear filling Wu Ying's nose.

Seeing the entire confrontation devolve, Wu Ying sighed and stepped forward while raising his voice. "Northern Lake Pearl! I thought I knew where those robes were from." Attention drawn to him, Wu Ying smoothly stepped to the side to ensure he allowed Zhong Shei space to clear his sword while also putting himself in front of the girl. "A pleasure to meet you all. Long Wu Ying, of the—"

"Verdant Green Waters Sect!" One of the previously silent cultivators gasped. "Senior!" He sketched a quick bow, followed by the other cultivators.

Wu Ying's eyes crinkled slightly as he noted how the others bowed and echoed greetings. All but Ji Cheng, who still glared at Zhong Shei and, now, Wu Ying. Wu Ying might be younger than these inner sect cultivators in age, but by the politics of sect seniority and prestige, he was their senior as a fellow inner sect member.

"So what if he's a Verdant Green Waters cultivator?" Ji Cheng sniffed. "Our problem has nothing to do with him. It is with this useless guard and woman."

"I was willing to let you go, but I think it's time for you to spend a night in the jail," Zhong Shei replied. He placed a hand on his sword as he glared at Ji Cheng.

"Har! As if you could." Ji Cheng reached back, grabbing his waiting sword sheath with one hand before reaching for the hilt with the other.

Future events flashed through Wu Ying's mind in a blur. Even if Zhong Shei won this fight, the cultivator would be injured and angry. So would the sect. And if Zhong Shei didn't win immediately, three other members would join in. Rather than let things devolve further, Wu Ying decided to act.

Two quick steps allowed him to cross the space separating him and Ji Cheng. As the opposing cultivator shifted, ready to block a grab at his sword or arm, Wu Ying struck. A simple palm strike, placed just below the man's sternum. Rather than put all the energy into the attack to injure, Wu Ying kept pushing inward and upward. This launched his opponent away, his feet clipping the table and striking the plates as he flipped over backward. Ji Cheng body flew, sending drinks and food scattering before he smashed into the opposite wall. The impact shook the wall, sending dust and packed earth to the floor.

"How dare you not greet your Senior!" Wu Ying snapped, pulling himself up to his full height. "What kind of manners are they teaching you at your worthless sect?"

Inwardly, Wu Ying could only cringe at the words he leveled. But it was the best way he could think of to focus attention on himself. The other three cultivators bristled in anger at Wu Ying's insults, but held off on taking action as Ji Cheng clambered to his feet.

"How dare you lay hands on me!" Ji Cheng said. "I'll have your head for this."

"Then meet me in a sparring ring," Wu Ying said. "If you dare. Unless you are too afraid to fight a real cultivator, being only willing to strike defenseless mortals." He clamped his mouth shut against the next insult that floated into his mind, deciding against plying additional insults on their sect. He wanted to divert attention and take the fight out from the dining room, not make it a giant brawl.

191

"Your challenge is accepted!" Ji Cheng said. "I will see you at the dueling ring."

"Now?" Wu Ying said, cocking a single eyebrow. "Or do you need to clean up?" He let his gaze roam over the man's body, his robes and body stained with foodstuff, in a dismissive sneer. "Unless you are happy for others to watch you be doubly humiliated."

Ji Cheng grew rigid with fury, and one of the other cultivators hurried to speak for him. "In an hour! We will leave and see you at the central fighting ring in an hour."

Wu Ying nodded, and Ji Cheng, his arm grabbed by one of his friends, was dragged out. The remaining cultivators scooped up their weapons, stalking by Wu Ying. The guardsman, on the other hand, stood to the side, grinning.

"Make sure to pay the proprietor!" Zhong Shei called, making the last cultivator freeze.

Rather than argue, he reached into his purse and tossed a tael at the host. Done, he stomped out with the rest of his group, leaving Wu Ying and Zhong Shei amid a group of thankful restaurant employees. A few heads had popped out to watch the proceedings, but seeing it was a matter between cultivators, had retreated. Mortals should not get involved in such matters.

"Well, now you've done it," Zhong Shei said, shaking his head. "I'm surprised you managed to pull that off. Very haughty."

Wu Ying grinned weakly, placing a hand surreptitiously on a chair to hold himself up. "I was just copying some nobles I knew."

"Yin Xue?"

Wu Ying offered a nod.

Zhong Shei burst out laughing, while the restaurant employees offered weak smiles. "Let us hope you don't lose too badly after all that grandstanding."

Chapter 18

Once the initial shock was over, the host and hostesses were quick to lay on their thanks, explaining that such incidents were normally handled in-house. But with cultivators, their usual methods of placating and ejecting angry guests had not worked. After a quick assessment, they took the injured hostess away, sending her home in a palanquin while Zhong Shei and Wu Ying finished paying their bill. They both refused the offer to leave their bill on the house, knowing the hostesses who had joined them would lose out in that case.

Outside the restaurant, the pair found the road well-lit as the lanterns from other restaurants kept the sidewalk easily navigable. They strolled over to the main thoroughfare that led to the central fighting rings located just north of the magistrate's house in the center of the city. Here, exhibition matches and the occasional public duel were handled.

In a society where everyone trained in martial arts, a public dueling ring was mandatory. Even Wu Ying's village had a designated field where intractable matters of honor or prestige were dealt with. Of course, the field in his village was left unused by the villagers, the Elders and family heads easily heading over such matters in the small village.

As they walked, Zhong Shei kept shooting Wu Ying a look before looking away. This continued for blocks before Wu Ying finally said exasperatedly, "Just speak."

"I could've taken him," Zhong Shei said.

"Of course you could," Wu Ying said. Even the initial struggle had told Wu Ying that much. While Zhong Shei might not have as many energy storage meridians open, he had progressed his body cultivation further. His strength was higher, and having spent time in the army, it was likely that Zhong Shei was a better fighter too. "But if you had fought, the others would have gotten involved. And then that nice restaurant would have been wrecked."

Zhong Shei huffed. "Damn cultivators. Not you, of course."

Wu Ying grinned.

"But all of these others. Idiot Magistrate, choosing to hold an auction. We are too small to deal with this kind of trouble," Zhong Shei said.

"Too small?"

"We don't have enough high-level cultivators. There are only three Energy Storage guards in the city, not including the captain. And none of us are core cultivators. So far though, at least the core cultivators have been polite."

Wu Ying's jaw dropped a little as he realized the implications. "Then the auction materials being stored—"

"Are safe," Zhong Shei reassured Wu Ying. "The auction house itself is being guarded by the Lim family auctioneers. It's the rest of the city that is the problem." The guardsman shook his head. "The auction can't start fast enough, if you ask us."

Wu Ying could see how Zhong Shei and the rest of the guards would have to tread a very fine line. They couldn't let the cultivators, from sects or wandering, tread all over their dignity. Guardsmen were always outnumbered by the populace. Only the illusion of authority and the threat of punishment kept the civilian population in check. Cultivators were but a special subset of the population. One whose individual strength made them dangerous to cross, but when placed against the might of the kingdom bureaucracy, they were but ants.

"But I could have handled that better," Zhong Shei said after a while, shaking his head. "I could have tried to calm matters. But when I saw Ah Mei on the ground, I lost my temper. To strike her..."

"I understand. Losing one's temper like that, striking those below, there is no honor in that." Wu Ying shook his head. It seemed Zhong Shei was much more familiar with the ladies here than he had believed initially. "Arrogance takes us all at times. It is too easy, as a cultivator, to forget that those beneath us are as important to the Heavens as we are. We walk the same roads, bask in the same sunlight, and drink from the same water."

Zhong Shei cast a sideways glance at his friend. The guard's lips curled up a little, but he forbore speaking on the topic. "Do you think you can beat him?"

"If you can, obviously so can I," Wu Ying said the words confidently, almost teasing his friend.

Inwardly, Wu Ying had to admit he was not so certain. It was one thing to fight another unarmed but place a sword in the same hands and they could become a devil. Whatever the case, angry as either party might be, this was a friendly spar. There would be no deaths here, not on purpose. Neither party would dare overstep the bounds of honor, not with their sects overlooking the final results. And if he lost, well... Wu Ying had lost before. He would again.

When they reached the small town square that hosted the city's fighting ring, Wu Ying found it empty and dark but for the reflected lights from nearby restaurants. The pair moved around the square, lighting the nearby lamps and brightening the square further. As they did, curious onlookers arrived, drawn by the light at first then by rumors of the upcoming duel. A battle between two cultivators in the main ring was bound to be good entertainment.

As Wu Ying stretched and settled his mind, Zhong Shei moved around the square, finding a pair of wandering guards and tasking them with dealing with the growing crowd. Once he was done, he returned to Wu Ying's side to glower at the people about him.

Five minutes before the bell tolled the start of the hour[19], the other cultivators arrived. Ji Cheng was dressed in a new pair of robes, slightly tighter to allow for better movement during the duel. It was then that Wu Ying cursed underneath his breath.

Zhong Shei frowned. "Problem?" He eyed the group, wondering what it was that had made his friend swear.

"I don't want to dirty my robes. Or tear them," Wu Ying replied. After all, he only had so many undamaged robes.

Zhong Shei chuckled, his humor drawing glares from the newly arrived cultivators. Without taking time to ready himself, Ji Cheng jumped onto the stage, clearing the five feet difference in height with one easy bound.

Wu Ying looked at the hexagon-shaped stone stage where Ji Cheng stood, then jumped up himself. Overlapping light circles from the numerous spirit stone lanterns lit the stage well, leaving only the audience in shadows. The stage itself had been swept recently, leaving it bare and clean. Wu Ying drew his sword once he was on the stage, saluting his opponent. Ji Cheng echoed the motion.

From below, Zhong Shei called, "This is a friendly match. No deaths! Anyone who kills their opponent will have to face the magistrate for breaking his peace."

Ji Cheng and Wu Ying glanced at Zhong Shei before dismissing him, refocusing on one another. Almost in unison, the pair began to circle one another, edging into distance. Wu Ying eyed the dao his opponent used,

---

[19] Ancient China used bells to tell time on the hour as well. Incense sticks – and incense clocks – were a common method of telling time as well, with incense sticks being carefully marked to indicate amount of time. The amount of time an incense stick burnt varied, depending on size and use. The day was broken up in two hour portions, and also in 'ke' which these days is the equivalent of 15 minutes. It gets a lot more complicated (as always), so we're just sticking to minutes and hours.

noting its quality and the pretty golden edging on the guard. Compared to Wu Ying's utilitarian straight sword, it was certainly nicer looking.

As if Wu Ying's brief glance down was a signal, Ji Cheng threw himself forward in a blazing fast series of strikes. Wu Ying blocked them, weaving Dragon paints the Sunset as his defense and letting each blow shed its energy around him. As they fought, Wu Ying tried to grasp his opponent's skill and style.

The dao lent itself to fast cuts, powerful attacks that could crush or shatter an opponent. It spun and chopped, meant to overwhelm the opponent. Ji Cheng's style focused on drawing upon this strength of the weapon to increase the speed and strength of his blows. Rather than face each attack head-on, Wu Ying had to shed the attacks, parry them at an angle and divert the momentum.

Each block sent Wu Ying's sword jittering back, each resounding meeting of blades ringing through the square. Wu Ying was forced to retreat and circle, dodge and block constantly. The momentum of the fight was all his opponent's.

Yet the flaws in Ji Cheng's style, in his practice soon appeared.

Wu Ying moved, using Cloud Steps to shift his position, staying at maximum range and eking out the couple of inches advantage his thrusting weapon had over his opponent. More importantly, he used Cloud Steps to work angles of attack. A dao, and a dao in the style used by Ji Cheng, required significant movement to defend the center line. However, Ji Cheng didn't move his feet enough, didn't pay attention to the subtle angles a jian could exploit.

A quick wrist cut here. A short extension of the arm there. In short order, Wu Ying had injured the man once, then again. But he still held back, each cut only a trivial injury, surface wounds that looked bloody but did nothing to stop his opponent's movements. He held back because the next stage of the fight was about to erupt.

Realizing he was out-classed in pure technique, Ji Cheng jumped back, twisting in mid-air and releasing a blast of sword chi. Wu Ying returned the attack in kind, energy projection meeting energy projection. His attack was clear, without color, as unaspected chi looked like nothing more than a heat-haze. His opponent's attack was wider and purple-colored. Metal chi struck Wu Ying's own and overwhelmed it—all but the center, where Wu Ying's focused attack broke through.

Dispersed chi and sword intent rippled around Wu Ying, throwing his hair from his head, kicking up dirt and clouding the air. The defensive formation in the arena flickered to life, nullifying the attack before it could pass out of the stage. In so doing, it muted the roar of approval of the audience for a second.

"Now we're starting." Wu Ying's body vibrated with anticipation. For the first time, he was taking part in a real duel at the Energy Storage stage.

In rapid sequence, the pair unleashed their sword intent at one another, sending strikes flying across the space. It wasn't just flashy attacks but extensions of simple cuts or thrusts that made such duels different from those at the Body Cultivation stage. A lunge that might be dodged by the sway of the body became dangerous when the opponent increased the width of their sword by an inch through chi projection. A cut was impossible to just lean aside from if said cut became a sword intent projection. A feint became a true attack when sword chi pulsed through the weapon.

Dodges became wider, sword positioning became more important as the pair fought. Wu Ying threw himself into the third form, switching styles as he fought and utilized the stored energy in his meridians. Flashes of sword chi erupted from blades, smashing into the barrier and tearing at the stone

199

arena floor. Dust choked the air and was dispersed with each motion. Eventually, blood bloomed as strikes landed.

A cut across a cheek. A thrust plunging half an inch deep into a shoulder. A swipe tearing at trailing robes and leaving traces of blood behind. Injuries piled up as Wu Ying's greater skill and control began to tell.

He could not help but grin, confidence increasing with each exchange of blades. His opponent had a larger chi store, had more of his meridians open. At the edges of Ji Cheng's attacks, his control of the released energy was firmer, more controlled. But his very movements were overly large, his attacks sweeping through unneeded space. It made his greater pool of chi deplete faster, the density of his chi less.

It was, in the end, a one-sided battle. Wu Ying cut, sliced at exposed arms and legs, wending his way in deeper and deeper to Ji Cheng's defense with each passing moment. And if he dragged out the fight a little, eked out some experience, it was hard to tell.

A single rap, the dao pushed aside, then a half-step close. A hand shifted, placing itself in the path of the returning arm. And suddenly, Wu Ying's blade was at Ji Cheng's neck, just under his chin. His opponent froze, the hand holding his dao dropping. Then it twitched, starting an attack.

"No, no, no." Wu Ying raised the blade, forcing his opponent to rise on his toes.

Ji Cheng's hand stilled as the threat was made more apparent. Ji Cheng muttered something, too low to be heard under the rumbling roars of approval of the audience.

"I'm sorry. I didn't hear you," Wu Ying said.

"I said, I lose. You win!" Ji Cheng raised his voice, almost shouting his loss now. His eyes grew red, and he blinked fast.

"Thank you." Wu Ying stepped back once, then again, to clear the distance. Wu Ying sheathed his sword as he continued speaking. "Good fight."

Ji Cheng blinked furiously, then turned away as he slammed his own blade back into its sheath. He made it most of the way to the arena edge, its defensive formation already flickering, before he stopped. His next words were bitter and curt. "Thank you for the guidance, Senior."

Ji Cheng descended the stage and joined his friends. The group shot Wu Ying one last angry look before they left through the crowd. Wu Ying exhaled threadily, taking his hand off his sheathed sword. It seemed that the matter was settled. And without major bloodshed too. As he turned his attention to the crowd, he could not help but blink.

The crowd was a mixed lot, from rustic peasants in their subdued hemp clothing to waitresses and hosts in colorful robes, scholars of the government exams grouped close to one another, and a smaller gathering of martial cultivators in the varied colors of their sect robes. Amidst them all, Zhong Shei cajoled those who'd bet with him to pay up.

"Something wrong?" Zhong Shei asked Wu Ying as the cultivator came down, head turning from side to side as he caught the scent of those in the crowd.

"Just a weird smell," Wu Ying said. He could not place it, but that smell had been wrong. Too sharp, too strong, and yet familiar. A difficult thing to explain.

"Har. It's probably you." Eyes gleaming with humor, Zhong Shei rattled his coin purse. "You couldn't have held off winning for a few more minutes? I nearly had another win."

Wu Ying rolled his eyes. "Should a guard be betting?"

"The fight was perfectly legal," Zhong Shei said. "Good job. I was worried when you all projected your chi, but you've improved." His eyebrows creased, as he added beneath his breath, "A lot."

Wu Ying shrugged. What could he say to that? His friend had chosen to relax, to stop pushing as hard. When it came to cultivation and the martial arts, persistence and practice paid off. If you stood still, friends and enemies would pass you by.

Too long in the same spot, and you would be irrelevant. At least, martially.

"Well. Now that I have more coin, we should drink!" Zhong Shei said, shaking off his glum mood and smacking Wu Ying on the shoulder. "And I should introduce you to some people."

"Who?"

Wu Ying's puzzlement disappeared as Zhong Shei dragged him toward a group of smiling young women dressed in thin, almost translucent strips of cloth that hid little of how cold the night air had become. All of them offered Wu Ying and Zhong Shei wide smiles of welcome, eyes fluttering and silken handkerchiefs rising to cover delicate mouths. Wu Ying could not help but groan mentally, even as his protests to his friend were soundly ignored.

This was going to be a long night.

Chapter 19

Light streamed in through the slats of Wu Ying's room, striking the cultivator in the eyes. He groaned, twisting from side to side as he attempted to get away from the light. A searching hand found the thick silk blanket supplied by the inn, but a pair of futile tugs showed Wu Ying that he was lying upon the bed covering. For long moments, Wu Ying debated moving again and weighed it against his exhaustion.

Memories of the previous night—this morning—flitted through Wu Ying's mind. After his win, Zhong Shei and their new friends had been brought to a restaurant. Their first bottle had even been paid for by the restaurant owner, as thanks for a "great show." Behind Wu Ying and Zhong Shei, the other cultivators and audience members had come along, filling the restaurant within seconds.

After the first bottle, another one came as wandering cultivators all made to introduce themselves to Wu Ying. Drinks had flowed without stop, and Zhong Shei's fattened purse quickly depleted. Faces of merchants and wandering cultivators, all who wished to speak with Wu Ying, blurred together. Food arrived next, as the hostesses plied late night snacks and more alcohol on all those present. And then…

Then.

Wu Ying touched his lips, blinked, and turned sideways. He exhaled in relief, grateful to note he was sleeping alone. And in his own bed. Or the inn's. It was the same thing.

Relief was short-lived though, as a loud and insistent knocking rose from his bedroom door. He glared at the noise and stayed silent. Rather than going away, the knocking sped up and grew louder. Wu Ying's head throbbed in time to the pounding and he let out a muffled groan.

"I can hear you in there!" Lei Hui's voice called. "Open the door!"

Wu Ying forced himself to his feet, gently circulating his chi to help with the nausea and pounding headache. He made his way to the door and threw it open to see Lei Hui outside.

The thin apothecarist thrust a lidded teacup at Wu Ying. "Drink."

"What?" Wu Ying muttered as he took the teacup.

"Drink!" Lei Hui snapped.

Wu Ying complied, gagging at the sour and oily taste. It was like a group of fermented fish had taken residence and procreated. Gagging, he took the next bottle thrust at him by Lei Hui and washed down the taste with lightly brewed tea. "What was that?"

"Medicinal tonic for drinking and over-eating. Now, Elder Yang wants to speak with us at lunch," Lei Hui said.

"Lunch?" Wu Ying turned his head to stare at the sun streaming in. It looked much stronger than dawn light, now that he was actually paying attention.

"In half an hour. Best get dressed and washed." He looked at Wu Ying's soiled robes and added, "Even your peasant clothing is better off."

Wu Ying made a face, then thanked Lei Hui for the tonic. Already, he felt it warming his stomach, reducing the nausea and the pounding headache. He shut the door, stumbling only a little as he made his way to the washbasin in his room, trying to piece together his memories of last night.

Because there were a few hours, including how he got back, that were missing. And a potentially angry Elder awaiting him.

***

The rest of the team were in their private dining room, already waiting for him when Wu Ying arrived. Tou He flashed him a quick smile, while Lei Hui ignored Wu Ying entirely. Yu Kun offered a lascivious grin, even going so far as to waggle his eyebrows. As for Wang Min, she shot Wu Ying a cold glare. In juxtaposition to the rest of her team, Fa Yuan seemed to ignore the entire byplay between the inner sect cultivators and just waved Wu Ying to his seat.

As if they had been waiting for Wu Ying to arrive, waitresses appeared from the side doors, bearing simple dishes. Tofu, mixed greens, minced meat, and white rice all arrived in large quantities, with thin slices of spirit beast meat scattered throughout. Wu Ying even noticed traces of spiritual herbs grown in a high chi environment mixed into the dishes. All in all, the smell that rose from the meal set his stomach rumbling.

Conversation among the cultivators focused on their activities the day before, each party detailing their part as they supped. Tou He was the simplest, having wandered the city in search of snacks before returning to cultivate. Yu Kun had spent his time in local taverns, visiting with wandering cultivators he had met in the past. Wang Min had initially spent the time in the inn before she journeyed out at night to listen to other musicians within the city. As for Lei Hui, he declined to detail his experience.

"And we know of your evening." Yu Kun grinned at Wu Ying. "You've become the talk of the town."

Wu Ying winced. "What are they saying?"

"That a dashing—and they're quite insistent on that word—Verdant Green Waters Sect cultivator fought a lecherous cultivator for the honor of a mere hostess and killed him," Yu Kun said.

"I didn't kill anyone!"

"I heard it was for the hand of a noble lady. And that he fought four of them—at the same time. And beat them all," Tou He supplied. "But yes, definitely dashing."

"Two guards who were accosting a wandering cultivator," Lei Hui said.

"I heard the inner sect cultivator from the Green Water Sect was actually a lecher. And spent the evening in the company of multiple paid women," Wang Min said. "He wined and dined the ladies and everyone who praised him."

Each additional sentence made Wu Ying shrink into his seat in embarrassment. "I get it, I get it."

"I was told one of my inner set cultivators, one of the team members I had carefully chosen for an important expedition, had gone out of his way to humiliate one of the Northern Lake Pearl sect members. I was told of this matter early in the morning by Elder Toh," Fa Yuan said, fixing Wu Ying with her heavy gaze. "The Elder was looking for recompense. Luckily, all he wanted was a dinner date."

Wu Ying winced at Fairy Yang's tone of voice.

"I should mention, Elder Toh is both very old and very venerable. He's a man well-known for his kindness, as his previous three wives would attest," Fa Yuan said, tone completely dry. "In fact, his great-granddaughter I believe is only around my age. And his great-great-granddaughter might be of interest to you, Wu Ying. She's supposedly very pretty."

Wu Ying twitched as Fa Yuan drove her words home with that dry, acerbic tone. He felt himself shrinking into his seat, trying to hide. Only when she stopped did he straighten. "I'm sorry. I should have not put you in a position like that. But I did not humiliate him. We fought. Because he was sullying the honor of all cultivators."

Fa Yuan arched a single eyebrow, waiting for Wu Ying to explain. Murmurs of agreement rose from the other cultivators, as interest over the night's events overtook their desire to tease him. Seeing that he had their attention, Wu Ying proceeded to relate his evening. He chose not to shade the actions he took, going for a simple and plain statement of facts. Even if the fact that he did spend his evening with paid companionship lowered Wang Min's estimation of himself. After all, he'd only paid for companionship, conversation, and the meal. Nothing else. Or at least, he was pretty certain he hadn't paid for anything else.

Now, if he only could recall that memory of a kiss, that firm pressing of self against his body properly. Jasmine perfume as he tilted his head down. The feel of bare flesh on his arms as he held a figure close. Water beneath the bridge, lapping at the edges of the stone canal.

He shook his head, dismissing the memory. Pleasant, but unimportant.

"Interesting. If what you said is true, I will not punish you. Though I desire that you seek a more suitable method for managing confrontations next time," Fa Yuan said after she considered Wu Ying story. "I will tell Elder Toh what you have told me. And if he refuses to see the justice in your actions, I will meet him in the arena myself for a second fight."

"Oh, there's already a second, third, and fourth fight at the arena," Yu Kun said. "It seems that our little dragon here has started a trend. The cultivators have been challenging one another. Even some of my friends want to meet our little dragon and exchange pointers[20] with him."

"I do not like drawing attention to ourselves like this," Fa Yuan said disapprovingly.

Wu Ying could not help but nod along to her words.

Yu Kun offered Fa Yuan a small smile. "Of course. But are we allowed to watch?"

---

[20] Exchanging pointers is another term for dueling. It denotes a slightly more formal form of sparring, often conducted between martial arts groups or between senior and junior students. The idea is that during the process of sparring, both participants learn something from the fight. Depending on the skill level difference, these exchanges could even be a form of guidance.

Fa Yuan inclined her head in agreement to that.

"And bet?"

"Bet?" Fa Yuan said.

"You bet on the prowess of other cultivators?" Wang Min sniffed, in disparagement.

"It is good training, to understand what each fighter brings to the table. It could be a useful skill for you in the future," Yu Kun said to Wang Min.

Lei Hui could not help but nod, stroking his chin. Then, catching himself agreeing to something that Wang Min disagreed with, he stopped, a stricken look crossing the apothecarist's face. However, none of that seemed to have caught Wang Min's attention as she sniffed at Yu Kun.

"And what is being bet?" Fa Yuan said curiously.

"Coins, taels obviously. But also spirit beasts cores, some natural meats, even a few equipment treasures," Yu Kun said. "It all depends on the bettors."

"And are there a significant number of such bets?" Fa Yuan said. At Yu Kun's nod, she leaned back, picked up her teacup, and turned it around in her hand. She sipped on the drink, letting herself enjoy the warm comfort before her gaze fell on Wu Ying again. "And they want to fight our little dragon."

"Yes," Yu Kun said, the grin that he'd been trying to hide creeping up on his face.

Wu Ying looked back and forth between the pair before he shook his head. He was not particularly enthused by where this conversation seemed to have gone. But he caught Fa Yuan's gaze going to her spirit ring, where the accumulated wealth between her and his Master rested. It was a lot, though not as much as he would have believed. After all, part of the problem of not wanting any ties with anyone was that you also missed out on a number of opportunities. Between that and his earlier year's quest with Fa Yuan, Elder Cheng had depleted his meager resources. Or at least, as Fa Yuan had expressed as being true for an Elder. To Wu Ying, the amount mentioned was astronomical.

"I'm going to be fighting again, aren't I?" Wu Ying said grumpily.

Fa Yuan offered him a small smile, though Wu Ying caught the glint of greed and amusement in her eyes. Yu Kun, on the other hand, was chuckling and rubbing his hands together. Tou He stared between the group before shaking his head and uttering a prayer under his breath. And Lei Hui was stroking his beard as he leaned forward, ready to begin plotting Wu Ying's future.

***

"Are you sure this is going to work?" Wu Ying muttered, walking alongside his companions.

Fa Yuan had left earlier to join the other sect Elders who had made their way to Hinma. All of them, as reported by Yu Kun, had taken residence in a private room of a restaurant overlooking the central fighting stage to watch for good seeds and watch how their own harvest had grown.

The stage itself and the surroundings had changed in the light of day. Rather than the initially bare square, it was now packed with onlookers. Multiple members of the guard moved around the crowd, keeping the peace and an eye out for the pickpockets who worked the crowd. Along the edges of the square, enterprising food hawkers had set up, offering food and drinks to the audience. And along three cardinal points, local gang members had set up stalls, taking wagers from commoners and nobles alike as the fights went on.

All of that paled to the main spectacle, which was the pair of cultivators fighting on the main stage. To Wu Ying's surprise, they both used polearms. One, a long spear. The second was more unusual, wielding not an actual weapon, but a giant oar. The wooden implement, weighted toward the end, was capped with metal, giving the entire wooden tool a deadly edge.

Wu Ying took a deep breath, extending his senses as he made a quick judgment of the pair. They were only Body Cleansing cultivators, not yet at the stage of Energy Storage. If he had to guess, Wu Ying would place them in the top edge of Body Cleansing. More interestingly, Wu Ying turned his head and spotted the large clusters of cultivators that had gathered at either end of the stage, where the two staircases that led up to the stage were located.

The groups were split between sect members and wandering cultivators. In between were a few enterprising individuals, making their way between each group, small pieces of paper clutched in their hands.

"Those are the brokers?" Wu Ying asked Yu Kun.

The ex-wandering cultivator nodded, his gaze raking over the pair. He sniffed, seeing that one was a wandering cultivator, the other a sect member, before he straightened his robes, conjuring up his own slips of paper and a pen. "I need to get to work. Remember, hold off on joining immediately."

As a group, they pushed to the edge of the crowd and broke into the clear no-man's-land around the arena's edge. This space was as much a matter of practicality as courtesy. If one stood too close, it would be impossible to catch all the action on the raised platform.

A slight decrease in the volume of conversations arose as both mortals and cultivators noted the presence of the Verdant Green Waters Sect cultivators. There was a brief hesitation before the group was waved over to join the sect cultivator group.

Without a better option, the group, sans Yu Kun, walked over as the battle between the two Body Cleansing cultivators approached its end. As strong as the larger, oar-wielding cultivator might be, the hardwood weapon he wielded was riddled with tears, its edge blunted and chipped by the fast-moving spear. A crack resounded through the square as the oar finally gave way, leaving the panting, weaponless cultivator at the mercy of the spear-wielder sect cultivator. Rather than lose without grace, the wandering cultivator raised his hands, indicating his loss.

All around, his loss was met with muttered groans and cries of celebration from the crowd as the pair left the stage and cultivators rushed to charge the protective enchantment around the stage.

"Seniors!" Shouted greetings from the various sect cultivators arose from the crowd once the loss had been assessed and absorbed.

Wu Ying and his friends passed on their own greetings, offering martial hand clasps and bows, all the while making the necessary introductions.

"Are you here to fight?" one of the new cultivators asked Wu Ying, her eyes gleaming with interest. A quick recollection placed her name—Cultivator Liu Fan Yi.

Another cultivator, clad in light yellow and white, on her way to the staircase for her fight, paused. She turned as her senior held up a hand to make her wait for Wu Ying's answer.

"Not at all. I have had my turn." Wu Ying gestured to the waiting cultivator in yellow, offering her an encouraging smile. "I'm just here to watch for now."

"A pity." Fan Yi batted her eyelashes at Wu Ying before she waved her junior on.

Across the stage, another cultivator had managed to ascend. Wu Ying ignored the glares and the considering looks he received from the other side of the stage. The divide between wandering cultivators and sect members was a longstanding divide born of the fates of the gifted, the lucky, and the hard-working.

"How are we doing?" Lei Hui asked, one corner of his mouth turned up in a sneer as he stared at the wandering cultivators.

Yu Kun had joined the group of wandering cultivators, plying his trade, making bets.

"Obviously, we are winning," Fan Yi said. Wu Ying considered briefly before he recalled that she was from the Eternal Spring Crane Sect. "We have won a total of seven out of the twelve matches this afternoon."

"Only seven?" Lei Hui said with distaste. "Why so low?"

"We did not bring many Body Cleansing cultivators." Fan Yi shrugged. "Those who are here weren't necessarily chosen for their fighting ability."

"Then what were they chosen for?" Tou He asked guilelessly.

Wu Ying could not help but wince a little, having already guessed.

But Fan Yi did not seem to have any compunction in explaining the matter. "Status and money. After all, we are here for the auction. There is little use in bringing those who could not afford to shop."

And, Wu Ying added in his mind, for the wandering cultivators who came, it was those who could fight who could afford to buy anything. After all, the vast majority of such cultivators made their money hunting spirit beasts or hiring themselves out to local nobles and magistrates.

"Then why are we not fighting their Energy Storage cultivators?" Lei Hui asked, his gaze roaming over their competitors.

Wang Min snorted, cutting in before Fan Yi could reply. "Can you not sense the difference? Unlike us, the wandering cultivators have fewer such cultivators."

"Oh!" Lei Hui said, realization dawning.

At least in the square, the wandering cultivators were heavily weighed toward those in the first stage of cultivation.

"What I don't understand is why we are separating in this manner," Wu Ying said, gesturing. "Surely it would make more sense for us to just practice against those of the same cultivation level. Whether they are wandering cultivators or sect inductees."

Fan Yi and a few of the other more senior sect cultivators shot Wu Ying an incredulous look. Eventually, realizing that he really did not know, they answered.

"We are fighting for the right to use the stage entirely. We must show them the difference between us and them," another cultivator—this one sporting an exemplary beard, large and bushy that almost covered half of his blue and black striped robe—spoke up. From his introductions, Wu Ying recalled that he was of the Greater Tiger Ridge sect. Their headquarters were just a couple hundred li from Hinma actually, which resulted in a larger number of members than the other sects being present. "It was they who laughed at us, saying that it's no surprise our sects were beaten so badly. They taunted us, saying that other than the Verdant Green Waters, the rest of us might as well be wandering cultivators."

Wu Ying winced. Though he did feel a bit of pride upon hearing that statement. The Verdant Green Waters Sect was the premier sect in the kingdom for a reason.

"Bah! I do not believe they are that good," another voice said, this one high and scratchy. Clean-shaven, the youth in his purple and white robes glared at the Verdant Green Waters group. "I would like to test them out."

"Perhaps after the most recent group of bouts is finished," Yu Kun said, having made his way over.

Above them, the young lady used a pair of short swords, each of them barely longer than three feet. The shortened jian were wielded in quick succession to beat against her opponent's paired axes. Like the previous opponents, they were both Body Cleansing cultivators, and as such only had their skill of arms to showcase. Even so, they moved faster and hit harder than any low-level Body Cleanser could hope to replicate.

What was particularly interesting were the flashes of aspected chi that Wu Ying sensed being wielded by the pair. The woman utilized air chi, gifting herself greater speed in quick bursts. Her opponent, the wandering cultivator with the axes, was unaspected, but his axes had hints of fire and metal chi imbued in the blades. Small, runic scripts on the heads indicated that the weapons were probably enchanted rather than being manipulated by the cultivator directly.

More importantly, it was quite clear that the sect cultivators were about to lose another fight. As skilled as the female cultivator was, she lacked experience. Too often, she left herself open to a follow-up attack and her dodges were growing ever more erratic.

A quick engagement and the end appeared in short order. Low cries of warning erupted, but too late to do any good.

The axe-wielder's most recent retreat was but a feint to draw in the overly aggressive jian-wielder. He had shifted his upper body but not his legs, giving the impression of movement without adjusting his measure. When she slipped into range, he kicked upward. He caught her between her legs, striking the upper portion of her thigh with a resounding crack. The nerve that ran on the inside of the thigh was vulnerable and rarely trained.

She crumpled and an axe whistled through the air. It stopped a bare half-inch from her face, flickers of chi along its edge sharpening the weapon to an unnatural edge. The woman whimpered, dropping her swords to indicate her loss.

"I believe they might be open to another form of competition. The red flag?" Yu Kun said.

Wu Ying rolled his eyes but said nothing. He knew this had been set up by the other cultivator even as he collected bets from the wandering cultivators.

"And who will hold the flag to begin with?" Shen Wei, the bushy-bearded cultivator from the Greater Tiger Ridge sect, asked.

"If this humble one could offer, he would advance his name," Tou He spoke.

The group looked at the ex-monk and frowned, eyeing the muscles in his arms, on his legs, and the staff propped on his shoulder. Eventually, they nodded. After all, he was from the Verdant Green Waters. He should be able to offer a decent showing.

Wu Ying, of course, knew that Tou He would do more than that. Even if he might not be a martial cultivator, he had the skills to be acknowledged by them. Having advanced his plan, Yu Kun quietly cajoled the various sect members to make bets on how long Tou He would last.

"Three opponents to win," Fan Yi said, handing over a tael and receiving back a jotted down script of paper from Yu Kun.

"Two," the clean-shaven youth spoke next, offering a pair of taels. He sent a challenging glare at Tou He as he made the prediction.

If Tou He was concerned, he did not show it.

With the floodgates opened, the bets poured in. When it began to slow, as the cultivators paid attention to the new fight going on on the stage, Wang Min spoke.

"Seven."

A hush dropped over the crowd at her bold bet.

"Foolish girl!" the clean-shaven youth, who Wu Ying finally recalled was named Lu Ren, snapped. "Seven is too many."

"Then will you take my bet?" Wang Min challenged.

Lu Ren growled and fished in his pouch. He pulled out not a tael but a large beast core. A quick pulse of chi from Wu Ying told him it was no demon beast core but the more expensive, rare spirit core. This one was at the Energy Storage stage.

Rather than take the core, Wang Min snorted. "Just one?"

Rankled, Lu Ren glared at her, but still did not move to offer another beast core. Instead, he spoke. "You can just offer a small Body Cleansing core."

Before she could speak, Lei Hui interrupted the pair and shoved a core at Yu Kun. "Here. I will pay for her."

Wang Min froze then sniffed, turning away from Lei Hui. Grinning, Lu Ren handed Yu Kun the core to hold as well, receiving in return a written note. Of course, neither bettor paid attention to Yu Kun as he grumbled about not receiving anything for his troubles. Seeing Lu Ren make the bet, others streamed over, passing over small beast cores to Yu Kun, who in turn adjusted the bet, taking counter bets from Lei Hui, who fished from his pouch in increasing unhappiness.

By the time they were done, two more sets of cultivators had finished their matches above. Wu Ying had paid only slight attention to the betting, having let his gaze roam over the surroundings, taking in not only the cultivators, but the crowd and the Elders above. When he caught sight of his martial sister staring at them, he offered her a nod.

A few more minutes, as word was passed and agreements made, before Tou He made his way up, staff on his shoulder. In the short delay, Yu Kun spoke with the other two betting agents, adjusting the odds between each other and passing on bets, all to earn a little coin playing go-between.

Once all three were satisfied, they waved to the two groups. In turn, a heavyset female strode onto the stage, bearing an overly long jian, to face Tou He.

Licking his lips, Wu Ying cast his gaze around one last time. Hopefully matters would play out as they'd planned.

Chapter 20

"Liu Tou He, inner sect cultivator of the Verdant Green Waters Sect." The ex-monk announced himself to his opponent, placing both hands together in a prayer pose as he bowed to his opponent. He did this while cradling his staff on one arm, balancing the entire thing expertly while never bowing so low that he lost sight of her feet.

Wu Ying knew the last fact since he had once seen another martial specialist try to surprise his friend to give him a "lesson" on proper bowing procedures. That he then ran into the tip of Tou He's staff and ended up vomiting his breakfast had been quite amusing to Wu Ying.

"Lin Lan Ying, wandering cultivator," the female cultivator called out in return. Unlike Tou He, she'd placed the blade of her long jian along her right arm, allowing her to clasp her fist and hand in the usual formal martial bow.

"Thank you for the pointers you will bestow upon me," Tou He said as he shifted his stance. Setting oneself in guard with a staff was a simple matter. A case of taking the weapon in both hands and pointing it at your opponent. You could spin it—and Wu Ying knew Tou He could do that with ease— but for standing in guard, you just needed to keep it still. Until your opponent committed.

Lan Ying grinned good-naturedly and stomped forward. Or, Wu Ying had expected her to stomp. She had when ascending the stage. But the moment the fight started, she floated, moving with a grace and a lightness of foot that belied her size. It was as though she danced and the sword but an extension of her arm.

"Sense of the Sword," Wu Ying breathed in surprise out loud.

"And very good qinggong skills," Fan Yi added. "Impressive. For a wandering cultivator."

Wu Ying nodded, having already sensed her stage of cultivation. Unless they had suppressed their auras, most cultivator levels were simple enough to gauge. Lan Ying was in the middle stages of Energy Storage, like Tou He.

Even as the pair talked, the first exchange had finished between the combatants. A couple of quick strikes at Tou He's weapon had set it moving, and the ex-monk never let it stop after that. Around and around his hands, twisted from his wrists and elbows, around his body. He showcased his monastery's resident style—the Mountain Resides—and batted away her attacks.

Once the first exchange had finished, Tou He moved forward, never letting his weapon stop. Meeting the challenge, Lan Ying threw herself at him, only for her lighter weapon to be deflected. Underhand strikes, over-shoulder swooping angles, it all threatened her and her balance after each aborted attack. Again and again, Lan Ying retreated.

"Mistake," Wu Ying said, watching as she backed off.

"Oh?" Fan Yi asked, curious.

"Tou He's offense is his defense," Wu Ying said.

As if to highlight his point, Lan Ying hit the edge of the stage. Unable to retreat, the large woman blocked desperately, even going so far as to deflect with the palm of her free hand. Tou He stopped, standing just within his range but not hers. His staff kept moving, striking at her, bouncing from one deflection to the next as he wielded both ends of the staff. Overwhelming her thin defense.

"Now…" Wu Ying breathed.

As if on cue, the staff stopped and stabbed out, just once. It slipped past Lan Ying's hasty defense to land on her chest. It was a gentle push and the woman caught herself as she fell, flipping over to land gracefully.

But off the stage.

"You know his style well," Fan Yi said, glancing at Wu Ying.

"We've fought often."

"That's one," Lei Hui called, crowing his victory even as Tou He walked back to his side of the stage.

Once he arrived, Tou He turned around and stared at where his opponent would ascend the staircase, his breathing quickly regulating itself. It helped that there was an argument going on among the wandering cultivators as they discussed who would take the next battle. Yu Kun had made his way over to that side of the arena, egging them on as he attempted to take more bets.

"I noticed you did not place a wager," Fan Yi said to Wu Ying.

"True."

When she realized that Wu Ying was not going to explain further, she prodded. "Is there a reason?"

"I'm a poor peasant. Ex-peasant," he corrected himself. "I don't exactly have the spirit cores to lose."

"Even for a certain win?" Fan Yi asked, eyes glinting with amusement.

"As my father used to say—in gambling, a certain bet is a fool's bet." Wu Ying pursed his lips before he added. "Though he only ever said that when we were racing grasshoppers. Just before mine was blown off course…"

Wu Ying's eyes narrowed at the memories. A niggling suspicion bloomed as he considered how chi—sword chi or just energetic chi—could be projected. His father might have been at the Body Cleansing stage, but he could easily project enough energy to push a grasshopper off course mid-jump.

"That cheating… cheater!" Wu Ying shouted as suspicion became certainty. "He always took my share of the tang yuan[21]!"

---

[21] Rice balls. Often cooked in a sweet dessert-soup base. Black or red sesame versions are most common.

Quite a few faces had looked at Wu Ying at his first declaration, eyes narrowed in suspicion at Tou He. Then, realizing he was shouting about sweet desserts, their interest disappeared. All but Fan Yi, whose eyes crinkled in amusement.

"That damnable, cursed man. How could he do that to his only child!" Wu Ying complained to her, even as Tou He faced his new opponent. This one wielded a jian like Wu Ying, and while Wu Ying would normally be interested, this time he had a bigger concern that had to be vented.

"My sister would tell me my parents were calling for me when the long xu tang[22] hawker came by the house," Fan Yi offered, making a face. "Then she'd buy and eat my portion before I got back. And said it was for my own good, so that I didn't get fat."

Wu Ying looked at the slim martial artist.

She grinned at Wu Ying's incredulous look. "Oh, my sister is Fairy Xi."

Wu Ying blinked, then his jaw dropped. "Oh, I didn't... well. I..." He drew a deep breath. "I never had many chances to eat long xu tang. It was too expensive."

"Understandable," Fan Yi said.

While sugary products were not impossible to purchase, they were expensive. The sugar canes that one had to purchase often came from farther south, so blocks of sugar would be transported, raising the overall price of the commodity.

Wu Ying sighed and calmed himself. By the time he paid attention to the fight above, it was over. The wandering cultivator was walking away, his sword sheathed as he cradled his injured hand. Wu Ying winced, knowing it was likely from a simple strike to the top of the hand. It didn't take much

[22] Translates as dragon beard candy. Yes, that Long.

force to crack the bone in the hand connecting wrist to thumb. As he well knew.

"Hun dan," Wu Ying cursed. "I missed the fight."

"Well, maybe you should have considered shutting up and watching." The voice that spoke behind them was curt and irritated.

Wu Ying turned around and glared. But he had to admit, the man had a point.

Having been told off, Wu Ying fell silent and paid attention. Fan Yi, noticing his change in demeanor, also kept silent as she watched Wu Ying and Tou He at the same time.

Over the next few fights, Tou He acquitted himself well. It was the fifth opponent who pressured him at first before he slipped and fell. The sixth fight was a hard-fought battle of whirling spears and staff, of hard strikes and close misses, all peppered with weapon intent and chi infused strikes and defenses. And so, as the seventh round began, the inevitable occurred.

It was something Wu Ying had been concerned about since the beginning of the game. Tou He's smaller-than-normal dantian ensured he'd have less chi than his opponents. And while some of the fights, like the first, had little use of the energy, others, like the sixth and fourth, were almost exclusively fought using sword and staff projections. Even in the easiest encounter, a couple of chi blasts would be released, pushing Tou He to protect himself by imbuing his own aura.

Wu Ying had noticed the signs after the fifth fight. Tou He had managed to hide it from everyone else, Wu Ying figured. At least, those down here. No guarantees with the Elders above. But Wu Ying knew his friend, had fought him enough to know when he was flagging. Now, everyone else did as Tou He leaned against his staff and breathed deeply in the wake of his sixth fight.

As Tou He's latest opponent strode up, Wu Ying winced at the man's weapon. He wielded a ji—an axe-halberd, which was a long polearm with a small axe-head on the side and a dagger affixed to the top. It could both cut and stab with lethal results. Like the spear, it removed Tou He's reach advantage while adding a lethality his simple staff missed. More so, the wandering cultivator proceeded to extend the dimensions of his weapon by another foot with his chi once the normal salutations were given.

Rather than wait, Tou He leapt into action. He jumped, twirled, and blocked with his staff, using the full length of the stage to his advantage. Wu Ying noted the way the ex-monk attempted to avoid the attacks with his body, utilizing his physical prowess rather than his chi aura to guard himself.

Even so, Tou He's attempts at defense were being beaten aside, overpowered as he was slowly cornered, forced to block and utilize the remnants of his energy. Each strike sent flurries of dust and chipped stone across the stage, sparked gold and red auras. Each second saw Tou He stagger, his attacks growing ever sparser.

Behind and beside Wu Ying, the crowd was screaming, the bettors teasing Lei Hui, goading him about his future losses. The thin apothecarist quivered, hands held by his sides as he took the abuse from the other sect members.

"It seems your friend will not last," Fan Yi said. "A good thing then that you did not bet. But a pity that you did not have confidence in your own friends."

"I trust Tou He when it matters," Wu Ying replied.

As if to punctuate Wu Ying's words, the axe-halberd wielder released a loud cry from the stage. "The Light of the Heavens—Twice Sown!"

As the ji-wielder spoke, light collected around the already glowing edge of the weapon. Light in the dull, black color of good soil drank in nearby light, absorbing it and seeming to cut apart the natural world. The axe grew in size with each word, deepening in color. At the end of his cry, the wandering cultivator brought down his raised polearm.

Tou He, cornered, exhausted, and without a place to dodge could only block the attack. He angled his staff, filling it with the flames of his own chi. But his fire chi was a weak thing in comparison to the earth-generated axe that plowed into his conjured defense. Hasty defense was shattered, broken, and buried under the dark, loamy soil of his opponent's chi. Wind and dust kicked up, shrouding the stage and hiding the individuals within.

"No!" Wang Min cried, moving toward the stage.

Wu Ying did not move, instead tilting his head from side to side, surreptitiously sniffing the air as he tested what his extended aura had told him. When he confirmed his senses, he relaxed, even as Wang Min finished dismissing the defenses. Covered in dirt that slowly faded as the chi holding it in reality dissipated, the ex-monk allowed himself to be brought down from the stage by the worried female cultivator.

"That was… surprising," Tou He said. His eyes were a little glassy, but otherwise he seemed unhurt.

"That was dangerous!" Wang Min snapped. "This entire production is dangerous. What use is there in this if you are too injured to continue the expedition?" Wang Min turned and glared at the wandering cultivator. "And you! Unleashing such a powerful attack in a sparring match was irresponsible."

"I was careful!" the axe-wielding wandering cultivator protested, then quailed as she released Tou He entirely and stalked over, scolding him. The wandering cultivator shrank back a little, but Wu Ying could see a little glint in his eyes as she continued to scold him.

"Some men, they'll do anything for a woman's attention," Fan Yi muttered. Wu Ying glanced at her and she made a small gesture to the pair.

Wu Ying felt a wry smile cross his face, while Fan Yi turned her attention fully to Wu Ying. "And some are just oblivious."

"Hmmm?" Wu Ying frowned, already looking away as he spotted Tou He getting mobbed by other cultivators. He wanted to make sure his friend was really all right, but from the way he was smiling and replying while drawing in the ambient chi, it seemed so.

A look to the side, where Lei Hui and Yu Kun were being mobbed by another set of cultivators for a very different reason, made the slight surge of happiness at seeing his friend's lack of injury disappear. Voices were raised as they demanded payment, along with the incessant teasing that made his friends grit their teeth. Wu Ying could only shake his head at their actions.

"It seems you have lost much on this bet," Fan Yi said.

Wu Ying shrugged. "That's Lei Hui's problem. He should have known not to bet. And Yu Kun I'm sure has done well on taking the bets..." Or at least, he thought he did. That was how the brokers made their living after all. Not on expecting one side or the other to win, but on the margin between bets.

"I told you the Verdant Green Waters Sect is nothing," Lu Ren said, raising his voice enough that it managed to quiet the crowd.

Fan Yi placed a hand on Wu Ying's, but then removed it when she saw that the youth was not making any motion to accept the challenge. On the other hand, Lei Hui finally had enough.

"As if you know any better! You bet and lost at two opponents," Lei Hui snapped.

"Perhaps I underestimated him, but it was because I had not realized how poor the competition would be," Lu Ren said, sniffing and raising his nose. "He would not have lasted even three real opponents."

"Three!" Lang Ying roared, the woman stomping over. Tou He's first opponent glared at Lu Ren, who turned to face the female wandering cultivator and the other, enraged wandering cultivators who had arrived behind her. "Say that again, I dare you!"

"I dare. Three real cultivators would have beaten the monk," Lu Ren sneered.

The attention of the group turned toward Tou He. The ex-monk blinked as he gulped down the mouthful of meat he had been provided. He tried to hide the meat skewers that had found their way into his hands behind his back as he offered a guileless smile. "Yes?"

"You can fight again, right?" Lei Hui said, gesturing at Lu Ren. "He's saying you can't even beat three sect cultivators."

"Don't change the subject. I want this skinny, pimple-faced nobleman to back up what he's saying!" Lang Ying snapped. "We are just as good as these sect cultivators."

Yu Kun eyed Tou He, noted his situation, and shook his head. "No. He can't." Yu Kun straightened up. "I can fight in his stead."

At the chorused shouts of no from both wandering and sect-based cultivators, Yu Kun ducked his head.

"Of course you'd turn down a real challenge. As I said, you Verdant Green Waters cultivators are nothing," sneered Lu Ren.

"A little far, do you not think so?" Shen Wei said.

"Not far enough," a smaller man with a cut that extended across his left eye, making him look like a true ruffian, snapped. The eye itself was unharmed, though its surroundings were bloodshot. When he spoke, even Lan Ying stepped back.

"And who are you?" Shen Wei said. There was no antagonism in his voice, just curiosity.

226

"Wo Chi Yun," the ruffian announced. "Tell me, do you dare bet that you can beat a Verdant Green Waters Sect opponent faster than us? Seven opponents, was it not?"

Fan Yi, who had been silent thus far, snorted.

But already Lu Ren was leaning forward, almost snarling his reply. "Of course!"

"Then show me this bet," Chi Yun said. "And I'll match it."

Lu Ren reached into his storage ring and extracted a fist-sized beast stone. Even from where Wu Ying was, he felt the chi it emanated. "This is the core of a Twice-Born Metal Commorant. Core level creature."

"A good start." Chi Yun turned his hand around and showed a beast core of his own. "Jade Mountain Goat from the Qu Yi passes. Core level."

"Good," Lu Ren said, his eyes flicking over the core.

But before he could agree to the bet, Chi Yun continued. "Yes, it is good. To see how little the honor of the sect cultivators really is worth."

"How little!" Lu Ren bristled.

"You want more?" Shen Wei said, rumbling, and strode over. He made a scroll appear, dropping it onto Lu Ren's hand. "Spirit level movement skill— The Whistling Grasshopper."

"This is the Gold Protection Necklace of the Third Princess of the Hanju tribes. It will stop a single strike from a Core level cultivator."

"Ever-Returning Throwing Knives forged by Master Yu."

"A blade control exercise. It will double your sword chi projection distance if trained well."

Wu Ying shook his head as one after the other, the two groups of cultivators stacked beast cores, enchanted equipment, cultivation and aura training exercises on top of the two speakers' arms. It quickly overflowed, at which point another cultivator was brought out to carry the items. Yu Kun, beside the pair, was scribbling desperately, his actions copied by the other two betting agents.

At a certain point, as nearly everyone had placed their contributions and it had started devolving to Body Cleansing level spirit stones, Fan Yi raised her voice. "But who will fight on the Verdant Green Waters side?"

Both groups froze as they realized the issue. They looked between one another, eyes landing on Lei Hui, who shook his head furiously. Then they turned to Wang Min, who offered them a small, mysterious smile. As if in silent agreement, the group turned away from her. It would be unfair to choose either cultivator—both of whom were quite clearly not martial cultivators. After all, Tou He was a strapping, powerful young man. And the pair were not.

Yu Kun was soiled, as both a wandering cultivator previously and now a Verdant Green Waters Sect cultivator. He could not be considered a proper cultivator of either kind.

Eventually all eyes landed on Wu Ying.

"No."

"You refuse!"

"Coward," Lu Ren spat. The crowd rumbled in agreement.

"I promised my martial sister I would not get into any more trouble," Wu Ying said. "And this looks like trouble."

"Now, Wu Ying," Yu Kun wheedled, "she can't really blame you for this. It's for the Sect's honor!"

Wandering cultivators and sect cultivators nodded in unison.

Wu Ying snorted and turned his head upward, to where Elder Yang was staring at the crowd with the other Elders. "You tell her that."

His actions and words made the group freeze. It was one thing to have their fun. Another to bother the Elders. Still…

"Surely a small series of duels would not cause too much anger," Shen Wei said.

Wu Ying hesitated, then shook his head. "I have no reason to do this."

Disappointed groans rose from all around.

Fan Yi leaned over to Wu Ying, having caught his words. "And what if we gave you a reason?"

"Like?"

Fan Yi shrugged and looked at the pair of ringleaders.

Chi Yun caught on faster, eyes narrowing, making the scar on his eyebrow pucker, before he grinned. "Fine. I'll give you a lesson. In my Seven Star Sword Style."

"I have a sword style," Wu Ying said.

"Not like mine!" Chi Yun puffed out his chest. "I killed the bandit Frog-Leg Xun with it."

There were a few muttered words of awe, though Wu Ying had not heard of him. Still, from the reaction, it seemed to be a decent name.

"And I'll train you in my family's fist art," Lu Ren said.

"Your family?" Wu Ying said.

"The Fu family Thrice-Struck Nerve," Lu Ren said.

"Oh." Wu Ying sighed, then looked between the group before he glanced up at where his martial sister was looking down at them. He met her imperious gaze for a second then exhaled heavily. "Fine."

Muted cheers rose up as Yu Kun ushered the group to a table that had been located for them to deposit the bets. At the same time, another argument had arisen among the sect cultivators, all of them wanting a place in the lineup. Almost all of them wanted in, which raised the hubbub again.

In the meantime, with the stage empty, a pair of wandering cultivators had gone up and fought one another—to the boos of the mortal crowd who'd gotten used to the more spectacular fights between the Energy Stage cultivators.

Amidst all that, Wu Ying nearly jumped when a voice spoke into his ear, the words almost a caress. "I expect you to make it up to me."

"What?" Wu Ying blurted, turning to look at Fan Yi.

"For helping with your little play," Fan Yi said.

Wu Ying continued blinking, even as she sashayed off as the other senior sect members called for her participation in the discussion.

"Is it the innocent obliviousness?" Tou He asked, making Wu Ying jump again.

When Wu Ying turned to his friend, he was met with the sight of a stick of meat in his face. As he breathed in, Wu Ying could not help but note the lightly charred sweet-glazed meat, combined with the scent of water chi.

Meat stick waggled in the air. "Snake gizzard?"

"What do you mean?" Wu Ying asked grumpily as he took the skewer.

"Your ability to attract the strangest of women," Tou He said. "Be careful of her. She's much slyer than Li Yao. And from another sect."

Wu Ying glared at his friend and bit into his meat. Still, he could not help but glance at Fan Yi, as she argued among the other cultivators, before shaking his head.

No. His friend was wrong. There was no way the young noble lady, at least a few years older than him, was interested in Wu Ying in that sense. She probably just wanted some of the taels they'd conned out of the group.

That was it.

Definitely.

Chapter 21

Twice in less than twenty-four hours. Wu Ying shook his head as he stood on the stage and looked around. As the defensive formations were yet to activate, he could see the crowd without an issue. Throughout the day, the numbers had kept growing with each fight. Now, midday had come and gone, and the mid-afternoon sun beat down on Wu Ying through wispy clouds. He made note of where it was and the angle it would hit. Not too high, not too low. It'd probably not get into the eyes. Not unless he jumped.

The smell of the crowd, the scent of mingling chi came back to Wu Ying as he stood on the stage, carefully regulating his breathing. The sharp smell of the Elders, of strengthened dantians until they had become a core of power, told him that even more Elders had joined Fa Yuan in the restaurant. If things went well, she was likely placing bets too, earning what she could from them.

And below, he knew, Yu Kun would earn a little for the sect whichever way this fight played out. But to cover their losses, the money Lei Hui had lost, Wu Ying would need to beat Tou He's record. And, unlike what others might think, the ex-monk had not tried to lose. His loss was real.

It was just that Fairy Yang and Wu Ying knew of Tou He's weakness. In an endurance battle, he could not last. So they had planned for his loss. Just in case. Because the one thing Wu Ying could do was endure. He could push on, be stubborn, and win even when he was tired. And if he was no genius martial artist, neither were the sect members attending the auction.

These were the flowers of their sects, blooming with promise. These were people who had bought their way to success, who would rather visit a city for an auction than fight a war, cultivate, or run another assignment. And compared to them, Wu Ying could win.

Or so they hoped.

Noise at the other end of the stage drew his attention to the present moment. Wu Ying drew a deep breath and unsheathed his sword as his first opponent, a young lady with a piece of rope wrapped around one arm and a small dagger on the end, ascended the platform.

Rope dart. Joy.

Wu Ying pushed his feelings aside, his thoughts on their plan. Now, all he had to do was beat seven sect cultivators.

As simple as turning over one's hand.

As if.

***

The rope dart was a unique and specialized weapon that was probably the most flexible weapon among the eighteen weapons of wushu. It had immense range, speed, could curl around simple defenses, and punch through hasty blocks. It required immense skill to wield, but in the hands of a master, it could slay dozens. Add the ability to project chi to make its greatest weakness—its rope—as hard as steel, and as a weapon, the rope dart was unequaled in a duel.

To simplify, it was a pain to fight.

Wu Ying cuts sideways, beating the flying dagger off course. It flew up into the air before it shifted directions again at the tug of the rope. Not that Wu Ying was letting the opening go. He stepped forward, attempting to close the gap. And was defeated, as the returning weapon nearly cut off his ear.

Snarling, Wu Ying blocked and tried a lunge, only for his sword tip to be wrapped in the hardened rope and yanked off line. Another attack forced him to jump, twisting his sword in the rope and tearing at the bindings. The rope held, reinforced by her chi. Through his blade, Wu Ying felt the energy sent within, strengthening each strand of rope and the weapon itself. He could even smell it, the way rope and wood chi flowed, mingling together.

232

Chi bound, strengthened, but not sharpened. It never reached the end of her blade. There were traces, but her wood chi focused on the rope itself, binding it tight.

Wu Ying landed, drawing his sword to his face as he brought up his guard, and his assailant returned her weapon to herself, sending it spinning back around her arm to keep its momentum.

"Very annoying," Wu Ying muttered to himself.

No more time to complain, as she launched the weapon once more. This time, it was a shortened attack, jerked back just before Wu Ying could block. The weapon flew untouched by his blade but a threat as it returned and built more momentum.

Wu Ying threw himself forward, following the returning weapon. She had repeated this motion three times already. Foolish.

Even as she wrapped the weapon around her arm, the blade twisting about and coming toward Wu Ying at greater speed, he was ready. He snatched his scabbard from his belt and, covering it with his sword chi, blocked the attack. His lunge, aimed for her face at the beginning, dipped low to plunge into her foot as he extended the blade by a few inches with his aura.

Blood dripped from the sword aura, falling to the stone as he retracted it. The pain froze his opponent's attacks long enough for Wu Ying to step deeper and launch a roundhouse kick into her side. The impact caught her in the short ribs, throwing her to the side. Before she could recover, a foot on her still rope blocked her weapon and a blade to her throat made her yield.

Then he helped her stand. "Good move. But too repetitive."

His opponent grimaced but nodded with thanks as she hobbled down.

Wu Ying felt a little bad for her, but he knew that injury would heal quickly, especially under the ministrations of the pills her sect members were already plying her with. And in truth, it was better to learn now than later.

Even as he walked back to his corner, Wu Ying churned his dantian, drawing in the chi of the world. He could have finished the fight a little faster if he had not been trying to cultivate at the same time. But he needed to last.

One.

***

His next opponent was simpler, at least to Wu Ying. His opponent stood before him, holding a jian in each hand, and beckoned Wu Ying toward him. Right foot forward, back foot on the ball of his foot to give him the explosive movement his style required.

Another clash of swords, and Wu Ying threw a series of quick wrist cuts to deflect a pair of attacks. He felt his opponent's water chi thrum through the swords as they met. Muted, like his previous opponent's wood chi. Unsuited, but still part of the weapon. More, Wu Ying could smell it on his opponent's body, in the traces in the air as they circled. Sensed the way it made him a little more fluid, how it helped adjust his opponent's body a little, made him react faster. How Wu Ying's own jian slid off the blade a little faster, a little more smoothly than it should have.

After a half-dozen exchanges, Wu Ying shook his head at the dual-wielding jian cultivator.

"Who told you that you should dual wield jian?" Wu Ying said.

In the half-dozen confrontations, he'd learned that his opponent had the Sense of the Sword, but it was muted. Muted by having to pay attention to two weapons at the same time instead of a single weapon. The jian, with their similar long lengths, were ill-suited for anyone but a master to dual wield.

"What's it matter to you?" the youth sneered. He drew a series of cuts at Wu Ying as he spoke, bok choy green and silt brown robes flapping.

A simple falling dodge, back foot placed behind Wu Ying's body, was all he required to angle himself away and out of his attacker's line of control. Wu Ying left his hand in the same location though, only going so far as to raise the hilt of his sword, while leaving the point in place. Almost as though it was magic, it slid past both swords into the gap, just over his opponent's defense.

"Because I want to thank them," Wu Ying replied, pushing a little forward so that the tip of the blade sat facing the cross-eyed teenager's eyes. "For giving me such an easy win."

A beat, then his opponent stepped back and sheathed his weapons. Unwinding himself, Wu Ying did the same. They did the formal thanks at the end, though Wu Ying could tell his opponent did not feel it. In truth, he should not have taunted his opponent. But the teen had hurt Wu Ying's sense of pride as a swordsman. You did not pick up two weapons, wield them, and act as though you knew what you were doing until you were the master of one.

Wu Ying drew a deep breath, returned to his position, and continued churning his dantian as he dismissed the man and the echoes of his father's words from his mind.

Two.

***

"Crossbow!" Wu Ying exclaimed angrily. Even as he spoke, he dodged from side to side, his sword weaving in the Cloud Hands and Dragon pins the Sunset mixed defense form he was using. Each motion was aided by the projection of sword chi, cutting fast-moving bolts out of the air and sending the wooden skewers clattering to the stone floor.

"It is a legitimate weapon," the grinning opponent on the opposite side of the stage replied, pausing only long enough to slap another box of crossbow bolts to the repeating crossbow he used.

Wu Ying growled, cursing the fact that the additional speed offered by the cultivator's cultivation stage had taken away one of the crossbow's greatest weaknesses. Now, all Wu Ying could do was wait for his opponent to either run out of crossbow bolts or risk charging in.

Another series of projectiles flew at him, and Wu Ying managed to dodge and block all but one. A light injury resulted from a bolt sliding across his ribs, tearing at his skin. Air chi—a mixture of wood and fire—was not imbued into the bolt itself but wrapped around the wooden shaft and metal tip. Wu Ying hissed then drew another breath, the stuffiness of an enclosed arena filling his nose for a second as the buzz of the working protective shielding penetrated his focus.

Even as he recovered, his opponent switched the box of ammunition beneath the repeating crossbow for a new box. Wu Ying darted closer, only to be forced to back off as a series of caltrops—small metal balls with spikes on them—were thrown on the ground, blocking his way.

"What kind of fighting is this?" Wu Ying said as he ducked, sending a blast of chi parallel to the ground to blow away the impediments. He even almost managed to send one into his opponent's legs, but received another light wound across his shoulder for his efforts as a bolt cut through the air.

"The Black Nightingales care about winning, rather than silly concepts such as proper battles," his opponent replied. "Now, taste the Three Shadows."

To Wu Ying's mild surprise, rather than three bolts, he spotted five. Four in front, and a fifth that had formed from pure chi behind the first wave. He cut and ducked, using his sword sheath to help block the attacks, and dispersed the final chi bolt with a flaring of his aura.

"You…" Wu Ying growled.

But a sudden cessation in attacks made Wu Ying freeze. To Wu Ying's astonishment, his opponent was slapping at the edges of his weapon, trying to dislodge a stuck bolt.

Wary of a feint, Wu Ying rushed his opponent. The slight widening in his opponent's eyes, his lack of balance, told of a man who was likely actually surprised. And if not…

The Sword's Truth glowed as Wu Ying pushed the aura in his chi to the maximum. It flowed around him, glowing yellow and white as his blade plunged toward his opponent. Even a hasty attack of a trio of throwing knives did nothing to slow Wu Ying, the simple attacks missing and deflected by his solidified aura.

Out of options, his opponent solidified his aura, taking the attack as he crossed his arms. Metal struck metal as the opponent's hidden bracers protected him from being skewered. They did nothing for Wu Ying's built-up momentum, however. Light flared and the Black Nightingale cultivator was thrown backward, off the arena to crash into the ground.

"Lucky," Wu Ying heard muttered from the crowd.

But he had no time to listen to them. He had chi to gather and wounds to bind.

Three.

***

Weapons clashed, sparks flew. Wu Ying growled, pulling back and shedding another attack. A small motion at the corner of his vision wanted his attention, but he forced himself to focus as he fought. He knew what the glinting, flying distraction was. Just another chip of his weapon, shaved off as he and his opponent dueled.

Metal chi infused his opponent's weapon, making it sharper than ever. It was so sharp that it was impossible for Wu Ying to block the infused chi attack directly. Instead, he focused on infusing just enough chi to make sure his weapon did not break upon clashing while he used angles and shedding blocks to slide his opponent's weapon away. Better to conserve his chi and win this the old-fashioned way.

Unfortunately, his opponent, like himself, had focused his studies on the sword. His opponent might not be able to release large waves of sword intent, but the intent he infused into his weapon made it difficult to block his attacks. In the meantime, he used his technical swordsmanship skills to find gaps in Wu Ying's defenses, leaving thin cuts across Wu Ying's arms and chest.

Of course, it was not entirely one-sided. In a high-speed battle like this, where both opponents flipped, ducked, and slashed, wounds accumulated on both sides. Wu Ying had the advantage of a form that took full use of his Energy Storage channels, allowing him to expand and divert energy into his sword at regular intervals. His opponent, on the other hand, was limited to a more mundane style.

A cut, high then low, Greeting the Sunrise before Claws across Water and then Stroking the Painting. Each blow followed by a surge of chi or a retraction, making the size of Wu Ying's weapon unpredictable, its length dangerous. His opponent took injuries, but more importantly, was forced to widen his motions, expend more energy in defense.

"Beating the broken Forge!" A shout, punctuated by a cut downward.

Wu Ying took the attack on his raised jian, stepping sideways as he did so and angling his weapon to slide the attack off the blade. A chip caught, his opponent's weapon dipped, and suddenly, Wu Ying was missing two feet of his sword.

Acting on instinct, Wu Ying moved inward. Northern Shen Wind Steps combined with the qinggong Twelve Gale exercise had Wu Ying slide into his opponent's blind spot. A roundhouse kick sent him stumbling back as his opponent recovered from his sudden success. An extended chi blade cut at the raised weapon arm as his opponent brought his own weapon back in guard. A surge of will made the chi blade blunt as he struck, bruising but not incapacitating his opponent.

Wu Ying fell back, drawing his chi into his body, circulating his energy. Bleeding from wounds on his thigh—how did that happen?—and his chest and arms. Old wounds, opened. He eyed his opponent, curious if he would acknowledge the attack.

"You won," his opponent spoke, clasping his hands together. "Thank you for the pointers."

"And thank you for yours," Wu Ying replied. He had learned a lot, watching his opponent. Grasped at another piece of the puzzle about what sharpness was. How to utilize it.

Wu Ying returned to his corner, struggling to control his breathing, knowing he would fail to get it under control before the next fight. He tossed the remainder of his weapon down the steps, calling forth another jian from his spirit ring.

Four.

***

Polearms were Wu Ying's bane. The extended reach meant that he constantly had to work his way inward, going from the edge of his opponent's full measure to the edge of his own. It was part of the reason why he focused so often on his footwork, to cross that deadly distance.

Polearm flails were the worst. The weapon was exactly what its name implied—a flail attached by a metal chain to the end of a long polearm. To wield the weapon, all you needed to do was swing the weapon around, allowing the flail to speed up and strike. The entire weapon was all about momentum—but when it gained enough speed, the flail's attack could shatter any defense Wu Ying chose to put up.

So he didn't.

He ducked and dodged, leaned from side to side to avoid the swinging end of the polearm. Each attack, Wu Ying grew to learn the pattern of the attacks. A weapon like this had one major disadvantage—the momentum it built also meant that attacks could only follow specific patterns. You could not suddenly stop and swing it back, not without forcing a significant pause. Once Wu Ying understood those patterns and the most likely response by his opponent, he could work his way in.

So he ducked and dodged, on occasion deflecting the weapon when he had no choice. Each deflection cost him, making his fingers tremble, wrist hurt, and shoulders ache as he blocked the attacks. He did not face them directly, instead cutting at the weapon at angles or blocking with a twist, just to ensure the attacks did not impact directly. And even then, his fingers were growing numb.

240

But he was learning patterns. Movements at specific timings, the tells his opponent exhibited before he completed the next change in trajectory. Each pass, Wu Ying ascertained his opponent's patterns. A retraction of the polearm as Wu Ying shed the attack made the flail swing backward. It struck his back, earth chi giving weight to the flail end, imparting greater momentum and force to the flail end. It forced him to roll on the ground after being struck, roll and rise to his feet as the scent of baked clay filled his nose.

Another injury, added to his others. But he was learning.

On the twelfth pass, Wu Ying made his move.

First, a projection of sword intent. Directed at his opponent, forcing him to block with the weapon. It shifted the polearm shaft to an angle to Wu Ying's body and his opponent. The swinging flail followed the initial motion. Then a follow-up wrist cut, one aimed at the flail, following the same trajectory of its initial motion. A third cut and projection of energy added speed and momentum to the flail end.

The attack disrupted his opponent's plans, forced him to readjust his forms as he pulled back. In that time, Wu Ying used Wind Steps to rush in. Past the initial danger zone, inside the polearm flail end. He pushed forward, putting his forearm against the shaft to restrict motion.

A twist at his opponent's hips, and the shaft smashed into Wu Ying's arm. It formed a bruise and made his bones creak, his arm throb. A switch in grip, and the opponent began to bring the butt of his weapon into play.

Too little. Too late.

Another step and Wu Ying's blade was there. At his opponent's throat.

Breathing ragged, bruises forming on arm and back, Wu Ying saluted his opponent and gave his thanks.

Five.

***

Wu Ying dueled his opponent, their jians dancing in the space between each other. His opponent in grey and red robes, his face pudgy, but arms and legs long like a swordsman's should be. He was skilled, maybe even better than Wu Ying, with a form that made full use of the chi they both wielded.

Wu Ying danced, flowing between forms, exhaustion edging his consciousness, encroaching on his concentration. Each motion was part of the forms, each breath part of his moving cultivation. Chi flowed as he cultivated, as he swayed and cut, the flow of his chi healing his wounds.

Healing perhaps, but still bleeding. Injuries accumulated across his various duels dripped onto the floor, staining it and bringing wafts of the copper scent to his nose. He had to win this one, so he matched skill and chi directly against his opponent. No longer holding back.

The scent of his own chi filled Wu Ying's senses. The smell of his own body, of his own energy filled his lungs, leaving a slight taste in his mouth. He felt it thrum through his body, down his arms, along his legs. He felt his sword through the Sense of the Sword, the way he wrapped it up in his own unaspected energy. Sensed his aura flicker and grow and thin as he willed it.

The Sword's Truth—extended—became Heron stalking the Marshes, flowing to a dropped front foot and a series of quick kicks at his opponent's ankles. He watched as his opponent backed off, raising his foot as he retreated with each motion.

A crescent kick—the Falling Moon—sent a projection of chi that was blocked by his opponent's own blade. Another drop, again into Heron stalking the Marshes, and his opponent was on guard, jumping in the air and thrusting with his sword at Wu Ying's face.

The blade closed in, filling Wu Ying's vision with each passing moment. He leaned sideways, letting the attack cut his aura, waste its projected chi on the reinforced defense. A hand reached upward, gripped the hilt. Twisted his body and his opponent's.

Wu Ying threw both of them, wrapping his opponent up in his own body as they flew backward, through the arena. Putting his opponent beneath his body as they landed. An elbow, carefully positioned, slammed into his midriff.

A forced, painful exhalation.

Arm wrapping his opponent's. Leg twisting as he continued to place weight on his opponent. A quick series of motions, and Wu Ying had the arm gripped between leg and shoulder. A slight twitch of his body, and it would break. Firmly held, he knew he had won. Cheated by grappling when he should be sword fighting.

It was just a question of if his opponent would give up now or after Wu Ying broke his arm.

Wu Ying huffed, feeling the slickness of his opponent's skin on his, wet with sweat and blood. Smelled a whiff of cooking meat brought from outside the formation as the crowd roared its approval. He was nearly done, even as he pushed against the arm to still his opponent's struggles and remind him of his place.

Six.

Chapter 22

A familiar face. Well, they had all been familiar. But he had spoken with this one. Lu Ren, the clean-shaven sect cultivator in purple and white robes, stood before Wu Ying. To his chagrin, Lu Ren used a polearm too—a trident. Shorter than the traditional polearms, thankfully, but with its three tines, it could catch and break his weapon if Wu Ying was not careful.

Yet unlike many of the other fights, even before he had made the usual salutations, Lu Ren had started speaking. "Is this all there is? To a Verdant Green Waters cultivator? A martial specialist?" Lu Ren sneered. "Struggling to win through luck and dirty tricks?"

Wu Ying offered a half-smile, his breathing still ragged. He cultivated, trying to slow down the bleeding in the wounds that had reopened through the last fight's energetic battle. He breathed slowly as chi filled his depleted dantian.

"Do you not have anything to say?" Lu Ren said.

"Is there anything I can say that would convince you otherwise?" Wu Ying said, eyeing the weapon in his opponent's hand. "It seems my blade must do the talking."

"You will not beat me. You can barely stand," Lu Ren scoffed.

Wu Ying shrugged, knowing how much of his statement was true. His opponents were more skilled than the wandering cultivators Tou He had faced. They knew how to use their energy properly; they had received the training from multiple teachers to perfect their forms. And just as importantly, they fought with more conviction.

The wandering cultivators had fought Tou He for fun. For a little bit of money on the side, but mostly, to learn. It was no life-or-death spar, no great matter of honor when they had battled the ex-monk. They had not taken the matter seriously.

Wu Ying's opponents all had. He'd had to break his last opponent's arm to make him declare his loss. Break his arm—for a simple sparring match.

That was how far some of them were willing to take it. So his fights had required more chi, expended more of his energy, injured him when Tou He was only tired and bruised.

"Maybe. But I am still standing," Wu Ying said, raising his sword in impatience. He could delay for a few more breaths. but the difference would be negligible. Better to get this over with. "Long Wu Ying, of the Verdant Green Waters Sect."

"Fu Lu Ren, direct disciple of Elder Hsu of the Heavenly Lake Sect," Lu Ren said. He brought his trident upward, setting his feet apart.

Announcements made, the pair stood in silence. Even the crowd grew silent, watching the two square off. Wu Ying felt his heart rate slow slightly, his breathing calming and regulating. He watched his opponent—not his eyes or his hands, but his body. Letting his peripheral vision take in the rest.

Small twitches, the tightening of a hand, the adjustment of the angle of an elbow, the shifting of weight on the foot. Wu Ying took it all in, the smallest motion alerting him then discarded. Wu Ying shifted in reply, letting his body adjust to the minute motions his opponent made, closing off lines of attack—or leaving them open to invite a response.

Dueling was as much a game of chess, of creating openings for the opponent's pieces as it was a physical fight. Shift your guard to allow your governor to be attacked in his palace in a certain direction. Leave a space for the chariots to rush but be careful of the knights and cannons[23] that might avoid your trap.

Each motion, each gap, had to be different too, for each piece your opponent used. A trident could attack with any of its three tines. It had more

[23] The Chinese version of chess is somewhat different than the Western version of chess. It consists of seven different types of pieces, with movements of some similar (the horse/knight, chariot / rook) and some quite different (the cannon).

range and could capture blades. A jian was simpler but more agile, able to swiftly change direction and strike at any angle.

A duel was a chess match of bodies and weapons, of forms and physicality. A game of mind and body, and one that Wu Ying had joined tired, aching, his mind fogged while his opponent was fresh, his chi full. No surprise then that the first to move was Lu Ren.

A step to the left, and then again. Wu Ying idly noted his opponent fought with his left hand leading. A left-hander. That would matter to some, like wandering cultivators who had insufficient practice. To someone like Wu Ying, who'd been trained to fight with both hands, who'd faced his father either-handed, who'd met opponents in his Sect who wielded weapons in either hand, it made little difference.

Just a different board setup.

They fought, weapons seeking each other's throats. Searching for a way to win, to beat their opponent. Wu Ying moved, probing with each motion of his sword, shifting his feet to create new angles, new options. And Lu Ren, for all his mouthiness, followed Wu Ying's placements, cutting off lines of assault, his heavier weapon aiming to thrust, to cut, to break.

Arm. Leg. Sword. It didn't matter, not to the trident. Three different tines, easy to catch his weapon, easy to injure or target multiple areas.

A dozen passes, jian flicking forward, cutting, stabbing, chopping. Each attack dodged or, more often, struck aside. His weapon was of decent quality but chipped under the assault. Metal chips flew through the air as the pair dueled.

Dragon blocking the Sunset.

Chip.

Wings splayed for the Mate.

Chip.

246

Heron stalking the Marsh.

Missed.

Wu Ying's sword arm sliced across once, a push cut that left a thin line of flesh shaved off the forearm. A twist from the trident nearly tore his weapon out of his hand at the last second.

In turn, he made his opponent bleed too. Just a little. A tip slid across the top of the shoulder, skipping off the trapezius. A retraction after a block, the edge skimming against the extended thigh, damaged edges catching against folds of cloth and skin.

Deep inside, Wu Ying knew he was losing. His reaction times were down, the strikes by the trident making the already tired, slow fingers on his hand less and less responsive. His motions grew larger with each second, more energy used with each motion. His weapon continued to be chipped away, his opponent reinforcing the trident with his own chi. A chi that smelled burnt, slightly rotten. It made Wu Ying's nose scrunch up even as he fought. Another unneeded distraction.

He was losing, and no matter how much Wu Ying churned his chi, drew upon the energy within his body and the environment, he could not win. The attacks were stronger, harder than he had expected. His opponent, a higher level of cultivation. Faster. Maybe not more skilled, but it was a hair's difference.

Wu Ying could not get close, could not grapple or use other forms. The trident took away his range advantage, the butt of the weapon threatening, striking him whenever he closed in. Already, Wu Ying's shin hurt from a shaft that had caught a roundhouse kick. He had to learn a unique weapon, a unique form. And all the while, Lu Ren knew Wu Ying's tactics, knew what he would do, having studied him for six duels.

A step deep into Wu Ying's guard and a shoulder shove by Lu Ren sent Wu Ying stumbling. The trident came up within Wu Ying's guard, swinging cross-body to tear open Wu Ying's chest. A downward block, an arm reinforced with chi got in the way of the shaft before momentum could be built up.

Too little, too late.

The impact resounded through the stage. It caught the attention of all those watching. It made even the uninitiated wince. Wu Ying's hand numbed, his fingers falling open as he lost all sensation. The air flooded with the burnt chi smell as his opponent reinforced his attack at the last moment. More, much more than a simple Energy Storage cultivator should have been able to achieve.

Wu Ying retreated, instinct retracting his sword, bringing it to point at his opponent's face to buy time. His left arm hung by his side. Useless. A change in stances, angling away as he retreated.

His loss, Wu Ying knew, but you never let your guard down until the duel was truly over. He opened his mouth to call out his loss, regret and stubbornness holding his lips closed for a second as he retreated rather than speak immediately.

Too little. Too late.

Wu Ying's jaw snapped shut, words choked off. A sweeping tine nearly took off his nose. A stab sought his eyes. No taunting, no hesitation. Lu Ren rushed forward, throwing attacks again and again, even as the crowd stirred restlessly. The burnt chi smell grew stronger, choked Wu Ying in its intensity.

A slight haze formed around Lu Ren, the trident stabbing at face, chest, face, leg. Kicks targeted Wu Ying's damaged hand. Reverse shaft strikes to beat his sword aside.

Wu Ying's leg reached backward, found nothing behind it, and retracted. He froze, unable to retreat farther. Instinct kept his hands moving, his balance centered over the stage. Seconds had passed from the initial injury to his arm to his retreat. Not enough time for the audience to do much but exclaim, for his friends to move toward the stage.

Caught out, Wu Ying's sword became predictable. The trident swept in, twisted as it caught the jian, locking the blade in place. A surge of strength ripped it out of Wu Ying's hand. The tines of the trident raised to the sky. Then, it came down.

A hasty block, reinforced by both hands crossed over one another against the shaft of the weapon. Wu Ying took the attack on the Woo Petal Bracer, guarding himself even as pain from his already injured arm flared. The attack drove Wu Ying to his knees. Lu Ren flared his chi again, driving his strength to a level that Wu Ying could not match. It reminded Wu Ying of the taotai, the strength of a Core level monster. Impossible to handle as an Energy Storage cultivator.

On his knees, Wu Ying saw Lu Ren retract the weapon to thrust forward. There was no hesitation in Lu Ren's eyes. Blood lust, killing intent flowed from it, that sneer fully capturing his face. He thrust, and Wu Ying copied the action.

No sword, no defense. Instinct and epiphany mixed. Knowledge from the fights before, the manipulation of chi formed and coalesced in Wu Ying's mind. First, let the chi within his body flow, faster and more fluidly like the water chi opponent. Draw metal chi from the Bracer to form a sword. Wrap the weapon with his own chi like the crossbow bolts, give it weight like the flail, and project the attack through the Dragon's Breath. Enforce the concept with his understanding of the dao of cutting, of sharpness.

It was a single motion, a thrust with all the chi left in Wu Ying's body, a pair of fingers leading the way. The chi-created sword struck Lu Ren high in the chest, just below the trachea. The blow was blunted, the moment of enlightenment incomplete.

But sufficient.

It threw his opponent back, made his own attack go off course. A tine tore at Wu Ying's ear, making it bleed as it passed. The others missed. Lu Ren staggered back, his weapon falling, choking and breathless.

The formation around the arena flickered off. Figures flew down, a hand raised to strike Wu Ying, only to be blocked by Fa Yuan in her familiar green and grey robes. Words shouted at one another even as Wu Ying's chi-bereft body sagged, his friends clustering around him as they ascended the stage.

Then...

Enlightenment. And darkness.

***

Wu Ying came to hours later in his own room in the inn. Pain radiated from his arm, from his numerous wounds, and took his attention first and foremost. He breathed in, feeling stitches across his bare chest pull, the silk blankets he was laid under shift. Gingerly, Wu Ying clenched his fist, attempting to close it. Pain flared again, making Wu Ying's breath hitch.

"Stop that," Lei Hui's voice came, breaking across Wu Ying's self-examination. "We just finished cleaning you. If you can move, you should instead drink this." A hand offered a shallow bowl full of a brownish-grey, foul-smelling concoction.

"What happened?" Wu Ying asked as he levered himself up with his uninjured hand. He felt… good. Better than he should have. Even his arm, which still hurt, seemed to hurt less.

"You beat Lu Ren at the last moment. Do you remember your strike?" Lei Hui pushed the bowl at Wu Ying again.

The cultivator sighed but took it, draining the concoction that smelled like crushed dung ants and rotten lotus roots in one swift gulp. "Vaguely." Wu Ying breathed through his nose after pushing the bowl aside. He focused on his arm, flexing it gently rather than his mouth, where the cloying taste, bitter and crunchy, still lingered. Tea helped. A little. "It was a sword strike. Without the sword."

"You formed a sword with your chi," Lei Hui agreed. "Impressive. Mostly late Energy or Core stage cultivators can do that. Or, well, will do that. It takes a lot of chi."

Wu Ying made a face, memory flooding back. How drained he'd felt as he used up every available dreg of chi within his dantian. He still had energy left, of course. There was no way to really use it all—not without burning your life force, the stable reservoir of chi that made up one's core of their dantian. But he'd used what was available.

"How long was I out?" Wu Ying asked, probing his own energy. To his surprise, he noted the Never Empty Wine Pot cultivation exercise had been running even while he slept. It explained why he was filled, but not fully.

"Just over an hour. You don't recall what happened after?" At Wu Ying's shake of his head, Lei Hui continued. "You nearly killed Lu Ren. His Master tried to kill you in retaliation. But Elder Yang stopped him. She and, well, some other Elders blocked his rampage. Lu Ren is healing, though you nearly shattered his trachea with your attack."

Wu Ying nodded, remembering the attack. And now, glimpses of what Lei Hui said. But his memory was filled with something else. A warm glow, a rush of chi, a sense of peace. A sharp smell, of burning metal and the scent of a freshly oiled sword. Understanding, grasped.

"You remember," Lei Hui stated.

Wu Ying looked up, hearing the tinge of jealousy in the apothecarist's voice. "Enlightenment."

"Yes. What did you—" Lei Hui stopped, shook his head. "Never mind. Forget I asked."

"No, it's fine," Wu Ying said. It was impolite to ask about others' enlightenment. After all, it was a personal thing. But Wu Ying could understand Lei Hui's point. Gaining enlightenment always jumped one's cultivation, made it easier. The more you had, the easier it was to progress. And to step into the final stage, to gain immortality, you needed sufficient enlightenment. "It was about the nature of chi. Of the elements. Of sharpness and cutting. When you put them together when you wield each element…"

He trailed off, then stopped. He tried again, attempting to find the right words to explain the glimpse he had of reality, of the Dao. "It's all the same, but separate. You must weave them together but keep them separate. But it can't be separate, right?"

Lei Hui raised a hand, stopping Wu Ying. "Enough. You've tried. But I'm just getting more confused. Some understanding cannot be explained. Only experienced." Lei Hui's eyes crinkled a little. "Or you could just be bad at explaining."

"Maybe. Sorry."

"No need."

"Where are the others?" Wu Ying asked even as he forced himself to his feet.

Lei Hui frowned as Wu Ying pulled out new peasant robes of hemp to put on. After all, his other Sect robes were damaged. All but a single pair left, and he was not going to get those messed up.

"Dealing with the aftermath. Yu Kun was dealing with the cultivators and our bets. There were some disputes if you won or Lu Ren." At Wu Ying's frown, he shrugged. "Your last blow was lethal. And he had already injured your hand. Had you on the ground. If he'd stopped…"

"I would have lost," Wu Ying said. If he had stopped, Wu Ying would have given up.

"Tou He is helping him, while Wang Min is accompanying Elder Yang. She is dealing with Lu Ren and the attack."

Wu Ying winced. "Do you know why he tried to kill me?"

Lei Hui shrugged. "Elder Yang might know better. But I've been here."

At Lei Hui's insistence, Wu Ying took a seat once more on his bed and cultivated, reinforcing both his understanding of the enlightenment that he had failed to explain and the chi within his body. There was little left to do until the others returned.

***

Late that night, Yu Kun and Tou He finally returned, glowing triumphantly. Wu Ying had stopped for a short while to drink and eat with the others before returning to his bed to cultivate. The hard rosewood bed was spacious and comfortable, and in his room, he had peace to contemplate the day. Neither of his friends had much to report, only able to confirm they'd managed to deal with the bets and keep their share of the fees. A small fortune for them all to split.

Of course, the plan had revolved around the bet. They knew Tou He might lose, but it would give them the opportunity to make the bets bigger, to earn more both betting on Wu Ying himself and in the management of the bets. It earned them funds without much risk. At least, that had been the plan.

But more importantly, Elder Yang would do the same above. Where the real fortunes would change hands, where she could make wagers with the Elders of other sects. Gain additional help, taels, or spirit cores. She was the linchpin…

Or meant to be.

But she had not returned, even after supper. And so, Wu Ying cultivated. Patience, instilled by years of cultivation, left him seated on his bed, breathing in the fresh night air as wind blew from the rivers to him. Letting him heal slowly.

A presence slowly intruded on his mind and drew him out of his cultivation. He looked up to see the Elder seated across from him, holding his damaged jian. She was idly sharpening the weapon, working out chips with a whetstone on a side table set between them.

"Another moment of enlightenment," Fa Yuan said, a half-smile on her face. "I do envy you. To be so young again."

Wu Ying greeted her, bowing from his seated position. "I've been lucky. And received much guidance."

"Mmm… yes. Wise guidance," Fa Yuan said, taking her hand off the weapon to place against her chest. "You might make it to the Core stage, if you keep it up." Wu Ying raised an eyebrow and she shrugged. "Many stall at the late Energy Storage stage. More and more chi is required for each breakthrough. Each blockage requires greater force behind it. Even normal cultivation might be insufficient.

"Enlightenment deepens the pool, allowing one to force more chi into the blockage. Enlightenment itself makes the dantian larger or denser. Makes the chi within one's veins thicker."

"Or?" Wu Ying said as he uncrossed his legs. He moved gingerly, making sure he had not frozen his feet. Ever since he passed the Body Cleansing stage, it never happened, but old habits died hard.

"Or. Or it might do something else." Fa Yuan shrugged. "It varies for each person. Each enlightenment."

"Oh," Wu Ying said. "And you had many of these?"

"Almost all Core cultivators do. Enlightenment in the early stages is easy," Fa Yuan said. "You grasp at small facets of the world, peer through the gaps in the walls and see something that you feel is important. It is," she clarified before Wu Ying could object. "But later on, those small gaps are insufficient, nothing more than a brief blink in your understanding of the Dao. As you progress, your understanding must be more than a small thing. The field that feeds your body must be larger."

Wu Ying considered her words. In the silence, Fa Yuan returned to sharpening the sword. Eventually, Wu Ying blinked, glanced at the sword and his martial sister before deciding against objecting. If it amused her, who was he to say anything? And while it was an intimate act, it was not wrong. She was his martial sister after all.

"About Lu Ren..." Wu Ying said. "His Master..."

"Tried to kill you. Or cripple you at the least," Fa Yuan replied, her voice hinting at the anger she kept contained. "We stopped him. But they are refusing to honor their agreement on the bet. Saying you cheated. As if enlightenment could ever be a cheat."

Wu Ying winced at the acid in her statements. Still, he could not help but ask, "Why?"

"Did you smell it?"

"Huh?"

"Their chi," Fa Yuan said. "I know Master taught you his smelling chi exercise. Did you smell Lu Ren's chi?"

"Yes. It was impossible to miss," Wu Ying said.

"Then that is your answer." Fa Yuan placed the sword on the table. "Finish caring for your weapon. And maybe buy a proper one at the auction." She walked to the door, leaving Wu Ying still puzzling over her answer. "Cultivate well."

Wu Ying picked up the sword when she left, leaving him alone late in the night. He blinked, realizing how scandalous it might seem to others, and was grateful that no one would know. Still, as he sharpened his sword, he turned over her answer in his mind. Her answer, and the smell. Where...?

A hint, a memory. Of when he'd learned the chi smelling exercise with his Master. The smell coming from Elder Cheng himself, soaking his sweat. Burnt wood, soiled earth. Something wrong, something sickened.

Eyes wide, Wu Ying froze. The hiss of his sword sliding against the whetstone paused as conclusions were drawn. He exhaled hard and started the process of readying his weapon. He would need it.

Then he paused as he found his hands trembling on the whetstone, on his blade.

It seemed their enemies were not going to let them just act without interference.

Chapter 23

Four days passed in a blur as Wu Ying stayed at the inn and cultivated. He reinforced the gains he had achieved, practiced his form, and tried to grasp the entirety of the moment of enlightenment he had achieved during the sparring match. In between, he occasionally left their residence to enjoy the city with his friend Zhong Shei. However, unlike their earlier escapades, they were always accompanied by at least one other cultivator.

In fact, none of the Verdant Green Waters Sect cultivators were allowed to travel by themselves—with their obvious exception of Fairy Yang. The restriction on their activities grated upon the other cultivators, especially as Elder Yang and Wu Ying would not explain their reasoning. Better to let them assume it was to reduce trouble with the other sects and wandering cultivators than to think that the pair were jumping at children's stories. One was a plausible explanation, the other just eroded trust.

Only to Tou He did Wu Ying tell the truth. As usual, the amicable ex–monk but hummed a little before nodding in acceptance. When asked why he did not seem surprised, Tou He explained himself with a single Amitabha.

In this way, the four days between Wu Ying's fight and the auction passed in a blur. Yu Kun and Wang Min partook of the dueling rings in the interim period, but they only earned a little more. After the initial burst of wagering, the cultivators had grown wary of additional losses, especially as the auction grew closer.

On the day of the auction, Wu Ying and the team walked to the auction house in a group. The auction itself was held in a large hall, most commonly used for opera and musical performances and the occasional dining festivity. The building was located to the east of the magistrate's residence, close to where the affluent merchants resided and where the breeze from the conjoined rivers constantly blew, providing relief from mosquitos and summer heat in equal order.

The outside of the building was relatively bare, the large two-story wooden building's exterior painted white. Across the front and along the eaves of the windows, red silk drapes hung, giving the hall a festive air. Large banner scrolls were placed on either side of the main doors, announcing the auction to one and all.

A large crowd had gathered around the hall—mostly commoners in the lower ranks of Body Cleansing cultivation and their children. They milled about, pointing and murmuring words of awe and wonder as they spotted the cultivators who entered the building.

As Wu Ying walked through the crowd with his friends, he overheard the conversations all about him.

"Look at him, Mama. He's got such a great big beard!"

"Who's the red-faced man? Is that bandit Cho?"

"I think so. But he's not a bandit anymore, so don't use that title. He's in the middle stages of Energy Storage and could squash us like bugs!"

"Is that the Blistering Axes? I hear their men are really manly. If you know what I mean..."

"Ah Liu!"

"It's true!"

"Look at that sword, I bet it's enchanted."

"That's the Eight Flower Spear. I hear it was given to Elder Gan's direct disciple. What was his name... Li? Lee? Liu?"

As they made their way deeper into the crowd, a silence fell over the nearby individuals as they caught sight of Fairy Yang. They would stare, many men not even daring to breathe as they drank in the rare beauty among them. Yet none of them dared to make a move, the subtle hint of her killing intent, the pressure from her aura denying any crass action at the pain of death.

In this silence and a slowly growing murmur behind their backs, Wu Ying and the expedition entered the auction hall. Guards, including a familiar face, stood before the main entrances, checking invitations before allowing the cultivators within. Fairy Yang, who proffered her invitation, was waved in without hesitation, Zhong Shei not even bothering to glance at her invitation.

"Elder Yang, your booth will be on the second floor." Zhong Shei gestured within, glancing at the crowd and at Wu Ying before he continued. "I can send one of my men to show you the way, if you wish."

"You wouldn't want to do it yourself?" Fa Yuan said, her voice dropping in register and growing husky. Wu Ying could almost swear that she batted her eyelashes at his friend.

Zhong Shei gulped, straightened his back, and shook his head. "I would be honored. But I have my duty." He turned and looked at the other guards, spotting how each of them was silently vying for the honor and privilege of spending more time with the Elder. "Senior guard Yun could show you the way."

Wu Ying's lips twitched, for the female guard called upon beamed.

Unfortunately, her interest was crushed moments later as Fa Yuan spoke. "It is fine. I know my way there."

Having said her piece, Fa Yuan swept through the room, leaving Wu Ying and company to hurry after. He could only cast one last glance back at his friend to glimpse Zhong Shei wiping his face as he consoled the unlucky female guard.

A few quick steps took Wu Ying toward his martial sister's side, allowing him to speak with her and still stay half a step behind as was proper. "Why did you tease Zhong Shei?"

"Perhaps I was interested in him?" Fa Yuan said. At Wu Ying's narrowing of his eyes, she smiled. "I was curious to see the kind of man you had made friends with."

"Oh."

They ascended the wooden stairs and turned down the hallway. He absently offered bows and greetings to the various Elders they passed, mimicking his fellow cultivators.

It was only when they stepped into their private room that Wu Ying asked, "And what did you think?"

In reply, Fa Yuan smiled.

Wu Ying sighed, knowing his martial sister was unlikely to answer him. She got into these moods at times, when she tried to play enigmatic teacher and came off as an annoying older sister instead. Or perhaps that was what she was going for. It wasn't as if he had an older sister to compare to. Rather than pursue the matter, he surveyed their room.

The viewing box that extended from the room was not large, with barely enough space to cram in the half dozen chairs required to fit all the members of the Verdant Green Waters Sect. Soft curtains and a single painting of a standing white crane added to the ambience of the room, while the lone table hosted a tea set, the rising steam from the pot of water indicating its recent addition to the room.

Tou He moved toward the tea set, beginning his practice and brewing the provided refreshment. The only other mildly amusing addition was the set of placards in the room to indicate the auction number they had been allocated.

Moving toward the balcony, Wu Ying looked at the hall below. Even a half hour before the auction was scheduled to begin, the hall was teaming with cultivators. A push of his senses allowed Wu Ying to sense the widely mixed chi below. Too much chi, too many overlapping auras hid everything from his senses at first. There was no way for him to pick out individuals. Not easily. So he settled for trying to spot faces that he knew.

Individuals moved around the hard benches that ringed the stage, offering seating on the ground floor for the majority. Most of those below were wandering cultivators and the smaller sects unable to acquire one of the limited viewing boxes on the second floor. To Wu Ying's left, a mezzanine floor provided additional seating for the poor and the curious, while independent viewing boxes, set on the second floor and separated by wooden walls and silk curtains, gave the Sect Elders privacy and a view of the auction itself.

"Do you see them?" Fa Yuan said to Wu Ying as she joined him at the edge of the balcony. With practiced ease, she ignored the pointed fingers, the inclined heads that turned toward their box at her appearance.

"Who?" Then Wu Ying finally turned his head to view the viewing boxes directly opposite them. He spotted his assailants, the members of the Heavenly Lake Sect. The Elder was looking at them, glaring at the pair with undisguised distaste. "Do you expect problems?"

"Problems? Certainly. Violence? No," Fa Yuan said. She tapped her finger against the wooden bannister, long nails drumming slightly in nervousness. "But it is always worthwhile paying attention. Trouble can arise from directions you least expect."

Taking his martial sister's words to heart, Wu Ying turned his gaze away from the known problems to continue searching for others that might cause issues. More than once, he spotted cultivators staring at them, regarding their box with jealousy, lust, or avarice. But he also spotted a number of guards from the auction house and the city guards. A few minutes before the auction was to begin, even Zhong Shei arrived, standing at the back doors as they closed.

The chime of a small metal gong, set just below the stage, drew the attention of the crowd. It signaled the imminent start of the auction and cultivators hurried to take their seats. A couple of brief scuffles broke out between wandering cultivators as they attempted to acquire the same resting spot. They were dealt with by the guards via harsh words and threats of being rejected.

The second chime indicated the true start of the auction. From the back of the stage, an older man walked out, flanked by two stout and muscular individuals. Rather than the long, coiled hair of the people of Wei, these were northerners who had shorn their hair to their shoulders and woven it into a single knot. Both wore metal scalemail armor, and each held a large, unsheathed sword.

For all their visible menace, it was the older man Wu Ying paid attention to. Instinct had Wu Ying focus his senses on him, searching for a reading. In a few seconds, he leaned over to speak to his martial sister. "I cannot sense his aura at all."

"True."

From that simple answer, Wu Ying drew a rather dire prediction. That old man, with his long white whiskers and simple brown and black robes, was at least at the top end of Core cultivation. More than that, as Wu Ying stared at him, he noted how the old man was perfectly balanced, how he'd automatically spread his weight across both feet, and his gaze rested on the crowd with simple assurance. He had no fear of potential violence. At least, not violence conducted against him.

It would take true bravado to launch an attack here. While most of the auction house guards were at the upper ends of Body Cleansing, there were a few Energy Storage cultivators. And deeper in the building, Wu Ying could feel the quiet, steady strength of at least another Core cultivator. Perhaps two. As he watched the back curtains, his eyes widened as he noted the magistrate's daughter peeking out, her eyes sweeping over the crowd before she stepped back behind the curtain.

"August personages and great Elders, I would like to extend Magistrate Song's and my gratitude for your attendance at the first spirit cultivation auction of Hinma. As you may know, the midlands of the State of Shen have long been missing such a gathering, and it was only with the wisdom and bravery of the magistrate that this matter was viable." The old man's voice carried to the far reaches of the auction hall with ease.

Wu Ying felt the slight vibrations in the air, the way the old man had sent his chi into the environment to carry his words to everyone in equal measure. Another chi projection trick, one that Wu Ying had yet to learn. Useful though...

"I am Hall Master Li, of the Most Auspicious Grey Heavens Auction House. Any issues with the auction and the way we run the proceedings can be brought to myself at the end of the auction. Any violence will see the participants rejected. All bids must be paid immediately or as otherwise arranged with the magistrate and myself." He paused, sweeping his gaze over the crowd. "Are there any questions?"

When the crowd only returned silence, the old man smiled. "Then let us begin. We start this auction with the very first lot, a trio of Tiger Blood Amber. The contents of the amber have been verified to contain the blood of a primeval Metal Tiger, caught in the prime of his life. Mixed with the right alchemical potions, the Tiger Blood Amber can enhance the physical robustness of an individual and his reflexes. Obviously it is best suited for a metal cultivator, with those in adjoining elements able to gain some degree of benefit."

A susurration of sound grew from below as Elders and cultivators stared at the three amber blocks. Wu Ying wondered how droplets of such blood could occur, what events had led to the spirit beast's death. How long those droplets had been suspended. A primeval creature was one from the times of the Yellow Emperor at the very least, or maybe even older. That would make it thousands of years old, with blood and potency greater than any present-day animal.

"Bidding on a single amber will begin at fifteen spirit stones at the Core cultivation stage." The old man declared the opening bid casually, but the sudden hisses and exclamations from the crowd told Wu Ying exactly how high the opening bid was.

He definitely could not even hope to join the initial bidding, no matter how much he had earned through their machinations and betting. Before they had arrived at the auction hall, Yu Kun had provided Wu Ying his share of their earnings, more than quadrupling his current wealth. But compared to the asking price for a single amber piece, he was but a penniless vagrant.

"Fifteen," the elder opposite Wu Ying, from the Heavenly Jade Lake Sect, cried out his bid.

Even before the echoes of his words had ended, another voice called from the back of the hall, "Sixteen."

Bids erupted then, as if a dam had broken. The price rose at an intemperate rate. Wu Ying's eyes continually widened as fortunes that could buy and sell his village—including the people within—were offered. A hand landed on his before withdrawing.

"Breathe." Fa Yuan said, her lips turning up into a sardonic smile. "And lean back. We are not bidding on any of these."

Wu Ying could only comply stiffly before whispering, "Is it that good?"

"With the right apothecarist? Yes," Lei Hui replied, his lips curled up in a sneer at Wu Ying's ignorance. The apothecarist kept darting glances at the stage where the box of amber stood open, held by one of the female stage attendants. "A single amber could improve the strength of a Core cultivator. If all three were taken together, maybe even a Nascent Soul Elder."

Wu Ying sighed and fell silent as the numbers kept climbing. In the end, it was the Elder of the Heavenly Lake Sect who won two of the three ambers and a wandering cultivator the third. The moment he had won the third amber, the wandering cultivator made his way to the corner, where he paid for and received his prize, before exiting the building.

"He looks worried," Tou He muttered, inclining his head at the wandering cultivator who had left.

"It is not common, but banditry and theft do happen at such events," Fa Yuan said. "If he only came here for this, he is better to leave now. That forces potential assailants to choose to attack him and leave the auction now or wait to see what else might turn up."

Wu Ying nodded. Most of the auction items had been made known to the general public, but the magistrate and the Auction Hall leader had made sure to keep some of the contents of the auction—the most powerful, the most expensive, or the most in demand—hidden to build anticipation and reduce issues. It was why being provided the list in full earlier was both a sign of trust and respect.

Wu Ying watched the man leave until his attention was drawn to the stage again when the auctioneer announced the next item, the attendant walking back and forth with the sword resting across her arms, the scabbard set beside it.

"The Wavering Water Sword was made by the famed Blacksmith 'Iron Foot' Teoh during the sixth year of his mastership of the flame. Made using water steel, the blade was further enchanted using metal chi during its processing, and an additional, unrecorded alloy was added," Hall Master Li announced.

At his gesture, the young lady walked to a small stand where multiple bars of iron had been placed. Wu Ying watched with interest as she pushed a small amount of chi through the blade she held one-handed. It hummed, and the wave-like marks on the blade glowed. Even from his seat, Wu Ying could feel the metal chi that the blade now emanated. He unconsciously licked his lips as the woman swung at the iron bars and sliced through them as though they were tofu.

"Good blade," Wu Ying whispered, staring at the simple straight jian. He wished he could hold it, see if it suited itself to him. But with his Sense of the Sword, he could make it work even if it was marginally longer or shorter than his preference. It was part of the benefits of understanding a weapon to that degree.

When Hall Master Li judged the silence was ripe, he spoke again. "As you can see, this is a high Spirit level weapon. While not unique, many of the weapons created by Blacksmith Iron Foot have been lost to time. They would serve both collectors and wielders in equal measure. Bidding will begin at one Core-level spirit core."

Wu Ying's eyebrows flashed up, surprise catching him off guard. He found himself raising his auction paddle, as greed—and his minor flush of funds—drew him. But even before he could be acknowledged, wandering cultivators in the hall below had shouted out their bids. In short order, the bid had breached four Core-level spirit cores and Wu Ying brought his hand down, folding it in front of him.

"You were never going to win it," Fa Yuan said in commiseration to Wu Ying. "He started the bidding low to create interest. It will be a while before weapons that fit your purse arrive."

Wu Ying grunted, folding his hands in front of him in pique. He could not help but feel angry at having the weapon taken away so quickly. Yet it was no one's fault but his own that he was that poor. Both Fa Yuan and his Master had warned him that his actions last year, of moving the village, would have consequences. And this was but one of them.

He sighed, dismissing the concerns and watched the auction below, idly feeling at his pouch. Perhaps if the herbs he had gathered finished selling early on in the other vending hall, he would be able to pick up something here. A brief tour of the other hall had shown most of the items in the high mortal tier of quality, meaning that they had little interest for the inner sect cultivators. Even if they did for a large number of other wandering cultivators.

Better to wait and watch. And hope that the others spent their funds fast.

***

Hours later, Wu Ying shifted on his hard rosewood seat once again. Below, the excitement had died down as hours passed and items trended toward the mundane. Among the group, Yu Kun and Lei Hui had purchased items, Yu Kun picking up a scroll of a new water cultivation exercise while Lei Hui had purchased a variety of herbs and pill materials. Of them all, it was Tou He who was the most bored, seating himself in the back with his legs crossed, cultivating as the drone of the auctioneer's voice continued.

"Twenty-seven tael and three Energy Storage demon cores. Current bid," the Hall Master called. "If there are no further bids"—a pause—"then the cultivator from the Crane Boneyard has won the Gold Flame Bone Spear."

Scattered applause met Hall Master Li's announcement while the inner sect cultivator jumped to his feet in excitement. He rushed out from the benches, tripping on his robes and nearly face-planting, drawing laughter. However, instead of being embarrassed, the man kept moving, his eyes fixed on his prize.

With practiced eye, the Hall Master gauged the crowd's enthusiasm before he clapped his hands. "This brings to an end the first portion of the auction. We will begin the auction again in an hour, after repast has been taken. For those who have not collected their purchases, we request that you do so now. Our attendants are awaiting your presence."

The Hall Master nodded to the side where multiple attendants stood, their hands clasped while the magistrate's daughter, watched over them all. The Hall Master walked to the back of the stage, where he was met by his assistants. He spoke with them while the magistrate, seated near the front of the hall, hurried onto the stage to join the conversation. Around the hall, voices rose as cultivators congratulated the winners and commiserated with the losers, all the while streaming out of the building to find lunch.

"Come. I have a room booked for us at a nearby restaurant." Fa Yuan rose from her seat, smoothing her robes. She swept her gaze over the milling crowd below. "Let us take the side exit."

The group followed the Elder, only to find themselves stymied in the corridor by the presence of other auction attendees. Immediately, one of the younger Elders swept forward to Fa Yuan's side.

"Fairy Yang." He offered a low bow. "You might not remember me. We met two nights ago? I am Elder Kho Yun Er of the Three Springs Vista Sect."

Fa Yuan turned, offering a small bow in return. "I do remember you, Elder Kho."

Wu Ying snorted slightly as the man flushed in pleasure at her acknowledgement. Wu Ying raked his gaze over the man, noting the long, thin limbs, pointed chin, and slightly longer than handsome nose. Still, he had beautiful pale skin and there was a fluidity to his movement that spoke of his sect's preoccupation with water chi. Overall, a decent-looking suitor.

"Would the Elder grace us with her presence at lunch? We have a room booked in a nearby restaurant," Elder Kho said, gesturing back to the waiting sect members.

"I'm sorry, but we have prior reservations," Fa Yuan gracefully answered.

"Ah, it's a pity. The Pink Pearl restaurant is well known for its twice-boiled peach wine chicken, and we ordered a triple serving of their chicken butts[24]," Elder Kho said.

Fa Yuan hesitated, and Wang Min, standing beside her, tilted her head at Elder Kho. Wu Ying had to admire the man's shamelessness. Never mind the expensive dish; the triple serving of the delicacy—known to help make the skin smoother and paler—was a blatant ploy at Fa Yuan's known weakness.

"Go," Yu Kun spoke up. "We can go to the restaurant ourselves."

Still, the Elder hesitated and Elder Kho threw out his last bait. "We did purchase the Liu Valley Yin Spring tea leaves at the auction and wanted

---

[24] Yes, this is real. You'd be surprised the kind of fights that occur around the dinner table on who gets to eat the (cleaned) chicken tail (basically, the butt which is fleshy and fatty).

your—and your sect member's—opinion on its potency." Elder Kho tilted his head toward Wang Min, offering the female cultivator an enticing smile. "It is supposedly quite effective at the Energy Storage stage."

Fa Yuan glanced at Wu Ying one last time and he made a small gesture, shooing her off. Turning to Elder Kho, Fa Yuan acceded to his request and the pair headed down the corridor, the Elder already trying to ingratiate himself with her further as he discussed the auction.

Tou He looked at the departing group before grumbling, "I'm the tea practitioner here."

"But you're not very pretty," Yu Kun replied.

Bemused, Wu Ying watched the group troop off. Hopefully the Yin Spring tea leaves would do as promised and help Wang Min and Fa Yuan further improve the clarity of the chi that flowed through their veins.

"So… does anyone know where this restaurant that Elder Yang booked is?" Lei Hui asked after a moment.

"Hun dan!" Wu Ying cursed and smacked himself on the forehead.

Chapter 24

"You're late," Elder Yang rebuked Wu Ying and his friends as they hurried back into their private auction room after lunch.

As Wu Ying slid into his seat, he glanced down at the auction hall, noting that the room itself was still as packed as the morning. That was no surprise, since Wu Ying had noted how winners from the morning who had purchased what they needed had sold their invitation tokens to those waiting outside. The auction house had turned a blind eye to those proceedings, wanting to keep the seats filled no matter what.

As Wu Ying turned his attention to the stage, he noted that the starting item of the afternoon session was once again a rather expensive item. What anyone would want with the lacquer shadow puppet box, Wu Ying did not know. Sure, it created shadow illusions that could be used to protect a building, and with enough chi it could even form shadow warriors, but the expense involved would easily pay for a half-dozen strong Body Cleansing cultivators to do the same job for the next twenty years.

"My apologies, martial sister. You forgot to inform us of which restaurant you had booked. We had to visit nearly half of those around before we found it," Wu Ying replied.

Once they'd realized their mistake, the group had scrambled down the stairs but had been too late to catch Fa Yuan. Rather than bother her, they'd decided to visit each restaurant around the auction house to locate the reservation. Unfortunately, between the crowds and the business of the dining establishments, it had taken them longer than they had expected to find their room. Even rushing through lunch had not let them return on time.

"Ah…" Fa Yuan raised a hand to her nose, her long sleeve covering her mouth. "Well, it is good you found it. You'll need your energy for this next part."

Wu Ying's eyes narrowed in suspicion, but not being able to see behind her sleeve, dismissed his concerns. "Did you have a good meal?"

"Definitely!" Wang Min said, literally vibrating in her seat. "They were so kind to us. And the Yin Spring tea leaves were very potent."

"I can see that," Yu Kun said sardonically. "Though I would have thought the Yin chi would have calmed you."

"It will," Fa Yuan replied. "She is but expelling surplus Yang chi."

"Ah," Yu Kun replied, eyeing the jittery cultivator. "Well, that's good."

"Hush," Lei Hui snapped as the auction below came to an end and another item was brought forth.

Wu Ying sighed, seeing it was an onyx jewel. Beautiful, but useful only to the craftsmen in the audience. Shaking his head, Wu Ying settled himself in for a long few hours.

Swords, maces, apothecarist cauldrons, rare metals and chiseled spirit stones, talismans and formation flags, even manuals and cultivation exercises all showed up, one after the other. The drone of the auctioneer's voice became a pleasant background noise, the hubbub from below fading in Wu Ying's consciousness as wandering cultivators warred with sect members over the items.

Anything in demand by craftsmen went for relatively high prices. Apothecarist items sold for the most, followed by metals and hammers and other instruments for blacksmiths. For secondary occupations outside of those two— such as the formation flags and talisman masters—had the materials they needed sold at a lower price. It was a clear indication of importance and wealth of the various secondary occupations. To Wu Ying's amusement and disappointment, there wasn't a single set of seeds or book of herbs insight. Such items were specialty purchases, unlikely to draw a bidding war in an auction.

Somewhere in the middle of the afternoon, one of the attendants arrived in their room, bringing Wu Ying's earnings from the sale of his herbs in the other hall. He collected the purse filled with gold taels, unrolling the short parchment paper that listed his sales, and smiled. Even if he did not earn much per individual sale, the ability to gather large numbers of herbs and care for them to ensure their quality meant that he'd made up in bulk for his earnings. In time, he might sell some of his gathered herbs directly at the auction hall, but first, he'd have to level up his gathering skills. And, of course, locate some rarer herbs.

"Next, we have a living world spirit ring. This ring was created by famed formation master and blacksmith Er Hu and will allow the deposit of living materials within. The living world within encompasses a thirty-foot by twenty-foot area. The ground within has been thoroughly drained of nutrition, but under the care of a proficient spirit gardener, the ring will return to full functionality."

Wu Ying frowned, turning his head and speaking to Fa Yuan. "Why would they put this on an auction? Few could make full use of this spirit ring."

Fa Yuan gestured down to the stage, where the Hall Master had finished announcing the low starting bid for the ring. To Wu Ying's surprise, rather than sitting in significant silence, the wandering cultivators below had begun a fierce bidding war, raising the price twice and three times over.

"Eight Energy Storage spirit stones," a wandering cultivator snapped, turning around and glaring at a shorter individual clad in dirty rags who had been bidding against him.

"Nine," his competitor said.

Wu Ying kept one ear on the bidding below while he ran estimates of the funds he had. The sale of the herbs had netted just over one hundred sixty taels. His portion of the demon and spirit beast cores they'd sold—animals killed while they had traveled through the wildlands—had added another thirty-three tael. Unfortunately, it had been mostly demonic beasts they'd fought, since the smarter spirit beasts had avoided their party with Fa Yuan present.

It was the won wagers that made up the bulk of his fortune, increasing his total funds to just under a thousand one hundred taels. From the various wagers, they'd managed to acquire spirit stones, manuals, and other unnecessary items, which they'd sold and converted into taels and, in a few cases, intermediate-sized spirit stones. Those intermediate-sized stones were being used as currency, with the value of an Energy Storage spirit stone considered to be between twenty-five to thirty taels. In this case, the auction house was valuing such stones at twenty-five tael. They were willing to convert stones for taels and vice versa, having already published the conversion rates for all to see.

It was, of course, disadvantageous to do such a conversion through the auction house, but it did give Wu Ying a way to enter the auction and the value of the bids at the moment.

"Rubbish. You wandering cultivators should just go home if that is all you can afford," a voice called from a balcony box. A young woman snorted at those below before turning to the Hall Master. "One Core spirit stone."

Rather than being the ostentatious display of wealth she expected, her words caused an eruption of laughter among the wandering cultivators. A single Core spirit stone was valued at three hundred tael, or twelve Energy Storage spirit stones, so her bid was only a marginal increase.

"Did you mean to say Nascent Soul?" the vagabond said, taunting her. "Because if it was Core spirit stones, I have one too!" He reached into his pouch and pulled out a stone, waving it. This one was jagged and slightly off-kilter, glowing a cool and pale blue-white, reminding Wu Ying of fluffy clouds on a clear spring day. "And this one is from the White Cloud Fox."

At his words, the Hall Master gestured. An attendant hurried over, taking the Core spirit stone and bringing it back to be evaluated. One of the senior attendants peered at the stone, flushing chi into it before he looked at the Hall Master. He flashed a quick series of hand signs before the Hall Master spoke, ignoring the woman who vibrated with anger at being shown up so publicly.

"It is confirmed. As a rare spirit stone from the White Cloud Fox, we shall value it at five hundred taels. If that is suitable?" He raised a single eyebrow at the owner.

The vagabond frowned deeply, but when he glanced upward at the gloating woman, he nodded. In short order, the bidding started again at the much higher value, while Wu Ying bit his lip, debating joining the bidding. He needed one such ring, but already, the bidding was worth two-thirds of his fortune. If he purchased it, he would have no funds to purchase a weapon.

The ring could earn him funds in the future. But a strong weapon could save his life. Chewing on his lip, Wu Ying listened to the bidding as first one then another bidder dropped out. The sect cultivator stayed in stubbornly, though from his vantage point, he could see her making pleas for funds from her various sect mates. Below, the vagabond cultivator that Wu Ying had realized was another gatherer like him fiddled with his storage ring and rubbed the dirt on his hands as the bidding crested the equivalent of eight hundred taels.

"Two regular intermediate Cores, nine Energy Storage spirit stones," intoned the Hall Master. "Do we have further bids?"

"Are you going to bid?" Tou He asked Wu Ying, leaning forward between the seats to speak. His sudden appearance made Wu Ying jump a little in surprise.

"I don't know... I need a sword."

"You have a sword. In fact, you have a few."

"It's not a *good* sword," Wu Ying pointed out. "None of them are."

"Every weapon is a good weapon in the right hands. Is that not what you realized? That the Dao can cut if given the right impetus?" Tou He said.

Wu Ying opened then shut his mouth. It wasn't just that idea of course—his epiphany had included more. Still, there was truth there too. A blade was sharp, because he could will his chi to be sharp. He could make it stronger, tougher, with his own energy and understanding of the Dao. But his understanding was a small dao at best, a tiny shard of enlightenment. Still, perhaps it too could be sharpened if he continued to rely on what was, in effect, a blunted blade compared to the dao.

When he cast a glance at his martial sister, seeking reassurance, she just offered him an enigmatic half-smile. As if she expected him to make his own decision.

"Congra—"

"Eight hundred fifty taels," Wu Ying interrupted the Hall Master.

The vagabond frowned, doing the math quickly before he shook his head. "Nine hundred tael then!"

"One thousand," Wu Ying replied. Hopefully, that would drive out the vagabond. He hoped so, because that was nearly all his new fortune.

From his position, Wu Ying watched the way the wandering cultivator clutched at his hands, trying not to tremble and shame himself. "One thousand taels too. But I'll trade my White Cloud Fox core and another intermediate Core and make the rest up with taels."

Wu Ying moved to protest, but Fa Yuan interrupted him by shaking her head. "Let the Hall Master verify with the owner. This is normal, for some items are more in demand than cash."

Grimacing, Wu Ying could only subside. He had a little funds—ha! A few years ago, it would be a fortune—but he was uncertain if it mattered. All he could do was wait. The Hall Master's lips moved as he sent his words straight through the hall to the owner of the ring. Even as Wu Ying stretched his senses to work out who it was, he failed to do so.

A short conversation later, the Hall Master looked back at Wu Ying and the vagabond cultivator. "Thank you for your patience. The spirit ring will be sold to the honored member from the Verdant Green Waters Sect, unless the honored wandering cultivator would be willing to raise his bid further?"

At the cultivator's shake of his head, the Hall Master swept his gaze over the room one last time to ensure no one else had a bid.

"Congratulations," Tou He murmured.

"Yeah…" Wu Ying said. He touched his full purse, mentally wincing at his sudden plummet from fortune. So easy to be rich, then poor. Now, there was only the spirit stone of the Ben that they had to worry about.

***

It amused Wu Ying a little, as he fiddled with his new living world spirit ring, how some cores—from common beasts—were used as currency, and in other cases, like the Ben's Spirit Stone, were an auction item. The difference in rarity, the difference in uses in an apothecarist's recipes or as a central aspect of a formation made such a difference.

"Fourteen Core spirit stones," Fa Yuan called, shooting a glare at her competitors.

To Wu Ying's lack of surprise, their main competitor for the Ben's spirit stone was Lu Ren's master from the Heavenly Lake Sect.

"Fifteen."

"Sixteen," Fa Yuan snapped.

"Seventeen," Lu Ren's master replied without hesitation.

Wu Ying watched the pair go at it, neither even looking at the Hall Master below to acknowledge their bids. Their eyes were focused on one another, as if daring their opponent to step back. Each rebuttal raised the price to eyebrow-raising levels, but none more so when Fa Yuan spoke next.

"One"—as Lu Ren began to smirk, she continued—"Nascent Soul spirit stone."

Silence filled the hall before the Hall Master spoke. "Elder Yang, while I do not wish to besmirch the good name of the Verdant Green Waters Sect—"

"Catch." Fa Yuan tossed the pouch to the Hall Master without a care, the leather container flying unerringly at the Hall Master. He caught the pouch then peeled the inscrolled leather purse open to stare at its contents.

The spirit stone within was not particularly large, no more than a small fist's size. Yet it glowed with an internal strength that caught the entire hall's attention. Everyone stared at the spirit stone as it pulsed with a soft, gentle yellow light. As Wu Ying stared at it, he could almost swear he saw the image of a burning bird within.

"A Two-Tail Fire Crane, slain when it attempted to challenge the Sect's borders twenty-four years ago," Fa Yuan announced. "I was there."

Below, more than one cultivator stared at the object with lust. Using such a spirit stone in their cultivation, even unenhanced by a pill or potion, could cut years off a cultivator's journey. The Dao secrets held within, especially for a fire cultivator...

Wu Ying glanced back, only to find Tou He still seated calmly, meditating. His fingers continued to pull at the prayer beads, counting them one after the other as he cultivated. Wu Ying's lips quirked in amusement as his friend ignored the treasure before them all for his own internal world.

"Confirmed," the Hall Master murmured. Whatever he had done to confirm its authenticity, Wu Ying had not noticed the chi fluctuations, reaffirming his belief that the Hall Master must have been at Core cultivation at the least. Otherwise, his control of chi couldn't be so precise and controlled. "The bid stands at one Nascent Soul spirit core."

Sneering, the Heavenly Lake Sect elder spoke. "Did you think you are the only one?" He reached into his pockets and tossed down a pouch.

When the Hall Master revealed its contents, silence once more filled the giant hall. Wu Ying found his breathing shortened, the pulse of chi within the room seeming to flow around the stage. Two Nascent Soul spirit stones stood revealed from the Heavenly Lake Sect elder's pouch, and the very chi in the hall flowed around the trio of spirit stones. Every breath of chi pulsed with power, the very presence of the stones commanding the environment's chi, stretching the edges of reality and revealing the Dao around the room.

Eddies in the air, small wisps of wind currents flowed, highlighted by the water and earth chi that floated within. Fire chi, as part of the heat in the air, shimmered more closely around certain cultivators. The wood grain on the bannister under his fingertips pulsed. Reality stretched with each second.

In the halls above, and even in the hallway itself, small whirlpools of energy formed around the youngest, newest cultivators. Those individuals who were on the edge of enlightenment or were just lucky enough to glimpse something that touched upon their understanding of the world. One after the other, they began their process of enlightenment.

Reality pushed against his senses and Wu Ying pushed back. He exhaled hard then inhaled, catching the hint of burnt wood and soiled earth again. A moment of concentration made him narrow his eyes. It came from the two newly revealed spirit stones on the stage.

The Hall Master stared at the revealed stones—blue and brown, both dark and dirty—for moments that seemed an eternity. Then he closed the bindings on the pouches, cutting off the radiating dao truths from the revealed stones. Silence pervaded the hall, broken only by the deep and regular breathing of those still descending from their moment of enlightenment.

"The bid is two Nascent Soul spirit stones."

Fa Yuan frowned, then shook her head at the Hall Master's inquiring gaze. At her acknowledgement of defeat, he turned to her rival.

"You have won the Core Spirit Stone for the Ben." The Hall Master smiled slightly, gesturing backward. "If I'd known the demand, I would have placed this as our last lot. I fear our next item will be of little interest after such a spectacular display of wealth. Still…"

Wu Ying tuned out the Hall Master as he turned to his martial sister. "What now?"

Fa Yuan stared at the Hall Master's hands, at the spirit ring which he had made the spirit stones disappear into, her lips pursed. She shook her head slightly, as if dismissing her thoughts. "Now? Nothing. I will speak with the Hall Master and magistrate tonight."

Wu Ying frowned, but before he could continue speaking, a knock on their door interrupted him. Lei Hui opened it to reveal an inner sect member of the Heavenly Lake Sect.

"My apologies for bothering you, Elder Yang. But Elder Hsu would like to invite you to speak about the item you were bidding on. Tonight," the inner sect cultivator blurted under the glares of the Verdant Green Waters Sect cultivators within.

"Tonight?" Fa Yuan considered. "Very well." Once the inner sect cultivator had left after providing their address and location, she continued. "And it seems, I'll also be seeing Elder Hsu."

Chapter 25

The rest of the auction had ended with little fanfare. Even the last few items—including the remnant pieces of a Saint-tier jian and a lost third manual of a cultivation style—did not elicit the same level of bidding that the Ben spirit stone had generated. While they had lost the spirit stone, there was an unexpected benefit to the entire matter.

Due to the knowledge of Fa Yuan's rather expansive wealth, the Elder was able to purchase a number of useful items—like new attack talismans, a series of messenger talismans, a Spirit-tier jian, an enchanted tea set, and a set of Saint-level sewing needles—with minimal competition. Only the most desperate or needy dared to compete with her, knowing the true extent of her purse.

Once the auction was over, the group left with haste, declining offers to dine left and right. Back at their residence, with a simple meal on the way, Wu Ying and the rest of the expedition tried to dissuade the Elder from visiting Elder Hsu, only to fail. After a brief snack and a requisite bath, Fa Yuan swept out of their rooms to visit the magistrate and the auction hall elder, leaving the team to their own devices that night.

"I don't like this," Wu Ying complained to Tou He as they picked at the remnants of their dinner. He waved a stalk of bok choy with his chopsticks as he talked. "It's got to be a trap."

"In the middle of the city? After she spoke to the magistrate and the hall master?" Lei Hui said. "It would take much daring to launch an attack with so many eyes on them."

"Then why would they invite her?" Wu Ying asked.

Wang Min arched a graceful eyebrow at Wu Ying. "She is the Fairy. And stop waving your food around, it's rude."

"That takes desire to a whole new level. That's two Nascent Soul spirit stones!" Wu Ying pointed at Lei Hui and Yu Kun. "You both had epiphanies just from being in the presence of them."

"Three. We had epiphanies from three," Lei Hui corrected. "And it was a minor one."

"There is no big or small, just enlightenment," Tou He said softly. His words cut through the group, silencing them with the simple conviction in his statement.

"I beg to differ," Lei Hui said. "That barely helped with my cultivation."

"Enlightenment and the road to immortality is not something you should judge like a trip to the river," Tou He said, tapping the rim of his teacup. "Breaking the cycle of samsara and achieving an awakened mind cannot be achieved by strict adherence to how many meridians we form, how many layers of our Core we have achieved. The final form of your newborn spirit is not the sum of your body, but of your soul."

"That's what you think," Lei Hui snapped.

"And don't you mean joining the Dao?" Wu Ying said, frowning at his friend's use of Buddhist terms. Tou He shrugged, and Wu Ying had to dismiss the matter. "My point stands. They paid too much just to court her."

Yu Kun put down his rice bowl, placing the chopsticks on the empty bowl and fixing Wu Ying with a firm gaze. "Then what are you worried about? It seems it's more than her chastity or vague concerns that worries you."

Wu Ying hesitated while the other two new cultivators stared at him with interest. Only Tou He seemed calm, happily picking at the remnants of the meal.

"Speak. You had us stay home because you feared something would happen before the auction. Now you're worried about the Elder, the strongest of us all," Yu Kun pushed. "What are you not telling us?"

"It's about our mission. And Elder Cheng," Wu Ying said finally. "We think his attackers might be in the city."

"Think or know?" Lei Hui sniffed.

Wu Ying hesitated. "Know."

"How?" This from Wang Min. Her voice was gentle still, but insistent.

"Their chi. At times, it's… wrong."

"Twisted and spoiled," Tou He said. "Their karmic balance is perverted, such that it affects the very things they touch."

"You knew?" Yu Kun asked.

"I paid attention." Receiving the glares of all three other cultivators, Tou He smiled enigmatically and popped the last spare rib into his mouth. That made Wang Min at least look away.

"It doesn't matter if he knew. We didn't tell you because—"

"You think it's a dark sect," Yu Kun said. As Wu Ying's jaw dropped, Yu Kun snorted. "Did you think those of us who joined your Sect have not seen the signs? We are not blind. The rumors have grown among us. If anything, it is you orthodox sects that are slow to this realization."

"That's impossible. They were all wiped out!" Lei Hui protested. The thin cultivator leaned over the dining room table, his robe dangerously close to being stained by the dishes. "There are no more dark sects. Not in the State of Shen."

On the other hand, Wang Min focused on Tou He and Wu Ying, looking between the pair of inner sect cultivators. Humming to herself, she turned to Yu Kun, who met her gaze and offered her just the slightest of nods.

"Don't tell me you believe this bucket of waste herbs they're trying to sell us," Lei Hui said to Wang Min.

"They believe it. Enough to warn us against the matter and face ridicule. Enough to join a Sect when they refused to before," Wang Min replied neutrally. "More. The poison we are trying to cure—its origins are from the very same sects you say are destroyed."

"It's possible to use poison without being a member of the dark sect," Lei Hui rebutted. "Many of my recipes have varied origins."

"Yes." Wang Min opened her hands sideways. "I choose to believe they believe. And will act accordingly. After all, they are not asking us to do more than be careful, no?"

Wu Ying hesitated, looking out the door to where Fa Yuan had departed. "I…"

"You want to follow her," Yu Kun said.

"The Elder asked us to stay out of this. To stay in," Lei Hui said, crossing his arms. "Defying her will reflect badly upon her evaluation of us to our own Masters." Turning pleading eyes on Wang Min, he continued. "And even if they are right, what can we do?"

Wang Min shrugged one graceful shoulder. "If we are not there to choose, how would we know?"

"You're willing to come?" Wu Ying said.

Her nod greeted his words, but Yu Kun raised a hand. "Before we go anywhere, let's talk about what we intend to do. It's not as if we can just walk in and demand they not hurt the Elder, now can we?"

Wu Ying made a face but had to agree. Whatever they chose to do, it would have to be well considered. It was one thing to have a duel, another to attack the residence—temporary or not—of another sect. The second could result in a blood feud or the entire group being disowned.

"Do you have a suggestion?"

***

Staking out the residence of the Heavenly Lake Sect was easier than Wu Ying had expected. At the end of the block that the sect had taken residence within was a restaurant that stayed open late into the night. They were more than happy to host the group on the top floor, giving them a window that overlooked the street and the way toward the sect's residence. That they had to kick out a group of diners celebrating their grandparent's ninetieth birthday had made Wu Ying wince enough that he paid for their dinner.

The restaurant itself was of significantly lower quality than the ones they had been visiting, more focused on serving the local populace than a high-class restaurant meant for cultivators. There was no spirit beast meat on the menu, and only a single dish trumpeting the use of a demonic chicken was present. Even the decor, sparse as it was, was of lower quality, the artwork from unknown local artists.

For all that, Tou He did not hesitate as he ordered, burdening the waiter with his rapid-fire requests for dishes such that the waiter almost missed Yu Kun's demand for wine. Wang Min kept silent while Wu Ying had his attention focused on the building in the distance.

"We should have found a closer place," Wu Ying complained.

"Where?" Yu Kun replied, waving down the street. "It is all residential and closed retail. Unless you wanted to hide on the rooftops…" His eyes narrowed. "You did, didn't you?"

Wu Ying shrugged uncomfortably.

"I will not. I am a cultivator, not a… a… cì kè[25]!" Wang Min said.

Wu Ying grimaced but relented. The cike held a strange position in the jianghu[26]. The cike was as much a series of martial arts styles as a way to describe a group of sects that focused their activities on assassinations. Due

---

[25] Technically translates as an assassin. Yes, the Chinese have their own version of the ninja, just less glamorized.

[26] Translates literally as "rivers and lakes," but in this case, in the book refers to the world of martial arts. It comes from the poem by Fan Zhongyan which states (roughly) – "Living in temple and palace, I will help the poor peoples. Living near rivers and lakes, I will worry about the emperor."

to the nature of their style and their focus, the sects were either heretical or dark sects, depending on their dao focus. Because they walked such a fine line, they were viewed with distaste by the more orthodox sects like the Verdant Green Waters, resulting in the kind of response Wang Min showed.

"But I can't see what's going on," Wu Ying said.

"That's why you brought me along," Yu Kun replied.

He moved around to the window and placed his hands on the windowsill. As he moved his hands away, Wu Ying was surprised to see a yellow paper stuck to it, talismans that Yu Kun proceeded to attach all along the windowsill. When he was done, Yu Kun sent a surge of chi through the talismans.

A gasp from the waitress who had arrived caught the cultivators' attention. Wu Ying could understand, for the talismans had shifted the window opening, making the chi flows outside visible. Furthermore, Wu Ying felt that with a small exertion of his will, he would be able to extend his perception, allowing him to see—to sense—the chi flows within the residence of the Heavenly Lake Sect.

Yu Kun took his seat, waiting for the waitress to depart after supplying the jars of wine before he explained. "If there is a fight, we should easily sense it brewing. Even if the sect attempts to hide such an occurrence, these talismans should allow us to know."

Wu Ying nodded but a part of him worried that they might try something a little more underhanded. What if they poisoned her? Struck her so fast that she never had a chance to protect herself? What if they overwhelmed her in an all-out attack before Wu Ying and the others could arrive?

All of those questions and more ran through his mind as dishes arrived and he stared out the window. While his friends supped on the dishes, commenting on the taste and generally playing at being unconcerned, he watched. He knew there was little he could do, but still, he watched.

Two hours later, Elder Yang finally made her appearance. She strolled down the street, passing through the ill-lit passages without need of a lantern, her spirit sense more than sufficient to guide her way. She stopped in front of the sect's residence, briefly looking around before she rapped the door and was guided in by a servant.

Wu Ying's murmured acknowledgment of her arrival elicited grunts and nods of acknowledgement from the group. As usual, Tou He continue to eat without concern, while the others slowed down, picking at the dishes. Only Wu Ying's bowl of rice lay untouched.

Hours passed with only the continual slurp of meals being eaten, of commoner diners chattering in the background to disturb Wu Ying's focus. Each time the chi in the window fluctuated, he tensed. Almost always, it was a minor fluctuation in the environment, the passing by of a strong cultivator or a practice session within the residence. None of it was of the same strength or intensity that Wu Ying would have expected from a fight.

The ongoing tension wrung his nerves dry, made him rub the hilt of his sword over and over in nervous worry. Assurances that they would catch it, requests that he relax were all greeted with a grunt before he turned back to watching the residence.

So it was a surprise that when matters escalated, he was the least ready of the group.

***

A hand struck the door leading into their dining room. It stayed aloft, catching the swinging door on its return with contemptuous ease as the intruder strolled in. Behind him, others crowded the doorway. Tou He paused, one hand falling to his side where his staff rested against the table, the other holding aloft a pork skewer, half consumed. Yu Kun, closest to the door, was on his feet, his swords already drawn and facing the intruders. Lei Hui and Wang Min were only a fraction of a second behind, standing as the intruders entered the room.

Only Wu Ying, intently focused on the residence, wrung out after so many hours, reacted slowly. He caught sight of flashing blades as he turned, as the first entrant to the room engaged Yu Kun.

"You dare to spy on us! You Verdant Green Waters Sect offal, die like the wandering dogs you are!" Lu Ren exclaimed, making sure to pitch his voice such that everyone in the restaurant could hear. "How dare you attack us, using those spells!"

Even as Lu Ren accused them, acting the part of the victim, Wu Ying noted that the cultivators who engaged his friends in combat were all clad in plain martial robes. None of them wore clothing that denoted their true alliances, though a couple of the faces were familiar from the duels. Certainly not all of them were wandering cultivators or members of the Heavenly Lake Sect.

His surprise and musings were cut short as the flare of energy he had been waiting for—as well as the roar of structural destruction—arose from behind Wu Ying. He twisted his head, his sword drawn from his side, only to catch sight of the newly destroyed second and third floor of the residence tumbling down. Even as he watched, swirls of blue and foam-green chi formed around a familiar female Elder's form as she rose in the sky, sword light gleaming as she battled another.

"Watch out!"

Wu Ying jerked his head aside, barely dodging the sword thrust that sought his life. He riposted automatically, finding himself engaged in battle with Lu Ren again. Behind the cultivator, the rest of Wu Ying's party was fighting in close combat, one of the cultivators engaged with Wang Min sporting a half-eaten barbeque skewer sticking out of his arm.

"Your interference ends now," Lu Ren snarled, thrusting at Wu Ying and catching him in a high bind. Sword blades and guards pressed together, Lu Ren sent a surge of chi through his body, filling the room with that burnt chi smell as he shoved Wu Ying.

Unable to hold his position, Wu Ying was thrown backward into the wall with Lu Ren following, blades still engaged in the bind. The flimsy, common-made wall could not handle the energy imparted to it and shattered around their bodies. Together, the pair tumbled from the third floor of the restaurant, broken wooden beams and compressed mud walls showering them as they fell to the street.

Sword freed finally as they tumbled, Wu Ying began a series of cuts, sending his own chi surging through his weapon. His feet, kicking in the air, connected with a beam. A surge of energy imparted itself into the beam. He changed directions in mid-air, even halting his fall for a second. The sudden change caught Lu Ren by surprise. An underhand cut, a twist of Wu Ying's wrist, and the blade bit into flesh.

Blood filled the night air, staining his blade.

Wu Ying landed, the loud, ungainly thump of Lu Ren's graceless fall preceding his. The other cultivator staggered upright, clutching the back of his neck, which had been sliced open. Blood pooled from his fingers as Lu Ren raised his blade.

Not intending to give the man time to recover, Wu Ying threw himself forward. Blades flashed as Wu Ying executed Clearing the vermin from the

Doorstep and then Dragon greets the Sunrise, again and again. Cuts scored Lu Ren's body, the fast attacks breaking open his opponent's guard. Before Wu Ying could finish the job, a whistle blew.

"Halt! No fighting in the streets!" Behind the screaming guard lieutenant, a troop of Body Cleansing city guards appeared, all armed with long spears and metal scalemail armor.

"That mean we can keep fighting up here?" Yu Kun called from above, even as the clash of blades and thump of wood continued.

"Stop fighting!" the lieutenant screamed again, face flushed and incensed.

Wu Ying debated stabbing Lu Ren and finishing the matter anyway, especially when the swooning and injured cultivator smirked. Wu Ying's sword trembled a little, but he stepped back and swung his sword, cleaning it of the man's blood and the stink of his chi. Killing him in cold blood and in front of the guards would bring more trouble than Lu Ren was worth.

Wu Ying did wonder how exactly Lu Ren and his Master had managed to hide their affiliation with the dark sects, what with the rather obvious clues. It was something he'd ask Elder Yang…

Eyes widening, he looked around, searching for his martial sister. But their battle had shifted from the residence, through the sky, and across rooftops at speeds Wu Ying could not hope to match. Only the sudden pulse of chi in the distance spoke of their continued battle.

"Don't worry, that fight will be handled too," the lieutenant said. "Now, all of you, sheathe your weapons and follow us back to the jail."

Wu Ying frowned, but seeing Lu Ren put away his weapon and the guards raise their weapons threateningly, he complied. He could only hope that Fa Yuan could manage the battle herself. Because it looked as though they would be stuck in jail instead.

Chapter 26

To Wu Ying's surprise, his elder sister was led into the same jail that contained him and his teammates in the early hours of the morning. Zhong Shei was the one leading her over, though he separated her from Wu Ying and placed her in an adjoining cell alone. The guardsman was extremely apologetic to the Elder, murmuring things about procedure and necessity while assuring her that the magistrate would have this settled in short order.

When Zhong Shei left, Fa Yuan looked around the jail cell, meeting Wu Ying's gaze before she perused the environment. The cell itself was made of compacted earth plaster, overlaid on top of clay fired bricks. The entire cell was fully reinforced by simple enchantments to increase durability, much like the wooden doors, reinforced with metal bars, that shut them in. To Wu Ying's surprise, the jail cell itself was not particularly redolent, the straw within recently changed and the cell itself scrubbed of refuse. Still, it was a far cry from their usual accommodation.

"Are you okay?" When Wu Ying realized he'd echoed Fa Yuan's question, he could not help but smile. He gestured back to the group when she waited for his answer. "We are uninjured mostly. If anything, it was the *others* who came out of the fight worst."

He could not help but be proud at that turn of affairs. The worst injured among them was Lei Hui and the apothecarist had managed to blind his attacker with a carefully dispersed pouch of powder. On the other hand, since Wang Min was fussing over Lei Hui's injury, wrapping his injured arm with a bandage and making sure he was taken care of, Wu Ying had a feeling the apothecarist would have taken twice the injuries for the result.

"I am fine. Elder Hsu had more strength than skill." Fa Yuan's lips curled in a smirk. "It is what happens when one rushes for strength and cultivation more than skill. Much like his disciple."

"He wasn't that bad the day before," Wu Ying protested. Though his recent fight with Lu Ren had been more one-sided.

"There were extenuating circumstances then." When Wu Ying made an inquiring noise, Fa Yuan answered. "There is a kind of cultivation exercise that burns potential to give strength and speed. It requires sacrifice, and if we are right, not necessarily their own. The greater the sacrifice, the greater the benefit. Temporarily."

Wu Ying's eyes widened. That kind of thing, it was anathema to cultivators. To waste one's potential for the present would cut short one's immortal journey. To draw on another's potential, to force that kind of sacrifice... "Wait. Was that why they asked you to meet with them?"

"Yes. They offered the Ben's spirit stone if I offered them some of my own life blood," Fa Yuan admitted.

"You didn't give them any, did you?" Lei Hui spoke up, struggling to stand and being pushed back by Wang Min. "They can do more than just use it for your potential."

"Of course not." Elder Yang shot a contemptuous look at Lei Hui, which made him wilt. She drew a deep breath, settling her emotions. "I would never do such a thing. Our initial negotiation for the spirit stone took some time before they raised the issue. My refusal did not anger them at first. Eventually, they chose to stop the civilities."

The group fell silent, knowing the rest of the story. Except...

"Did you kill him?" Yu Kun asked.

"I did," Fa Yuan replied coldly.

Wu Ying winced. Not at the death of their enemy but what it would mean for them. Killing another sect Elder would have consequences. Never mind the fact that it happened in the middle of a city. Battles in the woods, in the wilds were issues that the jianghu dealt with privately. Battles in cities added in unwanted local bureaucracy, making things much more complicated.

"Good." Yu Kun nodded, going back to take a seat.

"How is that good!" Lei Hui said, waving his hand around. He winced and was pushed back down to his seat by Wang Min, who muttered something about idiotic apothecarists to Wu Ying's amusement. The fight in the restaurant must have been intense to create the shift in Wang Min's regard of Lei Hui. "We were trying not to kill our opponents!"

"We were?" Wu Ying said, surprised.

"We were," confirmed Tou He.

"Huh."

"And it was a good thing that you did not. I asked you to not get involved," Fa Yuan said coldly, her arms crossing. "It might not have devolved if you had not made your presence known."

"We were trying to not draw attention," Wu Ying muttered.

"Hiding a block away was not exactly subtle."

He winced again, looking for support from his friends. He found Tou He seated, counting his prayer beads in quiet meditation. Lei Hui and Wang Min were arguing about Lei Hui's recent movements, while Yu Kun had found the waste bucket suddenly engrossing. Glaring at the group doing their best to avoid confronting the Elder, Wu Ying turned back. Some friends they were.

"Sorry, Elder Sister." Wu Ying cast his gaze down, lowering his head in supplication. When all else failed, rely on one's familial ties. Which, he knew, was the reason his friends were leaving him to confront her. It wasn't a card they could play.

The snort his words elicited told him his blatant ploy was not unnoticed. But when he looked up, he saw the slightest tug of a smile on her lips, quickly squashed.

"Still, Lei Hui was right—"

"I told you!"

"The death of Elder Hsu would be troublesome in most circumstances." Fa Yuan smiled grimly. "It is a good thing I made arrangements."

Wu Ying grinned, turning around to shoot an "I told you so" look at Lei Hui. The apothecarist just sniffed and turned back to Wang Min as they discussed healing pills.

"So now what?" Wu Ying said.

"Now, we wait."

***

It was late morning when the magistrate himself and the hereto-unseen captain of the guard arrived. The captain was a massive man, more bear than human it seemed, so overflowing was his follicular nature. He was clad in a dark scalemail chest armor that reached beneath his hips and carried a pair of crossed daos on his hips. Even in the jail, the man was wearing his helmet as he glared about him, stray tufts of hair escaping the open face of his helm and around the end of his helmet.

"Elder Yang, thank you for your patience. I apologize for this taking so long. Much of what you said was true, though it took more effort to have the Hall Master to allow me to view the spirit stones," Magistrate Song said. "While it seems the allegations are true upon first perusal, we have a problem."

Fa Yuan arched an eyebrow at the magistrate, who wiped at his forehead at her displeasure.

"You killed a sect Elder in the city. Whether you were justified or not, we cannot just free you," the captain of the guard said. "I've been dealing with a half dozen others complaining about your actions."

"What sects were they from?" Fa Yuan asked, her voice cold.

"Does it matter?" the captain said. "You did kill him."

Cutting off Fa Yuan before she could speak, the magistrate waved his robed hands, the long sleeves flapping in the musty air of the jail and creating a small breeze. "I know why you asked, Elder Yang. And we are looking into the other matter"—he flicked his gaze toward Wu Ying and his team—"but such accusations… well, it's not something a simple magistrate like me can handle."

"This is not what you told me before," Fa Yuan said disapprovingly.

"Well, it has become a bit more of a problem, you know…" Magistrate Song said, wringing his hands. "We're calling a tribunal of other Elders— from the orthodox sects—to look into the matter. I have reported the entire matter upward and the Provincial Magistrate is sending his own investigator."

"Really," Fa Yuan said.

"Yes. And because of that, well…" He coughed, glancing back at the captain.

"You will stay in jail until the trial," the captain growled.

Wu Ying bristled, his hands clenching on the jail cell bars. He wanted to say something but knew that doing so would cause just as many problems. Instead, he listened in growing angry silence.

"And you intend to keep me here? In this room?" Fa Yuan's eyes flicked around the cell with contempt. Wu Ying knew with a little exertion of strength, she could break out.

The guard captain probably knew too, for he puffed out his chest. "Not here. We're not entirely unused to handling ornery Elders."

"Please, please, there's no need for all this." The magistrate wiped his head, the silk handkerchief he was using damp from accumulated fear. Wu Ying's nose wrinkled a little, catching a whiff of the acrid smell of fear the man was pouring out, mixing with his own uncontrolled expulsion of chi. "We just ask you for your patience. And in turn, we can release your expedition members now. While we don't allow fighting in public, all indications are that they were attacked first."

"And my quest?"

The magistrate looked uncomfortable, wringing his hands. Fa Yuan glared at the group, at the guard captain who stood there uncaring, before she jerked a single nod.

"Fine. Let them out. I will need to speak with my martial brother." When the guard captain shifted, she added in a clipped tone, "Alone."

The magistrate let out a relieved sigh and cut off the guard captain, gesturing for Wu Ying and his friends to be released. Quick words were passed between Wu Ying and the team, arrangements made for them to meet up at their residence. And then, Wu Ying made his way over to his martial sister's cell.

"It seems you'll have to finish this quest alone," Fa Yuan said.

When Wu Ying was close, she reached forward and placed a hand over his own. He frowned when he felt a heavy presence in his hands that she'd extracted from her spirit ring. Eyes wide, Wu Ying looked at a familiar bag. "Is that...?"

"Yes. I took it from his corpse."

Wu Ying quickly deposited the spirit stone of the Ben in his ring before Fa Yuan composed her thoughts and spoke. Mostly, she outlined the major steps Wu Ying needed to take, the actions that were left. With only one of the three materials they needed located, Wu Ying had much to do. Still, at least in this case, Wu Ying knew most of what she had to say since he had been party to the expedition from the start. Their conversation was filled with half-spoken sentence fragments, portions of ideas that did not need to be completed.

A short forty minutes later, the pair were done and Wu Ying walked out the jail—only to find the hirsute guard captain glaring at him.

To Wu Ying's surprise, rather than being belligerent like before, he softened his tone. "Will she stay?"

Wu Ying nodded.

"Good. It would have been difficult to control her if not."

"Why did you act so… so…"

"Hard-headed?" The guard captain grinned, and Wu Ying was surprised to note he had a missing front tooth. "If I hadn't, the magistrate was going to call for more help. And the closest help are other sect Elders."

Wu Ying frowned. Considering what they suspected about the dark sect's infiltration…

"This way, he'll let us guard her." A hand clapped down on Wu Ying's shoulder, making the smaller cultivator stumble. "The magistrate and your Elder have told me of your concerns. Whether it's a child's fairy tale or not, I will not allow her to be damaged while in my custody. But I wouldn't take too long on your journey. And you might want to contact your sect."

Wu Ying nodded, rubbing his shoulder. "Why are you helping us?"

"I'm not. I'm helping myself," the guard captain said. "I didn't retire to be a guard captain just to fight more Core cultivators."

Wu Ying snorted, then his eyes narrowed. Thinking quickly, he spoke up. "The people we fought, you're still holding them?"

"We are." The guard captain sounded wary.

"They might have friends who might be unhappy with us," Wu Ying said. An innocuous statement on the surface. And true too.

"My lieutenants—Zhong Shei among them—and the other guards are keeping an eye on the remaining cultivators. We won't have another such incident in my city."

Wu Ying could only hope the man was true to his word. At the least, Fa Yuan had told him that they had let her keep her spirit ring, which contained her weapons. She was not entirely unarmed if things went badly. As for themselves, he was not so naïve as to think the other cultivators were the only ones being watched.

"Then thank you." Wu Ying said. He made sure to offer the necessary and polite farewells before he hurried away. There was much to do if he was to take advantage of the captain's largesse.

Once back in his room, he penned a note to the Sect on the spirit messenger paper Fa Yuan had passed to him. All he had to do was write on the paper before folding the message into a paper crane, then the spirit paper took on a life of its own and flew out of his hands. The message would take days to arrive, compared to the weeks a normal message would take, but he sent a pair of mundane messages too, just in case.

After that, the team had much to do to get ready. Hopefully they had already begun the necessary preparations. Because they still had two material pieces to deal with. And active opposition to handle.

Chapter 27

"Is this a good idea?" Yu Kun asked Wu Ying as he kicked his horse to catch up with the cultivator.

On the dusty road that led out of Hinma, they rode their horses at a decent clop in the early morning. They passed the farmers who pulled their morning produce to the city in the dawn's light, headed for the bridge that spanned over the eastern river.

"Leaving?" Wu Ying nodded. "We've finished our preparations."

Every time they had left the inn, they had been trailed—subtly and not so subtly—by the guards in the city. Luckily, they had few enough preparations to complete, what with spirit rings and the sect's lone branch member in the city working to supply their needs.

"In broad daylight."

Wu Ying shrugged. "Did you think we could sneak out? Or that our departure would have long been hidden?" He shook his head, running a hand down the side of his horse's neck to calm it when it tossed its head at his motions. "Better to leave early and get a move on the day."

The frown Yu Kun shot told Wu Ying he did not agree. But Wu Ying was in charge now that Fa Yuan was no longer with them. And so, Yu Kun let his horse fall back. The ex-farmer did notice, when he looked back later, that Yu Kun had taken the time to put a bow and a quiver of arrows on his saddle. Added to Wang Min's repeating crossbow, Wu Ying could not help but be happy at the ranged attacks they had gained. He even had his own crossbow in his ring, but in a surprise attack, his ability to project sword intent would be faster and more flexible.

The team rode for hours, crossing the covered bridge that spanned the western river, continuing on the road that would lead them farther west and into the wilderness. Their initial stated goal to the branch member was a particularly large lake known to host the Ben when they came south. At their current pace, Wu Ying knew it would take them just over four days to arrive at the lake, two of them on the road and two more cutting through the forest itself.

By this point, they were nearing the edges of farmed civilization, the rice fields that had dominated the surroundings giving way to clumps of forested land. These clumps grew in size as they journeyed, finally ending in an unbroken stretch of trees that denoted the start of the lowland forest that bordered this part of the county. The team had their senses fully extended, wary of an ambush or attacks by demon beasts drawn to the thoroughfare for easy meals.

Wu Ying pulsed his aura, pushing it out with a rush of chi, allowing him to extend his senses. Not sensing any human contact within his expanded range other than his team, Wu Ying held his hand up and called a halt to the expedition.

"We will be dismounting here and journeying north through the forest from this point." Wu Ying suited action to words, slinging his feet off the beast. "Yu Kun, please take the back. We will be relying on you to cover our path. Lei Hou, you mentioned a dust you have that might aid Yu Kun."

At first, the group looked puzzled, but soon broke out into grins.

"We'll talk later. Let's move quickly now," Wu Ying added.

Together, they led their horses through the thick undergrowth, pushing aside brush as they took themselves out of sight of the road. Wu Ying could only hope that Yu Kun could cover their tracks well enough. His experience as a wandering cultivator would be important now, as would the powder Lei Hui provided. It would disperse signs of their passing while enhancing the growth of vegetation in their wake.

Of course, all that predicated upon the fact that someone was looking for them. And that that someone would follow their tracks in a mundane manner, rather than guessing at their destination and trying to meet them there directly or using another enchanted object. If that was the case, there was little Wu Ying could do, other than choose a different destination. Unfortunately, his options were limited to some extent.

An hour and a half later, they broke into a small clearing and Wu Ying called for their first halt since they had left the road. As the team worked to care for their mounts, brushing out burrs and checking hooves, while feeding and watering the animals, Wu Ying spoke.

"We will be looking to locate and harvest the Sun Lotus first, avoiding the marshlands to the northwest. While the swamp in the northwest is well known to contain a number of Chan Chu, finding one with a sufficiently large heart might be difficult. It is also the most obvious option for us to journey to, after visiting the lake," Wu Ying said.

"Won't the Sun Lotus location be obvious too?" Lei Hui asked.

"Perhaps. The first location we are journeying to was marked by Master Li. I saw no reference to it in other, more widely distributed records," Wu Ying said. All that time in the libraries had not been for nothing, at least Wu Ying hoped. "I'm trusting that they do not know of this location, allowing us to pick the Sun Lotus without issue."

"Then what? Is there another location for the Chan Chu close by afterward?" Tou He asked.

Wu Ying nodded. "Yes. Three, two old, one with relatively recent indications of their habitat. We will check them all out if necessary."

"And the Ben?" Yu Kun said.

"We have that one already," Wu Ying said grimly.

"How…" Wang Min shook her head. "Of course. Taken off his corpse?"

Wu Ying nodded. "We'll search for the Chan Chu once we harvest the Sun Lotus. All but Lei Hui."

Lei Hui started, his head rising from where he'd been stroking his mare. "Why not me?"

"Because I want to send you back to the Sect with both ingredients once we collect them." Wu Ying rubbed his chin before he added, "I'll contact my martial sister to join you on the way back if she is released in time. Once we know which city you'll be headed towards, we'll make arrangements then." The last portion, he had hesitated on. Taking on the Chan Chu would be difficult, especially without Elder Yang. On the other hand, it would be a waste if they lost the materials.

"But why send me away?"

"Security. With two of the three materials, we have a much better chance of acquiring support within the Sect to finish the cure. Having you make it on hand was always going to be the last choice," Wu Ying said. Of course, Lei Hui had known that—it had been explained to him on hiring. But Wu Ying and Fa Yuan had wanted an apothecarist with them, just in case.

"But we only have one spirit stone," protested Lei Hui. "What if I'm found? What if those people attack me?"

Wu Ying's eyes narrowed as he realized there was a slight whiteness to Lei Hui's lips as he pressed them together after speaking. He noted how Lei Hui's hands clenched and released again and again, as if no one could see the twitch. Realization hit that fear drove Lei Hui's protests as much as anything else. "We'll make sure that you are hidden before you break off. If anything, our attackers will come for us."

"But what if they don't?"

"Then you'll survive," Wang Min said, riding closer to Lei Hui and placing her hand on his clenching fists. She smiled at the apothecarist. "I know you can do it. You're a lot stronger than I thought. Than you think."

Lei Hui glanced at the hand covering his own. He licked his lips then straightened his back as he replied. "You're right. And I've got a number of pills and potions to hide my tracks. I could even cook up a face-changing potion." He touched his own face with his uncovered hand. "Though it would be a shame to alter this handsome face."

A round of coughing broke out from around Lei Hui, and even Wang Min cracked a small smile.

Lei Hui glared at the amused group before he smiled too. "You're risking a lot, sending away the only spirit stone."

Wu Ying shook his head. "The Ben are flying down at this time. Their spirit stones should start flooding the market soon enough. With the Sect's resources, if we can get them the other components, we should be fine. And anyway, it's not a risk. I trust you."

As much as Wang Min's feminine encouragements, his words made Lei Hui puff up in pride. The blunt, irascible apothecarist grinned before the group fell silent.

And Wu Ying had to admit, if only to himself, that what they sought from the Chan Chu was dangerous. If he could send the two materials away, even if they failed, his Master would have a chance.

***

Once the group had rested sufficiently, they resumed their trek north. Toward the end of the night, Wu Ying dropped backward, extracting small yellow talismans from his bag to place across their pathway. After half the day, they had stopped covering their tracks directly. The dense undergrowth, combined with the time taken to do so, forced that decision. Hopefully, by that point, they had lost their pursuers, if any. They had taken other precautions as well, even going so far as to ride their horses through shallow streams and cross rocky regions when they found them in a bid to obscure their tracks. But now, Wu Ying took one additional precaution.

The talismans he used were simple warning talismans. Strung across the trail, the talismans formed an invisible net, one made of air chi. Gossamer webs of chi expanded from each talisman, connecting with the next in line, and covered the trail, invisible to the naked eye. Even with Wu Ying's extended aura senses and his breathing exercise while knowing what he was looking for, he could still not pick out the threads with ease.

Of course, he knew that he was limited by his cultivation and experience. It was quite possible that their enemies might have someone specialized in tracking or of a higher cultivation level. Still, it was the best he could do. Once he finished the job, he returned to the group, which had ridden ahead of him, clutching the last talisman of the set.

If their enemies were tracking them, when they passed through the net, his talisman would burn up and warn them. It was the best option they had, beyond leaving Yu Kun a little behind to watch for their enemies. But that would only work if they had not gained a significant lead on their enemies.

Precautions taken, the group headed deeper into the woods. They kept their senses peeled, for the spirit and demon beasts around them were increasing in strength the deeper they went.

Three days later, they had their first major encounter. The yellow-throated marten—its beast core in the high Energy Storage stage—had slunk close, its belly low to the ground before it attacked. Its low-slung but overly large body had managed to hide it as it crept close, its instinctive use of wood chi aiding the demon beast. When it burst from hiding, it took Tou He by surprise, forcing the cultivator to block with his arm.

Together, the pair tumbled off Tou He's horse and crashed into the undergrowth in a rolling ball of fur and cultivator. In retaliation for the scratches and bites he accumulated, Tou He reacted by flaring his chi, wreathing his body and hands in flame. The marten let out a shrill eek, its body twisting away as it disengaged.

A final kick sent the burning, wood-based demon beast into a nearby tree, its fur smoking and the unmistakeable smell of burning flesh and ash filling the air. As the lengthy creature twisted back to its feet, a trio of bolts sprouted from its fur as Wang Min unloaded her repeating crossbow into the monster. The creature continued flailing, desperate to escape and put out the fire, before Wu Ying finished it.

Beheaded, the monster lay on the ground, burning, muscles still spasming as Tou He clambered to his feet. A grasping and clenching motion with his hand brought the fire chi he'd released back into his hands, leaving the fur smoking but no longer burning.

"Are you okay?" Yu Kun called to Tou He.

"I have some injuries, but nothing grievous," Tou He replied. He touched the bleeding wounds on his arm where the creature had bitten him and along his sides, where he'd been scratched.

Lei Hui unseated himself from the horse and bandaged the ex-monk, passing the man a healing pill to consume. In the meantime, Yu Kun stripped the marten, muttering about wasted fur as he did so. Wu Ying ignored the trio, working with Wang Min to watch for additional trouble. Breathing deeply, he focused, trying to locate additional problems. Thankfully, that marten had focused its initial attack on the most incompatible cultivator, and thus doomed itself from the start. Their next encounter might not be so fortunate.

***

Days passed, and to Wu Ying's minor relief, the talisman never burnt itself. It stayed inert until such time as Wu Ying discarded the talisman. The minor charge within the talisman would run out soon, and rather than leave a trace, he set the entire set burning with a thought.

Afterward, they kept searching the forest for their prey.

Wu Ying no longer led the team in a single straight line but instead followed the contour of the ground, searching appropriate environments for the Sun Lotus blossom, or cresting hills to review nearby lakes in search of migrating Ben. While his Master had provided Wu Ying a map, it had only provided a rough location. Day after day they rode, heated battles with demon beasts and the occasional spirit beast increasing in frequency.

Hungry, egg-laying demonic flies swarmed them in the morning, seeking a place to grow their children. A liberal application of an apothecarist's rub kept the smaller examples of the monsters away. Still, the larger, more aggressive demon beasts had to be fought as their fist-sized proboscises attempted to tear through flesh.

In the afternoon, they faced a cloud leopard spirit beast, one whose newly acquired Core status left the team sans an extra horse. A quick retreat had the team backtracking from the creature who seemed content with its offering of horse flesh.

An overgrown and twisted demonic snake swallowed Yu Kun whole in one sudden gulp, only to be torn apart from the inside as the cultivator broke free as his friends fought the snake's children. And only careful scouting allowed them to avoid a costly battle with a mid-stage Energy Storage wolverine whose size had grown to that of a full-grown tiger.

But it was the evenings, when flying demonic barred owls and massive, fist-sized flame and air-aspected mosquitoes came out to play that protective talismans were used. Luxuries like daily baths were set aside as the group collapsed in mental exhaustion night after night under the protection of necessary campfires and protective formation flags.

For all that, Wu Ying and his team found no sign of the materials they required. No Chan Chu miraculously appeared in areas they were not meant to, and the few Ben they did see were flying so far overhead they might have been figments of their unfulfilled desires. As for the blossoms, the single plant Wu Ying managed to locate was too young to provide a flower.

Transplanting the immature Sun Lotus took Wu Ying half a day of tense work, as he shifted the plant to his ring. Over the course of their journey, he had begun the process of revitalizing the world spirit ring. He had removed the old, lifeless soil and replaced it with new, well-tended soil purchased from a local gardener before they had left the city. A small portion of the ring had been set aside for a compost pile, one that was liberally seeded with remnants of spiritual herbs Wu Ying had gathered. Unused, unneeded spirit herb cuttings were discarded into the pile, while other parts and soil from chi-rich locations were worked into the soil in his ring.

To care for the Sun Blossom and transplant it, Wu Ying needed to alter the temperature, humidity, and the chi flow in his ring. He had to dig out a small pond, fill it with water, and ensure a constant flow of nutrients. All of that required a careful application of chi through the ring itself, as well as the addition of formation flags. Thankfully, spending time with Ru Ping had provided Wu Ying a basic understanding of managing environmental chi flows, and the addition of crushed beast stones in the right aspect covered for his shortcomings. In the short term, it would last, though he would need to perfect the formations and the environment in the Sect.

While he worked, his friends cultivated and watched, dealing with a couple of inquisitive demon beasts. Without Elder Yang, they were forced to fight more than ever, but thus far, they had managed to deal with such attacks well enough. Still, injuries accumulated faster than their boosted healing could recover. All that they could do was keep moving, day after day.

Chapter 28

Nearly two weeks after they had left Hinma, the group arrived at their destination. A short half-day ride was left for them, and within the valley, amidst the small lakes, as the sun beat down on them on this clear day, a field of floating Sun Blossom Lotuses arose.

"That it?" Yu Kun asked.

"That's it," Wu Ying confirmed. He kicked his feet into his horse, taking them off the ridge that had opened up before them and down into cover again. He rode forward for a while until the team regrouped with him, out of sight of potential enemies.

"Why are we stopping?" Lei Hui asked. "It's right there. As close as a meat bun to Tou He's mouth."

"What!"

Snorted laughter arose, a brief break of levity that was much needed.

Wu Ying waved, bringing the humor to an end. "We need to make sure there are no enemies awaiting us. Yu Kun and I will scout the surroundings. You all will continue to make your way down, slowly. We'll meet at the south edge of the main lake, at the portion that hooks up near the outflow."

"What do we do if we arrive first?" Lei Hui asked.

"Have lunch," Wu Ying said. "Watch for trouble and set up camp. It's unlikely they're here, and even if they are, it's unlikely they'll attack you first. Better to either kill Yu Kun and me separately or attack us all together." He did not add that as he was the only Gatherer in the group, all their enemies needed to do was finish him off to end the quest.

There were nods from the group. Wu Ying swung his feet off his horse, dismounting and handing over the reins. Yu Kun copied his motion, and in short order, the much smaller expedition started riding down.

"Left or right?" Yu Kun said.

"Left." Wu Ying added, "Don't engage. Just find them, if you can. We'll decide what to do once we know."

On foot, the pair loped into the forest in their respective directions. Wu Ying moved easily, churning his chi and holding his aura close, much like Yu Kun. Of the group, the pair of them had the best aura control and woodsman craft. If anyone could ascertain if others had arrived and lay in wait, it would be either of them.

It might be a little paranoid, but Wu Ying had vowed to himself that he would not make a mistake. Not when so much rode on his decisions.

***

Hours later, as the midday sun had passed its zenith and crept toward the horizon, Wu Ying arrived at the meeting spot. To his amusement, the expedition had set up a camp including a small cooking fire. Tou He manned the fire while Lei Hui added formation flags around their temporary encampment, boosting its defensibility. Wang Min had her guzheng out, her fingers playing the instrument, yet no sound arose. A small formation circle around her dampened all noise, allowing her to practice without alerting anyone or endangering the camp.

When Wu Ying parted the underbrush and stepped out, he was gladdened to note the group's instinctive motions. Wang Min shifted her hand, her repeating crossbow appearing in it. Lei Hui placed his on the formation flag he'd just planted, ready to activate the defenses. Only Tou He did not make any overt moves, though his hand had never strayed far from his staff.

"Any problems?" Lei Hui asked, relaxing and moving to the next location. These flags were simple to set up and had the advantage of being useable when not completely distributed. The flags and written talismans of melded metal and jade were all created to channel both external and stored chi for their effects. In this case, a simple attack formation against those breaching the initial line of defenses.

"None that I noticed," Wu Ying said.

The group smiled while Wu Ying made his way to his horse to extract a water bottle. While he had one in his storage ring, it was better to drink those out here first. The horses themselves were stabled a short distance away in the clearing, staked down at a convenient tree and close enough to a trickling stream that they could water themselves as needed.

A short distance away, Sun Lotuses in various states of bloom bobbed in the water. Many had blossomed, the golden and pink flowers casting reflections of the midday sun across the valley. It was a tranquil sight, and Wu Ying set aside the worries of command, the concerns for his martial sister and Master, and reveled in the natural beauty. As water played and waves lapped at the shore, Wu Ying breathed and cultivated.

A noise behind him made Wu Ying pivot, hand falling to his sword. He had it drawn and pointing at the interruption before he thought, only to spot Yu Kun. The other cultivator's eyes had widened, hands raised to block the attack that never came.

"Those were good reflexes," Yu Kun said. "Wu wei[27]?"

"Yes," Wu Ying said. Speaking, thinking, threw Wu Ying from that moment of peace, of oneness with the world, and he found himself sighing.

Achieving wu wei, acting without acting, was always difficult. He grasped it sometimes when he sparred, when he dueled. That brief moment of oneness with nature and his body, when the gap between thinking and acting, choosing and moving, disappeared. There was no thought anymore, for action was effortless because it was perfectly in line with the flow of life.

---

[27] Translates literally as "non-doing" or "inaction."

There was no more individual desire or thought, and so, there was no more consideration before action was taken. It just… happened.

"Beautiful," Yu Kun praised.

And it had been. So fast, so effortless that Yu Kun had had no chance to react. Not unless he had achieved that state of mind too. It was what they all strived for, in their own ways. Finding a place in the Dao.

"Thank you. I assume you didn't find anything?" Wu Ying said as he assessed the relaxed nature of Yu Kun's comments, the way he strolled over to Tou He to procure lunch.

"No cultivators. No tracks of other large beasts either," Yu Kun said.

The way he said the last sentence made Wu Ying pause. He considered his own experience, considered what he'd seen, then frowned. This was a watering hole, a location to gain freshwater. While not the only one in the region, it was an easy-to-reach location. So why would the local wildlife stay away from it?

"Problem?" Lei Hui asked.

"Maybe." Wu Ying turned back to the lapping waves of the lake, the serene sight suddenly taking on a different sheen. He looked from side to side, taking in the water.

Seeing his distraction, the group left him to it and continued to set up the camp for the day.

A short ten minutes later, Tou He was by Wu Ying's side. He held out a soft, pliable bun overflowing with stir-fried meat and vegetables. "Eat."

Wu Ying took the bun without a word, biting into it and chewing. The taste of the bouncy, lightly floured rice bun soaked in meat juices filled his mouth as the fresh vegetables crunched as he chewed. But it was the savory taste of the meat and the slight rush of chi that made Wu Ying release an unintentional moan of pleasure. After he swallowed his second bite, Wu Ying finally freed himself from his gluttony to ask, "Marten?"

"Yes. Soaked it in some peach wine," Tou He said. His eyes twinkled. "I got the cast-off versions from your friend."

Wu Ying snorted. Zhong Shei's family's version of unsuitable wine was considered top tier nearly anywhere else. As he bit into the bun again, stuffing the remainder into his mouth to chew and to free his hand to accept another from Tou He, he caught sight of a firefly. The demon beast insect was the size of a large cat, nearly two feet in length with its wingspan doubling that. It hovered before flying down to perch on one of the Sun Lotuses.

A bulge in the water, silent before the explosion, was all the warning they received. The dragonfly, reacting on instinct, had begun to take off, but it was too late. The oversized carp that erupted from the lake took the two-foot-long dragonfly in its mouth, serrated teeth crunching down and cracking wings, before the fish's leap ended, its body and tail disappearing into the water once more.

Wu Ying's jaw dropped open, food nearly dribbling out.

Yu Kun's laconic voice from behind said, "Well, now we know why there are no beasts drinking from the lake."

***

"Are you sure this is a good idea?" Tou He asked as he stared at the now-shirtless cultivator. "There are other lakes."

"But those flowers have already blossomed. They've grown to quite an extent. How long would it take to find another? What if they've stopped

314

blossoming by then?" Wu Ying said. "Another location might not have the same."

"Also, no giant spirit carp in the Core cultivation stage," Tou He pointed out. "I'm all for fish, but mostly as a meal. Not being the meal."

Wu Ying nodded over to where Wang Min sat, the guzheng before her. She had finished tuning the instrument and now just awaited Wu Ying. Lei Hui stood by her, ready to activate their formation flags around the campsite if necessary. When she began playing, there would be no muting of her music this time.

Yu Kun was gone from the camp, ranging the hills in an attempt to spot potential problems. If there were attackers, Yu Kun could hopefully spot and potentially deal with it all beforehand. As for Tou He, he would keep an eye on the water and Wu Ying. Hopefully he would be able to haul the cultivator back on the rope wrapped around the ex-farmer's waist.

"Are you sure this will work?" Tou He asked.

Wu Ying shrugged. In theory, the music Wang Min would play would calm the monster. But it was only in theory. They weren't trying to decrease its chi or make it lethargic during a fight, as they had planned with the Chan Chu. Instead, the song Wang Min would perform would just reinforce the natural, placid nature of the carp.

After all, Wu Ying was not its natural prey. Nor was Wu Ying going to agitate the monster. His only goal was to acquire the Sun Lotus blossoms. In theory, this should work.

In theory.

Drawing a deep breath, Wu Ying slathered himself down with the oil Lei Hui had handed him. The oil would mask his chi and scent better, while also keeping him warm in the frigid cold lake. Preparations complete, Wu Ying waded into the water, the hemp rope playing out behind him. He kept walking until he was forced to swim, taking long and slow strokes to drive himself toward the closest Sun Blossom.

With so many to choose from, Wu Ying was intent on getting only the best of the flowers. More so, he intended to pick at least two, and potentially a third in its entirety to plant within his spirit ring. Of course, he had not admitted the full scope of his plans to his friends, wary of the objections they might raise. But Wang Min would either manage to calm the spirit carp or she would not.

Long, gentle, slow strokes brought him close to the floating lotuses. He pushed aside one of the leaves, paddling gently as his eyes focused on his target. The large, resplendent flower gleamed in the slow setting sun, its petals almost seeming to be on fire as it reflected sunlight. In the water, Wu Ying could smell, could sense the flow of chi, the disparate elements of fire of the Sun Lotus and the water chi in the lake sharp, painful contrasts.

A buzz above Wu Ying made his head turn. An unnaturally large mosquito fly, seeking a place to land and deposit its eggs. Something brushed his legs, then water rose and splashed as the mosquito was eaten. Gone in a flash of silver-white scales as a carp—only four feet long—acquired its meal for the day.

Wang Min continued to play, the gentle notes of her guzheng thrumming through the air. Wu Ying felt the slight pressure on his aura, felt the tune's gentle persuasion to relaxation that it engendered within him. He took control of his mind, forced it to focus on his objective.

There were things that tickled his feet, that brushed against his arms underneath the murky water as he paddled. There were monsters beneath the water.

And he ignored it all.

He had a job, and as he reached the blossoms, he began the process of completing it.

Separating the Sun Lotus blossom from the lotus pad itself was not difficult. To keep the Sun Lotus alive, he would need to use wood and water chi while plucking the blossom. To separate the stalks, he had specialized implements to grip and hold the flower. But this close, Wu Ying sensed another issue.

The fire chi within the Sun Lotus blossom was so intense, he felt his face and hand blister. What he had expected to take time with, he realized, he would need to hurry. All of the documents he had read had mentioned this problem, but only in passing. Unfortunately, the other Gatherers who had written the books were in the Core cultivation stage. As such, they had a natural defense against the heat that beat upon Wu Ying's skin.

Paddling beside the flower, Wu Ying made up his mind quickly. There was no point in worrying about incomplete information or his own lack of understanding. He could curse himself out later for not grasping the details. Now he had to work. And work fast.

His breathing hitched as Wu Ying kicked more vigorously in the water, feet brushing against plants and creatures below. His hands moved, grasping the implements, filling them and his own arms with his unaspected chi, reinforcing them with his aura. Then he stuck his hands forward.

Burning. His hands were on fire, his face too. He cut and pulled, dislodging the blossom and harvesting it as quickly as he could. A small motion and he extracted an ice jade box into which the Sun Lotus blossom was deposited. Wu Ying hurriedly closed the box, pushing his chi into the enchanted storage, reinforcing its natural ability to seal. Another exertion of will sent the box into his world spirit ring.

The heat disappeared as Wu Ying stopped paddling. He sank, water covering his face, his arms, providing blessed relief. At first, Wu Ying had his eyes closed, but he pried them open to see small darting fish floating beside him, among the waving tendrils of the lotus roots. And beneath his feet, far beneath, he caught sight of something bigger.

Something much bigger. Languidly swimming, tail flicking in slow motion.

He watched for a time as his breath grew short. Watched the monster paddle, ignoring all around it. And Wu Ying grinned. This could work. As he kicked upward and broke the surface, Wu Ying smiled.

This really could work.

***

The third target. This was going to take the longest, for Wu Ying was working to free dangling roots, cutting them when needed and preparing the land within the ring. The pond he had created needed to be deepened, some of the rich spiritual water he swam in replacing the current liquid within. As he swam, he debated whether it was worth the risk. But Wang Min had played well, and thus far, no issues had arisen even after he had acquired the second Sun Lotus.

Now, hands beneath the water, cradling the large lotus pad, Wu Ying readied himself to send a surge of chi into the plant to extract it from the water and deposit it into his ring. It would be the largest outflow of his energy since he had entered the water, which should not matter. He was only taking one of dozens of plants. And thus far, the carp below him was placid, rising up only twice to snap at larger-than-normal insects.

Inhale, exhale. Then, inhale again. On the exhale, Wu Ying sent his energy through the plant, wrapping it around leaves and flower all at once. He strained, expelling chi in greater quantities as he realized the enormity of the task. Uncontained by the ice jade boxes, the Sun Lotus fought his acquisition, refusing to allow him to send it into another dimension.

His breathing grew short, his legs kicked harder as he fought the plant. Long seconds, an eternity of struggle, and the plant disappeared with a plop. Water flowed into the gap and he breathed in relaxation and enjoyment. For a second.

For something had changed.

The moment Wu Ying took away the Sun Lotus, the fish all around him had begun moving faster. Deep in the water, Wu Ying felt a shudder tear through the environmental chi as Core-stage carp pushed against the music lulling it to rest.

"Wu Ying!" Wang Min cried. The fear that laced her voice was a clear indication of the trouble he was in, even as she poured additional chi into each note to combat the struggling monster.

Making a quick decision, Wu Ying stroked over to the nearest lotus leaf. He channeled chi through his body, triggering the Twelve Gale Steps cultivation exercise, and placed a hand on the leaf. His actions drew the nearby carp to him, and they bit at his body, drawing blood as they unleashed their anger at his theft.

A surge of energy, and Wu Ying pushed down on the leaf, leaping out of the water. He flipped, landing on a nearby floating plant, then kicked off again. He dared not stay long, even as he burnt the chi within his body, as he manipulated both his own and the water and wood chi around him to lighten his steps and increase his speed.

He raced across the many floating plants, feet touching against leaf pads, brushing against burning petals and scalding his skin. His clothing stuck to his body, in parts wet but slowly drying amidst the intense heat that emanated from the flowers. Carp, agitated by the expulsion of chi, by his presence, threw themselves into the air, attempting to bite him, knock him aside. The rope played out behind him, pulled in by Tou He as the ex-monk mouthed encouragement.

Beneath him, another shudder.

This was followed by a scream as Wang Min rocked backward, blood erupting from her nose and mouth as her enchanted tune was broken forcefully by the spirit carp. Wu Ying sensed beneath him the agitated, moving fish as it neared.

A hundred feet and he would be safe. Only seconds were required to run that distance. Wu Ying poured energy through his body, feet pushing against yielding green fronds. Bare feet rubbing against petals and burning. He felt the movement, a flicker of energy, smelled the wave front of expanding water chi.

He dropped low. Not daring to stop, Wu Ying shifted chi to his arms, pounding forward on all four limbs, brushing against petals that seared and made him scream.

Above him, the graceful lunge of the spirit carp. Jaws opened then clamped shut on open air, missing him by inches as he'd dropped. He continued to run, bounding onto his feet as momentum overtook balance, forty feet to shore. Landing in the water, plunging deep, the large fish disappeared with a flick of its tail, splashing Wu Ying and shifting floating vegetation with casual ease.

Trouble came next in the form of a school of flying fish, all of them smaller than their behemoth relative. But angry still, intent on bowling Wu

Ying over. Hands held up to his face, protecting his body, Wu Ying ran as creatures clamped on, tore at skin.

Only to realize, through the gaps between his arms, that there was no more vegetation as he neared the edge of the lake. With no choice now, he took one last flying leap, twenty feet left. Just water and fast-moving flashes of spirit carp, some clamping onto his body, wearing away at his skin. Their attacks buffeting themselves against his aura.

Feet landed on water. They pushed against the water, allowing him to keep moving. Chi flowed, reacted against water chi in the waves, solidifying the water briefly as he ran. Desperation gave him energy, gave him strength, clarified understanding. What had eluded him before worked now.

Eight feet.

Five.

Then, the water before him opened up. Water parted, and for nearly a foot beneath his feet, there was but air. He stumbled when his foot met air instead of water. Pace disrupted, Wu Ying pitched forward as he sought purchase.

Tumbled. Into the water.

He surged upward, tried to push against the shallow water here. So close. But the smaller carp swarmed, tore away at his control of the water, refusing to let him solidify it as they attacked him. They weighed him down, tearing at his aura, his skin, and his muscles. Blood flowed as Wu Ying struggled, drowning in a few feet of liquid.

Then the tug at his waist increased. Pulled, drawing him forward. Another heave, and suddenly, the water that had been like mud gave away, throwing his body onto cool, dry land. Threw him and the squirming carp that refused to give up their prey. A wave, coming from the depths, rushed out, splashing and battering the pair of cultivators, throwing them farther from the lake. As if it was casting them out like a pair of ungrateful guests, arriving with ang pow or mandarins at a banquet.

***

Wu Ying lay beside a crackling fire, Lei Hui wrapping his numerous but shallow wounds. He groaned again as he felt the warmth reach up to him, a sharp contrast to the cream slathered across his extremities that pulsed with cold. Above, the nearly full, risen moon and its companion stars illuminated the lakeside camp.

Wu Ying shifted, feeling soft sand beneath his back, silk robes laid across his legs and waist.

"Don't move. Cultivate if you are bored. I just stopped the bleeding and won't have you moving further," Lei Hui said.

Wu Ying complied, though he found it hard to concentrate. There was a delectable smell in the air, rising from the numerous carp being grilled near the fire. Others had been filleted and set aside to be smoked. As always, Tou He worked the fire, checking on the food while he continued to strip and clean the last few fish that had followed Wu Ying to shore. All in all, Wu Ying spotted at least a dozen of his assailants.

"When...?"

"At least another twenty minutes, he says," Wang Min said from where she sat near the fire. Fingers played across her pipa, idly strumming the instrument as she watched the meal and the rice pot hung over it.

Wu Ying yelped as a bandage pulled around his body roughly. "Not so tight!"

"Oh, I'm sorry. Maybe if I didn't have to work around the remnants of your pants, it wouldn't be so bad."

"Sorry." Wu Ying grimaced.

As the apothecarist continued his ministrations, Wu Ying tried to return to cultivating. It was difficult, especially when Wang Min kept looking over—he was somewhat less dressed than he would prefer. On the other hand, her attention was mostly focused on Lei Hui.

His musings were interrupted as Tou He, oblivious to the interplay—or playing at oblivious—walked over to Wang Min with a leaf plate of fish fillets. Tempted by the delectable smell, she placed her pipa aside and ate. In short order, Yu Kun managed to make his way back, lured by the promise of food.

"So did you get it?" Yu Kun asked as he took a seat beside Wu Ying.

"I did. We'll escort Lei Hui to the nearest road and begin the next steps."

"Already?" Tou He said, frowning at Wu Ying's injuries.

Wu Ying shook his head, even if it made his neck ache. He must have pulled a muscle—or had one bitten—during his flight. "It's mostly superficial. My pants took more damage than my body."

Lei Hui's lips thinned, but he reluctantly nodded in agreement. Wu Ying kept his face turned from Wang Min, though he smelled the shift in her chi, the way it flared as his words spoke. It had been rather embarrassing when he realized exactly how much of his clothing had been torn aside.

"No need to be ashamed. You have a nice buttocks," Tou He said.

Another flare of chi and Wang Min turned even redder.

Lei Hui spoke up, his voice angry. "Stop it. We're not discussing Wu Ying's buttocks."

"Or his tendency to take off his shirt?" Yu Kun said teasingly. "Not that I mind, mind you."

Wu Ying growled, eyes narrowing at the ex-wandering cultivator. Did he have to have words with the man? It was not a major issue, especially since they were all cultivators and thus not expected to advance the family line directly. But seeing that the other man was only joking, Wu Ying relaxed and watched the byplay between the group as they burnt off excess adrenaline by joking.

"Maybe we should focus on our preparations?" Lei Hui said, rising to the bait.

"It's okay, your buttocks are quite nice too," Yu Kun said. "Isn't that right, Wang Min?"

"You... you... you don't ask a lady that!" Wang Min flushed even more.

Wu Ying was amused to note that she glanced at Lei Hui's bottom involuntarily at Yu Kun's teasing. And that she grew even redder when they caught her looking. Lei Hui looked conflicted, his face warring between embarrassment, anger, and a little pride.

"Enough," Wu Ying said, his voice cutting through the group. He eyed the rising moon, wincing as he felt the sunburn on his face pull against his body. "We should rest soon. Once we're done eating, cultivate and get ready. Yu Kun, we'll be relying on you to watch for a little more. We have what we came for. We leave the lake tomorrow morning." Wu Ying met each of the now-sober group members' regard. "The next objective will be even more difficult."

Chapter 29

"Remember, keep the box closed. I've watered it and made sure it'll survive. But it won't last forever, not without care. This has to reach Elder Li within the next two months," Wu Ying said, reiterating the point as he held the ice jade box out to Lei Hui.

The apothecarist rolled his eyes, tugging the box from Wu Ying's hands. "Enough. I know how to take instructions. I am an apothecarist. I have written down all you have said that was relevant. It is a simple matter."

"As for the spirit stone—"

"Don't take it out of the spirit ring. But don't keep the ice jade box inside the ring with it." The apothecarist rolled his eyes again. "I am no fool. Now, stop with this. Or do you really wish me to go?" Lei Hui's eyes narrowed, and he shot a glance at Wang Min, who stood by their sides. "I can stay…"

"No. You should go." Wu Ying pointed down the road. "The village should be just a few li down the road. You should be able to buy or rent a boat to reach a major canal. From there—"

"I know."

Wu Ying clamped his mouth shut. Lei Hui sounded truly irate. Still, Wu Ying could not help but open his mouth to add another warning, only for Wang Min to grab his arm and pull him back.

"You're done. Let the rest of us speak with him," the musician said, pushing Wu Ying out of the way.

Forced back, Wu Ying glared at the back of her head, even as the musician led Lei Hui a short distance away. To his surprise, a moment later, a sound barrier enveloped the two. Wu Ying frowned, fists clenching and unclenching in agitation as he stared at the pair.

"You're acting like a worrying new mother bitch," Tou He said, prodding Wu Ying in the leg with his staff to get his attention. "He will be fine."

"Or not."

Tou He nodded agreeably. "It will be as it will be."

"That is not comforting," Wu Ying groused. He crossed his hands over his body and looked down the simple dirt road they stood beside.

Yu Kun was out scouting again, checking both sides of the road for potential problems. It was he who had stumbled across this rarely used track within the woods. It had not been marked on any map they had, but with some triangulation, they had ascertained their location and that of the upcoming village and river. Use of the lucky path and their attendant fishing craft should save Lei Hui time on his journey. And once he was on a boat, the cultivator would release messages for both the Sect and Elder Yang.

With a little luck, Lei Hui, with the two material pieces, should easily make his way to the Sect or a nearby town branch. Depending on where he traveled to and how Hinma was handling Elder Yang's imprisonment, he could have reinforcements soon after. At least staying in one of the Sect branches would keep him and the materials safe until another Elder arrived.

As for themselves, Wu Ying could not help but be grateful for the fortunate location of the path. His initial plan had involved a few additional days of tracking through the forest to locate the river. Now, they could just cut through the forest in a more direct route, saving multiple days of travel.

Whatever conversation Lei Hui and Wang Min were having drew slowly to a close. The pair parted with small smiles exchanged, and if Lei Hui had a new handkerchief, none of the other cultivators mentioned the matter. The apothecarist offered the group one last nod before he rode off, back ramrod straight.

Wu Ying bit his lip, forcing himself to not call out any further last-minute pieces of advice. At least Wu Ying still had one of the three materials on him. And, if they were lucky, they would locate the other two needed materials soon afterward. If not, it did not matter, so long as they had one set. But he'd prefer two.

If they didn't die acquiring one from the Chan Chu.

***

Down a second member of the expedition, Wu Ying had to admit that their desire to keep numbers low might have been a mistake. Unlike his first expedition, they were significantly understrength. If they could have gotten additional help, perhaps…

But the truth was, as many as they would have liked to acquire, neither Elder Cheng nor Elder Yang had enough contribution points. And while some might have been willing to help without payment—beyond Fairy Yang's company—it would have created its own issues. Not everyone was like Tou He, happy to receive his contribution at a later time or not at all. The more powerful the aid they gained, the greater the obligations they would have incurred.

And, reflecting on the list Wu Ying had received of those dismissed, too many of the Verdant Green Waters Sect's men were paper tigers. They had reputable martial forms, high cultivation levels, but it all came from training and not real-world experience.

Regret warred with worry as the expedition rode onward. The constant need to keep an eye out for trouble meant that Wu Ying could not take his mind off matters too often, but he still found himself gnawing at his worries. It was only when he missed noticing the return swing of a branch and received a branchful of leaves in his face that Tou He rode forward.

"Amithabha, Wu Ying," Tou He said, bringing a hand before him in prayer, the other still holding onto the reins.

"Not that easy," Wu Ying groused. "We're being attacked more because there aren't enough of us. And for the Chan Chu…"

"We will defeat it."

"If Buddha wills it," Wu Ying muttered wryly.

"Yes."

"How can you be so... so..." Wu Ying threw his hand up in the air.

"Serene?"

"Yes."

"Amithabha," Tou He repeated. "Your Master will live or die as is his fate. And we will survive or not, by our actions. Worrying about the future will not change it. Nor will regretting choices that made sense before."

"But—"

"Amitabha."

Wu Ying kicked his horse, making it dance as his frustration got the better of him. It took him a few seconds to calm the animal before they continued to ride. Tou He watched his friend for a short while before he let his horse fall back, smiling.

And Wu Ying had to admit, he felt better. It was not perfect. They could still fail. But he was beginning to realize that perhaps nothing in this world was perfect except the Dao. And worrying about the future would not change it.

Drawing another breath, he focused within and cultivated, forcing himself to be in the present and improving himself in the now. For whatever the future would bring, it could only be fixed by action in the present, not worrying about the future.

***

A week later, a dirty, disheveled, and injured group found themselves at the edges of the marsh they had been aiming for. By this point, even Wu Ying's multiple sets of hemp robes had proven to be insufficient and he wore clothing that had been torn apart multiple times and—badly—stitched together again. His companions were no better off. The attacks by the monsters had grown in such frequency and fierceness that even the durable silk of the Sect robes had parted. Of course, they each kept a single, untouched piece of clothing for later use in civilization. All of which left their current attire even more prone to abuse.

For all that, their gains had grown significantly. The hardships and constant cultivation had pushed Tou He through a blockage, and they'd had to wait half a day as he broke through then consolidated his cultivation. The ex-monk was now over halfway through the Energy Storage stage with five open Energy Storage meridians.

Other improvements were more subtle. To Wu Ying's surprise, Wang Min had revealed another ability based off her studies as a musician—vocal singing attacks. During battles, she would hum or sing a short verse, infusing the music with her chi in an aural attack. It was still new, and even when the attacks worked, they were less powerful than her instrumental attacks.

But vocal attacks were more flexible and allowed her to disrupt creatures during critical moments, like the family of monkeys that had found them days ago. A simple harmony had set the entire family against one another when an accidental thrown stick had struck another simian attacker. A flare of irritation, a hummed discordant note, a howled rebuke, and suddenly, a gang of close-knit monsters had become a brawling, shit-flinging nest that the expedition managed to escape.

Yu Kun had complained about the loss of demon stones, but his complaints had been overruled by the already dirty and tired group. No need to add foul-smelling substances to their clothing, especially since demon beast fecal matter somehow stuck even better than normal waste.

It amused Wu Ying how few of the epics of his peasant past, how few stories he'd read discussed the logistics of trampling through the countryside for weeks on end. How the heroes of his favorite stories never concerned themselves about torn and bloody clothing, at most having a single, artful tear in a sleeve. The reality of an expedition was mostly one of dirt, hunger, and exhaustion.

And what gains there might be, might be little or ephemeral. Yu Kun, like Wu Ying, had achieved a point in his current development that sudden increases in his cultivation were unlikely. Minor improvements in awareness and skill with martial forms accrued, as did Wu Ying's bag of herbs.

"One moment," Wu Ying called.

The group ground to a halt and, seeing him dismount, followed suit. They were not surprised to watch the Gatherer walk away from the group after tying his horse off, head pivoting from side to side as he neared his goal. Around a tree, the cultivator bent, brushing aside leaves and branches to locate the mushrooms he had smelled.

"White and purple spots. Spores are…" Wu Ying lightly tapped the mushroom while holding a knife beneath it, making sure to tap it with a convenient stick. He brought the knife up to his eyes, careful not to breathe while he verified the color. "Pale yellow. Nearby plants are correct too." The Gatherer grinned and began the process of digging up the mushrooms to transplant into his ring.

"What did you find?" Tou He asked, having made his way over.

"Purple-eyed forest mushrooms." Even while talking, Wu Ying was taking care to dig around the tree and the fungi, pulling the ground up around the mushroom while mentally carving the same gap in his world ring. It required a deft use of chi to do the same within the ring, a manipulation of the formations that made up the ring itself. But once done, he deposited the entire mushroom beside a smaller tree he'd transplanted earlier, all situated near the pond he'd created for the Sun Lotus. "They're not particularly useful for apothecarists, but they help manage nearby chi flows. It's one of the types I was looking to add to my ring."

"You smelled it?" Tou He asked. At Wu Ying's nod, he continued as the pair wandered back to the group. "How did you know what it smelled like?"

"I didn't. I can just... sense the difference. The way it interacted with the surroundings. I could tell what the smell meant, in general, and then because of how it interacted, I assumed it was something good," Wu Ying explained. "I wonder if Master Cheng knew..."

To his surprise, the use of his new sense of smell for chi had widened his range for his search for herbs. And while Wu Ying was busy learning to differentiate the various smells in the wild, his living world spirit ring was nearly filled to the brim with plants he'd transplanted. Even his horse was weighed down by what he'd located, the various herbs carefully arranged to dry, keep moist, or were otherwise stored. The few that could be stored in his other spirit ring, he had.

"Ask him, when you return," Tou He said.

Wu Ying flashed his friend a tight smile, reminded of why they were there. Once he'd thanked everyone for their patience, he pointed at the marsh, so similar to the one before. "Our objective lives in there. Objectives, perhaps."

Trees dotted the terrain before them, marking areas of shallower water and firm ground, with tall roots and murky water everywhere. In the marsh itself were wisps of mists obscuring sight, while colorful plants, both beautiful and poisonous, threw yellow, purple, green, and red splotches of color across the shaded landscape.

"Reports in this region indicate that the Chan Chu are common in the marsh before us. Due to the lack of easy routes within, and the danger from spirit and demonic beasts this far in, few cultivators bother them. As such, it's unlikely that the Chan Chu have been wiped out since the last report a decade ago," Wu Ying said, reiterating points he'd brought up before to the cultivators as they rode. But he could not recall what he'd said and what he hadn't to each of them, so he repeated himself. "The marsh itself is only mildly dangerous. The plants within are poisonous, but Lei Hui has left us with enough pills that we should be protected. Just try not to touch anything colorful."

The group broke into laughter at Wu Ying's words, but soon calmed as he raised his hand.

"Take what you need, leave behind what you don't require. We'll tether the horses and set up a formation to keep them and our belongings safe, but…" Wu Ying shrugged and the rest nodded in understanding.

They were in the wilds, and while they had a decent formation for defense, without a cultivator to keep it safe, there was no guarantee. Chance could just as easily send a Core Formation beast nearby as it could keep their belongings safe.

"If there are no questions, we leave tomorrow." A pause. "And thank you. All of you. Again."

***

The next morning, the group set out on foot. Training, experience, and a little enlightenment had progressed all their skills in qinggong to such an extent that they no longer feared the water. As a group, with Wu Ying leading and Yu Kun taking up the rear, they ran across the marsh, feet tapping against the liquid that flowed and shifted beneath them. Of course, they made sure to stop at dry spots of land whenever they could to recharge their dantians and allow Wu Ying to watch for signs of their prey. Even so, their journey through the marsh was much swifter.

Left unspoken was the greatest concern—the issue of locating the three-legged frog. They no longer had an Elder to expand their search radius with her senses, nor could they afford to be blatant in their attempts. They had no idea what lived in the swamp, what they might attract if they conducted themselves like Elder Yang.

Worse, the amphibians were not known to be easily baited. Hunters would often place numerous traps, using time and experience to locate and bring back their prey. The cultivators had neither in great quantities, so they could only hope that Wu Ying's expanded senses and the sparse expedition notes would lead them to the creatures.

Day after day, the group trooped through the marsh. At night, they set up sparse formations, built using simple talismans to ward off insects and other spirit creatures. They hid their presence through the day and night as they searched for signs of the Chan Chu. Twice, they were attacked by powerful monsters, including once by a Core formation mutated water strider, as large as one of their horses, with a pair of pincers that glowed when it cast waves of water at them.

Tou He nearly drowned, trapped in a bubble of chi-formed water by the angry water strider due to his flame attacks. Only the combined attacks of Yu Kun and Wu Ying managed to crack the creature's shell and end it. Luckily, as an insect, it was significantly weaker than a larger, Core formation spirit beast.

The second attack was by a Chan Chu, but only in the Energy Storage stage. The smaller animal had latched his tongue around Wu Ying's arm and tried to drag the swordsman into the water. Dealing with it had been a simple enough matter, such that it would have barely been worth noting, except for its origin. As a member of the species they hunted for, it gave them hope that they would find an appropriately sized monster. Unfortunately, the smaller heart was unlikely to be sufficient.

And so, the group continued to search, trudging through the marshes, skimming along the water and batting aside the occasional evolved insect. They swallowed anti-poison pills daily, the acrid taste of the pills leaving a lingering bitterness on the tongue and causing nausea for a few hours after they were swallowed.

All the while, the team moved carefully, wary about their enemies. Yet, neither sign of enemies nor three-legged frog appeared in the days that passed. Their long circular search had them nearing their entrance location when Wu Ying called a halt to the expedition.

"We have a heart. It isn't great, but we have one. If we take any longer, the heart will degrade even further. And whether or not our prey is here, we have not found them," Wu Ying said. "I think it is time for us to go."

The group was silent, all of them watching him and their surroundings. He noted how their shoulders were bowed, their hair damp and plastered to dirty faces, hair oily from lack of washing. Clothing that was once pristine had stained and torn even further, making them all look like vagrants rather than upright sect members. Yet Wu Ying felt a flash of pride as not a single one of them jumped at his suggestion.

"Thank you again," Wu Ying's said. "Tomorrow morning, we turn back and retrieve our horses." He looked around the simple, mushy ground, in the bowels of the trees that rose around. "We'll rest here for tonight."

Chapter 30

The morning found Wu Ying up before the others, having taken the last watch of the night. Whatever malaise he might have felt over having to choose to use an imperfect material for his Master's potion, he had driven it away. Instead, he bounced around the group cheerfully, goading them on with promises of a warm meal at the end of the day's trek.

Encouraged by the cultivator, the team members dressed and washed quickly before following the running cultivator. They stopped much less frequently, only long enough to ensure that their chi reserves were close to full, barely checking for signs of the Chan Chu.

It was perhaps fated then that, as they neared the entrance to the marshes, Wu Ying smelled a familiar scent. He nearly lost his footing on the water, sinking half an inch into the brackish liquid before he exerted his chi and bounced away onto a root. Perched on the slimy wooden sustenance-giver, Wu Ying breathed deeply, head tilting from side to side as he confirmed what he sensed.

"Trouble?" Yu Kun asked, hand on his swords as he scanned about him.

"No... a Chan Chu. A big one too." Wu Ying hesitated, looking at his friends. He wasn't surprised to see flashes of conflict on their faces, emotions of disappointment, fear, and anticipation crossing them all. A powerful Chan Chu was dangerous. And they were so close to being done. Choosing to attack it put them all at risk.

Not choosing to do so...

"Whatever Buddha wills, it seems," Tou He said. "So what do you suggest we do?"

Wu Ying couldn't help but smile at the ex-monk's words. Yu Kun looked resolved, while Wang Min was a little paler than normal.

Wu Ying gestured for them to come closer and pointed at the female cultivator. "You should tune your instrument as best you can. When we find it, we will need you to be ready."

She nodded and sat, extracted her guzheng, and tuned it, having already laid out a simple sound-blocking formation around herself.

Seeing the musician settled, Wu Ying turned to the others. "Unless there's a reason to change, we will follow the basic plan. Tou He, you will have to hold its attention. Yu Kun and I will do our best to kill it, but we will not strike until Wang Min has frozen the creature."

The ex-monk nodded. His role meant he would have to bear the brunt of the attacks for a few minutes, but if the others unleashed their attacks too soon, it would definitely spell failure. None of them could catch the spirit frog if it truly meant to run.

Wu Ying looked over as Tou He hummed, then continued. "I will see if I can find the Chan Chu while we wait. Yu Kun, please verify that there are no additional dangers."

Orders given, the group split up with Tou He staying behind to guard the musician. As Wu Ying moved through the water, he paid careful attention to how much chi he dispersed. Too much and he would be found before he located the creature himself.

***

They set up on a small hill, not far from where the Chan Chu rested. Like most of its kind, it lay half-submerged in the water near the edge of dry ground. It was covered by brackish water, sand, and vegetation lapping at the edges of its body. Only portions of its head and eyes showed, nostrils poking out of the water as it slowly breathed. It lay in wait, and if not for Wu Ying's expanded senses, they would have likely walked right past the creature.

Wu Ying shook his head again, marveling at the flows of energy he sensed and smelled. The Chan Chu cultivated as it rested, offering Wu Ying a glimpse into a greater dao. It emanated a sliver of chi from its body, manipulating the flow of energy around it within a couple of li radius. It was a subtle, almost imperceptible alteration of the environment, akin to the way Wu Ying and the others manipulated the environment with their own qinggong exercises.

But instead of making its body lighter, the Chan Chu's manipulation formed a vortex that drew the environmental chi toward it. In this way, the Core formation spirit beast was able to draw in a greater than normal amount of chi by concentrating energy within its surroundings. Once it drained an area dry, it would leave. And if a meal came along, drawn by the flow of chi, well, dinner was served.

The fact that the Chan Chu was currently cultivating was an opportunity for the expedition. Until it was ready to move along, they had an opportunity to set up and attack. Wang Min was seated with her guzheng out, gently strumming the instrument and verifying its tuning. Unfortunately, she could only tune the instrument to a certain extent while she was blocked off from the environment. It was no simple matter of tuning notes but tuning the environment and making the song work against the creature in question. As such, she needed to sense the environment and the creature's chi-aspect to complete her job. Once she released her formation, they would face the greatest danger as the Chan Chu could choose to attack at that time.

If it did not, Wang Min would finish her tuning before leading the assault against the spirit beast. Careful application of her music would affect the creature's chi flows, both blocking the environmental flows going in and out and also disrupting its defensive aura. Done well, it would leave the creature defenseless to Wu Ying and Yu Kun's attacks.

Together, Wu Ying and Tou He made their way to another hill a short distance away from the one the team had set up on, in between the Chan Chu and the other pair of cultivators. Wu Ying moved ahead a little farther, setting up a series of trap talismans. He licked his lips, sweating as he finally returned to his position beside Tou He.

The moment they were ready, Wang Min dropped the formation, and the first of her delicate notes entered the atmosphere. They struck Wu Ying as he crouched low, sword in hand, and he felt the notes press upon his skin, his aura. He pushed back automatically and extended his senses.

Every breath was controlled to allow him to sense the chi all around, to smell the rotten, brackish water of the marsh, the poisonous mists that floated through the air. He felt the winds, bearing the pollen of poisonous and aromatic plants, brush against his skin, pushing his tattered robes tight. The grip on his sword was comforting, the leather of the hilt absorbing the moisture from his palms, the cool metal engravings of his scabbard drawing away heat.

He expanded his senses and waited.

Fingers strummed, filling the air with musical notes laden with chi. Wu Ying sensed his friend shift beside him, the tip of Tou He's staff creeping into his vision, pushing ahead of his position. Depending on what happened, either Tou He or Wu Ying would meet the creature first. After the initial clash, they would transfer the monster's attention away from Wu Ying if needed, allowing the monk with his Mountain Resides staff form to keep the creature away.

"It's moving," Wu Ying warned his friend.

Moments later, the water trembled. The washed-up mud and debris that had sat upon the previously inert monster shifted, trembling as they fell aside. At first look, it could have been mistaken for an errant wave, maybe an errant breeze. And then, a bigger change. The creature shifted, pushing against the water and the mud around it as it jumped. A single bound took it two-thirds of the way toward Wu Ying and Tou He.

The pair did not need to speak, having worked together for so long now. Tou He jumped, meeting the Chan Chu as it leaped through the air again. Staff raised over his head, the ex-monk swung the wooden implement, pouring his chi into the attack. The staff lit aflame, as did the monk himself. Faint shimmers of a mountain, tall and implacable, formed around the man as he fell.

In retaliation, the Chan Chu imbued its aura with its chi as ever more earth and water sloughed off its body. Wu Ying groaned mentally as it revealed its aspect, though he'd already guessed. It was a metal-aspected Chan Chu, the hardest kind to fight.

Fire and metal met in the air, the chi auras of the combatants flaring as they impacted. Wu Ying watched as Tou He's staff bent under the force of their collision. The Chan Chu was redirected downward, its trajectory altered as it crashed to the ground in a spray of water and mud. Tou He was thrown backward as the momentum of his attack rebounded, sending him flying into the distance.

Already, their plan was disrupted. Wang Min's playing kept going at the same serene pace, but Wu Ying could barely hear it as he rushed the slowly rising monster. An arrow buried itself beneath the frog's left eye, just missing blinding the creature, as Yu Kun fired at it. Another arrow was knocked aside by a fast-moving tongue, one that forced Yu Kun to throw himself aside as it shattered his bow.

Trap talismans, forming spikes of metal chi, erupted from the surroundings as the Chan Chu waddled forward. Its own metal aura deflected the attacks, the monster delivering a loud croaked rebuke. As its feet bunched beneath it, Wu Ying finally caught up.

Sword chi imbued with the full strength of the Dragon's Breath attack of the Long family style struck the back of the Chan Chu's only rear leg. It caught the rear tendon of its left foot, tearing at metal-chi hardened flesh and leaving a long bleeding wound. Another croaked rebuke as the creature twisted to assault Wu Ying, ignoring the noisome but ineffective Wang Min for the moment.

Wary now, Wu Ying raised his sword and scabbard. His caution paid off as the monster opened its mouth, releasing the fleshy protuberance at him only to be deflected with a flick of Wu Ying's wrist. Even as he retreated, hand and sword shaking from the force of the attack, chi-formed duplicate tongues assaulted the cultivator at multiple angles.

"Metal copies!" Wu Ying shouted, just barely dodging an attack that tore at his robes. He twisted and cut, deflecting with scabbard and sword the chi-created copies.

As strong as his body was, Wu Ying was more focused on his aura, using it to batter at the copies. In forming his own aura around his defenses into sharp edges, he cut at the metal chi the creature formed, breaking the chi formations and dispersing the attacks.

Even as he retreated, Wu Ying attempted to launch his own attacks. The projected sword intent barely left more than a scratch on the Chan Chu— often not even that much. Ineffective or not, the attacks were sufficiently annoying to keep the monster focused on him. Yet each moment saw Wu Ying in growing danger as the creature's strikes grew closer, forcing him into desperate acrobatics and wild defenses. Soon enough, attacks of any form were no longer an option.

Before he was entirely overwhelmed, the monster let out a croak. Its muscles twitched, blood flowing from a cut along its flank as Yu Kun dug his hooked swords into it. He twisted and pulled, tearing at the hardened flesh, attempting to widen the wound.

A flare of cold iron, of rusted metal rose from the monster. Wu Ying's eyes widened as he reset his posture, feet skidding along the water as he called out a warning. Too late.

The Chan Chu flared its aura, and for a second, it looked like a reptilian, slimy porcupine as spikes of metal chi rose from its body. Yu Kun barely dodged the initial formation. He failed to dodge the explosion as those spikes flew from the monster's body. Wu Ying too was subjected to the explosive aura attack, adding a number of surface wounds to his litany of injuries.

Falling backward, Yu Kun clutched his arm, a hooked sword fallen to the ground. Rather than leave the weapon, Yu Kun used his other weapon, hooking them together with a sweep of his uninjured arm. The weapons became a long whip, swirling around him as he channeled his water chi to stop the bleeding.

"You okay?" Wu Ying called.

"I'm fine. Soon!" Wang Min replied, reminding the cultivator that Yu Kun was not the only one in danger.

Worries about the musician fell away as the monster redirected its anger at Yu Kun. Whether it sensed the other cultivator was injured or it just wanted revenge, it hopped over to the other man, injured back foot bunching as it leaped. At the apex of its jump, the monster opened its mouth, unleashing a new attack of small, chi-laden metallic spitballs at Yu Kun.

Hooked swords spun in a circle, pulling water from the marsh as Yu Kun retreated from the bulky frog. Water formed around the blades, creating a circular shield of metal and liquid that intercepted the spit-laden metal chi.

"Don't ignore me!" Wu Ying snarled, sheathing his blade and crouching low.

"No! My turn." Tou He's voice interrupted Wu Ying just before the swordsman attacked.

Like before, Tou He attacked with a jump strike, flying through the air to swing his staff down. Wrapped in fire chi, he plummeted with his staff leading the attack, the mountain reforming as he fell.

Metal yielded to fire and the frog sank into the ground, water splashing in a wave of loathsome liquid. The ex-monk did not stop, instead redirecting his energy to land a short distance away on an outcropping of land. Then Tou He pirouetted, fire dimming. Staff raised, Tou He waited for his opponent.

And come it did. The Core Formation stage Chan Chu was not knocked out, even if Tou He had managed to land a strike that had dented the creature's head. Fire and Metal were anathema, with fire having the advantage over metal. That gave the ex-monk's strikes a strength that the other pair lacked.

Yu Kun backed off, crouching low as he worked to stop the bleeding in his wounds more permanently. A water cultivator might not be able to injure the Chan Chu without effort, but he could take temporary measures to heal himself. A pill slipped into his mouth helped stabilize Yu Kun's chi flows, creating a calming center as his body stitched itself together.

In the distance, protected by the trio, Wang Min began to play for real. Chords struck, mixing with the attacks that the Chan Chu launched, mingling with the crunch of iron and bronze spikes impacting wood as the monster fought Tou He. Her playing sped up, the timing continuing to be impeccable as notes from her song, imbued with her air chi, drove deep into the Chan Chu. Each note worked deeper into its body, invading muscle and meridians.

At first, the Chan Chu ignored her. But perhaps somewhere deep within, it recognized the greater danger the woman held. The monster shuddered; its aura flared as it attempted to push away the aural assault. Taking advantage of its distraction, Wu Ying ducked in and cut at its injured back leg again. His attack tore at the skin and exposed tendons, fraying them further and distracting the monster once more.

Another flare of power, its aura pulsing with the same spiked defense and attack. Wu Ying jumped backward, attempting to get as much distance as he could before the spikes exploded. Tou He formed a flaming defense in front of the monster, blocking its view of Wang Min, while Yu Kun ducked behind an outcropping of earth, sinking into the water.

Too close, Wu Ying could not block all the attacks. A spike slammed into his left shoulder, burying itself in his wounds before it disappeared, the chi attack dispersed by his own aura. Blood flowed and strengthless fingers dropped his scabbard. As it sank into the water, Wu Ying raised his sword, spotting the jagged, chipped edges of the blade.

"Another blade!?!" Wu Ying groaned. While his unaspected chi allowed him to protect his weapons and himself, it was nowhere as powerful as earth or metal chi in that respect. And now, more than ever, as he continued to fight stronger and stronger opponents, it was showing its weakness. He had one other blade in storage, after which he'd be forced to rely on the damaged blades he still kept. "Cao nei mah!"

Thankfully, his inattention cost him nothing. Tou He blocked the Chan Chu's progress, the ex-monk breathing hard, his flame aura guttering as it was assaulted by the frog. By Tou He's side, Yu Kun darted out with his linked hooked swords, whipping the blades across the creature's eyes and face. Tearing at it, distracting the monster when Tou He required a moment's respite.

Joining the pair, Wu Ying attacked from behind, threatening its leg, forcing the creature to reposition itself constantly or be maimed.

It was, to Wu Ying's surprise, an easier fight than he had expected. The creature was powerful, each of its attacks so intense that they often threatened to cripple or kill with a single strike if they were not deflected or shifted to non-vital areas. But at the same time, the beast was simple, artless in its aggression and form.

Its greatest ability was the greater defense its metal attunement gave it. Crippling attacks became nothing more than light wounds, blinding strikes doing little more than annoy it. Each attack had to be reinforced with chi, forcing them to expend greater and greater energy.

"How much longer?" Wu Ying called as he dodged. He knew Tou He would never ask, would never complain. But Wu Ying could tell, he could sense that his friend was lagging, his smaller than normal chi reserves draining away.

"I can do it," Wang Min called, her fingers never stopping playing.

If anything, Wu Ying sensed that she sent even more chi into her aural attacks. The Chan Chu shuddered, rage growing as it tried to near her and was stymied again.

"Then do it in five breaths!" Wu Ying enjoined her, shifting position.

As if they had rehearsed it—and they had—Tou He dropped back, giving ground. The frog followed, eager to finish the ex-monk and the one it protected. Yu Kun stopped attacking, retreating to the side as he grabbed his sword from his other blade and took hold of both in either hand. His wounds flowed again, but the cultivator ignored it.

There was no need to speak, for the change in notes was signal enough. A harsh, discordant chord was struck. It made the air, the chi shudder. Wu Ying sensed the way the discordant note made the remnant air chi twitch.

Buried in the Chan Chu's body, the dregs of Wang Min's aural assault rippled, tearing at meridians and muscles, locking it in place as pain shot through the monster. For a second, its aura failed entirely.

Together, Wu Ying and Yu Kun struck.

Yu Kun jumped forward, his swords swinging, hooks digging deep into the wounded side. Searching for a grip, for tendons and muscles to pull away.

As for himself, the Sword's Truth combined with Dragon's Breath—the Dragon's Truth—formed Wu Ying's attack. He pushed sword intent into the tip of his sword as he lunged, targeting just above the monster's front legs. Aiming for the creature's heart.

A straight lunge, with everything Wu Ying had within him. All the strength that flowed through his dantian, all his chi formed into a single cutting edge empowered by his understanding. Power flared and his blade sank deep into the monster. When his attack finished, when the initial impetus died, he dug his feet into the soggy ground and pushed, driving his sword deeper.

The Chan Chu threw itself from side to side, spinning in a circle and splattering blood from the open wound Yu Kun had created. Blood, smelling heavier of rusted iron than ever, stained the ground, flooded the shallow waters.

Wu Ying slipped and twisted, gripping his embedded sword with every ounce of strength. As shoulder and wrist jolted with each twist, a snap resounded as his blade broke off within the monster. A moment later, the cultivator was struck by the spinning body and sent tumbling into the water. As he struggled back to the surface, feet finding purchase on yielding, muddy ground, he noted the monster still standing. Its movements had grown slower, but even if the monster was not as stupidly enduring as an Earth-attuned creature, it was still strong.

Tou He had returned to the fight, but his strikes were slower and less powerful. Wang Min had switched her attacks, launching blades of air at the monster rather than burrowing deep within with her music. As for Yu Kun, he was back, attempting to widen the wound that poured blood in ridiculous amounts.

Thankfully, the Chan Chu was raging, shooting edged spikes at the cultivators and the surroundings without care. A spike nearly tore into Wu Ying's face as he struggled to pull himself out of the water, hand on a nearby root.

"It's flagging," Wu Ying cried as he struggled to his feet. The frog was dying. It just required a little more, just a little more... "Just add more oil[28]!"

---

[28] This is more a direct translation of jiā yóu, meaning 'more energy' or 'more focus'. Normally, I don't use direct translations, but it's one of those amusing translations.

Chapter 31

Wu Ying panted, face bleeding, leg bleeding, shoulder aching as he stood over the corpse of the Chan Chu. He leaned heavily on the sword buried in the monster's skull, the scent and taste of raw blood and sodden marshlands filling his nostrils. Surrounding the beast, the others slowly made their way closer, limping and injured. They had killed it, but not without cost.

Tou He moved slowly, ribs broken, one leg dragging as he neared. He stood only by sheer force of will and the aid of his staff. Yu Kun was not much better, one arm mangled and his shoulder wound bleeding freely. Even Wang Min had finally been injured, the woman the only one not close to the monster as she stared at the destroyed guzheng, unmindful of the blood that dripped from her mouth.

"Is everyone okay?" Wu Ying called, just to check. He swallowed a healing pill, his dantian churning overtime as the Never Empty Wine Pot drew in the surrounding chi to refill his body and begin the healing process.

"I need. To. Sit down," Tou He forced out. And then, without waiting for acknowledgement, the ex-monk collapsed against the still-warm flesh of the Chan Chu, crossing his legs to cultivate. Wu Ying sensed the change was not just because of his injuries but from overdrawing his chi once again.

Wu Ying frowned at his friend and looked at Yu Kun. The ex-wandering cultivator waved a tired hand, his body slowly filling as he churned the chi within his body and utilized the pill he had swallowed. Even if Yu Kun was standing, Wu Ying wondered if he could fight. If he himself could fight…

"Wang Min," Wu Ying called.

The female cultivator jerked, her gaze leaving the guzheng, and wiped her eyes hastily with the long sleeves of her robe. "Yes?"

"Can you set up a perimeter and watch? The others need to cultivate and heal." Wu Ying sent his mind into his own body, testing the efficacy of the pill he had swallowed and his injuries. "I'll begin harvest in a minute."

"Are you sure?" Wang Min asked, her brows drawing down in worry as she stared at him.

"The faster we—I—harvest the heart, the stronger it will be." Wu Ying flashed her a half-smile. "It's not as if I have a choice, do I?"

As experience had shown, you worked when there was work to be done. You stopped when the work was finished, not when you were tired or injured. He had too many memories of peasants limping into the field with open wounds, broken fingers, or running a fever when harvest day came. When it was time to plant.

Nature never waited for a time to be convenient. And you could only choose to act, to finish the job. Or lose an entire year's harvest. You did what you had to do. And rested when you were done.

Wang Min glanced at her hands, then at the monster before looking at Yu Kun. She assessed the group and laughed. The laughter was a little strained, a little hysterical, but it was laughter still. "I guess not."

She moved then, crossing the water to near the group even as she extracted yellow talismans from her ring. These would safeguard them for a few minutes, reducing the scent and smell of their battle and subtly driving away scavengers. Other talismans would create a barrier when triggered, to block those too strong or too bullheaded to be swayed.

Wu Ying watched the musician for a moment, then turned away to focus deeper within himself. He had a little while to heal himself, to replace his chi. Then he would have to cut apart the Spirit Beast and harvest its innards. Even if the metal chi the Chan Chu had gathered within itself was dispersing, cutting through the creature would be a struggle.

Luckily, Yu Kun had opened a nice hole...

***

Twenty minutes later, Wu Ying extracted bloody hands from within the Chan Chu's body. Arrayed before Wu Ying, bunched around his sodden trousers and stained cloth shoes, were the discarded innards of the monster, parts too damaged or too lacking in value to be worth bringing back. In Wu Ying's hands was an inert organ, the heart of the creature.

Inert to normal senses at least. But to Wu Ying's aura, to his extended olfactory sense, he could taste the metal chi, the lifeforce of the Chan Chu still trapped within the heart. As he pulled his body from the sucking cavity, chest and face stained with the blood he'd been forced to deal with, he extracted the storage box his Master had gone through such trouble to locate.

A simple motion had the heart deposited within, sealing the chi and reducing the speed of decay. The faster they got this stored away, the more effective the antidote would be. With two such hearts, Wu Ying felt almost confident that they would be fine. It was just too bad they had no second stone for the Ben.

As Wu Ying placed the storage box in his world spirit ring, he found a wave of weakness washing over him, draining his strength. He plopped down onto the discarded viscera, creating a small splash of blood and guts. He would have vomited, but even that level of energy and reaction seemed too much for him. It was all he could do not to collapse onto his back.

"Wu Ying!" Yu Kun cried, rushing over to the cultivator. A quick check showed that Wu Ying was not injured in any way—beyond the obvious damage—and the wandering cultivator eventually dragged him out of the viscera via his armpits. He propped the man against a nearby tree, nearby the flowing water. "Rest. You've done enough. I'll finish the harvesting."

"No…" Wu Ying protested, but his voice was so soft that Yu Kun either ignored it or just missed it entirely. Watching the man stride away, Wu Ying tried to protest again and even attempted to stand, only to collapse as his body enforced its exhaustion upon him. Forced to rest, he found his eyes drifting closed.

When he awoke, Wu Ying found that he had been washed off. He was shirtless and his pants were still slightly damp and stained, but the blood and viscera he had accumulated had been cleansed from him. Furthermore, the organs and the corpse of the monster had been stripped, simple scent talismans applied to make their life a little more pleasant.

As he pushed himself up, Wu Ying spent a moment perusing his body. His earlier collapse had come about due to the draining of tension, the release of stress that had built-up over the past few weeks. Now that it was gone, his body betrayed him, leaving him feeling listless and muggy.

"How long was I asleep?" Wu Ying asked. It was hard to tell in the misty surroundings of the marsh, the daylight sky covered by foliage and wisps of mist.

"Just over three hours or so," Wang Min replied. She walked over and handed him a few pieces of charred white meat on a stick, which he grabbed and wolfed down. By the time she returned with more, he was staring contemplatively at the bare sticks.

"Slightly slimy like fish but firmer, with a heavy dose of metal chi." Wu Ying met her gaze. "The Chan Chu?"

Wang Min nodded. After she handed over the next batch to Wu Ying, she pointed in the direction she'd come from. "Yu Kun started cooking once he was done, and Tou He took over when he woke. Yu Kun's now resting."

Grimacing, Wu Ying levered himself to his feet as he chewed and swallowed. The additional chi from the meat and the warmth of the meal was helping to restore his energy. Water from his waterskin helped as well, rejuvenating his body as he added another healing pill. Taking so many in such short order was dangerous. Too many pills would slow or even halt his progression. But they were in danger in the marsh, and such future concerns had to be set aside.

"Good. We should eat, rest up, and leave." Wu Ying glanced again at Wang Min, noting that her eyes were a little red and puffy. "I'm sorry. About your instrument."

"It is fine," Wang Min said automatically. Then, drawing a breath, she continued. "It will be fine. My Master warned me that taking part in expeditions would risk it. That we must all risk what we love to improve."

Wu Ying nodded, then gestured back to where she had sat. He noted that the remnants of the guzheng were gone. "Did it have particular importance to you?"

The cultivator stayed silent as they walked around the dead corpse, forced to tread carefully as they moved along the water's edge. Wu Ying kept a hand on his sword, eyeing the water for potential dangers, limping carefully as his shoulder ached from the newly scabbed over wound. They managed to traverse the distance with little trouble to spot the fire and Tou He.

"It was my first instrument. It was given to me by my mother," Wang Min said softly. "It was her first guzheng too. I had hoped..." She shook her head. "Hope is for a fickle future that betrays us at every turn."

The bitterness in her voice made Wu Ying frown. In truth, unlike Yu Kun, he knew little of her. When she was not practicing, Lei Hui had taken up her time. On rare occasions when Lei Hui had not been by her side, she had spent that time with Fairy Yang. Add her usual reticence and even months of journey together had revealed little. Wu Ying knew she was the daughter of a nobleman's second wife. But beyond that, he knew little else.

"I see," Wu Ying said. "Your mother...?"

"Lives, and is treasured," Wang Min said, shooting a look at Wu Ying. "She bore my father two sons after me." Wang Min shrugged. "As for me... I am best suited as a cultivator."

"Ah." Wu Ying fell silent. "Perhaps not all hope is a betrayal though. Like you and Lei Hui?" He flashed her a smile, trying for levity.

"Mmm... perhaps. He is... intense. But my mother always says the passionate studious ones are the least likely to stray."

Wu Ying blinked. Thankfully, their steps had carried them close to the fire and he was saved by Tou He turning around and thrusting cooked meat sticks at them. As she moved to the opposite side of the fire, Wu Ying could not help but sigh in gratitude. Were all women that mercenary in the choice of their affections?

"You good?" Wu Ying said, choosing a simpler concern.

"Tired," Tou He said. "I might not be... well..." The ex-monk shrugged. "I won't be able to fight at my full strength for a bit."

"Good thing that we aren't expecting any more fights." Growing grimmer, he eyed his friend. "Your dantian?"

"Drained. I might have... I might have damaged a meridian or two."

Wu Ying winced. He mentally checked his storage ring, wondering if he had anything for that. Overdrawing one's chi and damaging your meridians was a common injury. Common enough that such medicine was often kept on-hand. Except, of course, he hadn't the funds or contribution points to own such things just in case.

"I have some raw herbs. If you chewed it..." Wu Ying trailed off as Tou He shook his head.

"I have a Two-Color Spring Harvest Meridian Healing Pill," Tou He said. "Once I've healed further, I will take it."

"What colors?"

"Red and white."

"Oh, those are good." Wu Ying nodded. The Two-Color pills' strength varied, both on the strength of the pill itself and its interaction with the consumer's chi-aspect. A red pill would work very well with Tou He's flame aspect.

"Worry less. Eat more," Tou He said, pushing another piece of meat at Wu Ying. "We should leave soon. So best to finish what we can."

"Right, right," Wu Ying replied. "When you go to get your... well... for anything..."

"I'll ask."

"Good."

They were leaving the majority of the large toad behind, its house-sized body a prize for the scavengers. They had no way to store so much meat, nor any desire to do so. While its flesh was strong and filled with chi, it would do them little good by the time they reached civilization. They could bring enough for their own meals for a few days and store some of the more valuable portions, but that was it.

Chowing down, Wu Ying could not help but feel a small smile creep across his face. After all this time, they had succeeded. Now, so long as Lei Hui was fine or they met another Ben, his Master would be saved. And as for his martial sister... well, she'd be fine. She was the Fairy after all.

***

When the group exited the safe ground Wang Min had created by deploying the talismans, Wu Ying was startled to spot a number of scavenger beasts attempting to locate and track down the delectable aroma they had escaped.

Thankfully, the group had used additional aura- and scent-suppressing talismans on themselves, allowing them to sneak past the monsters.

Under the guise of the talismans, the group left the marshlands, burning taels rather than risk another encounter. They took their time as they exited, preferring caution over speed now. Only a single, semi-sapient plant attacked them, wrapping Yu Kun in its branches before Wu Ying's shouted warning could arrive.

They'd had to chop down the monstrous, blood-drinking tree, then had to wait longer as Wu Ying extracted pottery jars to store the bleeding sap. The Blood Drinking Water Asp sap could be used in apothecarist pills to help bind healing type pills together. It was one of many preferred binding agents, and a rarer type due to its great demand. It was a great find, even if it came at the cost of additional injuries to Yu Kun.

Eventually, the group found themselves by their horses. To their relief, their equine companions were safe and unharmed, though somewhat hungry and bored. Releasing the beasts, the group began their long ride back to civilization, wary of additional attacks. The plan was to get an hour away from the marsh and its dangerous denizens before they would camp and rest for the evening.

Over the next few days, the group moved with a lightness to their movements, a sense of peace and happiness. They took extra care with their travel, only shifting course once in a while when they found potential locations for the Ben. Once, they even encountered a flock of the creatures. But the flock was safeguarded by a Core-level pair of mated Ben, and the group chose to avoid the confrontation.

As they rode, they slowly healed, their wounds stitching together. The most grievous of their wounds scabbed over, minor injuries disappearing as the days ran on. Occasional encounters with monsters left the group tired, but luckily, no one received any further major injuries.

Once they reached the road on Wu Ying's map, they rode faster. A few days on the road and they would be at the city it led to, where they would alight on the fastest passenger ship they could locate. From there, they would travel back to the Sect, potentially meeting with Lei Hui, Elder Yang, or any incoming Elders. Once they had reached the road, Wu Ying released a spirit messenger to Elder Yang and the Sect, relating their success.

The evenings by the road were quieter, conversations lighter and more relaxed. Deep in the wilderness as they were, rest stops were hard to find and on one occasion, lay abandoned. Rather than practicing, the team spoke, recuperated and healed their wounds, and refilled their dantians while contemplating their recent experiences. Two evenings in, Tou He took his pill and spent the evening tossing and turning in pain as it forcefully healed his meridians.

The next morning, they rose early with excitement thrumming through their veins. At Wang Min's suggestion, the group changed into their last set of Sect robes, the only clean and presentable clothing they had. They were half a day away from their destination city and had to arrive with some dignity. As they rode, their spirits were light, laughter and idle conversations filling in the hours.

Hours later, before them on the road, a small group of cultivators sat waiting. And in their midst was a familiar apothecarist, trussed up, his thin, scholar's face beaten black and blue.

Chapter 32

Wu Ying slowed his horse with a gentle tug of his reins. His eyes swept over the half dozen cultivators before him on the road to the city. A single farmer was between Wu Ying and the cultivators before them, driving his produce to the side of the road and casting fearful glances back and forth between the groups of cultivators.

Neither party spoke as Wu Ying brought his horse to a halt a distance away, waiting for the farmer to clear out. As they sat, leaves rustled on the trees and bushes that hemmed in the dirt road on either side, the silence only broken by the nickering of their rides and the creak of the farmer's wagon. Wu Ying's team joined him in his regard of their opponents.

Wang Min eventually broke the leaden silence, whispering, "Lei Hui..."

The thin, scholarly apothecarist sat on his horse in the middle of the cultivators, his face bruised and beaten, his hands strapped to the saddle. Even from this distance, Wu Ying saw the fear and shame in the apothecarist's eyes, the way his too-red hands trembled. They looked wrong, twisted in a way that made Wu Ying's stomach fall.

Of the five remaining cultivators facing them, three were in the mid-stage Energy Storage like Wu Ying and his friends. The other two had closed off their auras, hiding their levels. One of those forgot—or perhaps did not know—how to stop his chi from emanating and staining the air, allowing Wu Ying to peg him in the lower stages of Energy Storage and an earth chi wielder. The last, the leader who sat with his jian resting casually on his saddle pointing at Lei Hui, Wu Ying could sense nothing from.

When the farmer had left and those behind them had moved out of the way, Wu Ying gently kicked his feet into his horse. The mare plodded forward while Wu Ying kept a hand on his sword. A muttered word of caution was all he managed to force out of his dry mouth as his gaze locked on the scared Lei Hui. As he rode closer, his guts twisted and churned, bile threatening to erupt. The other group of cultivators rode forward too, closing the distance until a bare twenty feet kept them apart.

Wu Ying raised his free hand, keeping the other hand on his jian. "That's close enough."

"Or what?" The leader smirked, his voluminous mustache and eyebrows twitching. He kicked his horse again, forcing it to take a few steps closer.

Wu Ying's hand clenched on his sword and Yu Kun raised his nocked bow. Tension grew between the groups as weapons were readied. As if his goading had done its job, the leader had his horse stop with a tug of his reins. Lei Hui's horse was guided forward to join the rest, leaving the groups to stare at one another again.

"Who are you?" Wu Ying said. "What do you want?"

"Did you think we'd just tell you our names?" The leader laughed mockingly. "And you know what we want. If you hand it over, we won't even have to kill your friend."

"Why do you need it?" Wu Ying said, shaking his head. "Haven't you taken what you need from Lei Hui?"

Lei Hui ducked his head low, his face burning. Shame that redoubled when the opposing group laughed. He clenched his tied fists then released them with a hiss, broken fingers and hand bones hurting.

"Oh, it was easy getting it from him. We barely had to beat him much," one of the other cultivators spoke up, patting his fat stomach. He licked his lips, leaning over his saddle to stare at Lei Hui. "I was looking forward to tasting his flesh too. Apothecarists all have a different flavor, depending on what pills they specialize in."

Disgusted looks flashed across Wu Ying and his team's faces. Interestingly enough, so did they on the opposition leader's and another of the other group's, while one nodded in thought and the last two just stoically stared ahead.

"You didn't answer the question." Wu Ying pushed down his disgust and fear, talking to buy time. He caught Wang Min looking between him and the leader, her eyes creased in worry.

"Because it's no business of yours. You just have to hand over what you have," the leader said. "Stop stalling. Or else I'll chop off a hand."

Lei Hui let out an involuntary utterance of negation, while the fat cultivator licked his lips.

"If you hurt him again, we fight," Wu Ying stated, his mind spinning with possibilities.

They were too far apart to launch a surprise attack and catch the others unguarded. Wu Ying could try it when they did a handover—if they let him get that close. But he doubted they would do that. They also outnumbered the expedition group, and Wu Ying's team was tired and still injured from their fights.

Their chances of winning were low. But not meaningless. Which was most likely why the other group was offering the trade. Better to cripple their chances this way, wait for reinforcements, and attack later than risk a close battle or deaths. They had little to lose, making this offer of trade.

"Then give us what we want," the leader reiterated. He gestured behind Wu Ying's group, and while Wu Ying did not take his gaze from his opponents, he saw Yu Kun shift to look behind. "Or do you intend to sit here, holding up the commoners all day?"

"I'm thinking about it."

"Wu Ying…" Wang Min murmured, her voice plaintive.

Lei Hui looked at Wu Ying, jaw clenched tight. Wu Ying had to admire the thin apothecarist, that he was refusing to beg for aid or demand that he make the deal. It made Wu Ying's job harder, deciding what to do. Who to betray. His friend, his teammate, or his Master? The man who had placed him on the path of true cultivation?

"Well?" The mustached leader shifted his hand a little, pushing the edge of the blade into Lei Hui's side. It pricked the skin of his arm, drawing blood before Lei Hui shied away from the blade.

As the smell of spilled blood stained the air, the fat cultivator grinned wide.

"Stop it!" Wang Min cried, then turned to Wu Ying. "You can't. You can't let them eat him."

"Wang Min," Tou He spoke up, laying a hand on her arm.

She jerked, surprised at the ex-monk's touch, and saw his placid gaze. Rather than calming her, she grew even more agitated. "No! I won't be quiet. You can't just give up one of our own. That's wrong!" Her eyes grew teary. "Look what they've done to him already. You know they'll kill him if you refuse."

"I know," Wu Ying said flatly. He did his best to keep his voice calm, but he could not help the trace of anger that ran through it. "But I can't just give them the materials. There's nothing stopping them from killing him and leaving with it then."

"There is a simple solution. Give us half of what you have. We will hand you your friend, and you can give us the other half. We know you have two of the materials you need," the leader said, having pulled back the sword.

Wu Ying glared but eventually nodded. He could not see another option. And as much as he wanted to save his Master, he couldn't just let them kill Lei Hui. He had to do something…

Wu Ying reached into his world spirit ring, extracting the jade box that contained the Sun Lotus. He hefted it in the air, and at the leader's insistence, opened it to showcase the contents. After verification, the leader beckoned Wu Ying to hand over the box. A simple underhand toss and the leader pocketed and stored the box.

"Let him go." When his men hesitated, the leader growled. "I said, let him go."

Reins were dropped and Lei Hui used his knees to guide his horse forward. Tension rose as the horse ambled through the gap between the groups, the opposing parties fingering their weapons, wary of betrayal. To Wang Min's and Wu Ying's relief, Lei Hui arrived without further trouble. Immediately, she cut his hands free with a small knife, then fed the apothecarist a healing pill.

"I'm sorry. They caught me when I was waiting for the Sect to arrive. They got me while I was sleeping in the inn. I tried to stop them, but there were so many... I really did. I'm sorry. I tried," Lei Hui blathered once he was free.

"It's okay. I should never have split the party," Wu Ying said. Now, his overabundance of caution, his double-guessing at the future, had resulted in them losing not just one precious ingredient but all of them. Lei Hui had nothing to feel guilty about. The fault was all his. He could not help but glance at Lei Hui's broken hands. "I'm sorry. I know you did your best."

"All right, all right. Enough. Now, hand over the second ingredient." Even as the leader spoke, his group tensed, ready to attack.

This was the most dangerous time for the other group since Wu Ying had Lei Hui now. He could launch an attack against the other party and maybe win back the materials. But he hesitated, switching his gaze from them to Lei Hui, who slumped in his saddle. He traced his gaze across the apothecarist, noting how his robes were slightly disarrayed, the scent coming from the other.

"Open your robes, Lei Hui."

"My robes?" Lei Hui said, puzzled.

"Stop wasting time," the leader called. But there was a hint of concern in his voice, one that even Lei Hui caught.

The apothecarist fumbled with his robes before Wang Min leaned over to help. That caused the pale apothecarist to flush, but she didn't notice. For beneath the outer robes, stuck to his inner robes, were talismans that glowed with the light of chi activation.

"Damn. I guess you're not that dumb."

"What is this?" Wu Ying said even as he shifted his horse away from Lei Hui. The others did as well, leaving only Wang Min next to Lei Hui.

"Insurance."

"These are… they're… explosive charms," Lei Hui got out, his voice breaking with fear as he stared at the talismans covering his body. "I didn't know. You have to believe me."

"I do," Wang Min assured him.

"Are they timed or…?"

"Chi-activated," she replied.

Wu Ying made a face, though he had guessed as much. Metal chi was imbued into the talismans, stinking up his nostrils even further. His eyes narrowed as the leader smirked. He held all the cards, for he had the material and Lei Hui as hostage still. What could Wu Ying do? Extracting the charms was not a simple matter. He didn't even have a clue how to do so, though from what he recalled, Wang Min had a little knowledge.

"So we give you the remaining materials and you kill our friend?" Wu Ying said. "It doesn't seem like a smart trade."

"Well, you have my word we'll play fair," the leader said, obviously gloating.

"Not good enough."

"Eh, we might be at an impasse then." The leader tightened his grip on the sword, lifting it up and over his animal's head, letting it rest pointed straight down. Readying himself for the fight.

"Do not be so hasty. Let me think about this." Wu Ying looked at Wang Min, whose head was lowered, staring at the charms. He murmured to her, "What's the range on the charm? If we get him away from them, could you turn it off? How far away before they cannot use it?"

She looked between him and the enchantment. When she spoke, it was hesitantly. "Maybe half a li?"

Wu Ying huffed. That made sense, since any further and an Energy Storage cultivator would have trouble projecting their energy. Even their senses only reached tens of feet. Of course, the energy to activate the talismans was aided by the fact that it was minuscule and part of the enchantment itself, but a fight could easily interfere with the transmission.

"Okay. Get it off as soon as you can," Wu Ying informed her. He turned to the opposing group. "I won't give you the materials, not yet. She'll ride him and herself away, and then we will trade. When he's out of your range."

"And let more of you escape?" The fat cultivator sneered.

The other cultivators broke into laughter as well.

"There are five of you. There will only be three of us. Are you that afraid that you will lose a fight?"

One of the previously silent cultivators growled, the top half of his face masked while the lower part twisted as he kicked his horse forward. He only stopped as a flash of chi from behind broke the ground before his horse.

"Don't. We'll be punished if we fail. You know that," the leader said, glaring.

Reluctantly, the masked cultivator rode backward.

The fractures in their opposition were interesting. If he had more time, perhaps Wu Ying could exploit it. But not right now. Still, seeing that there were no additional objections, he sent the pair off. Soon enough, they turned a corner, disappearing from sight as rolling hills and shrubbery took them away.

"How long do we wait?" the leader asked.

"Ten minutes," Wu Ying said. It would give his friends enough time to escape. And then… and then he would sully his honor further.

***

Long minutes passed with excruciating slowness, the two groups regarding one another in brittle tension. Wu Ying occasionally glanced back, noting the growing crowd of mortals that lurked off the road and behind trees. None dared to involve themselves in a standoff between cultivators. He wondered what they looked like, how it felt to them. In their Sect robes, Wu Ying and his group were easy to notice while their opponents were dressed in black and grey, devoid of their affiliation. Three of them even had their faces covered, though the slim bodies of two of those dressed and covered that way gave hints to their fairer sex.

Eventually, the dark sect group leader spoke up, having returned his sword to rest above the pommel of his saddle. "Did you really think we would let you spoil our plans so easily?"

"I didn't think you would be so blatant," Wu Yin said. "Acting against me and my martial sister in public, kidnapping my friend. Even stopping us here…"

"Bah! The peasants know nothing. And as for you all"—the leader stroked his beard—"do you think what you have to say matters? What proof do you have?"

Wu Ying's eyes narrowed. True, they had no true proof here. His martial sister might be able to prove that Lu Ren and the Heavenly Lake Sect might be corrupted, might be using banned cultivation types and exercises. But it did not mean they were part of a dark sect. The use of shortcuts to improve one's cultivation was not unknown. The desperate, the stymied, they all took ill-advised actions.

As for himself? Wu Ying had no evidence. Lei Hui's wounds could be dismissed as injuries on an expedition. Wu Ying's encounter could be ascribed as a desperate attempt to excuse his failure. He had no bodies—and even if he did, corpses would be of little use as proof. It was not as if the dark sect tattooed or branded their followers. Even if someone were to believe they were robbed, bandits were not an uncommon matter.

Still…

"We are inner sect cultivators of the Verdant Green Waters. We do not lie," Wu Ying said firmly. "Our words, our tale would be taken seriously."

"By some." The leader grinned.

"And they'll make themselves perfect targets." The fat cultivator laughed. "A good meal for me and my Master."

"You want us to help you draw out your opposition," Wu Ying said softly. He shook his head, his lips compressing tight. "I think you'll find your wishes might bring you more trouble than you believe. We are not prey for you."

"Har. As if we haven't done the same for a hundred years," the fat cultivator said mockingly.

The leader growled, shushing the man. "That should be long enough, no?"

"Yes." Wu Ying exhaled, then reached into his ring. He extracted the wood-and-earth imbued storage box from his ring. At the man's gesture, he pushed the top open, displaying the heart within. "Satisfied?"

"Good. Throw it over and we will be done," the leader said.

Wu Ying watched as the man's hands twitched down by his side, out of Wu Ying's direct line of sight.

"Of course." Not letting his face shift, Wu Ying let his hand drop lower, in preparation to lob the box underhand. As he did so, he whispered to his friends, "I'm sorry."

As if the entire group had been waiting for the signal, as the box soared through the air, both sides exploded into action. Weapons were drawn, bows were raised and arrows loosed. The hundred gates of hell broke open and Wu Ying could only hope it was not to accept him and his friends.

Chapter 33

Wu Ying's first act after throwing the box was to kick his horse into a canter, sending it into a jerking run to the side of his starting position. At the same time, he bowed his body low as he cross-drew his jian. His actions allowed him to dodge the thrown knife that whizzed past his face, the weapon empowered by air chi.

By Wu Ying's side, Yu Kun had unhorsed himself almost completely, leaning so precariously over one side of his ride that it looked as if he would fall at any moment. He fired his bow from that position before dropping the weapon and pulling his swords from his spirit ring as they closed on their opponents.

On the other side, Wu Ying heard the thunder and impact of attacks rebounding off Tou He's defense. He could only hope that his friend was doing well, for it was Wu Ying's turn to return the attacks. He swung his sword once, then again, using quick elbow cuts. The first was a feint, but his second cut sent a spiral of empowered sword chi at his target. Caught off-guard, his opponent managed to block the attack but failed to protect his horse, which was the farmer's main target.

Rearing in pain, the horse bucked and twisted, bleeding from its face and body. The wound had dug close to the creature's eyes, causing the creature to buck and twist, panicked. Its slim-waisted rider was forced to fight the mare as it turned and bolted, leaving Wu Ying and his team to face the other four.

Three, for Yu Kun's attack had lamed another mare as they closed.

"Cowards, attacking animals!"

The accusation was, to Wu Ying's amazement, coming from the fat, cannibalistic cultivator. He looked truly enraged and cut across in front of his leader to charge Wu Ying directly. The mustached leader had to pull his horse short as the fat cultivator swung his guan dao straight down at Wu Ying.

A lean to the side and a cut at the head of the heavy halberd sent the weapon away. True to all guan dao wielders, the fat cultivator was absurdly strong and reversed course of the weapon. Wu Ying could only pull his own sword into a block, aborting his riposte at his opponent's wrist to guard himself.

Caught in the rising blow, Wu Ying was nearly lifted off his seat. Hands trembled as Wu Ying's horse, frightened by the swinging weapon, kept moving forward, driving Wu Ying closer to the cultivator. Rather than let the opportunity pass, Wu Ying struck out with his fist, embracing the power within the Woo Petal Bracer and infusing his fist attack with chi.

The energy-infused chi blow struck the guan dao's shaft, punishing weapon and cultivator. Rocked by the attack, the fat cultivator failed to capitalize on Wu Ying's back, leaving Wu Ying free to face his next foe. The mustached leader.

Wu Ying goaded his horse closer, the pair traded blows with their jians, cutting and thrusting at one another. The mustached leader was good and forced Wu Ying to focus on him.

Meanwhile, Tou He stepped in to deal with the guan dao cultivator, the ex-monk meeting his opponent on his feet rather than on his horse, while Yu Kun battled the pair of other cultivators—one horsed, the other unhorsed—with his swords. The last enemy cultivator continued to attempt to return on his panicked horse, too stubborn or too inept to get off it.

Wu Ying caught glimpses of that as he and the leader spun round and round, lashing at each other. In short order, Wu Ying learned a few things. The leader was strong—at least high Energy Storage, if not peak. Each of his blows, the speed of his reactions, all told of the greater physical strength opening more meridians provided. Luckily, he was not overwhelmingly strong—Wu Ying's base constitution and strength from years of back-breaking work providing him an equalizing force.

Secondly, neither of them were experienced in mounted combat. More than once, cuts and blocks were fouled by the unexpected movement of the horses beneath them. Wounds on both sides collected as the creatures bucked, twisted, and dodged with the barest modicum of control placed upon them. Only long years of training kept the creatures in battle, guided by inexperienced riders as they were.

As for the third aspect, it was the only thing that kept Wu Ying in battle. For all the man's strength and speed, he lacked skill. Or, more correctly, he lacked a form that worked on horseback. And while the Long family style was not focused on horseback riding, it was complete and had passages devoted to it. Whereas his opponent lacked even that and often reverted to a few repetitive attacks that allowed him to miss injuring his own ride.

Time passed as blades clashed and horses reared. Wounds collected—a cut on the arm here, a gash on the leg there, a new bleeding wound on the cheek. Neither managed to land an effective hit, though both equine companions were flagging under the repeated goading of their riders.

A passing glimpse told Wu Ying the other cultivator had given up on his ride and was swiftly returning on foot. Another showed Yu Kun pressured, wounded, and tired. Tou He was winning his own fight, having struck away the guan dao of his opponent. Now, he was in the midst of finishing his opponent.

But with the returning cultivator, they were out of time. Whoever the returning cultivator aided would be put in a losing position. Hands trembling, cheek slick with blood, Wu Ying ran through his options. What could he do? How could he turn this around?

An idea… but dangerous. A sacrifice. To save his friends, to save those who followed him.

A worthwhile trade.

But he needed a gap, an opportunity. Another blow nearly staggered Wu Ying, his blade pushed so deep that it nearly cut into his body. Earth chi from Wu Ying's opponent gave his attacks strength, one that chipped at Wu Ying's jian and made his shoulder and wrist ache. Pushed, leaving him no chance.

A scream, a familiar voice. Wu Ying jerked his head to the side, surprise blooming on his face. Tou He was down, clutching his leg as his opponent smirked, floating, black wisps erupting from his hands. Wu Ying smelled that burnt wood, rotting earth scent. Making him choke.

A flash of light, and a twist. Wu Ying jerked in his seat, falling off the horse as the cut tore open his chest. He landed and rolled, the wound on his chest opening further, blood dribbling. A ground-level cut tore at the incoming horse's legs, crippling it before the leader could reach him. Even as the mare crashed to the ground, the leader flipped through the air.

Exhaustion tore at Wu Ying's will, leaving him unable to stand. Blood rushed from his chest as Tou He attempted to protect himself with flaming chi from the floating black dots the fat cultivator wielded. And Yu Kun retreated, bloody gashes on both arms, one arm barely holding on.

Wu Ying pushed, forcing himself to stand. Refusing to stay down. Even as he realized he'd failed. Again. Made the wrong decision, made the wrong choice.

Killed himself, his friends, and his Master.

As the fifth cultivator arrived, joining with the team leader, Wu Ying faced them, wounded, tired, and bleeding, sword in hand.

A failure.

***

Sword trembling, Wu Ying glared at the opponents sauntering toward him. There were no words, no further conversation. That final attack Wu Ying had swung had closed off all those options. But at least Lei Hui would not die, nor Wang Min. They would be able to escape—probably. He wished he'd passed Lei Hui or Wang Min his world spirit ring. With his death, they would have been able to keep the second set he had within. Another mistake.

Now.

Now it was too late.

Wu Ying's hands trembled, his jian's blade dipping and rising in time. His attackers spread out, and Wu Ying cursed. He should have, could have used that moment to try something, anything. But instead, he'd spent it thinking of the past, missing the opportunity.

The fifth cultivator attacked first. Rather than a sword, she wielded a mace, a weapon more suited for a peasant than a refined cultivator. The weapon she wielded had a blackened head, and as she swung it, inscriptions lit up with a yellow-red glow.

Wu Ying cut and blocked, careful to block at the handle rather than the mace head. The dark sect leader stalked in the distance, ready for an opening. On his feet, Wu Ying could tell, the leader was even more dangerous. A single opportunity and Wu Ying would fall.

Mace and blade clashed as Wu Ying tried to maneuver himself around the attacks and away from the leader. The metallic chime of their weapons meeting, the shuffle of feet and forced exhalations joined the tinkling of notes. Forming a subtle tune.

Dragons rises in the Evening blocked a blow swung at his collarbone on the right. His scabbard, gripped in his left, managed to push the leader's jian off-line. It still cut, drawing blood along Wu Ying's lower ribs, nicking bone. Wu Ying hissed, a susurration of sound.

And then, a twist in the notes. A break before it struck. Their chi, moving to the music that had enveloped them, stuttered to a stop. They all felt it, were all caught. The aural attack had come subtly, sliding beneath their awareness as they fought, and it caught them all, freezing them in place.

Wu Ying was frozen, his movements slowed. His sword fell by his side. His eyes darted across the road. Tou He was on his knees, his fires dimmed, the staff on the ground. His opponent's dark mist attack dissipated, bleeding from his mouth. Yu Kun, hands held aloft, blocked both attacks, eyes glazed as his opponents fought through the attack, their bodies locked.

And Wu Ying. Free. For a second.

The Never Empty Wine Pot was used to hold off chi that was unaspected. The simple umbrella aura strengthening qinggong exercise gave him further protection as his aura constrained external chi from entering his body. It all helped slow down the insinuation of Wang Min's chi attack into Wu Ying's body.

Made the effects less.

Allowed him to move.

A rising cut, chi drawn not from his still-sluggish meridian but from the Woo Petal Bracer flowing through the blade. Wu Ying cut upward and sideways, sending the attack across the road. It struck, tearing at muscle and bone, flaying the backs and sides of his targets. A little of it clipped Yu Kun, but his opponents were staggered, injured by the unexpected attack.

Motion resumed as the other cultivators regained control of their body.

Tou He and the dark sect leader recovered next, the ex-monk smashing his staff upward between the legs of his fat opponent. His opponent crumpled, face white and eyes rolled back. There was no time to rejoice. The dark sect leader attacked Wu Ying, blade snaking out and targeting his back.

Wu Ying crumpled forward, dodging as best he could and failing. Flesh and robes parted under the weapon. Blade grated on reinforced bones, cutting and chipping but failing to penetrate as Wu Ying dodged. He fell and rolled, back and wound impacting the ground and forcing a strangled scream from his lips.

Coming to his knees, Wu Ying turned and cut, throwing everything he had, everything he could into a projected sword intent attack. It struck at both his opponents, but the attack was dispersed with ease. An aural attack of compressed air chi followed Wu Ying's attack, doing more damage than his own. It staggered the pair, leaving light wounds on their arms.

"Finish the girl! I'll deal with this cockroach," the dark sect leader snapped.

The female opponent slipped away, mace swinging in counter-time to Wang Min's sonic attacks. Air chi met air chi, creating explosive blasts of air that kicked up dirt and leaves on the road. A pebble shattered and cut the dark sect leader's face, leaving a thin line of blood and infuriating him.

Still, the leader did not lose focus as he threw cuts at Wu Ying, forcing him to defend. Defend with his sword by constricting his aura, reinforcing it against the chi-imbued attacks. As blood dripped, as the leader closed to finish, Wu Ying could only defend.

Another cry of triumph. Wu Ying glanced to the side as he was blasted off his feet and onto his back. The leader rushed over with his sword raised to finish him. Wu Ying saw Yu Kun rip his hooked blades across another neck, severing the head.

His friends were winning. They would survive.

Good enough.

The blade slid into Wu Ying's chest as he failed to block it. He thrashed, coughed as blade twisted. Felt searing pain as it was withdrawn.

Then.

Nothing.

Chapter 34

Wu Ying woke slowly, his head muggy, his body hurting. Cool glass was pressed to his lips, a liquid forced into his mouth. He drank reflexively, his throat bobbing as he choked down the bitter, spicy brew that tasted so much like mud water.

The moment it entered his throat, he felt warmth spread through his body, reaching out from his stomach, digging warm tendrils into torn and abused muscles and open wounds. As sense, as his thoughts grew firmer, as he awoke, Wu Ying realized that was not the only source of warmth. His body was wrapped in a warm liquid.

Eyes caked with sleep, with crusted blood, at first refused to open. When the cup was removed from his lips, he let out a little groan, and words, unintelligible words, were murmured around him. Wu Ying ignored it all, forcing his eyes open. It was a struggle, a greater struggle than raising his first sword at six.

Eventually, his eyes cracked open to see his friends. His tired, injured friends and the same road they had fought on. And, at the edge of his sight, the oval curve of a cauldron. Wu Ying's head lolled down, and within the cauldron—within the cauldron he was in—was a boiling liquid.

"Wha—" he croaked.

"Easy. Just rest. Cultivate if you can," Wang Min ordered him. Her hands were holding him up, had fed him the drink.

"Yes. Definitely cultivate," Lei Hui said. "The medicinal bath can only last so long. If you do not finish closing your wounds before it is over, you will die."

Wu Ying turned his head to the side, spotting the apothecarist. The man had a large ladle strapped to a broken hand, allowing him to stir the liquid within the cauldron. In his other hand, fingers trembling, the apothecarist was attempting to gauge certain medicinal ingredients.

"What is happening?" Eyes widening, Wu Ying stared as a familiar flower blossom floated past him. It glowed and boiled the water as it did so, but he could tell that the Sun Lotus was already dimming. Anger and fear flared in him, giving him strength. "Why are you using the Lotus?"

"To save your life, you idiot!" Lei Hui snapped. "Now stop talking and cultivate."

Seeing Wu Ying's face grow mulish, Wang Min moved to block Wu Ying's gaze from the irritable and angry apothecarist. "You were bleeding out. We managed to stabilize you long enough for Lei Hui to create this medicinal bath, but to give it strength, we needed the Sun Lotus blossom. We used it and the Heart of the Chan Chu, the smaller one you gave away. Along with some other herbs we found."

"Exactly! Found. This is not a proper bath," Lei Hui grumbled. "This is, this is… a soup! A body healing soup, and it'll fail if you don't cultivate."

Wu Ying wanted to object, for now that he was awake, he realized he was feeling quite good. Even the wounds he had, the one on his back and front, the hole through his chest, they didn't hurt. It was quite warm really.

Then his brows snapped together. He remembered bleeding out. Turning his head, he spotted the portion of the road where he had lain. And the large splotch of blood, some of which that had yet to soak through the ground. That much blood…

"You're lucky you did Body Cultivation before," Lei Hui grumbled, his voice hitching on occasion as he threw in another handful of herbs, making the entire soup flare. "You can withstand this better. But you're burning up from within. If you don't cultivate, you'll die."

Wu Ying met Wang Min's gaze. He had one more question, but like before, the musician anticipated it. "They are fine. Mostly. They're cultivating to heal themselves. But you were the worst injured."

Nodding in gratitude, Wu Ying let his eyes drift close. Let his attention drift inward to the warmth that wrapped around his chest, his torso. To the wounds and the chi that raged through his body, burning him from within. Supporting his life until it burnt his meridians to cinders and left him to die of his wounds.

A breath, an inhalation and exhalation, and he focused. Pulling at the chi within him, filtering it through his dantian, trying to reengage the Never Empty Wine Pot cultivation exercise. Trying to heal himself, borrowing from the medicinal bath. He started the Reinforced Iron Bones cultivation method, knowing that he would need it to help filter the soup.

In the heat, in the warmth of the boiling soup of expensive herbs and spilled lifeblood, Wu Ying cultivated.

And healed.

***

Wu Ying floated in the center of his being, wrapped in the warmth of the liquid, feeling chi flow through his body. It burnt his meridians, seeped into bone and muscle, soaked tendons and organs. His Reinforced Iron Bones Technique was taking full advantage of the medicinal bath, of the torn and damaged wounds to stitch him together better. Now that he was awake, Wu Ying took active control of the process.

Inhale, his face held barely above the bath, propped up by Wang Min. Draw in chi, filter out the ones that he did not need, churn it through his meridians.

Exhale, pushing chi through his dantian, through his meridians, through his lungs into his breath. Removing impurities, removing what he did not need.

Inhale, pulling in medicinal ingredients to fix his body, to integrate it within his body.

Exhale, push away the waste ingredients, push away the cut flesh, the broken and chipped bones.

Inhale and repeat.

Exhale and repeat.

Again and again, Wu Ying cultivated. His chi moved through his meridians, in his dantian according to the Yellow Emperor's methods. Each moment, strengthening himself, wearing away at impurities, advancing the size of his dantian.

Blood vessels, cut open, stitched together. Muscles grew close, tightening then relaxing as scar tissue was burned away by the flow of chi and the medicinal baths. Skin closed, leaving it mostly unblemished. Wounds and injuries, even the one in his chest and lungs, closed ever so slowly.

The water was replaced, more herbs were added. The fire beneath the cauldron renewed as Lei Hui worked in silence. Hands propping up Wu Ying changed, as he felt his body change. It grew warmer, his skin crisping and burning, skin sloughing off only to be replaced. Flesh and bones grew tougher as the earth-aspected Chan Chu's heart entered his body, refining it further.

He sat and cultivated, healing. And if the herbs being used, the ones they'd found in the cultivators' rings, that he had given from his own ring, that the others had taken from their stores were more expensive than anything Wu Ying had ever used... none spoke of it.

Time stopped having meaning. The cost of what had been used was no longer a concern. The possibilities of his Master's antidote failing washed away in the bubbles that surrounded him. All that mattered was the cauldron and the flow of chi.

Wu Ying inhaled.

Cultivated.

And exhaled.

***

Eventually, Wu Ying opened his eyes, the warmth that had surrounded him gone. His breathing settled and stilled, the chi that had churned through his body slowing in its processing, fading into that background process that had become part of his existence. Wu Ying shifted, surprised that he was holding himself up in the cauldron without thought, and slowly stood. An easy jump sent him well over the lip of the cauldron and he stumbled a little as he fell, his body feeling different. Stronger. Heavier.

He frowned, checking within. His meridians were the same, his dantian slightly larger. His cultivation had not advanced, but his body itself... his body had changed.

"About time."

The familiar voice made Wu Ying snap his head to the side to spot his martial sister. He looked around further, taking in the shaded pathway, the compressed dirt road and the curious passersby who stared at the half-naked cultivator and the cauldron. What he did not see this cloudy afternoon was his friends. Just his martial sister.

"Sister Yuan?" Wu Ying called hesitantly, unsure what to even start with as a question.

"Your friends are fine. I sent them back to accompany Elder Po with your ring," Fa Yuan said. "I elected to stay here to watch over you."

"My ring?" Wu Ying said confusedly. He looked at his left hand, spotting his spirit ring on it.

"The other one."

A look to his other hand where his world spirit ring had rested made Wu Ying's eyes widen with realization. The one that contained the remaining Sun Lotus—still growing—and the metal Chan Chu's heart. But...

"It's still linked to me."

"A small matter. The Patriarch will break your link and access the ring." Fa Yuan waved, dismissing the matter.

"But the Ben's spirit stone was lost," Wu Ying said disconsolately. Then, hope bloomed. "Did they find it? On their corpses?"

"No. They got rid of the spirit stone immediately after taking it from your friend," Fa Yuan said. When Wu Ying's face fell, she continued with a smile. "Smart, but not smart enough. They did not notice—like you—the twist of chi I left on the box itself. It allowed me to track the spirit stone when I arrived in the city." Her face grew grim. "Elder Yun is interrogating the merchant they sold the spirit stone to. Perhaps we will learn more of the dark sect's tendrils."

"Then the Sect believed you?" Wu Ying said. It was the only explanation he could find for her presence here, for her being released from Hinma.

"Eventually." Fa Yuan's beautiful face grew petulant for a moment. "It took quite a bit of convincing, but we were able to locate additional traces of their actions. Not enough to convince all the sects, but enough for the magistrate. Once I was released, we hurried over to meet your friend but were too late."

"So Master will be fine." Wu Ying exhaled, his shoulders relaxing again. The tension he had not realized he carried disappeared, especially when Fa Yuan confirmed his belief.

"Now, if your questions are done, perhaps you could get presentable."

At his sister's gesture, Wu Ying found a set of robes waiting for him beside the cauldron. He flushed, realizing his robes were once again a ripped and torn affair, stained with the dark liquid of the bath he had been in.

As Wu Ying walked out from the nearby woods after dressing, he slid his jian into his belt. He frowned as he walked back, the weapon taken from his spirit ring half-extracted from its sheath. He'd meant to have it fixed, but it was so chipped, he wondered if it was worthwhile. Sadly, it was also the best of his remaining weapons.

"You're still wielding that?" Fa Yuan snorted. "Here." A hand twisted, and she tossed him a jian extracted from her ring.

Wu Ying caught the weapon, pulled it from the sheath, and whistled. It was a familiar weapon, for it was one she had bought at the auction.

"I ask for your forgiveness. I should have given it to you when we parted." Fa Yuan's face grew pensive as she reflected on the past and Wu Ying's troubles. "It slipped my mind, and then it was too late."

"It's fine. A small matter," Wu Ying said, sheathing the blade and bowing to his martial sister as he held it in his hands. "This is a great gift."

"As is our Master's life," Fa Yuan said, gesturing for him to put it on. As Wu Ying replaced his weapon, she walked over to the cauldron and placed the entire thing, water and all, in her own spirit ring. "What you faced was more than we had expected."

"We?"

"Did you think Master Cheng and I did not have numerous conversations about your presence in this?" Fa Yuan said. "You are only at the Energy Storage stage. And while you have progressed at a commendable pace, you are still new to the jianghu. Having you participate was always going to be dangerous."

"And yet you did."

"We did." Fa Yuan's lips twisted in a sardonic half-smile as she walked down the side of the road to where their horses grazed on nearby bushes. "Master Cheng believes your karma, your fate, might be more turbulent than what you would prefer."

Wu Ying burst out laughing. "Toil and trouble is my fate in this life?"

"Perhaps." Fa Yuan led her horse back onto the road, seating herself with a single graceful motion.

As they rode off, Wu Ying could not help but turn around to stare at the unremarkable strip of land where he had nearly died. And now, had been reborn with greater strength and even more scars. He still remembered the plunging sword, the way his back had burned as torn and cut muscles twitched, and the warmth of the cauldron. A click of the tongue ahead made him return his gaze to the front, where his martial sister awaited.

"In only a few years, you have joined multiple expeditions. Left the Sect, returned, and left again on missions of mercy and spite. You've met Nascent Soul Spirit Beasts and fought armies. All the while, struggling to achieve some form of understanding of the Dao." Fa Yuan fell silent while Wu Ying urged his horse to catch up to the beauty. She turned to the side, regarding her younger martial brother, a somber look in her gaze. Somber and… expectant? "It is almost a story for the scholars. Perhaps it might be. If you survive."

Under those heavy words of portent and doom, the pair rode to the city. Sensing that Wu Ying needed time to think, to process not only her listing of his recent accomplishments but his own brush with death, his martial sister stayed silent. Leaving the ex-farmer, ex-outer sect member, ex-Body Cleansing cultivator to ponder the journey he had been on.

And what awaited him in the future.

***

The next few hours passed in a blur. They found a boat to take them back, and to the chagrin of both his martial sister and the sailors, Wu Ying took his place on the oars, kicking off an entire row of the merchant galley's rowers. He struck the oars, and in short order, the Captain had to add a third person to the oars on the opposing side.

It was not planting rice or turning the earth. It was not digging up canals or bending over for hours, pulling out weeds that persisted in their attempts to choke out their vegetable garden. It was not even the days' long process of reaping rice stalks. But it was work. Hard, necessary, repetitive work that gave Wu Ying time to think.

The world's chi churned and pushed at his aura, in turn pulled toward his center and pushed away by his cultivation. Each stroke, each breath, saw him working his way through his thoughts, his experiences. Each moment saw him finding some semblance of further calm, of acceptance.

There was no rush of chi, no acknowledgement from the heavens. Enlightenment was the process of understanding the Dao—of placing one closer to the true Way in thought and action. But what Wu Ying did was more of an acceptance of his past, of his decisions and choices and what had happened.

And yet, acceptance of who he was, what he had done, and what might come was as important to Wu Ying as any acknowledgement of the heavens. For the process of accepting allowed him to put what had happened—the fear, the pain, the anger—aside.

He no longer carried the burden of the past and his failed decisions. And in doing so, each step into the future would be lighter.

Chapter 35

"Tsifu." Wu Ying bowed low, pressing his head to the ground.

Beside him, his martial sister copied Wu Ying's movements. The flagstones of the courtyard pressed against his forehead; the smooth texture of the stone already cool in the late evening. Body shadowing the grey stone, Wu Ying's eyes picked out the grains of the stone, the twisting pattern as the full moon shed light on his back.

"Stand," Master Cheng said, his voice resounding with strength.

Wu Ying raised his head then stood as requested, taking in his Master. Only a few days after receiving the antidote, his Master had bounced back to health with remarkable speed. In fact, Wu Ying felt a new strength emanating from his Master, a deeper heaviness to his scent that had been missing before. If he had to guess, the long-limbed swordsman had had his own moment of enlightenment.

Such things were not uncommon. In the throes of depression and death, when pushed, clarity occurred. Though, clarity seen through the haze of fevers and pain might be less than an optimal long-term investment in one's dao.

"It is good that you have recovered, Master," Fa Yuan spoke, brushing her clothing idly.

"I am yet to fully recover," Elder Cheng said, making a gesture to dismiss her words. "But you have my thanks. You, and your friends."

Together, the pair bowed at his words.

"I have made arrangements for your friends to be repaid. Though some…" Elder Cheng shook his head. "Some prices might be a little more difficult to fulfill."

"Master?" Wu Ying said.

"Lei Hui. His hands were damaged. They used a poison to cripple the tendons," Elder Cheng replied. "It was how they broke him and made him give up the location of the materials he had hidden as a precaution."

"But I saw him…" Memories of trembling fingers, of roughly chopped herbs and handfuls tossed in by the exacting apothecarist crossed Wu Ying's memories.

"Yes. You understand. The poison has left his system, but the damage remains. His Master and I are looking into solutions, but the poison used was… vicious."

Wu Ying made a face, regret flashing through him once more. He began to understand his Master's position a little, for he could almost feel the way the thread of karma bound his Master to Lei Hui, to Yu Kun and Wang Min's future. And yet, he could not find himself regretting it.

"Never mind those matters. The debt is mine," Elder Cheng said, waving and dismissing the topic, long sleeves trailing. "The question I have is what payment I must make to my willful disciples? What form of gratitude do you desire?"

Fa Yuan was the first to speak, bowing from the waist with her hands clasped before her. "Nothing, Master. It is our duty to support you. For all that you have taught us, for all you will teach us."

"Yes, Master. There is no need." Wu Ying echoed.

"I see." Master Cheng fell silent, letting his gaze roam over the pair before he gave a firm nod. "Very well. Fa Yuan, the Patriarch and the Sect protectors want to speak with you about your experiences." When Fa Yuan still stood, he gestured at her to go. Fa Yuan's eyes widened, and she shot a glance at the dark sky, to which Elder Cheng shook his head. "I fear rest will be in short supply in the next few years."

"Yes, Master." Another bow and Fairy Yang disappeared out the doorway, green robes flaring behind her as she hurried, leaving but the hint of her perfume and the memory of her passing.

"As for you…" Master Cheng smiled at Wu Ying, his hand falling to his own belted sword. "Show me what you have learned."

"Master?" Wu Ying said hesitantly, even as he took hold of his own weapon.

"If you intend to throw yourself into such situations, it falls to me to ensure you survive your youthful follies." His eyes glinting, the Elder drew his weapon. "There will be even less rest for you in the coming months."

Wu Ying drew his weapon automatically, taking a stance across from his Master.

Just before his Master engaged, he spoke one last sentence. "A storm is coming. And I will make sure that at least this dragon learns to dance in the winds of calamity."

The End

So ends Book 4 of A Thousand Li
Wu Ying continues on his journey to immortality in
book 5—**the Second Sect**

Author's Note

Thank you for continuing the journey with me and Wu Ying in A Thousand Li. As you can guess, the dark sect and their machinations will play a large part in the next arc, with Wu Ying attempting to climb in strength and power as well as beginning to gain a true glimpse of what his dao will be.

Writing during this time (2020) has been challenging. While I'm Canadian, watching the political chaos in the US is heart-wrenching. Covid has affected all of us, no matter where we lived. I'm grateful that I'm able to continue to earn my living during these trying times, telling the stories that live in my head. And perhaps, hopefully, provide a little joy and thoughtfulness to another person's life.

Sometimes, all you can do is exist. And move on, from day-to-day, doing the best you can for yourself and those around you.

Continue to follow Wu Ying's adventures in:
- The Second Sect (Book 5 of A Thousand Li)
  www.starlitpublishing.com/products/the-second-sect

I also host a Facebook Group for all things wuxia, xanxia, and specifically, cultivation novels. We'd love it if you joined us:
- Cultivation Novels
  www.facebook.com/groups/cultivationnovels

For more great information about LitRPG series, check out the Facebook groups:
- GameLit Society
  www.facebook.com/groups/LitRPGsociety
- LitRPG Books
  www.facebook.com/groups/LitRPG.books

About the Author

Tao Wong is an avid fantasy and sci-fi reader who spends his time working and writing in the North of Canada. He's spent way too many years doing martial arts of many forms and, having broken himself too often, now spends his time writing about fantasy worlds.

If you'd like to support Tao directly, he has a Patreon page where previews of all his new books can be found!

- www.patreon.com/taowong

For updates on the series and the author's other books (and special one-shot stories), please visit his website: www.mylifemytao.com

Subscribers to Tao's mailing list will receive exclusive access to short stories in the Thousand Li and System Apocalypse universes:

www.subscribepage.com/taowong

Or visit his Facebook Page: www.facebook.com/taowongauthor/

About the Publisher

Starlit Publishing is wholly owned and operated by Tao Wong. It is a science fiction and fantasy publisher focused on the LitRPG & cultivation genres. Their focus is on promoting new, upcoming authors in the genre whose writing challenges the existing stereotypes while giving a rip-roaring good read.

For more information on Starlit Publishing, visit our website!
www.starlitpublishing.com/

You can also join Starlit Publishing's mailing list to learn of new, exciting authors and book releases.
https://starlitpublishing.com/newsletter-signup/

Glossary

Aura Reinforcement Exercise—Cultivation exercise that allows Wu Ying to contain his aura, trapping his chi within himself and making his cultivation more efficient and making him, to most senses, feel like someone of a lower cultivation level.

Body Cleansing—First cultivation stage where the cultivator must cleanse their body of the impurities that have accumulated. Has twelve stages.

Cao—Fuck

Catty—Weight measurement. One catty is roughly equivalent to one and a half pounds or 604 grams. A tael is 1/16th of a catty

Cì kè (or cike)—Translates as assassin. It also refers to a type of dark or heretical sect and a form of martial arts taught to assassins or those trained just to kill.

Chi (or Qi)—I use the Cantonese pinyin here rather than the more common Mandarin. Chi is life force / energy and it permeates all things in the universe, flowing through living creatures in particular.

Chi Points (a.k.a. Acupuncture Points)—Locations in the body that, when struck, compressed, or otherwise affected, can affect the flow of chi. Traditional acupuncture uses these points in a beneficial manner.

Core formation—Third stage of cultivation. Having gathered sufficient chi, the cultivator must form a "core" of compressed chi. The stages in Core formation purify and harden the core.

Cultivation Exercise—A supplementary exercise that improves an individual's handling of chi within their body. Cultivation exercises are ancillary to cultivation styles.

Cultivation Style—A method to manipulate chi within an individual's body. There are thousands of cultivation exercises, suited for various constitutions, meridians, and bloodlines.

Dao—Chinese sabre. Closer to a western cavalry sabre, it is thicker, often single-edged, with a curve at the end where additional thickness allows the weapon to be extra efficient at cutting.

Dantian—There are actually three dantians in the human body. The most commonly referred to one is the lower dantian, located right above the bladder and an inch within the body. The other two are located in the chest and forehead, though they are often less frequently used. The dantian is said to be the center of chi.

Dragon's Breath—Chi projection attack from the Long family style.

Dark Sects— Sects that delve into the darker side of human and demonic nature, intent on progression of power and personal strength over morality. Dark sects are destroyed when found, as they often indulge in torture, cannibalism, blood magic, murder and other darker urges.

Elements—The Chinese traditionally have five elements—Wood, Fire, Earth, Metal, and Water. Within these elements, additional sub-elements may occur (example—air from Chao Kun, ice from Li Yao).

Energy Storage—Second stage of cultivation, where the energy storage circulation meridians are opened. This stage allows cultivators to project their chi, the amount of chi stored and projected depending on level. There are eight levels.

Huài dàn—Rotten egg

Hún dàn—Bastard

Jian—A straight, double-edged sword. Known in modern times as a "taichi sword." Mostly a thrusting instrument, though it can be used to cut as well.

Jianghu (Jiāng hú)—Is literally translated as "rivers and lakes" but is a term used for the "martial arts world" in wuxia works (and this one too). In modern parlance, it can also mean the underworld or can be added to other forms of discussion like "school Jianghu" to discuss specific societal bounds.

Li—Roughly half a kilometer per li. Traditional Chinese measurement of distance.

Long family jian style—A family sword form passed on to Wu Ying. Consists of a lot of cuts, fighting at full measure, and quick changes in direction.

Meridians—In traditional Chinese martial arts and medicine, meridians are how chi flows through the body. In traditional Chinese medicine, there are twelve major meridian flows and eight secondary energy flows. I've used these meridians for the stages in cultivation for the first two stages.

Mountain Breaking Fist—Fist form that Wu Ying gained in the inner sect library. Focused, single, powerful attacks.

Nascent Soul—The fourth and last known stage of cultivation. Cultivators form a new, untouched soul steeped in the dao they had formed. This new soul must ascend to the heavens, facing heavenly tribulation at each step.

Northern Shen Kicking Style—Kicking form that Wu Ying learned at the outer sect library. Both a grappling and kicking style, meant for close combat.

Qinggong—Literally "light skill." Comes from baguazhang and is basically wire-fu—running on water, climbing trees, gliding along bamboo, etc.

Iron Reinforced Bones—Defensive, physical cultivation technique that Wu Ying trains in that will increase the strength and defense of his body.

Sect—A grouping of like-minded martial artists or cultivators. Generally, Sects are hierarchical. There are often core, inner, and outer disciples in any Sect, with Sect Elders above them and the Sect patriarch above all.

Six Jades Sect—Rival sect of the Verdant Green Waters, located in the State of Wei.

State of Shen—Location in which the first book is set. Ruled by a king and further ruled locally by lords. The State of Shen is made up of numerous counties ruled over by local lords and administered by magistrates. It is a temperate kingdom with significant rainfall and a large number of rivers connected by canals.

State of Wei—The antagonistic kingdom that borders the State of Shen. The two states are at war.

Tael—System of money. A thousand copper coins equals one tael.

Tai Kor—Elder brother

Verdant Green Waters Sect—Most powerful Sect in the State of Wen. Wu Ying's current Sect.

Wu wei—Taoist concept, translates as "inaction" or "non-doing" and relates to the idea of an action without struggle, that is perfectly aligned with the natural world.

Printed in Great Britain
by Amazon